# DAMNED IF YOU DO IN THE
# NIGHTSIDE

## SIMON R. GREEN

SOLARIS

This omnibus first published 2010 by Solaris
an imprint of Rebellion Publishing Ltd,
Riverside House, Osney Mead,
Oxford, OX1 0ES, UK

*www.solarisbooks.com*

ISBN: 978 1 906735 62 3

10 9 8 7 6 5 4 3 2 1

A CIP catalogue record for this book is available from the
British Library.

Designed & typeset by Rebellion Publishing

Printed in the UK

# Hell to pay

And follow darkness like a dream . . .

# ONE

# The Hall of the Mountain King

The boundaries of that dark and secret place, the Nightside, lie entirely contained within the city of London. And in that sick and magical place, gods and monsters, men and spirits, go about their very private business, chasing dreams and nightmares you won't find anywhere else, marked down at sale price and only slightly shop-soiled. You want to summon up a demon or have sex with an angel? Sell your soul or someone else's? Change the world for the better or just trade it in for something different? The Nightside lies waiting to oblige you, with open arms and a nasty smile. And yet within the Nightside there are many different lands and principalities, many private kingdoms and domains, and even more private heavens and hells.

One such place is Griffin Hall, where the immortals live.

My name is John Taylor. I'm a private eye, specialising in cases of the weird and uncanny. I don't solve murders, I don't do divorce work, and I wouldn't recognise a clue if you held it up before my face and said *Look, this is a clue*. I do have a special gift for finding things, and people, so mostly that's what I do. But basically I'm a man for hire, so sometimes that means I have to go where the money is.

I drove my car along the long, narrow road that spiralled up through the primordial jungle surrounding Griffin Hall. Except it wasn't really my car, and I wasn't actually driving. I'd borrowed Dead Boy's futuristic car, to make a better impression. It was a long, silver bullet with many wondrous features, which had fallen into the Nightside from the future, via a Timeslip. It adopted Dead Boy as its owner and occasional driver. I get the impression he wasn't given much of a choice. I just sat back in the driving seat, enjoyed the massage function, and let the car drive itself. Probably had faster reactions than me anyway. I knew better than to try to touch any of the controls; the last time I even let my hands rest on the steering wheel, the car gave me a warning electric shock.

Griffin Hall stood at the top of a great hill, in the middle of extensive grounds surrounded by high stone walls, protected by all the very latest scientific and magical defences. The huge wrought-iron gates were guaranteed impenetrable unless you had a current invitation, and you could get turned to stone just for leaning on the bell too hard. Griffin Hall, inside the Nightside, but not part of it.

The Griffin family valued their privacy, and didn't care whom they had to maim, mutilate, or murder to ensure it. Only the very important and the very privileged were ever invited to visit the Griffins at home. Their occasional parties were the biggest and brightest in the Nightside, the very height of the Social Scene; and you weren't anybody if you didn't have your invitation weeks in advance. I'd never been here before. For all my chequered and even infamous background, I'd never been important enough to catch the Griffins' eye, until now. Until they needed me to do the one thing no-one else could do.

I wondered who or what had gone missing, so completely and so thoroughly that not even the mighty Griffins, with all their resources, could find it.

What had once been a truly massive and elegant garden, sprawling up the high sides of the hill, had been left neglected, then abandoned, possibly for centuries. It had fallen into a rioting jungle of assorted and unnatural vegetation, including some plants so ancient they'd been declared extinct outside the Nightside, along with others so strange and distorted they had to have been brought in from other dimensions. A great dark jungle of towering trees and mutant growths, pressed tight together and crowding right up to the edges of the single narrow road. The trees rose high enough to block out the starry expanse of the eternal night sky, leaning out over the road so their interlocking branches formed a canopy, a shadowy green tunnel through which I drove deeper and deeper into the heart of darkness.

They say he raised the hill and the Hall in a single night . . . But then, they say a lot of things about Jeremiah Griffin.

The car's headlamps blazed bright as the sun, but the

stark scientific light couldn't seem to penetrate far into the verdant growth on either side of the road. Instead, thick motes of pollen drifted between the trees, big as tennis balls, glowing phosphorescent blue and green. Occasionally, one would burst into a spectacular fireworks display, illuminating the narrow trails and shifting jungle interior with flares and flashes of vivid light.

Some of the plants turned to watch as the car glided smoothly past them.

There were trees with trunks big as houses, their dark, mottled bark glistening wetly in the uncertain light. Heavy, swollen leaves, red as blood, pulsed gently on the lowering branches. Huge flowers blossomed, big as hedges, garish as Technicolor, petals thick and pulpy like diseased flesh. Hanging vines fell like bead curtains over the narrow trails, shivering and trembling like dreaming snakes. Now and again some small scuttling thing would brush up against the tips of the liana, and they would snap and curl around the helpless creature and haul it up, kicking and screaming, into the darkness above. The squealing would stop abruptly, and blood would drip down for a while. Green leafy masses with purple flowers for eyes and rings of thorns for teeth lurched and crashed along the narrow paths, stopping at the very edge of the road to shake their heavy bodies defiantly at the intrusion of light into their dark domain.

I'd hate to be the Griffins' gardener. Probably have to go pruning armed with a cattle prod and a flame-thrower. As the car drove on, I thought I saw something that might have been a gardener, leaning patiently on a wooden rake at the side of the road to watch me go by. He looked like he was made out of green leaves.

The road rose before me, growing steadily steeper as I

approached the summit, and Griffin Hall. The jungle was full of ominous sounds, deep grunts and sibilant rustlings, and the occasional quickly stifled scream. Everything in the jungle seemed to be moving slowly, stirring and stretching as though waking from a deep sleep, disturbed by the intruder in their midst. I was safe, of course. I'd been personally summoned by Jeremiah Griffin himself. I had the current passWords. But I didn't feel safe. The car's windows were all firmly closed, and the future vehicle had more built-in weapons than some armies, but still I didn't feel safe. Being simply a passenger made me feel . . . helpless. I've always preferred to protect myself rather than rely on others. I trust my own capabilities.

A thrashing mass of barbed vines lurched suddenly into the middle of the road, stretching out to block my way. There wasn't time to slow, never mind stop, and the living barrier looked heavy and solid enough to stop a tank. I braced myself for the impact, and at the last moment a roaring circular buzz-saw rose up out of the car's bonnet. We slammed into the thorny mass at full speed, and the howling saw tore right through it, spraying green leafy fragments in all directions. Many of them were still twitching. The great green thing screamed shrilly, its thorns trailing harmlessly along the car's armoured sides as we punched through the green mass and out the other side.

Long, twisting branches lowered themselves into the road ahead, any one of them big enough to snatch up the car and feed it to the overhead canopy. The buzz-saw sank back into the bonnet, and twin flame-throwers rose up in its place. Vicious flames roared out to attack the branches, their flaring light bright and clean against the dark. The heavy branches shook and shuddered as the flames took hold, and they shrank back from the car. We drove on through the opening gap, while the burning branches tried to beat out the flames by slamming themselves repeatedly against the road with terrific force.

Nothing else bothered us. In fact, most of the vegetation seemed to draw back more than a little as we passed by.

It still took a long time to get to Griffin Hall, the road rising higher and higher, increasingly steep and twisting as I ascended far above the neonlit streets of the Nightside and all the little people who lived there. It felt like I was scaling the heights of Mount Olympus to meet with the gods, which was probably the intention. Griffin Hall stood at the very top of its own private mountain, looking out over the Nightside as though the whole area was the Griffins' own private preserve. As though they owned everything they could see, for as far as they could see. And if Jeremiah Griffin didn't actually own all of the Nightside, and everyone who lived in it, it certainly wasn't for want of trying.

In the past the Authorities had kept him in his place, but they were all dead and gone now, so who knew what the future held. Someone had to run the Nightside, and ensure that everyone played nice together, and certainly no-one was better placed than Jeremiah Griffin, the immortal.

I didn't give a damn who ran the Nightside, or thought they did. I was only here because I'd been summoned, by the man himself. A great honour, if you cared about such things, which mostly I don't. Of course, such an important man couldn't follow the usual route of contacting my office and making an appointment with my secretary. No, the first I knew was when his voice suddenly appeared in my head, booming *This is Jeremiah Griffin. I have need of you, John Taylor.*

"Dammit, turn down the volume!" I yelled, attracting the occasional glance from other people in the street. "God himself wouldn't be that loud, even if it was the Second Coming, and He was offering advance bookings for ringside seats. You're not God, are you? I've been good. Mostly."

There was a pause, then a somewhat quieter voice said, *This is Jeremiah Griffin. I have need of you, John Taylor.*

"Better," I said. "Now how did you get hold of this number? My head is supposed to be strictly ex-directory."

*You will come to Griffin Hall. There is work for you here.*

"What's in it for me?"

There was a rather longer pause. People like Jeremiah Griffin weren't used to being questioned, especially when they've lowered themselves to speak to you personally.

*I could have you killed.*

I had to laugh. People (and others) have been trying to kill me for as long as I can remember, and I'm still here, while mostly they aren't. To my surprise, the voice in my head laughed, too, just a little.

*Good. I was told you weren't the kind of man who could be threatened or intimidated. And that's the kind of man I need. Come to Griffin Hall, John Taylor, and you shall have more money than you have ever dreamed of.*

So of course I had to go. I didn't have any other cases, and the big money the Vatican had paid me for finding the Unholy Grail had pretty much run out. Besides, I was intrigued. I'd heard of the Griffin, the legendary human immortal—everyone in the Nightside had—but I'd never moved in the kind of circles where I was likely to meet him. Jeremiah Griffin was a man of wealth and fame and had been for centuries.

All the Griffins were immortal, and there are very few human immortals left these days, even in the Nightside. Jeremiah was the first and the oldest, though no-one knew for sure exactly how old he was. Impossibly rich and incredibly powerful, Griffin owned much of the Nightside and many of the businesses that operated there. And he'd always been very open about his intention eventually to run the whole Nightside as his own private kingdom. But he was never a part of the Authorities, those grey and faceless men who used to run the Nightside from a safe distance. They blocked him at every turn, denied him openings and opportunities, kept him in his place . . . because when all was said and done, to them he was just another part of the freak show they'd run for longer than he'd been alive.

Still, they were gone now. Perhaps it was the Griffin's time, come round at last. Most of the Nightside wouldn't care, too busy chasing their own chosen damnations and salvations, all the passions and pleasures that could only be found and enjoyed in the sleazy bars and members-only clubs of the Nightside.

No-one knew for sure how Jeremiah Griffin became immortal. There were stories, there are always stories, but no-one knew for sure. He wasn't a godling, a vampire, or a sorcerer. He had no angelic or demonic blood in him. He was just a man who'd lived for centuries and might live for centuries more. And he was rich and powerful enough to be very hard to kill. The Griffin's past and true nature were a mystery, reportedly even from the rest of his family, and he went to great lengths to keep it that way. I saw the severed heads of investigative journalists set on spikes above the main gates as I drove through. Some of the heads were still screaming.

The jungle garden came to an abrupt halt at the low stone walls surrounding the great open courtyard laid out before Griffin Hall. Rustling vegetation came right up to the walls but stopped just short, careful not to touch them. Long rows of curious carvings had been deeply etched into the pale creamy stone. The future car passed through the single opening into the courtyard, delicate filigree silver gates opening before the car as we approached and shutting themselves firmly behind us. The car curved around in a wide arc, its heavy wheels churning up the gravel, and stopped right before the main entrance. The driver's door opened, and I got out. The door then immediately shut and locked itself. I didn't blame it. There was nothing remotely inviting or welcoming about Griffin Hall.

I leaned against the car, and took my time looking around. Beyond the low stone walls, the jungle pressed forward here and there, over and over. Any part of the vegetation that touched the creamy stone immediately shrivelled up and died, but the jungle persisted, sacrificing small parts of itself in its tireless search for a weak spot, driven by the slow, stubborn relentless nature of plants. Waiting only for the day, however far in the future that might be, when the walls would finally fall, and the jungle press inexorably forward to overwhelm Griffin

Hall and all who lived in it. The jungle was immortal, too, and it had endless patience.

The Hall itself was huge, sprawling and subtly menacing in the shimmering silver light from the oversized moon that dominated the Nightside sky. All the windows were illuminated, dozens of them, blazing out at the surrounding darkness. It should have been impressive, but every single window was long and narrow, like squinting, mean-spirited eyes. The massive main door was made of some unnaturally dark wood I didn't recognise. It looked solid enough to stop a charging rhino.

I let my eyes drift up several stories. All those brightly lit windows, and not one face peering out. Up on the roof, dark, indistinct figures moved shiftily among the sharp-edged gables. The gargoyles were getting restless. As long as they didn't start throwing things . . . gargoyles delighted in toilet humour, and possessed uncanny aim. I took a deep breath, pushed myself away from the future car, and headed for the main door as though I didn't have a care in the world. Never show fear in the Nightside, or something will walk all over you.

I didn't have to worry about Dead Boy's car. It could look after itself.

The path to the front door was illuminated by Japanese paper lanterns on tall poles, each one decorated with a different screaming face to ward off evil spirits. I took the time to study a few close up, but I didn't recognise anyone. As I approached the front door, I realised for the first time that for all Griffin Hall's legendary age, its stonework was still clean and sharp, the creamy stone untouched by time or erosion or the ravages of weather. The huge building could have been built just yesterday.

Griffin Hall, like the family it protected, was also immortal, untouched, unchanging.

I stood before the door, carefully pronounced the passWords I'd been given, and rapped firmly with the old-fashioned brass knocker. The sound seemed to echo on and on beyond the door, as though travelling unimaginably long distances. After letting me wait a suitable time, the door swung smoothly and silently open, to reveal the butler standing solemnly before me. He had to be the butler. Only a butler can look down his nose at you while remaining impeccably polite and courteous. I think they teach them that on the first day at butler training school. Certainly there's no bigger snob than a servant of long standing.

"I'm John Taylor," I said.

"Of course you are, sir."

"Jeremiah Griffin is expecting me."

"Yes, sir. Do come in."

He stepped back only enough to let me get past, so I made a point of stepping heavily on his perfectly polished shoes. He closed the door, then inclined his head to me in what was almost a bow, but not quite.

"Shall I summon a servant to take your trench coat, sir? We could have it cleaned."

"No," I said. "It goes everywhere with me. It'd be lost without me."

"Indeed, sir. I am Hobbes, the Griffin family butler. If you would care to follow me, I will escort you into the master's presence."

"Works for me," I said.

•   •   •

Hobbes led the way through the huge entrance lobby and down a long hallway, back stiff, chin up, not even bothering to check if I was following. It probably never even occurred to him that I wouldn't be. So I strolled along, a few paces behind, deliberately slouching with both hands in my coat-pockets. You learn to take your little victories where you find them. The hallway was big enough to drive a train through, lit by a warm golden glow that seemed to come from everywhere and nowhere. Typical supernatural track lighting. I had a good look round, refusing to allow Hobbes to dictate the pace. I was genuinely interested. Not many people get to see the inside of Griffin Hall, and most of them had the decency and common sense to keep quiet about what they saw. But I've never been big on either. I was pretty sure I could make a tasty sum selling a detailed description to the Gracious Living section of the *Night Times*.

But . . . I have to say, I wasn't that impressed. The hallway was big, yes, but you soon got over that. The gleaming wooden floor was richly waxed and polished, the walls were brightly painted, and the high ceiling was decorated with a series of tasteful frescoes . . . but there were no standing suits of armour, no antique furnishings, no great works of art. Just a really long hallway with an endless series of paintings and portraits covering both walls. All of them depicting Jeremiah Griffin and his wife Mariah, in the fashions and styles of centuries past. Paintings hundreds of years old, celebrating two people who were probably even older. From formal stylised portraits where they both wore ruffs and the obligatory unsmiling expressions, through dozens of kings and more Parliaments, from Restoration to Edwardian and beyond. Some by artists so famous even I recognised them.

I spent so long admiring a Rembrandt that Hobbes had to come back and hover over me, clearing his throat in a meaningful manner. I turned to give him my full attention. Hobbes really was the archetypal butler, upright and stern in his formal black-and-white Victorian outfit. His hair was jet-black and so were his eyes, though his tight-lipped mouth was so pale as to be almost colourless. He had a high-boned face, and a long, pointed chin you could use to get pickles out of a jar. He should have been amusing, an anachronism in this modern day and age, but behind the arrogant servility there was a sense of enormous strength held in check, ready to be released in the service of his master. Hobbes . . . was creepy, in an utterly intimidating sort of way.

You knew he'd be the first person to lean over your shoulder during a formal dinner and loudly announce that you were using the wrong fork. He'd also be the first to toss you out on your ear, probably with a broken limb or two, if you were dumb enough to upset his lord and master. I made a mental note not to turn my back on him at any time and to fight extremely dirty if push ever came to shove.

"If you've quite finished, sir . . . ?" Implied threats filled the pause at the end.

"Tell me about Jeremiah," I said, not moving, just to be contrary. "Have you worked for him long?"

"I have had the honour of serving the Griffin family for years, sir. But you will of course understand that I cannot discuss the family's personal matters with any visitor, no matter how . . . well-known."

"I like your gardens," I said. "Very . . . lively."

"We do our best, sir. This way, sir."

It was clear he wasn't going to tell me one damn thing,

so I set off at a fast pace down the long hallway, and he had to hurry to catch up with me. He quickly resumed the lead, gliding silently along a careful two paces ahead of me. He was very quiet for such a big man. I felt like sticking my tongue out at his back, but somehow I knew he'd know, and wouldn't care. So I settled for ambling along again, making as much noise as I could, doing my best to leave scuff marks on the polished floor. Every now and again, other servants would emerge from side corridors, all of them dressed in old-fashioned Victorian outfits, and every time they'd crash to a halt and wait respectfully for Hobbes to pass, before continuing on their way. Except . . . *respectful* wasn't quite the word. No, they looked scared. All of them.

Jeremiah and Mariah Griffin continued to stare solemnly back at me from the walls as I passed. Clothes and hairstyles and backgrounds changed, but they remained the same. Two hard, unyielding faces, with unyielding stares. I'd seen portraits of kings and queens in all their finery who looked less royal, less sure of themselves. As Hobbes and I finally approached the end of the hallway, paintings finally gave way to photographs, from faded sepia prints to the latest digital clarity. And for the first time the Griffin children appeared, William and Eleanor. First as children, then as adults, again fixed and unchanging while the fashions and the world changed around them. Both children had their parents' strong bone structure but none of their character. The children looked . . . soft, pampered. Weak. Unhappy.

At the end of the hallway, Hobbes took a sharp right turn, and when I followed him round the corner I found we were in another great hallway, where both walls were lined with trophies of the hunt. Animal heads watched and snarled from their carefully positioned wall plaques, stuffed and mounted with glass eyes that seemed to follow you down the hall. There were all the usual beasts of the field, lions and tigers and bears, oh my, and a single fox head that creeped the hell out of me by winking as I passed. I didn't say anything to Hobbes. I knew he wouldn't have anything to say about it that I wanted to hear. As we progressed further down the long hallway, the trophies progressed from the unusual to the unnatural. No-one cares about permits in the Nightside. You can hunt any damn thing you take a fancy to if it doesn't start hunting you.

There was a unicorn's head, complete with the single long curlicued horn, though its pure white hide seemed drab and lifeless, for all the taxidermist's skill. Further along there was a manticore, with its disturbing mix of leonine and human features. The snarling mouth was full of huge blocky teeth, but the long, flowing mane looked as though it had been recently blow-dried. And . . . an absolutely huge dragon's head, a good fourteen feet from ear to pointed ear. The golden eyes were big as dinner plates, and I'd never seen so many teeth in one mouth before. The snout projected so far out into the hallway that Hobbes and I had to edge past in single file.

"I'll bet that's hell to dust," I said, because you have to say something.

"I wouldn't know, sir," said Hobbes.

Several hallways and corridors later, we came at last to the main conference room. Hobbes knocked briskly, pushed open the door, and stepped aside to gesture me through ahead of him. I strolled in like I did this every day, and didn't even glance back as I heard Hobbes close the door firmly behind me. The conference room was large and noisy, but the first thing that caught my attention were the dozens of television screens covering the wall to my left, showing news channels, business information, market reports, and political updates from all round the world. All blasting away simultaneously. The sheer noise of the babble was overwhelming, but no-one in the room seemed to be paying it any particular attention.

Instead, all eyes were on the man himself, Jeremiah Griffin, sitting at the head of his long table like a king on his throne, listening intently as his people came to him in a steady flow, bearing news and memos and files and urgent but respectful questions. They swarmed around him like worker drones with a queen bee, coming and going, clustering and re-forming, and competing jealously for the Griffin's attention. They all seemed to be talking at the same time, but Jeremiah Griffin had no difficulty telling whom he wanted to talk to, and whom he needed to listen to. He rarely looked at any of the men and women around him, giving all his attention to the papers placed before him. He would nod or shake his head, initial some pages and reject others, and occasionally growl a comment or an order, and the people around him would rush away to do his bidding, their faces fixed and intent. Impeccably and expensively dressed, and probably even more expensively educated, they still behaved more like servants than Hobbes. None of them paid me any attention, even when they had to brush right past me to get to the door. And Jeremiah didn't even glance in my direction.

Presumably I was supposed to stand there, at full attention, until he deigned to notice me. Hell with that. I pulled up a chair and sat down, putting my feet up on the table. I was in no hurry, and I wanted to take a good look at the immortal Jeremiah Griffin. He was a big man, not tall but big, with a barrel chest and broad shoulders, in an exquisitely cut dark suit, white shirt, and black string tie. He had a strong, hard-boned face, with cold blue eyes, a hawk nose, and a mouth that looked like it rarely smiled. All topped with a great leonine mane of grey hair. Just as he'd looked in all his portraits, right back to the days of the Tudors. It seemed he'd only come to his immortality when he was already in his fifties, and the package hadn't included eternal youth. He'd just stopped aging. He sat very upright, as though doing anything else would be a sign of weakness, and his few gestures were sharp and controlled. He had that effortless gravitas and calm authority that come from long years of experience. He gave the impression that here was a man who would always know exactly what you were going to say even before you said it, because he'd seen and heard it all before. Over and over again.

His people treated him with a deference bordering on awe, more like a pope than a king. Outside this room they might be people of wealth and breeding and experts in their field, but here they were just underlings to the Griffin, a position and a privilege they would rather die than give up. Because this was where the power was, where the real money was, where all the decisions that mattered were made, every day, and even the smallest decision changed the course of the world. To be working here, for the Griffin, meant you were at the very top of the heap. For as long as you lasted. Somehow I knew there was a constant turnover of bright young things passing through this room. Because the Griffin wouldn't stand for anyone becoming experienced or influential enough to be a threat to him.

Jeremiah Griffin kept me waiting for some time, and I got bored, which is always dangerous. I was supposed to just sit there and cool my heels, to put me in my place, but I am proud to say I have never known my place. So I decided to act up cranky. I have a reputation to live down to. I looked unhurriedly round the conference room, considering various possibilities for mischief and mayhem, before finally settling on the wall of television screens.

I used my special gift to find the channel control signal and used it to tune every single television screen to the same appalling show. I'd found it accidentally one night while channel hopping (never a good idea in the Nightside, where we get not only the whole world's output, but also transmissions from other worlds and other dimensions), and I actually had to go and hide behind the sofa till it was over. The *John Waters Celebrity Perversion Hour* is the single most upsetting pornography ever produced, and now it was blasting out of dozens of screens simultaneously. The various men and women hovering around Jeremiah Griffin looked up, vaguely aware that something had changed, and then they saw the screens. And saw what was happening. And then they started screaming, and puking, and finally running for their lives and their sanity. There are some things man is just not meant to know, let alone do with a moose. The conference room quickly cleared, leaving only myself and Jeremiah Griffin. He looked briefly at the screens, sniffed once, then looked away again. He wasn't shocked or upset, or even impressed. He'd seen it all before.

He gestured sharply with one hand, and all the screens shut down at once. The room was suddenly and blessedly quiet. The Griffin looked at me sternly. I leaned back in my chair, and smiled easily at him. Jeremiah sighed heavily, shook his head briefly, and rose to his feet. I took my boots off the table and quickly got to my feet, too. The Griffin hadn't become the richest and most powerful individual in the Nightside without killing his fair share of enemies, many with his bare hands. I struck a carefully casual pose as he approached me (never show fear, they can sense fear), and he came to a halt carefully out of arm's reach. Presumably he'd heard about me, too. We studied each other silently. I didn't offer to shake hands, and neither did he.

"I knew you were going to be trouble," he said finally, in a calm cold voice. "Good. I need a man who's trouble. So, you're the infamous John Taylor. The man who could have been king of the Nightside, if he'd wanted."

"I didn't want it," I said easily.

"Why not?"

It was a fair question, so I considered it for a moment. "Because it would have meant giving up being me. I never wanted to run other people's lives. I have enough problems running my own. And I've seen what happens . . . when power corrupts." I looked the Griffin straight in his icy blue eyes. "Why do you want to run the Nightside, Jeremiah?"

He smiled briefly. "Because it's there. A man has to have a goal, especially an immortal man. No doubt running the Nightside will turn out to be more trouble than it's worth, in the end, but it's the only real goal left for a man of my ambitions and talents. Besides, I bore very easily, these days. I have no peers, and all my dangerous enemies are dead. I have a constant appetite, a need, for new things to occupy and distract me. When you've lived as long as I have, it's hard to find anything truly new, anymore. That's why I chose you for this assignment. I could have had any detective, any investigator I wanted . . . but there's only one John Taylor."

"You seemed to be keeping yourself busy," I said, gesturing at the door through which his people had departed.

He made a short dismissive sound. "That wasn't business, not really. Just . . . makework. It's important that I be seen to be busy. I can't afford to be seen or even thought of as weak, distracted . . . or the sharks will start to gather round my operations. I didn't spend centuries building up my empire to see it all brought down by a pack of opportunistic jackals."

His large hands closed into heavy, brutal fists.

"Why would anyone think you weak?" I said carefully. "You're the Griffin, the man who would be King."

He scowled at me, but his heart wasn't in it. He pulled up a chair and sat down, and I sat down opposite him.

"My grand-daughter Melissa . . . is missing," he said heavily. "Maybe kidnapped, maybe even murdered. I don't know . . . and not knowing is hard. She disappeared yesterday, just forty-eight hours short of her eighteenth birthday."

"Any signs of foul play?" I said, doing my best to sound like I knew what I was doing. "No sign of a struggle, or . . ."

"No. Nothing."

"Then maybe she just took off. You know teenagers . . ."

"No. There's more to it than that. I recently changed my will, leaving everything to Melissa. The Hall, the money, the businesses. The rest of the family get nothing. It was supposed to be strictly secret, of course. The only people who knew were myself and the family lawyer, Jarndyce. But three days ago he was found dead in his office, butchered. His safe had been ripped right out of the wall and broken open. The only thing missing was his copy of the new will. Shortly afterwards, the contents were made known to every member of my family. There were . . . raised voices. Not least from Melissa, who had no idea she was to be my sole heir.

"And now she's gone. Nowhere to be found. No sign of how she was taken. Or how her abductors got into the Hall, unseen by anyone, undetected by any of my security people or their supposedly state-of-the-art systems. Melissa has vanished, without a trace."

I immediately thought *Inside job*, but I had enough sense to keep that thought to myself, for now.

"Do you have a photograph of your grand-daughter?" I said.

"Of course."

He handed me a folder containing half a dozen eight-by-ten glossies. Melissa Griffin was tall and slender, with long blonde hair and a pale face completely devoid of makeup or expression. She stared coldly at the camera as though it was something not to be trusted. She wouldn't have been my first choice to leave a business empire to. But maybe she had hidden depths. I chose one photo and tucked it away inside my coat.

"Tell me about the rest of your family," I said. "The disinherited ones. Where they were, what they were doing, when Melissa disappeared."

Jeremiah frowned, choosing his words carefully. "As far as I can ascertain, they were all in plain sight, observed by myself or others, perhaps even conspicuously so. It's not usual for them all to be present in the Hall at the same time . . . It was the same the day before, when Jarndyce's office was broken into, and he was killed. But I can't really see any of my family as suspects. None of them would have the backbone to go up against me. Even though they were all mad as hell over the new will." He chuckled briefly. "Actually horrified, some of them, at the thought of having to go out and work for a living."

"Why did you disinherit them?" I said.

"Because none of them are worthy! I've done my best to knock them into shape, down the years, but they never had to fight for things, the way I did . . . They grew up with everything, so they think they're entitled to it. Not one of them could hang on to anything I left them! And I didn't spend centuries putting my empire together with blood and sweat and hard toil, to have it fall apart because my successors don't have the guts to do what's necessary. Melissa . . . is strong. I have faith in her. I've since hired a new lawyer and had a new will drawn up, of course, replacing the lost document, but . . . for reasons I don't propose to share with you, the will is only valid if Melissa returns to sign certain documents before her eighteenth birthday. Should she fail to do so, she will never inherit anything. I need you to find her for me, Mr. Taylor. That is what you do, after all. Find her and bring her safely home, before her eighteenth birthday. You have a little under twenty-four hours."

"And if she's already dead?" I said bluntly.

"I refuse to believe that," he said, his voice flat and hard. "No-one would dare. Everyone knows Melissa is my favorite and that I would burn down all the Nightside to avenge her. Besides, there's been no ransom demand, no attempt at communication. It is possible she just ran away, I suppose, intimidated by the responsibilities lying ahead of her. She never wanted to be a part of the family business . . . Or, she might have been afraid of what the rest of the family might say, or do to her. But if that was the case, she would have left me a note. Or found some way to contact me. No, she was taken against her will. I'm sure of it."

"Any friends who might be sheltering her?" I said, to show I hadn't given up on the running away idea.

"She only has a few real friends, and I've had them all checked out carefully, from a distance. They don't even seem to know she's gone missing yet. And that's the way it has to stay. You can't tell anyone, Mr. Taylor. I can't be seen to be vulnerable, or distracted."

"An impossible case, with impossible conditions, and an impossible deadline," I said. "Why don't you just tie both my legs behind my back while you're at it? All right, let me think. Could she have fled outside the Nightside, into London proper?"

"No," he said immediately. "Impossible. None of my family can ever leave the Nightside."

"It always comes back to the family, doesn't it?" I said. I thought for a while. "If she's out there, I'll find her. But you have to face the fact that she could already be dead. Murdered, either by someone in your family's employ, to prevent her from inheriting, or by one of the many enemies you've made in your long career."

"Find my grand-daughter," said the Griffin, his voice cold and relentless. "And in return I will pay you the sum of ten million pounds. Find out what happened, and why, and who is responsible. And either return her to me safely, or bring me her body, and the name of the man responsible."

"Even if it's family?" I said.

"Especially if it's family," said Jeremiah Griffin.

He pushed a briefcase across the table towards me, and I opened it. The briefcase was packed full of bank-notes.

"One million pounds," said the Griffin. "Just to get you started. I'm sure there will be expenses. You get the rest when I get Melissa. Are you all right, Mr Taylor?"

"Oh sure," I said. "Just having breathing difficulties. Money is only numbers to you, isn't it?"

"Do we have a deal, Mr. Taylor?"

"We have a deal," I said, closing the briefcase. "But understand me, Mr. Griffin. You're hiring me to bring you the truth about what happened. All of the truth, not just the bits you want to hear. And once I get started, I don't stop till I get to the end, no matter who gets hurt in the process. Once you unleash me, even you can't call me off. Do we still have a deal, Mr. Griffin?"

"Do whatever you have to, to find Melissa," said the Griffin. "I don't care who gets hurt in the process. Even me. They say . . . you have a special gift, for finding things and people."

"That's right, I do. But I can't simply reach out and put my finger on your grand-daughter. That's not how it works. I need a specific question to get a specific answer. Or location. I need to know which direction to look in be-fore I can hope to pin her down. Still, I can try a basic search here, see if my Sight can reveal anything useful."

I concentrated, opening up my inner eye, my third eye, my private eye, and my Sight came alive as my gift man-ifested, showing me all the things in the conference room hidden from everyday gaze. There were ghosts all over the room, men and women reliving the moments of their murders over and over again, trapped in endless loops of

Time. Jeremiah had been busy here. I grabbed his hand so he could see them, too, but his face showed no emotion. There were other creatures, too, not in any way human, but they were only passing through, using our dimension as a stepping-stone to somewhere else. They're always there. And finally I got a glimpse of Melissa, running through the conference room. I couldn't tell if she was running to someone, or from someone. Her face was cold, focused, intent.

And then my Sight was blocked and shut down by some outside force.

I staggered backwards, and almost fell. My Vision of the greater world was gone, closed off from me. I fought to force my inner eye open again, to See Melissa again, and was shocked when I discovered I couldn't. This had never happened to me before. Only some incredibly powerful force could shut down my gift, like one of the Powers or Principalities. But that would mean the involvement of Heaven or Hell; both of whom were supposed to be barred from intervening directly inside the Nightside. Jeremiah grabbed my shoulder and thrust his face into mine, demanding to know what was happening, but I was listening to something else. There was a new presence in the conference room, something strange and awful, building and focusing as it struggled to find a form it could manifest through. The Griffin looked around sharply. Still linked to me, he could feel it, too.

The temperature in the room plummeted, hoarfrost forming on the windows and the walls and the tabletop. The air was full of the stench of dead things. Somewhere someone was screaming without end, and someone else was crying without hope. Something bad was coming, from a bad place, smashing its way through the Hall's defences with contemptuous ease.

I reached into my coat-pocket and drew out a packet of salt. I never travel anywhere without condiments. I drew a salt circle around the Griffin and myself, muttering certain Words as fast as I could say them. You don't last long in the Nightside if you don't learn the basic defences pretty damned quickly. But spiritual protections can only defend you against spiritual attacks.

All the television screens exploded at once, showering me and the Griffin with shrapnel. He started to flinch away, outside the salt circle, and I grabbed his shoulder, shouting at him to hold his ground. He jerked out of my hand, but nodded stiffly. Oddly, he didn't look frightened, just annoyed. I looked back at the shattered televisions. The electronic innards were crawling out of the broken sets, spilling out in streams of steel and silicon and plastic. And from this possessed technology the invading presence made itself a shape.

It stood up slowly as it came together, tall and threatening, manlike in appearance but in no way human. An unliving construct, made of jagged metal bones with silicon sinews, razor-sharp hands, and a plastic face with glowing eyes and jagged metal teeth. It lurched towards me and the Griffin, crackling with imperfectly discharging electricity. A purely physical threat, to which the salt circle would be no defence at all.

"The Hall's security defences should have kicked in by now," said the Griffin, his voice strained, but even. "And my security people should be bursting in here any minute, armed to the teeth."

"I really wouldn't bet on it," I said. "We're dealing with a major Power here. I'd bet every penny of the money you just gave me that it's sealed off this room completely. We are on our own."

"Do you by any chance carry a gun?" said the Griffin.

"No," I said, and smiled. "I've never needed one."

I cautiously tried my inner eye again. The Power had shut down my ability to look for Melissa, but the gift itself was still operating. I inherited it from my mother, that ancient and awful Being known as Lilith, and probably only the Creator or the Enemy themselves could take it away from me. So I eased my third eye open just a crack, hardly enough to be noticed, and sent my Sight hurtling out over the Nightside, searching for someplace where it was raining. The metal construct was almost upon us, reaching out eagerly with its jagged metal hands. I found a rain-storm, and it was the easiest thing in the world for me to bring that rain into the conference room and drop it on the construct.

The plastic face cracked as it cried out harshly, an inhuman squeal of static, and the whole form collapsed and fell apart as the pouring rain short-circuited it. The construct shattered as it hit the floor, scattering into a million harmless pieces. I sent the rain back where I found it, and all was calm and still in the conference room.

I looked around cautiously, but the feel of the invading presence was gone. The room was already warming up again, the hoarfrost running away in trickles from the walls and windows. I stepped outside the salt circle, kicked at a few metal pieces on the floor, then gestured for the Griffin to join me. We looked down at what was left of the construct. He didn't seem too upset, or even impressed.

"One of your enemies?" I said.

"Not as far as I know," he said. "One of yours, perhaps?"

That was when the Griffin's security people finally charged into the room, shouting and carrying on and waving their guns about. The Griffin yelled right back at them, wanting to know where the hell they were while his life was in danger. The security people started backing up, under the sheer force of his anger, and he quickly drove them all away with instructions to check the rest of the Hall for possible incursions, and not to report back until they'd found or done something to justify their jobs and expensive salaries.

I let him get on with it, while I considered the matter. The appearance of such a powerful Being complicated matters. Not least because I couldn't see where it fitted into a simple kidnapping. Or runaway. If I couldn't use my Sight to find Melissa . . . I'd have to do it the old-fashioned way, by interrogating everyone involved, asking awkward and insightful questions, and hoping I was smart enough to know when someone was lying to me. I said as much to the Griffin, when we were finally alone again, and he nodded immediately.

"You have my authority to question all members of my family, my staff, and my businesspeople. Ask them anything you want, and if anyone gives you any trouble, refer them to me." He smiled briefly. "Getting them to cooperate, and tell you what you need to know, is of course your problem."

"Of course," I said. "You realise I may have to ask . . . personal questions of your immediate family. Your wife, and your children."

"Ask them anything. Feel free to slap them about, if

36

you want. All that matters is finding Melissa, before it's too late."

"I'd be interested in hearing your impressions of your family," I said. "Anything you think I ought to know . . ."

I already knew the basics. The Griffins were, after all, celebrities in the Nightside, their every word and move covered by the gossip rags. Which I have been known to read, on occasion. But I was interested to see what he would tell me, and perhaps more importantly, what he didn't.

"Any one of them could be involved," he said, scowling. "They could have hired people, I suppose . . . But none of them would have the guts to oppose me so openly. They're only immortal because of me, but you can't expect gratitude to last forever. My dear wife Mariah is loyal to me. Not too smart, but smart enough to know where her best interests lie. My son William, my eldest . . . is weak, spineless, and no businessman. Though God knows I tried hard enough to make him into an heir worth having. But he has always been a disappointment to me. Too much of his mother in him. He married Gloria, an ex-supermodel, against my wishes. Pretty enough, I suppose, but all the charm and personality of a magazine cover. She married money, not a man. Somehow, they managed to produce my wise and wonderful grand-daughter, Melissa.

"My daughter Eleanor has only ever been interested in indulging her various appetites. She only married Marcel because I made it clear she had to marry someone. Couldn't have her running round the Nightside like a cat in heat all her life. I thought marriage would help her grow up. I should have known better. Marcel gambles. Badly. And thinks I don't know, the fool. They have a son, my other grand-child Paul. He has always been a mystery to me and his parents. I'd say he was a changeling, if I hadn't had him checked."

And that was all he was prepared to say about what should have been his nearest and dearest. I picked up the briefcase, grunting with surprise at the weight, and nodded to the Griffin.

"I'll let you know when I know something. Can I ask, who recommended me to you?"

"Walker," he said, and I had to smile. Of course. Who else?

"One last question," I said. "Why does an immortal feel the need to make a will, anyway?"

"Because not even immortality lasts forever," said Jeremiah Griffin.

# TWO

# QUEEN BEE

When in doubt, as I so often am, start with the scene of
the crime. Perhaps the criminals will have left behind
something useful, like a business card with their names
and addresses on it. Stranger things have happened in the
Nightside. After I left the conference room, I turned to
the butler Hobbes, and spoke to him firmly.

"I need to see Melissa's room, Hobbes."

"Of course you do, sir," he said calmly. "But I'm
afraid you won't find anything there."

Hobbes led me through another series of corridors and
hallways. I was beginning to think I'd have to ask someone for a map if Hobbes ever decided to give me the slip.
All the hallways and corridors seemed unnaturally still
and quiet. For such a large Hall, surprisingly few people
actually seemed to live there. The only people we passed

were uniformed servants, and they all gave Hobbes and me a wide berth, scurrying past with bowed heads and lowered eyes. And for once, despite all my hard-earned reputation, I didn't think it was me they were scared of.

We came at last to an old-fashioned elevator, with sliding doors made up of rococo brass stylings. Very art deco. Hobbes pulled back the heavy doors with casual strength, and we stepped inside. The cage was big enough to hold a fairly intimate party in, and the walls were works of art in stained glass. Hobbes pulled the doors shut and said *Top floor* in a loud and commanding voice. The elevator floor lurched briefly under my feet, and we were off. For such an old mechanism, the ride was remarkably smooth. I looked for the floor numbers and couldn't help noticing there were no indicators or controls anywhere in the elevator.

"I can't help noticing there aren't any indicators or controls anywhere in this elevator, Hobbes."

"Indeed, sir. All the elevators in Griffin Hall are programmed to respond only to authorised voices. A security measure . . ."

"Then how did Melissa's abductors get to the top floor?"

"An excellent question, sir, and one I feel confident you will enlighten us on in due course."

"Stop taking the piss, Hobbes."

"Yes, sir."

The elevator stopped, and Hobbes hauled the doors open. I stepped out into a long corridor with firmly shut doors lining both sides. The lighting was pleasantly subdued, the walls were bare of any decoration or ornamentation, and the carpeting was Persian. All the closed doors looked very solid. I wondered if the Griffins locked their doors at night. I would, in a place like this. And with a family like this. Hobbes closed the elevator doors with a flourish and came forward to stand uncomfortably close beside me. Invading someone's personal space is a standard intimidation tactic, but in my time I'd faced down Beings on the Street of the Gods and made them cry like babies. It would take more than one severely up-himself butler to put me off my game.

"This is the top floor, sir. All the family bedrooms are here. Though of course not every member of the family is always in residence at the same time. Master William and Miss Eleanor have their own domiciles, in town. Master Paul and Miss Melissa do not. Mr. Griffin requires that they live here."

I frowned. "He doesn't let the children live with their own parents?"

"Again, a security measure, sir."

"Show me Melissa's room," I said, to remind him who was in charge here.

He led the way down the corridor. It was a long corridor, with a lot of doors.

"Guest rooms?" I said, gesturing.

"Oh no, sir. Guests are never permitted to stay over, sir. Only the family sleep under this roof. Security, again. All these rooms are family bedrooms. So that every member can move back and forth, as the fancy takes them, when they get bored with the trappings of a particular room. I am given to understand that boredom can be a very real problem with immortals, sir."

We walked on some more. "So," I said. "What do you think happened to Melissa, Hobbes?"

He didn't even look at me. "I really couldn't say, sir."

"But you must have an opinion?"

"I try very hard not to, sir. Opinions only get in the way of providing a proper service to the family."

"What did you do before you came here, Hobbes?"

"Oh, I've always been in service, sir."

I could believe that. No-one gets that supercilious without years of on-the-job training. "How about the rest of the staff? Did none of them see or hear anything suspicious, or out of the ordinary, before or after Melissa disappeared?"

"I did question every member of the staff most thoroughly, sir. They would have told me if they'd known anything. Anything at all."

"On the evening Melissa vanished, did you admit any unusual or unexpected visitors to the Hall?"

"People are always coming and going, sir."

I gave him one of my hard looks. "Are you always this evasive, Hobbes?"

"I do my best, sir. This is Miss Melissa's room."

We stopped before a door that looked no different from any of the others. Solid wood, sensibly closed. No obvious signs of attack or forced entry. I tried the brass handle, and it turned easily in my grasp. I pushed the door open and looked in. The room before me was completely empty. No boy band posters on the walls, no fluffy animals, no furniture. Just four bare walls, a bare bed, and an even barer wooden floor. Nothing to show a teenage girl had ever occupied this room. I glared at Hobbes.

"Tell me her room didn't always look like this."

"It didn't always look like this, sir."

"Did the Griffin order this room emptied?"

"No, sir. This is exactly how I found it."

"Explain," I said, just a little dangerously.

42

"Yes, sir. Miss Melissa was supposed to join the rest of the family for the evening meal. The Master and Mistress have always been very firm that all members of the family should dine together, when in residence. Master William and Miss Eleanor were present, and her son Master Paul, but Miss Melissa was late, which was most unlike her. When she didn't appear, I was sent to summon her. When I got here, the door was ajar. I knocked, but received no reply. When I ventured to look inside, in case she was feeling unwell, I found the room as you see it now. Miss Melissa never was much of a one for comforts or trinkets, but even so, this seemed extreme. I immediately raised the alarm, and security searched the Hall from top to bottom, but there was no trace to be found of Miss Melissa."

I looked at him for a long moment. "Are you saying," I managed finally, "that not only did Melissa's kidnappers remove her from this Hall without anyone noticing, but that they walked off with all her belongings as well? And no-one saw anything? Is that what you're saying?"

"Yes, sir."

"I have a major slap with your name on it in my pocket, Hobbes."

"I feel I should also point out that no magics will function in Griffin Hall unless authorised by a member of the Griffin family, sir. So Miss Melissa could not have been magicked out of her room . . ."

"Not without her cooperation or that of someone in her family."

"Which is of course quite impossible, sir."

"No, Hobbes, nailing a live octopus to a wall is impossible, everything else is merely difficult."

"I bow to your superior knowledge, sir."

I was still thinking *Inside job*, but I wasn't ready to say it out loud.

I peered into the empty room again and tried to call up my gift, hoping for at least a glimpse of what happened, but my inner eye wouldn't open. Someone with a hell of a lot of power really didn't want me using my gift in this case. I was beginning to wonder if perhaps Someone was playing games with me . . .

Footsteps sounded in the corridor behind me. I looked round just in time to see a uniformed maid come to a halt before Hobbes and curtsy respectfully. Damn, the servants moved quietly around here. She bobbed a quick curtsy to me, too, as an afterthought.

"Pardon me, Mr. Hobbes, sir," said the maid, in a voice that was little more than a whisper. "But the Mistress said to tell you she wants a word with Mr. Taylor before he leaves."

Hobbes looked at me and raised an eyebrow.

"Oh please teach me how to do that," I said. "I've always wanted to be able to raise a single eyebrow like that."

The maid got the giggles and had to turn away. Hobbes just looked at me.

"Oh what the hell," I said. "Might as well talk to the Mistress. She might know something."

"I wouldn't bank on it, sir," said Hobbes.


The maid hurried off on business of her own, and Hobbes led me all the way back up the corridor to Mariah Griffin's room. I was curious as to why she would want to see me and what she might be prepared to tell me about her grand-daughter that Jeremiah wouldn't, or

44

couldn't. Women often share secrets within a family that the men know nothing about. We finally came to a stop before another anonymous door.

"Mariah Griffin's room, sir," said Hobbes.

I looked at him thoughtfully. "Not Jeremiah and Mariah's room? They have separate bedrooms?"

"Indeed, sir."

I didn't ask. He wouldn't have told me anyway.

I nodded to him, and he knocked very politely on the door. A loud female voice said *Enter!* and Hobbes pushed the door open and stepped back so I could enter first. I sauntered in as though I was thinking of renting the place, then trashing it. Even though it was what passed for midafternoon in the Nightside, Mariah Griffin was still in bed. She was sitting up in a filmy white silk nightdress, propped up and supported by a whole bunch of puffy pink pillows. The walls were pink, too. In fact, the whole oversized room had a kind of pink ambience, like walking into a nursery. The bed was big enough for several people, if they were of a friendly inclination, and Mariah Griffin was surrounded by a small army of maids, advisors, and social secretaries. Some of them grudgingly made way as I took up a position at the foot of the bed.

The elaborate and no doubt very expensive counterpane was covered with the remains of several half-eaten meals, even more half-consumed boxes of chocolates, and dozens of scattered glossy gossip magazines. An open bottle of champagne stood chilling in an ice bucket, conveniently near at hand. Mariah conspicuously ignored me, apparently intent on all the people milling around her bed, competing noisily for her attention. So I stood at the foot of the bed and studied her openly.

Mariah Griffin was on the plump side of pretty, pleasantly rounded if not actually voluptuous, from the old school of beauty. The hair piled up thickly on top of her head was so pale a yellow as to be almost colourless, but her face made up for that with bright gaudy makeup. Scarlet bee-stung lips, rouged cheeks, dark purple eyeshadow, and eye-lashes so thick it was a wonder she could see past them. Mariah looked to be in her early thirties, and had done for many centuries. Her strong bone structure gave her face what character it had, undermined by a vague manner and a pettishness in the voice. She looked more like an indulged mistress than a wife of long standing.

Various maids and flunkies clustered around her, attending to her every need almost before she could think of them; plumping up her pillows, offering her a new box of chocolates or freshening her glass of champagne, as necessary. Mariah ignored them all, giving her entire attention to the day's correspondence and the updating of her social diary. It soon became clear that her default expression was a pout, and whenever events seemed to conspire against her, she would lash out feebly with a plump hand at whoever happened to be closest at that moment. The maids and flunkies took the blows without flinching. The fashion and social advisors were all careful to stay just out of arm's reach, without being seen to do so. Those nearest to me studied me carefully out of the corners of their eyes, and after a few moments to raise their courage, began making pointed little remarks to each other, loud enough for me to hear.

"Well, well, look who it isn't—the famous John Taylor."

"Infamous, I would have said. I always thought he'd be taller. You know, more butch."

"And that trench coat is so last year . . . I could run him up something really daring in mauve."

"Ask for his measurements!"

"Oh, I don't like to!"

There's definitely something about the Nightside that brings out the stereotypical behavior in some people. Emboldened that I hadn't taken offence, a large gentleman in chin-to-toe black leather glared at me openly.

"Well, lo and behold—the Nightside's very own private dick . . . always trying to slip in where he isn't wanted."

"Lo *and* behold?" I said. "I can behold all you want, but if loing is required, someone's going to have to coach me. I've never been too clear on what loing actually involves . . . There ought to be an instructional booklet; *Loing for Beginners*, or *A Bluffer's Guide to Loing*."

"You start anything with me, John Taylor, and I'll summon security, see if I don't. And then there'll be trouble!"

"Will there be loing as well?" I said hopefully.

"Why is this woman still writing to me?" Mariah Griffin said loudly, waving a letter in one plump hand to draw everyone's attention back to her. "She knows very well I'm not talking to her! My rules are very clear: miss two of my parties, and you're Out. I don't care if her children had leprosy . . ."

She was looking at everyone in the room except me, but the whole performance was for my benefit. She carried on complaining about this and that to her various advisors, who all gave her their full attention if not their interest. Mariah desperately wanted to come across as

regal, but she lacked the necessary concentration. She'd
start off on one subject, switch to another, get side-
tracked, then forget where she'd started. She fluttered
from one topic to another like a butterfly, always attracted by something else that promised to be a little bit
more interesting or colourful. I got bored waiting, so I
started wandering round the room, looking at things,
picking them up and putting them down in a deliberately
careless way.

If that didn't work, I'd start tossing them out the
windows.

There were luxurious items as far as the eye could see,
delicate china figures, antique dolls, glass animals, and
porcelain so fragile it looked like it would shatter if you
breathed on it too heavily. All carefully laid out and presented on antique furnishings of the highest order. Some
deep-seated anarchist part of me longed to run amok with
a sledgehammer, or perhaps a length of steel chain . . . I
eased my inner barbarian by helping myself to chocolates
from the opened boxes. All the soft centres were gone,
but I made do.

Judging by the pile of still-unopened letters cascading
across Mariah's bedside table, she got a lot of correspondence. E-mail never really caught on in the Nightside—
far too easy to hack or intercept. And there was always
the problem of computers developing sentience, or getting possessed by forces from the outer dark . . . and
techno-exorcists don't come cheap. Handwritten letters
are the done thing these days, especially in what some
people like to think of as the Highest Circles. The immortal Griffins are the closest thing the Nightside has to its
own aristocracy, which meant every social climber in the
place was desperate to get close to them, in the hope that

some of the Griffins' standing and glamour would rub off on the more favoured supplicants. Snobbery is a terrible vice, as easy to get hooked on as heroin and as devastating to give up when you're no longer In, and going through withdrawal symptoms.

Even royalty came to sit at the feet of the Griffins and beg discreetly for boons and favours. We get them all in the Nightside—kings and queens in exile, princes of This and lairds of That, and every rank and station you can think of. They arrive via Timeslips from other worlds and times and dimensions, cut off forever from their own people, power, and riches. Some buckle down and make something new of themselves. Most don't. Because they don't know how. They still expect to be treated as royalty just because they once were, and get really upset when the Nightside makes it clear it doesn't give a damn. Mostly they hole up together in private little members-only clubs, where they can all address each other by their proper titles and spend most of their time angling for invitations to the Griffins' latest ball or soiree. Because acceptance by the Griffins validates their special nature in the eyes of all. Unfortunately, there are so many aristos running around that the Griffins can pick and choose. And they do. You get one chance to prove yourself interesting or amusing, and then you're Out. Zog, King of the Pixies, was notorious for continually trying to crash the Griffins' parties, even after it was made clear to him that he was not welcome, and never would be, no matter with whom he arrived.

(He peed on the floor. Apparently where he came from, a servant used to follow him around with a bucket. And a mop.)

Mariah had always had pretensions to taste and style,

but unfortunately possessed none herself, and so was dependent upon a series of fashion and social advisors to help her decide who was In and who was Out, and which fads and styles would be followed each Season. But it was Mariah alone who enforced these decisions, with a whim of iron. And so the advisors shoved and elbowed at each other to get closest to Mariah, and argued every point with loud and affected voices, accompanied by large, dramatic gestures. Which occasionally degenerated into blows or slapping matches. Advisors could make or break a social reputation with a word or a glance, and everyone knew it, which was why these poor unfortunates had many acquaintances but few real friends. If the truth were known, they were probably even more paranoid and insecure than the social climbers who hung on their every word.

In the end Mariah got bored or impatient pretending I wasn't there and abruptly ordered everyone else out of the room. Including Hobbes, still lurking by the door. Everyone left, with varying degrees of reluctance, bowing and scraping and blowing kisses all the way, until finally the door closed behind the last of them, and Mariah Griffin and I were left looking at each other. She studied me coolly, trying to decide whether I was someone who could be commanded or someone she would have to flatter a little to get her way. In the end she smiled sweetly, batted her long eyelashes coquettishly, and patted the pink eiderdown beside her.

"Come here and sit with me, John Taylor. So I can get a proper look at you."

I walked forward, pulled up a chair, and sat down facing her, careful to maintain a safe distance. She pouted at me and eased down the front of her nightdress a little more, so I could get a good look at her cleavage. She wasn't upset by my caution. I could see it in her eyes. She always liked it better if the prey struggled a little first. Up close her scent was almost overpowering, the reek of crushed petals soaked in pure animal musk.

"I have some questions," I said.

"Well of course you do . . . John. That is what you private investigators do, isn't it? Interrogate your suspects? I don't think I've ever met a real private eye before. So thrilling . . ."

"You don't seem too upset over your grand-daughter's disappearance," I said, to get things started.

Mariah shrugged. "She's simply being a nuisance, as always. Sanctimonious little dear. Never happy unless she's interfering in the way I run my life, and upsetting all my plans . . . This is simply another plea for attention. Run away from home, get her grandfather's undivided interest, then turn up safe and sound a few days later, happy and smiling and perfectly safe, looking like butter wouldn't melt in her arse, the little minx. And Jeremiah will take her back in as though nothing has happened. She always could twist him round her little finger."

"You don't believe she was kidnapped?"

"Of course not! The security built into this house has kept this family safe for centuries. No-one could have got in or out without setting off all kinds of hidden alarms, unless someone in the know had deactivated them in advance. It's another of her attention-getting schemes, the stuck-up little bitch."

"Am I to take it you two don't get on?"

Mariah snorted loudly, a very unladylike sound. "My children have always been disappointments to me. My grand-children even more so. Jeremiah is the only person in the world who has ever mattered to me, the only one who ever really cared about me. You don't know who I was, what I used to be, before he found me and made me his wife, and made me immortal. Of course you don't know. No-one does, anymore. I've seen to it, believe you me. But I remember, and so does he, and I will always love him for that." She realised her voice was getting a bit loud and made a deliberate effort to regain her composure. "Melissa's current whereabouts are a matter of complete indifference to me, John."

"Even though she stands to inherit the whole family fortune, while you and your children get nothing?"

She smiled at me with her bee-stung lips, red as blood, and studied me hungrily with her dark, hooded eyes. "You're younger than I thought you'd be. Even handsome, in a hard-used sort of way. You think I'm beautiful, don't you, John? Of course you do. Everyone does. They have for centuries . . . I will never grow old, John, never lose my looks or vitality. I shall live lifetimes, and always be lovely. That's what he promised me . . . Say you think I'm beautiful, John. Come closer, and say it to my face. Touch me, John. You've never felt anything like my skin, young and fresh and vital for centuries . . ."

My mouth was dry and my hands were trembling. Sex beat on the air between us, raw and potent as an elemental force. I didn't like her, but just then, at that moment, I wanted her . . . I made myself sit very still, and the madness quickly passed. Perhaps because Mariah was already losing her concentration. When I didn't immediately weaken, her butterfly mind moved on to other matters.

"Fashions come and go, but I remain, John, forever lovely as a summer's day . . . That's the one thing I do miss, you know. Eternal night may be very glamorous, but anything can get tiring when it goes on and on without changing . . . It's been so long since I felt the warmth of sunlight on my face and the caress of a passing breeze . . ."

She prattled on, and I listened carefully, but I didn't learn anything useful. Mariah had been a shallow creature before Jeremiah made her immortal, and centuries of living, if not experience, had done little to change that. Perhaps she was incapable of change, frozen the way she was when Jeremiah took her out of Time, like an insect trapped in amber. She was Queen of Nightside Society, and that was all she cared about. Other queens might arise to challenge her grip, but in the end she would always win because she was immortal, and they were not.

She stopped talking abruptly and studied me thoughtfully, as though she'd only just remembered I was still there. "So you're the famous John Taylor. One does hear such stories about you . . . Was your mother really a Biblical myth? Did you really save us all from extinction during the recent War? They say you could have been king of the Nightside, if you'd wanted . . . Tell me about your glamorous assistants, Razor Eddie, Dead Boy, Shotgun Suzie."

"*Glamorous?*" I said, smiling despite myself. "Not quite the word I would have chosen."

"I've read all about you, and them, in the tabloids," said Mariah. "I live for gossip. Except when it's about me. Some of those *reporters* can be very cruel . . . I've been trying to get Jeremiah to buy up the *Night Times*, and that terrible rag the *Unnatural Inquirer*, for years, but he's always got some silly answer why he can't. He doesn't care what they write about him. He only ever reads the financial pages. Wouldn't know who anyone was in Society if I wasn't there to tell him . . ."

"Tell me about your children," I said, when she made the mistake of pausing for breath. "Tell me about William and Eleanor."

She pouted again, looking around her for more chocolates and her champagne glass, and I had to ask her twice more before she finally answered.

"I had the twins back in the nineteen twenties, because it was the fashion. Absolutely everyone in Society was having babies, and I just couldn't bear to be left out. All my friends assured me childbirth was the most divine, transcendent experience . . ." She snorted loudly. "And afterwards, my lovely babies grew up to be such disappointments. I can't think why. I saw to it that they had the very best nannies, the very best tutors, and every toy they ever wanted. And I made it a point to spend some time with them every weekend, no matter how full my social diary was."

"And Jeremiah?"

"Oh, he was furious at the time. Absolutely livid. Actually raised his voice to me, a thing he never does. He never wanted children."

"So what happened?" I said.

"He had me sterilized, so I couldn't have any more." Her voice was entirely unaffected, matter-of-fact. "I didn't care. The fashion was past, and they weren't what I'd expected . . . And I certainly wasn't going to go through all *that* again . . ."

"Didn't you have any friends, any close friends, who could have helped you stand up to Jeremiah?"

Mariah smiled briefly, and her eyes were suddenly very cold. "I don't have friends, John. Ordinary people don't matter to me. Or to any of us Griffins. Because you see, John, you're all so short-lived ... Like mayflies. You come and go so quickly, and you never seem to be around long enough to make any real impression, and it doesn't do to get too fond of those who do. They all die ... It's the same with pets. I used to adore my cats, back in the old days. But I can't bear them around me anymore. Or flowers ... I had the gardens laid out around the Hall back in the seventeen fifties, when landscaped gardens were all the rage, but once I had them ... I didn't know what to do with them. You can only walk through them so many times ... In the end I let them run riot, just to see what would happen. I find the jungle much more interesting—always changing, always producing something new ... Jeremiah keeps it going as our last line of defence. Just in case the barbarians ever rise up and try to take it all away from us." She laughed briefly. It was an ugly sound. "Let them try! Let them try ... No-one takes anything that belongs to us!"

"Someone may have taken your grand-daughter," I said.

She gave me a long look from under her heavy eye-lashes, and tried her seductive smile again. "Tell me, John, how much did my husband offer you to find Melissa?"

"Ten million pounds," I said, a little hoarsely. I was still getting used to the idea.

"How much more would it take, from me, for you to simply ... go through the motions and not find her? I could be very generous ... And, of course, it would be our little secret. Jeremiah would never have to know."

"You don't want her back?" I said. "Your own grand-daughter?"

The smile disappeared, and her eyes were cold, so cold. "She should never have been born," said Mariah Griffin.

# THREE

# All The
# Lost Children

I explained to Mariah Griffin, carefully and very diplo-
matically, that I couldn't accept her kind offer because I
only ever work for one client at a time. That was when
she started throwing things. Basically, anything that came
to hand. I decided this would probably be a good time to
leave and retreated rapidly to the door with assorted missiles flying past my head. I had to scramble behind me
for the door handle, because I didn't dare take my eyes
off the increasingly heavy objects coming my way, but I
finally got the door open and departed with haste, if not
dignity. I slammed the door shut against the hail of missiles and nodded politely to the waiting Hobbes. (First
rule of the successful private eye—grace under pressure.)
We both stood for a while and listened to the sound of

weighty objects slamming against the other side of the door, then I decided it was time I was somewhere else.

"I need to talk to the Griffin's children," I said to Hobbes, as we walked away. "William and Eleanor. Are they both still in residence?"

"Indeed, sir. The Griffin made it very clear that he wished them to remain, along with their respective spouses, on the assumption that you would wish to question them. I have taken the liberty of having them wait in the Library. I trust this is acceptable."

"I've always wanted to question a whole bunch of subjects in a Library," I said wistfully. "If only I'd brought my meerschaum and my funny hat . . ."

"This way, sir."

So back down in the elevator we went, then along more corridors and hallways, to the Library. I was so turned around by now I couldn't have pointed to the way out if you'd put a gun to my head. I was seriously considering leaving a trail of bread-crumbs behind me, or unreeling a long thread. Or carving directional arrows in the polished woodwork. But that would have been uncouth, and I hate running out of couth in the middle of a case. So I strolled along beside Hobbes, admiring the marvellous works of art to every side and quietly hoping he wouldn't suddenly start asking me to identify them. There still weren't many people about, apart from the occasional uniformed servant hurrying past with their head bowed. The corridors were so quiet you could have heard a mouse fart.

"Just how big is this Hall anyway?" I said to Hobbes, as we walked and walked.

"As big as it needs to be, sir. A great man must have a great house. It's expected of him."

"Who lived here before the Griffins?"

"I believe the Griffin had the Hall constructed to his own designs, sir, some centuries ago. It's my understanding he wished to make an impression . . ."

We came at last to the Library, and Hobbes opened the door and ushered me in. I shut the door firmly behind me, keeping Hobbes on the other side. The Library was large and old-fashioned, almost defiantly so. All four walls were nothing but shelves, packed with heavy bound books that clearly hadn't been published anywhen recent. Comfortable chairs were scattered across the deep carpeting, and there was a single long table in the middle of the room, complete with extra reading lamps. This had to be the Griffin's room; he came from a time when everyone who was anyone read. Many of the books on the shelves looked old enough to be seriously rare and expensive. The Griffin probably had every notable text from the past several centuries, everything from a Gutenberg Bible to an unexpurgated Necronomicon. This last in the original Arabic, of course. Probably marked with dogeared corners, doodles in the margins, and all the best bits heavily underlined.

William and Eleanor Griffin were waiting for me, standing stiffly together to present a united front in the face of a common enemy. They didn't strike me as the kind of people who'd spend much time in a Library by choice. Their respective spouses stood together in a far corner, observing the situation watchfully. I took my time looking the four of them over. The longer I kept them waiting, the more likely it was someone would say something they hadn't meant to, just to break the silence.

William Griffin was tall and muscular, in that self-absorbed body-building way. He wore a black leather jacket over a white T-shirt and jeans. All of which looked utterly immaculate. Probably because he threw them out as soon as they got creased and put on new ones. He wore his blond hair close-cropped, had cold blue eyes, his father's prominent nose, and his mother's pouting mouth. He was doing his best to stand tall and proud, as befitted a Griffin, but his face refused to look anything but sullen and sulky. After all, his comfortable existence had been turned suddenly upside down, first by the revealing of the new will, then by his daughter's disappearance. People of his high station resent the unexpected. Their wealth and power are supposed to protect them from such things.

Eleanor gave every impression of being made of stronger stuff. Even though she was wearing an outfit that even Madonna would have turned down as too trashy. Hooker chic, with added gaudy. She wore her long blonde hair in what were obviously artificial waves, and used heavy makeup to disguise only average features. She glared openly at me, as much irritated as angry, and chain-smoked all through the interview. She stubbed out her butts on the polished surface of the long table and ground them under foot into the priceless Persian carpet. I'll bet she didn't do that when her father was around.

Over in the far corner, as far away as she could get and still be in the same room, William's wife Gloria, the ex-supermodel, was tall, thin, and so black her skin had a bluish sheen. She studied me thoughtfully with dark hooded eyes, her high-boned face showing no expression at all under her glistening bald skull. She wore a long white satin dress, to contrast with her night-dark skin. She had that intense, hungry look all professional models cultivate, and she still looked as though she could saunter successfully down any catwalk that took her fancy. Although she was standing right beside Eleanor's husband Marcel, her body language made it clear she was only standing there because she'd been told to. I don't think she looked at him once.

Marcel wore a good suit, but from the way it hung off him you could tell he was used to dressing more casually. Marcel was casual, in thought, word, and deed. You could tell, from the way he stood and the way he looked, and from the way he continued to look vague and shifty even when doing nothing at all. He gave the impression that he was only there under sufferance and couldn't wait to get back to whatever it was he'd been doing. And that he didn't care who knew it. I don't think he looked directly at me once. He was handsome enough, in a weak and unfinished sort of way and, like Gloria, remained silent because he'd been told to.

I looked from Walker to Eleanor and back again, letting the tension build. I was in no hurry.

I knew all about the Griffin children and their many marriages. Everyone in the Nightside did. The gossip magazines couldn't get enough of them and their various doings. I have been known to read the tabloids, on occasion, because they make the perfect light reading on long stakeouts. Because they don't take up too much of my attention, and you can hide behind them when necessary. Which means I end up knowing a hell of a lot about people who otherwise wouldn't interest me in the slightest. I knew, for example, that Gloria was William's seventh wife, and that Marcel was Eleanor's fourth husband. And that all Griffin spouses were immortal, too, but only as long as they remained married to a Griffin.

In fairness, Gloria and Marcel had lasted longer than most.

"I know you," William said to me finally, trying to sound tough and aggressive but not quite pulling it off. (Though it was probably good enough for most of the people he had to deal with.) "John Taylor, the Nightside's premiere private eye . . . Just another damned snoop, searching through the garbage of other people's lives. Muckraker and troublemaker. Don't tell him anything, Eleanor."

"I wasn't going to, you idiot." Eleanor shot a glare at her brother that reduced him immediately to sulky silence again, then she turned the full force of her cold glare on me. I did my best to bear up under it. "You're not welcome here, Mr. Taylor. None of us have anything to say to you."

"Your father thinks otherwise," I said calmly. "In fact, he's paying me a hell of a lot of money to be here, and I have his personal authority to ask you any damned thing I feel like. And what Daddy wants, Daddy gets. Am I right?"

They both stared back at me defiantly. Any answers I got out of these two would not come easily or directly.

"Why are you both here?" I said, because you have to start somewhere. "I mean, in residence at the Hall as opposed to your own houses, out in the Nightside? That's . . . unusual, isn't it?"

More silence. I sighed heavily. "Am I going to have to send Hobbes off to bring your father here to spank the pair of you?"

"We're here because of this nonsense about a new will," said Eleanor. That was all she meant to say, but she couldn't bring herself to leave it at that, not when she had

62

so much spleen to vent and a ready listener at hand. "I can't believe he's prepared to disinherit us all, after all this time! He just can't! And certainly not in favour of that holier-than-thou little cow, Melissa! She's only gone missing because she knows what I'll do to her when I get my hands on her! She's poisoned our father's mind against us."

William snorted loudly. "Changing his will at this late stage? The old man's finally going senile."

"If only it were that simple," said Eleanor, inhaling half her cigarette in one go. "No, he's up to something. He's always up to something . . ."

"What was Melissa's state of mind, before she . . . went missing?" I said. "What did she have to say about the provisions of the new will?"

"Wouldn't know," William said shortly. "She wasn't talking to me. Or Gloria. Locked herself away in her room and wouldn't come out. Just like Paul."

"You leave my Paul out of this!" Eleanor said immediately. "There's nothing wrong with him. He's just . . . sensitive."

"Yeah," William growled. "He's sensitive, all right . . ."

"And what do you mean by that?" said Eleanor, rounding on her brother with the light of battle rising in her eyes.

I knew an old argument when I saw one and moved quickly to intervene. "What are you two planning to do about the new will?"

"Contest it, of course!" Eleanor snapped, turning her glare back on me. "Fight it, with every weapon at our disposal."

"Even kidnapping?" I said.

"Don't be ridiculous." Eleanor did her best to look down her nose at me, even though I was a few inches taller. "Daddy Dearest would have us both whipped within an inch of our lives if we so much as looked nastily at his precious grand-daughter. He's always been soft on her. William wasn't even allowed to chastise her as a child. If he had, she might not have grown up into such a contrary little bitch."

"I say, steady on, Eleanor," said William, but she talked right over him. I got the impression that happened a lot.

"Melissa hasn't been kidnapped. She's hiding out, hoping the storm will blow over. Well it won't! I'll see to that. What's mine is mine, and no-one takes what's mine. Especially not my sweet, smiling, treacherous niece!"

"Assume," I said, "for the sake of argument and because I'll hit you if you don't, that Melissa really has been kidnapped. Who do you think might be behind it? Does your father have any serious enemies, or any recent ones who might choose to strike back at him through his grand-daughter?"

William snorted loudly again, and even Eleanor managed a small smile as she ground out her cigarette on the tabletop, scarring the polished surface.

"Our father has enemies like a dog has fleas," said William. "He collects them, nurtures them."

"Sometimes I think he goes out of his way to make new ones," said Eleanor, lighting another cigarette with a monogrammed gold Zippo lighter. "Just to put some spice into his life. Nothing puts a spring in his step and a gleam in his eye like a new enemy to do down, and destroy."

"Any names in particular you'd care to throw into the pot?" I said.

"Well, the Authorities, of course," said William. "Because they wouldn't let Daddy become a member of their private little club. Never did know why. You'd have thought they'd be perfect for each other. After all, they ran the Nightside, and he owned most of it. But of course, they're all dead now . . ."

"I know," I said. "I was there."

Everyone in the Library looked at me sharply. Perhaps realising for the first time that some of the many scary things they'd heard about me might be true. And that not answering my questions might not be a good idea, after all. I have a bad reputation in the Nightside, and I've put a lot of work into maintaining it. Makes my life so much easier. Though I haven't killed nearly as many people as everyone thinks.

"Well," said William, a little uneasily, "I suppose Walker is our father's main enemy now, inasmuch as anyone is. He's running things in the Authority's absence, inasmuch as anyone does."

I nodded thoughtfully. Of course, Walker. That quiet, calm, and very civilised city gent who'd spent most of his life doing the Authorities' dirty work. He could call on armies to back him up, or calm a riot with a single thoughtful look, and his every word and whim was law. When he used his Voice, no-one could deny him. They say he once made a corpse sit up on its mortuary slab and answer his questions. Walker had a history of being willing to do whatever it took to get the job done. And he wasn't afraid of anyone.

We had worked together in the past, on occasion. But

we were never what you'd call close. We didn't approve of each other's methods.

"Anyone else?" I said.

"You can add the name of anyone who's ever done business with our father," said Eleanor, tapping ash onto the priceless carpet, genuinely without thinking about it. "No-one ever shook hands with Daddy and walked away with all their fingers."

"But none of them would have the balls to threaten him," said William. "They might talk tough through their lawyers, but not one of them would dare strike at him directly. They know what he's capable of. Remember Hilly Divine? Thought he could muscle Daddy out of his district by sending an army of mercenaries to storm the Hall?"

"What happened?" I said.

William smirked. "The jungle ate the mercenaries. And Daddy ate Hilly Divine. Over a period of months, I understand, bit by bit. Of course, that was back before we were born. He might have mellowed since then."

"There are those who say some part of Hilly Divine is still alive, in some hidden dungeon under the Hall," Eleanor said dreamily. "That Daddy still keeps him around, for special occasions. When he wants to serve something special at a celebratory banquet."

"Never touch the finger snacks," said William, still smirking. "Daddy's had a lot of his enemies disappear . . ."

"Everyone's afraid of our father," Eleanor said shortly. "No-one would dare touch Melissa because they know what he'd do in retaliation. Everyone in the Nightside bends the knee and bows the neck to Daddy Dearest because of what he could do and has done in the past."

"I don't," I said.

Eleanor looked at me pityingly. "You're here, aren't you? You came when he called."

"Not because I was frightened," I said.

"No," said Eleanor, studying me thoughtfully. "Maybe you aren't, at that." She seemed to find the prospect intriguing.

I looked at William. "Tell me about Melissa. How you feel about her. You don't seem too upset about her being missing."

"We're not close," said William, scowling heavily. "Never have been. Daddy saw to that. Insisting she be brought up here, under his roof, ever since she was a baby, instead of with me and Gloria. For *security reasons*. Yeah, right. She would have been perfectly safe with us. But no, it had to be his way, like always. He wanted to be sure we wouldn't turn her against him. He always has to be in control, of everything and everyone."

"Even family?" I said.

"Family most of all," said Eleanor.

"You could have stood up to your father," I said to William.

It was his turn to look at me pityingly. "You don't say no to Jeremiah Griffin. I don't know why he was so keen to raise her himself," said William. "It's not as if he did such a great job raising us."

"So you let him take your children," I said. "Melissa, and Paul."

"We had no choice!" said Eleanor, but all of a sudden she seemed too tired to be properly angry. She looked at the cigarette in her hand as though she had no idea what it was. "You have no idea what it's like to have the Griffin as your father."

"I might have made a mess of things," said William, "but I would have liked to try and raise Melissa myself. Gloria didn't care, but then Gloria's never really been mommy material, have you, dear? I went along with Daddy because . . . well, because everyone does. He's just . . . too big. You can't argue with him because he's always got an answer. You can't argue with a man who's lived lifetimes, because he's always seen everything before, done everything before. I sometimes wonder what kind of a man I might have been if I'd had the good fortune to be born some other man's son."

"Not immortal," I said.

"There is that, yes," said William. "There's always that."

I liked him a little better for what he'd just said, but I still had to ask the next question. "Why did you wait until your seventh marriage to have children?"

His face hardened immediately, and suddenly I was the enemy again, to be defied at all costs. "None of your damned business."

I looked at Eleanor, but she glared coldly back at me. I'd touched something in them, for a moment, but the moment had passed. So I looked at Gloria and Marcel, over in their far corner.

"Do either of you have anything to say?"

Gloria and Marcel looked at their respective spouses and shook their heads. They had nothing to say. Which was pretty much what I'd expected.

I left the four of them in the Library, shut the door carefully behind me, and turned to Hobbes. "There's still one member of the family I haven't seen. Paul Griffin."

"Master Paul never sees anyone," Hobbes said gravely. "But you can talk to him, if you wish."

"You're really getting on my tits, Hobbes."

"All part of the service, sir. Master Paul rarely leaves his bedroom, these days. Those troublesome teenage years . . . He communicates occasionally through the house telephone, and the servants leave his meals outside his door. You can try talking to him through the door. He might respond to a new voice."

So back down the corridors to the elevator, and up to the top floor again. I hadn't done so much walking in years. If I had to come back to the Hall again, I'd bring a bicycle with me. We ended up before another closed bedroom door. I knocked, very politely.

"This is John Taylor, Paul," I said, in my best non-threatening *I'm only here to help* voice. "Can I talk to you, Paul?"

"You can't come in!" said a high-pitched, almost shrill teenage voice. "The door's locked! And protected!"

"It's all right, Paul," I said quickly. "I just want to talk. About Melissa's disappearance."

"She was taken," said Paul. He sounded as though he was right on the other side of the door. He didn't sound . . . troubled, or sensitive. He sounded scared. "They came and took her away, and no-one could stop them. She's probably dead by now. They'll come for me next. You'll see! But they'll never find me . . . because I won't be here."

"Who are *they*, Paul?" I said. "Who do you think took Melissa? Who do you think is coming for you?"

But he wouldn't say anything. I could hear him breathing harshly on the other side of the door. He might have been crying.

"Paul, listen to me. I'm John Taylor, and almost as many people are scared of me as are scared of your grandfather. I can protect you . . . but I need to know who from. Just give me a name, Paul, and I'll make them leave you alone. Paul? I can protect you . . ."

He laughed then, a low, small, and terribly hopeless sound. No-one that young should ever have to make a sound like that. I tried to talk to him some more, but he wouldn't answer. He might still have been on the other side of the door, or he might not. In the end I looked at Hobbes, and he shook his head, his grave face as unreadable as ever.

"Has Paul seen a doctor?" I asked quietly.

"Oh, several, sir. The Griffin insisted. All kinds of doctors, in fact. But they all agreed there was nothing wrong with Master Paul, or at least, nothing they could treat. Miss Melissa was the only one he would talk to, lately. Now that she's gone . . . I don't know what will become of Master Paul."

I didn't like to leave Paul like that, but I didn't see what else I could do. Short of kicking the door in, dragging him out of the Hall by force, and hiding him in one of my safe houses. Even if the Griffin had been willing to go along with it, which I rather doubt. In the end I walked away and left Paul alone, in his locked and protected bedroom. I like to think I could have helped him if he'd have let me. But he didn't.

Hobbes escorted me back to the front door and made sure I had my briefcase with me when I left. As if there was any way I was going to forget one million pounds in cash.

"Well, Hobbes," I said. "It's been an interesting if not

particularly informative visit. You can tell the Griffin I'll make regular reports, when I have anything useful to tell him. Assuming the jungle doesn't attack my car again on the way out."

Hobbes went so far as to raise a single eyebrow again. "The jungle attacked you, sir? That should not have happened. All authorised visitors are assured safe passage on their journey up the hill to the Hall. It's part of the security package."

"Unless someone didn't want me here." I said.

"I'm sure you get that all the time, sir," said Hobbes. And he shut the door in my face.

FOUR

# where every-
# body knows
# your name

Bottom line, I had a victim who might or might not be
missing, and a family who might or might not want her
found. And Somebody very powerful had blocked off my
gift for finding things. Some cases you just know aren't
going to go well. I got back into Dead Boy's futuristic
car, and it drove me back down the hill. And as we glided
smoothly through the brooding primeval jungle, the
plants all drew back from the side of the road to give us
more room. Nothing and no-one bothered us all the way
back down the hill, and soon enough we passed through
the great iron gates and back out into the Nightside
proper.

The car bullied its way into the never-ending stream of
traffic, and I sat thinking and scowling as it carried me
smoothly back into the dark heart of the Nightside. One

of the first hard lessons you learn in life is never to interfere in family arguments. No matter which side or position you take you can't win, because family arguments are never about facts or reason; they're about emotion and history. Who said what thirty years ago and who got the biggest slice of cake at a birthday party. Old slights and older grudges. It's always the little things that really haunt people; the things no-one else remembers.

The Griffins were held together by power and position, and precious little love that I could see. And anyone who'd lived as long as they had had to have accumulated more than their fair share of grudges and nursed resentments. I felt sorry for the grand-children, Melissa and Paul. Hard enough to be born into such a divided family without having grandparents who'd already lived lifetimes. Talk about a generations gap . . . Why was the Griffin so keen to raise his grand-children himself? What did he hope to make of them that he hadn't managed with his children? Had he succeeded with Melissa? Was that why he changed his will in her favour?

I might have a photo of her, but I still didn't have a clear picture of who she was.

So many questions and not an answer in sight. Luckily, when you're looking for answers, the oldest bar in the world is a good place to start. You can find the answers to almost anything at Strangefellows; though no-one guarantees you'll like what you hear.

I looked vaguely out the window at the traffic passing by. The road was crammed full with all the usual weird and wonderful vehicles that speed endlessly through the Nightside, and every one of them was careful not to get too close to Dead Boy's car. It had really vicious built-in defences, and a very low boredom threshold. There were taxis that ran on virgin's blood and ambulances that ran on distilled suffering. Things that looked like cars but weren't, and were always hungry, and motorcycle couriers that had stopped being human long ago. Trucks carrying unthinkable loads to appalling destinations, and small anonymous delivery vans, carrying the kind of goods that no-one is supposed to want but far too many do. Business as usual, in the Nightside.

The car took me straight to the Necropolis, where its owner was waiting for it. The Necropolis is the Nightside's only authorised cemetery, where *rest in peace* isn't a platitude, it's enforced by law. When the Necropolis plants you, you stay planted. Dead Boy was currently working there as a security guard, keeping the grave-robbers and necromancers out and the dearly departed in. (There's always someone planning an escape.)

Dead Boy was mugged and murdered in the Nightside many years ago and came back from the dead to avenge his murder. He made a deal, though he's never said with whom. Either way, he should have read the small print in his contract, because now he can't die. He just goes on and on, a trapped spirit possessing his own dead body. We've worked a couple of cases together. He's very useful for hiding behind when the bullets start flying. I suppose we're friends. It's hard to tell—the dead have different emotions from the living.

I left the car parked outside the Necropolis and walked away. It could look after itself until Dead Boy came to claim it at the end of his shift, and I had things I needed to be doing. I strolled along the dark neonlit streets, past sleazy clubs and the more dangerous, members-only establishments, and my reputation went ahead of me, clearing the way. There was still a lot of rebuilding going on, aftermath of the Lilith War. The good guys won, but only just. At least most of the dead had been cleared away now, though it took weeks. The Necropolis furnaces ran full-time, and a lot of restaurants boasted a Soylent Green special on their menus, for the more discerning palates.

The streets seemed as crowded as ever, teeming with people busy searching for their own personal heavens and hells, for all the knowledge, pleasures, and satisfactions that can only be found in the darkest parts of the Nightside. You can find anything here if it doesn't find you first.

Buyer beware . . .

I made my way to my usual drinking haunt, Strange-fellows, the kind of place that should be shut down by the spiritual health board. It's where the really wild things go to drink and carouse, and try to forget the pressures of the night that never ends. The bar where it's always three o'clock in the morning, and there's never ever been a happy hour. I clattered down the bare metal steps into the great sunken stone pit and headed for the long, wooden bar at the far end. I winced as I realised the background music was currently playing a medley of the Carpenters' Greatest Hits. Music to gouge out your eyeballs to. Alex Morrisey, the bar's owner, bartender, and miserable pain in the neck, must be in one of his moods again.

(Last time I was in, he was playing the Prodigy's "Smack My Bitch Up," with the lyrics changed to "Suck My Kneecaps." I didn't ask.)

All the usual unusual suspects were taking their ease at the scattered tables and chairs, while half a dozen members of the SAS circulated among them, soliciting donations with menaces. The Salvation Army Sisterhood was on the prowl again, and if you didn't cough up fast enough and generously enough, out would come the specially blessed silver knuckle-dusters. The SAS are hardcore Christian terrorists. Save them all, and let God sort them out. No compromise in defence of Mother Church. They burn down Satanist churches, perform exorcisms on politicians, and they once crucified a street mime. Upside down. And then they set fire to him. A lot of people applauded. The Sisterhood wear strict old-fashioned nun's habits, steel-toed kicking boots, and really powerful hand guns, holstered openly on each hip. They've been banned and condemned by every official branch of the Christian Church, but word is they've all been known to hire the SAS on occasion, on the quiet, when all other methods have been tried, and failed. The Salvation Army Sisterhood gets results, even if you have to look away and block your ears while they're doing it.

*We sin to put an end to sinning*, they say.

One of the Sisterhood recognised me and quickly alerted the others. They gathered together and glared at me as I passed. I smiled politely, and one of them made the sign of the cross. Another made the sign of the seriously pissed off, then they all left. Perhaps to pray for the state of my soul or to see if there was a new bounty on my head.

I finally reached the bar, unbuttoned my trench coat, and sank gratefully down onto the nearest barstool. I nodded to Alex Morrisey, who was already approaching with my usual—a glass of real Coke. He was dressed all in black, right down to the designer shades and the snazzy French beret he wears to hide his spreading bald patch. He slammed my glass down onto a coaster bearing the legend of a local brewery; SHOGGOTH'S OLD AND VERY PECULIAR.

"I'm impressed, Taylor, you actually scared off the SAS, and I once saw them skin and eat a werewolf."

"It's a gift," I said easily.

I rolled the Coke round in my glass to release the bouquet, and savoured it for a moment before looking casually round the bar, checking who was in, and who might be useful. Count Dracula was sitting at the end of the bar, a ratty-faced dry old stick in a grubby tuxedo and an opera cloak that had seen better days. He was drinking his usual Type O Negative and talking aloud to himself, also as usual. After all these years he doesn't have much of an accent anymore but he puts it on for the personal appearances.

"Stinking agent keeps me so busy these days, I never have any time for myself. It's all chat shows, and signings, and plug your new book . . . Posing with up and coming Goth Rock bands, and endorsing a new kind of vacuum cleaner . . . I have become a joke! I used to have my own Castle, until the Communists took it over . . . I used to have my vampire brides, but now I only hear from them when the alimony cheque is late. They're bleeding me dry! You know who my agent booked to support me on my last personal appearance? The Transylvanian Terpsichorean Transvestites! Twenty-two tarted-up nosferatu tap-dancing along to "I'm Such a Silly When the Moon Comes Out." The things you see when you haven't got a stake handy . . . I could have died! Again. I tell you, some night you just shouldn't get out of your coffin."

Not far away, half-spilling out of a private booth and ostentatiously ignoring the old vampire, was The Thing That Walked Like An It. Star of a dozen monster movies back in the fifties, it was now reduced to signing photos of itself at memorabilia conventions. There'd been a whole bunch of them in the week before, reminiscing about all the cities they'd terrorized in their prime. Now, if it wasn't for nostalgia, no-one would remember them at all.

(The Big Green Lizard was banned from the convention circuit because of his refusal to wear a diaper after the "radioactive dump" incident.)

A couple of Morlocks bellied up to the bar, and made a nuisance of themselves by being very specific about the kind of finger snacks they wanted. Alex yelled for his muscle-bound bouncers, and Betty and Lucy Coltrane stopped flexing at each other long enough to come over and beat the crap out of the Morlocks before throwing them out on their misshapen ears. There's a limit to what Alex will put up with, even when he's in the best of moods, which isn't often. In fact, most days you can get thrown out for politely indicating you haven't been given the right change. I realised Alex was still hovering, so I looked at him enquiringly.

"I'm offering a special on Angel's Urine," he said hopefully. "Demand's gone right off ever since word got out it wasn't a trade name after all, but more of a warning ... And I've got some Pork Scratchings in, freshly grated. Or those Pork Balls you like."

I shook my head. "I've gone off the Pork Balls. They're nice enough, but you only get two in a packet."

"Hell," said Alex, "you only get two on a pig."

Behind the bar, a statue of Elvis in his white jump-suit was weeping bloody tears. A clock's hands were going in opposite directions, and a small television set was showing broadcasts from Hell, with the sound turned down. A mangy vulture on a perch was gnawing enthusiastically at something that looked disturbingly fresh. The vulture caught me watching and gave me a long, thoughtful look.

"Behave yourself, Agatha," said Alex.

"Agatha," I said thoughtfully. "Isn't that the name of your ex-wife? How is the old girl these days?"

"She's very good to me," said Alex. "She never visits. Though she's late with the alimony cheque again. *Jonathon, leave the duck alone!* I won't tell you again! And no, I don't want the orange back."

"Place seems pretty crowded tonight," I said.

"We've got a very popular new cabaret act," Alex said proudly. "Hang about while I announce him." He raised his voice. "Listen up, scumbags! It's cabaret time, presenting once again that exceptional artiste, Mr. Explodo! Your own, your very own, and I wish you'd take him with you because he disturbs the crap out of me, yes; it's Suicide Jones!"

A very ordinary-looking man stepped bashfully out onto a small spotlit stage, waved cheerfully to the wildly applauding audience, then exploded into bloody gobbets. Messiest thing I'd seen in ages. The crowed roared their approval, clapping and stamping their feet. As cabaret acts went, it was impressive enough if a bit brief. I looked at Alex.

"It's not the blowing himself up that's the act," Alex explained. "It's the way he pulls all the little bits of himself back together again afterwards."

"You mean he blows himself up over and over again?" I said.

"Every night, and twice on Saturdays. It's a living, I suppose."

"Speaking of which," I said, "why are you still here,

Alex? You always said you only stayed because Merlin's geas bound you and your line to this bar in perpetuity. But now he's finally dead *and* gone, thanks to Lilith, what's holding you here?"

"Where else would I go?" said Alex, his voice flat and almost without emotion. "What else could I do? This is what I know and what I do. And besides, where else would I get the opportunity to upset, insult, and terrorize so many people on a regular basis? Running this bar has spoilt me for anywhere else. This . . . is my life. Dammit."

"How has Merlin's disappearance affected things here?"

"*Will you keep your voice down!* I haven't told anyone, and I'm not about to. If certain people, and certain other forces not at all people, knew for certain that this bar was no longer protected by Merlin's magics, they'd be hitting it with everything from Biblical plagues to the Four Horsemen of the Apocalypse."

"It's your own fault for short-changing people."

"Let us change the subject. I hear you and Suzie Shooter are shacking up together now. I can honestly say I never saw that one coming. How is everyone's favourite psychopathic gun nut?"

"Oh, still killing people," I said. "She's off chasing down a bounty, out on the Borderlands. She's got a birthday coming up soon; maybe I'll buy her that backpack nuke she's been hinting about."

"I wish I thought you were joking." Alex regarded me thoughtfully. "How's everything . . . working out?"

"We're taking it one day at a time," I said. My turn to change the subject. "I need to talk to someone who can tell me all about the Griffin and his family. Very definitely including all the things people like us aren't supposed to know about. Anyone in tonight who might fit the bill?"

"You're in luck, sort of," said Alex. "See that smartly dressed gentleman sitting at the table in the far corner, trying to charm someone else into buying him a drink? Well, that is no gentleman, that is a reporter. Name's Harry Fabulous. Currently working as a stringer for the Nightside's very own scurrilous tabloid, the *Unnatural Inquirer*. All the news that can be made to fit. He knows everything, even if most of it probably isn't true."

I nodded. I knew Harry. I caught his eye and gestured for him to come over and join me. He smiled cheerfully and sauntered up to the bar. Oh yes, I knew all about Harry Fabulous. Handsome, charming, and always expressively dressed, Harry was a snake in wolf's clothing. There was a time when Harry was the Nightside's premiere Go To man, for everything that's bad for you. And then he got religion the hard way, through a personal encounter he still won't talk about, and decided to become an investigative journalist for the good of his soul. I think the idea was to expose corruption and bring down evil in high places, but unfortunately, the only place that was hiring was . . . the *Unnatural Inquirer*. Which doesn't so much expose corruption as wallow in it. Still, we all have to start somewhere. Harry says he's working his way up. He'd have a hard job working his way down.

"Hello there, John," said Harry Fabulous, showing off the perfect teeth in his perfect smile. He grabbed my hand and shook it just that little bit too familiarly. "What can I do for you? I've got a line on some genuine Martian red weed, if you're interested. A very cool smoke, or so I'm told . . ."

"If you say it's out of the world, you will receive a short but painful visit from the slap fairy," I said sternly. You have to keep Harry in his place or he takes advantage. "I thought you were out of that line of business?"

"Oh, I am, I am! But one does hear things . . ."

"Good," I said. "What are you working on at the moment, Harry?"

"I'm chasing down a rumour that the Walking Man has entered the Nightside," said Harry, trying hard to sound casual.

"There have always been rumours," said Alex. "Your paper pays for sightings, but all it ever runs are friend of a friend stories and blurry photos that could be anyone."

"This looks like the real thing," said Harry, absolutely radiating sincerity. "The wrath of God in the world of men, sent among us to punish the guilty. And he's finally come to the Nightside! Which is a scary prospect for . . . well, pretty much everyone in the Nightside. A lot of people have disappeared from sight, no doubt hiding under their beds and whimpering until he's gone again. If I could get an interview . . ."

"He'd shoot you on sight, Harry, and you know it."

"If the job was easy, everybody would be doing it." Harry considered me thoughtfully. "So, you and Suzie Shooter are an item now? You're a braver man than I gave you credit for."

"Does everyone know?" I said.

"You're news!" said Harry. "The two most dangerous individuals in the Nightside getting it on together! Talk about a celebrity couple. The man who saved the Nightside during the Lilith War, and Suzie Shooter, also known as Shotgun Suzie, and *Oh Hell, Just Shoot Yourself in the Head and Get It Over With*. My editor would pay out some serious money for an exclusive about your living arrangements."

"Not interested," I said.

"But . . . everyone is fascinated! Enquiring minds have a right to know!"

"No they don't," I said firmly. "That's why Suzie has been knee-capping paparazzi, and laying down man-traps outside the house. But I'll tell you what, Harry, you help me with a case I'm working on, and I'll tell you something about Suzie that no-one else knows. Interested?"

"Of course! What do you want to know?"

"Tell me about the Griffin and his family. Not just the history, but the gossip as well. Starting with how he became immortal in the first place, if you know."

"That's all you want?" said Harry Fabulous. "Easy peasy!" He started to give me a superior smile, then remembered who he was talking to. "It's not exactly secret how Jeremiah Griffin became immortal. It's just that most people don't talk about it if they know what's good for them. Basically, some centuries ago the Griffin made a deal with the Devil. Immortality, in return for his soul. The Griffin thought he'd made a good deal; because if he never dies, how can the Devil ever claim his soul? But, as always there was a clause in the contract; Jeremiah could pass on his immortality to his wife, and even to his children, and their spouses . . . but not to his grand-children. Should a Griffin grand-child ever reach society's definition of adulthood, then the Griffin's immortality is immediately forfeit, and the Devil would come to claim him and drag him down to Hell."

"What about the rest of the family?" I said. "Would they lose their immortality, too? And their souls?"

"Unknown," said Harry.

"So how did the Griffin end up with two teenage grand-children?"

Harry smirked. "Jeremiah never intended to have any children, let alone grand-children. Word is he took extraordinary precautions to prevent it, including condoms with so many built-in protections they glowed in the dark. But there never was a husband whose wife couldn't out-think him in that department, and once Mariah was actually pregnant with twins, the Griffin reluctantly went along with it. Though he's supposed to have taken steps to ensure there wouldn't be any more."

"He had her sterilized," I said. "Mariah told me."

"You got that straight from the woman herself?" said Harry. "Now that I can use! That's a genuine exclusive . . . Anyway, after the two children had grown up, it didn't take them that long to decide they wanted children of their own rather more than they wanted dear old Dad around forever. Both Melissa and Paul were planned, conceived, and born in strict secrecy, only a few weeks apart, then presented to Jeremiah as a fait accompli. Word is he went mad, threatened to kill both his children and the grand-children, but somehow . . . he didn't. Ever since, everyone's been waiting for the other shoe to drop. But the grand-children grew up unharmed, even indulged . . . and a little weird. I suppose living with the constant threat of death hanging over you will do that. Because let's face it, it's either them or him, and he's got a hell of a lot more to lose . . . When word got out that he'd made a new will, leaving everything to Melissa, you could hear jaws dropping all over the Nightside."

"Hold it," I said. "You know about the new will?"

"Damn, John, *everyone* knows! It's the hottest piece of news in years! The information spread across the

Nightside faster than a road runner with a rocket up its arse. Absolutely no-one saw that coming. The Griffin prepared to die at last, and leave everything to quiet, mousy, little Melissa? All the other Griffins disinherited, at a stroke? A lot of people still don't believe it. They think the Griffin's running another of his horribly complicated and very nasty schemes, where everyone gets the shaft except the Griffin. That man never gave away anything that was his in the whole of his over-extended life."

"Except his soul," I said.

Harry shrugged. "Maybe this is all part of a plan to get it back. There are rumours . . . that the Griffin is responsible for Melissa's disappearance. That he's already had Melissa killed and only set up the new will as a smoke screen."

"Not with what he's paying me to find her," I said. "Oh, Alex, before I forget. Look after this for me, will you? I'll pick it up later."

And I handed over my briefcase full of a million pounds to Alex. He grunted at the weight as he accepted it and stowed it out of sight behind the bar. He'd held things for me before and never asked questions. I think he saw them as surety against me paying my bar bill. He scowled at me.

"It's not your dirty laundry again, is it, Taylor? I swear some of your socks could walk to the laundrette on their own."

"Just a few explosives I said I'd look after for a friend," I said blithely. "I wouldn't let anyone get too near it if I were you." I turned back to Harry. "If Melissa really was kidnapped . . . who would you put in the frame as likely suspects?"

"I think better with a drink in me," Harry suggested.

"Get on with it," I hinted.

"Oh come on, John, all this talking is thirsty business . . ."

"All right," I said. I looked at Alex. "Get this man a glass of Angel's Urine, and a bag of Pork Balls. Now talk, Harry."

"When it comes to the Griffin's enemies, I'm spoilt for choice," said Harry. "I suppose you'd have to include the Jasper Twins, Big Max the Voodoo Apostate, Grievous Bodily Charm, and the Lady Damnation. If they all ever end up in the same room at the same time, it's probably a sign of the Apocalypse. Any one of them could be a contender for Number One Scumbag in the Nightside, if the Griffin ever does actually pop his clogs. But I still wouldn't rule out the Griffin as your main suspect. That man is more devious than you imagine. In fact, he's more devious than you *can* imagine. Living as a complete bastard for centuries will do that to you."

"Melissa will be eighteen in a matter of hours," I said. "Legal age of adulthood. If I don't find her before then and take her back to Griffin Hall to sign some documents to validate the new will, then Mariah and the others will become legal inheritors again. Which gives them one hell of a motive."

"If you take her back to her grand-father," said Alex, putting a glass and a bag in front of Harry, "he'll probably kill her right in front of you, to safeguard his soul. That could be why he hired you. Maybe . . . someone kidnapped her to save her from him."

"If Philip Marlowe had had to deal with cases like mine, he'd have given it all up and become a plumber," I growled. "There are far too many questions in this case and nowhere near enough hard facts." I glared at Harry just because he was there. "How old is Jeremiah Griffin? Does anyone know for sure?"

"If they do, they're smart enough to keep very quiet about it," said Harry. He sipped his drink and made a surprised noise. "The best guess is several centuries. There are records of the Griffin's presence in the Nightside all the way back to the thirteenth century, but before that the records for everyone get spotty. Chaucer mentions him in the unexpurgated text of *The Canterbury Tales*, if that's any help."

"Not really," I said. "Look, the Nightside has immortals like a dog has fleas, and that's not even including the Beings on the Street of the Gods. There must be someone or something still around who was there when the Griffin first appeared on the scene."

"Well, there's Shock-Headed Peter, the Lord of Thorns, Kid Cthulhu, and of course Old Father Time himself. But again, if they know anything, they've gone to great pains to keep quiet about it. The Griffin is a powerful man, and he has a very long reach."

"All right," I said. "Tell me about his business. I mean, I know he's rich and owns everything that isn't nailed down, but how, precisely?"

"The man is very very rich," said Harry. "Centuries of continued effort and the wonders of accumulated compound interest will do that. Whoever does eventually take over the Griffin family business will own a substantial part of the Nightside and a controlling interest in a majority of the businesses that operate here. It's no secret that the Griffin has been manoeuvring to take over the position left vacant by the recently deceased Authorities. So whoever inherits his power base could end up running the Nightside. Inasmuch as anyone does, or can. Would the

Griffin really have put so much time and effort into becoming King of the Heap, just so he could die and hand it over to an inexperienced eighteen-year-old girl?"

"It doesn't sound too likely, when you put it like that," I said. "But I have to wonder what Walker will have to say. Last time I looked he was still running things, and I can't see him stepping down for anyone he considered unworthy."

"Walker?" Harry sniffed dismissively. "He's only running the day-to-day stuff because he always has, and most people still respect him. But everyone knows that's only temporary, until someone with real power comes along. Without the Authorities to back him up, Walker's on borrowed time, and he must know it. The Griffin isn't the only person working behind the scenes to take control, and any one of them could have kidnapped Melissa to put pressure on the Griffin to step aside or step down."

"Names," I said. "I need names."

"They're not the kind of names you say out loud," said Harry, meaningfully. "Don't worry, though, you keep digging, and they'll find you. What is this I'm eating, exactly?"

"Eat up," I said. "It's full of protein. Now, give me the latest gossip on what the Griffin family likes to get up to when no-one's looking. All the tasty stuff."

"Now you're talking," said Harry, grinning nastily. "Word is that William takes his pleasure very seriously, and he takes it to the extreme. An explorer on the outer edges of sensation, and all that crap. You might want to check out the Caligula Club. His wife Gloria could shop for the Olympics, but of late she's turned away from bulk buying in favour of tracking down rare collectibles. She's the kind that would buy the Maltese Falcon or the Holy

Grail, just so no-one else could have it. The only reason she hasn't been conned more often is because most of the people who operate in that area are quite sensibly afraid of what the Griffin would do to them if he found out. Last I heard, Gloria was negotiating to buy a Phoenix's Egg from the Collector himself. He's a friend of yours, isn't he?"

"Not really," I said. "More a friend of my father's."

Harry waited hopefully, then shrugged easily as it became clear I wasn't going to say anything more. "Eleanor Griffin likes toy boys. She's got through a dozen to my certain knowledge, and she's always on the lookout for the latest model. Word is she slept with every member of a certain famous boy band, and they were never the same afterwards. Their fan club put out a fatwah on her. Eleanor's husband Marcel gambles. Badly. Most of the reputable houses won't let him through the door because he has a habit of running up his debts, then telling them to collect from the Griffin. Which, of course, they would have more sense than to try. As a result of this unpleasant practice, poor old Marcel has to gamble in the kind of places most of us wouldn't enter even if we had a gun pressed to our heads. How am I doing?"

"Very nicely," I said. "Tell me about the grand-children, Paul and Melissa."

Harry frowned. "Very quiet, by comparison. They each have their own small circle of friends, and they keep to themselves. No big public appearances or scandals. If they have a private life, they're keeping it so secret that even the *Unnatural Inquirer* doesn't know about it. And there's not many can say that."

"I see," I said. "Okay, Harry. Thanks. That'll do nicely. See you around."

"Wait a minute, wait a minute!" he said, as I got up to leave. "What about my exclusive? Something about Suzie Shooter that no-one else knows?"

I smiled. "She's really not a people person. Especially first thing in the morning."

I only had a moment to enjoy the look on Harry's face before someone called out my name, in a loud, harsh, and not at all friendly voice. I looked around, and everyone else in the bar was already running or diving for cover. Standing at the foot of the metal stairway was a tall spindly woman in black, holding Kayleigh's Eye firmly in one upraised hand. I didn't recognise the woman, but like everyone else in the bar I knew Kayleigh's Eye when I saw it. I felt a lot like running and diving for cover myself. The Eye is a crystal that fell to earth from some higher dimension centuries ago in the primordial days of ancient Britain. The Eye was a thing of power, of other-dimensional energies, and it could fulfil all your dreams and ambitions if it didn't burn you out first. The only reason Kayleigh's Eye hadn't made some poor fool king or queen of the Nightside was that they didn't tend to live long enough. The Eye was too powerful for poor fragile mortals to use. Most people had enough sense not to touch the damned thing, but of late certain fanatical groups had taken to using it to arm suicide assassins.

I would have run, but there was nowhere to run to. Nowhere Kayleigh's Eye couldn't reach me.

"Who are you?" I said to the woman in black, trying to buy some time while hopefully sounding cool and calm and not at all threatening.

"I am your death, John Taylor! Your name has been written in the Book of Wrath, your soul condemned and your fate confirmed by the Sacred Council! The time has come to pay for your many sins!"

I'd never heard of the Book of Wrath or the Sacred Council, but that didn't necessarily mean anything. I've upset pretty much everyone worth upsetting, at one time or another. That's how I know I'm doing my job.

"The bar's remaining protections should have kicked in by now," Alex murmured behind me. "But since they haven't, I think we can safely assume that you're on your own, John. If you need me, I'll be cowering behind the bar and wetting myself."

"Harry?" I said, but he was already gone.

"He's back here with me," said Alex. "Crying."

The woman in black advanced slowly on me, still holding Kayleigh's Eye aloft. It blazed brightly in the bar's comfortable gloom, like a great red eye staring right at me. Leaking energies spat and crackled on the air around it. Everyone was either gone by now or hiding behind overturned tables, like that would protect them from what the Eye could do. The woman in black ignored them. She only had Eye for me. She gestured at the tables and chairs that stood between us, and they exploded into kindling. People cried out as wooden splinters flew through the air like shrapnel. The woman in black kept coming, still fixed on me. She had cold, wide, fanatic's eyes.

Betty and Lucy Coltrane came charging forward out of nowhere, propelled incredibly quickly by powerful leg muscles. The woman just looked at them, and an invisible hand slapped the Coltranes away, sending them both flying the length of the bar. They hit the floor hard and didn't move again. I could have run while the woman was distracted, used one of the many secret ways out of the bar I knew about, but I couldn't risk what the woman and the Eye might do to the bar and the people in it in my absence. Besides, I don't run. It's bad for my reputation. And my reputation has scared off more people than any weapon I ever had.

So I stood where I was and let her approach. She'd want to do it up close so she could look me in the face while she did it. It wasn't enough for fanatics to win; they needed to see their enemies suffer. And fanatics will drink that cup right down to the dregs, relishing every drop. She advanced slowly on me, taking her time, savouring the moment. My mouth was dry, my hands were sweaty, and my stomach churned sickly, but I stood my ground. Kayleigh's Eye could kill me in a thousand ways, all impossibly horrible, but I had an idea.

And as the woman in black finally came to a halt before me, smiling a smile with no humour in it at all, her wide fanatic's eyes full of a fire more terrible than the Eye's . . . I used my gift to find the hole between dimensions through which the Eye originally entered our world. It was still there, unhealed, after all these centuries. And it was the easiest thing in the world for me to show Kayleigh's Eye its way home.

*Free! Free at last!* An unearthly voice roared through my mind, then the Eye was gone, vanished, back to whatever other-dimensional place it came from. The hole sealed itself behind the Eye, and that was it. The woman in black looked at her empty hand, then at me, and smiled weakly. I punched her right between the eyes, and she slid unconscious across the barroom floor for a good dozen feet before she finally came to a halt. I gritted my teeth and nursed my aching hand. I always did have a weakness for the big gesture.

"All right," said Alex, reappearing behind the bar. "Who have you upset this time, Taylor? And who's going to pay for the damages?"

"Beats me," I said cheerfully.

"Maybe you shouldn't have punched her out," said Harry Fabulous, rising nervously up beside Alex, his drink still in his hand. "She could have told you who sent her."

"Not likely," I said. "Fanatics never talk."

Someone clearly didn't want me investigating Melissa's disappearance. But who, and why? Only one way to find out. I nodded good-bye to Alex and Harry and went out of the bar in search of answers.

# FIVE

# The people
# we turn to
# for comfort

Of course I'd heard of the Caligula Club. Everyone in the
Nightside has, in the same way you hear about rabies,
leprosy, and everything else that's bad for you. If you're
tired of parachuting off Mount Everest blindfolded, or
hang-gliding naked over exploding volcanoes, if you've
slept with everything that's got a pulse and a few that
haven't, if you really think you've done it all, seen it all,
and there's nothing left to tempt or deprave you—then
the Caligula Club is ready to welcome you with open
arms and shock you rigid with new possibilities. And if
you should happen to die on the premises with a smile on
your face or a scream on your lips, you can't say you
weren't warned.

The Caligula Club can be found in Uptown, where all
the very best clubs and bars, restaurants and shows form

their wagons in a circle to repel the riffraff. Only the very wealthy, the very powerful, and the very well connected are allowed in to sample the rarefied delights on offer in Uptown. Rent-a-cops patrol the streets in gaudy uniforms to keep the likes of you and me out. But somehow the private cops always find a pressing reason to be somewhere else when I come around.

The Caligula Club is situated right on the very edge of Uptown, as though the area is embarrassed or ashamed of it. It's the kind of place where the floor show consists of a sweet young couple setting themselves on fire, then having sex, where the house band consists of formerly dead musicians, some of whom were dug up as recently as that night, and the management have their own private exorcist on speed-dial. Do I really need to tell you that the Club is strictly members only? And that membership is by invitation only? They wouldn't have me on a bet, so I was looking forward to taking my first look around inside.

Uptown—where the neon come-ons are bigger and brighter than anywhere else but no less sleazy. Hot music hammers on the cool night air, insistent and vaguely threatening. Club doors hang alluringly open, while their barkers work the crowded pavements with practiced dead-eyed skill. Getting in is easy; getting out again with your money, wits, and soul intact is something else. Buyer very much beware, in Uptown. Here be entertainment, red in tooth and claw.

Men and women paraded up and down the streets, in the very latest and most outrageous fashions, out and about to see and be seen. Making the scene, no matter how dangerous it might be, because if you didn't, then you just weren't anyone. High Society has its own obligations and penalties, and the very worst of them is to be ignored. Gods and monsters, yesterday's dreams and to-morrow's nightmares, bright young things and smiling Gucci sharks, were all out on the town and on the pull, come to Uptown to play their vicious games. And Devil take the hindmost.

None of them looked pleased to see me, but I'm used to that. Without quite seeming to, they all made sure to give me plenty of room. I play too rough for their refined tastes.

I stopped outside the Caligula Club and studied it thoughtfully from a safe distance. Big bold neon crawled all over the front of the high-tech edifice, glowing multi-coloured graffiti on a steel-and-glass background. A lot of it depicted stylised sexual positions and possibilities, some of which would have made the Marquis de Sade lose his lunch. Cruelty and passion mixed together, to make a whole far nastier than the sum of its parts. You don't come to the Caligula Club for fun, or even excite-ment. You come to satisfy the needs and tastes no-one else will tolerate.

And somewhere inside this den of sweaty iniquity and furious pleasures . . . was William Griffin, father of the missing Melissa.

The front door was being guarded by a satyr of the old school. About five feet tall, handsome in a swarthy and entirely untrustworthy way, with a bare hairy chest, furry goat's legs, and curling horns on his forehead. Half human, half goat, and hung like a horse. He wasn't shy about showing it off, either. I hate these demon half-breeds. You can never tell how dangerous they are until they show you, usually in sudden and unpleasant ways. I strolled over to him like I had every right to be there, and he smiled widely at me, showing off big blocky teeth.

"Hello, sailor. Welcome to the Caligula Club. Looking for a bit of adventure, are we? Afraid it's members only, though, and I do mean members. Are you a fine upstanding member, sir?"

"Knock it off," I said. "You know who I am."

"Well of course, heart face. Doesn't everyone? But I have my orders, and it's more than my job's worth to let you in, not even if you was the queen himself. Management is very strict, and that's how most of the members like it. I am Mr. Tumble, and nothing gets past me."

"I'm John Taylor, and I'm coming in," I said. "You know it, and I know it, so do we really have to do this the unpleasant and probably extremely violent way?"

"Sorry, sweetie pie, but I have my orders. You couldn't be any less welcome here if you was a health inspector. Now be a good boy and run along and irritate someone else. It's more than my job's worth to let you get past me. You wouldn't want to see an old satyr down on his knees and begging, would you?"

"I represent the Griffin in this matter," I said. "So stand aside, or I'll have him buy this place and fire your fuzzy arse."

"Threats don't bother me, sailor. Heard them all, I have."

"I could walk right over you," I said.

Mr. Tumble grew suddenly in size, shooting up so fast I had to step back to keep from being crowded. He topped out at ten feet tall, with broad shoulders and a massive chest, and powerful arms ending in viciously clawed hands. He smelled of blood and musk, and it was obvious from what was now bobbing right in front of my face that he was getting quite excited at the prospect of imminent violence. He grinned down at me, and when he spoke his voice rumbled like thunder.

"Still think you can get past me, little human?"

Something large and trunklike twitched in front of my nose. So I reached into my coat-pocket, took out the mousetrap I keep there for perfectly legitimate reasons, and let it snap shut. He howled like a foghorn, grabbed at his pride and joy with both hands, and collapsed onto the pavement before me. He shrank quickly back to his normal size, unable to concentrate through the pain, and I did the decent thing and kicked him in the head. He sank gratefully into unconsciousness, and I stepped past his weakly kicking hooves and on into the Caligula Club.

You just can't talk to some people.


The reception lobby was big and echoing, with white-tiled floor and ceiling. Presumably so they could wipe off stains and spills more easily. There were no fittings or furnishings, only a simple reception desk with a bored-looking teenager stuck behind it, completely engrossed in that week's edition of the *Unnatural Inquirer*. The lobby clearly wasn't a place you sat around waiting. It was somewhere you hurried through, on your way to whatever awaited you. I stood before the desk, and the receptionist ignored me. The headline on her paper said *Tribute Princess Diana to Tour Nightside*. And at the bottom of the page, in somewhat smaller type: *Keep Your Queen Mother Sightings Coming In. We Pay for Photos!*

"Talk to me," I said to the receptionist. "Or I'll set fire to your tabloid."

She slammed her paper down on the desk and scowled

at me through her various piercings. The one through the left eyeball had to have really hurt. "Welcome to the Caligula, sir. Walk all over me, that's what I'm here for. I don't have to do this, you know. I could have been a doctor. If I only had a medical degree. Did sir have a particular service in mind, or would sir like me to recommend something particularly horrible?"

I got a bit distracted as a door opened on the other side of the lobby, and a crowd of mostly naked people paraded past the reception desk, not even glancing at me. From their animated chatter it seemed they were leaving one party and on their way to another. Some had patches of different-coloured skin grafted onto their bodies, and I had to wonder what happened to the donors. Others had patches of fur, or metal. Animal eyes looked out of some sockets, swivelling cameras out of others. There were those whose legs had three joints, or arms in sets of four, or faces on the back of their heads as well as on the front. Some had both sets of genitals, or none, or things I didn't even recognise as genitals. Bunch of show-offs, basically. They hurried on and disappeared through another door on the far side of the lobby. I looked at the receptionist.

"I'm looking for someone," I said.

"Aren't we all? Soon as I get my claws into a decent sugar daddy, this place won't see my pink little botty for dust. Did sir have a particular person in mind?"

"William Griffin."

"Oh, him," The teenage receptionist pulled a face. "He's long gone. Never comes around anymore. Seems we weren't extreme enough for him."

I had to admit, I boggled slightly at the thought of tastes so extreme that even the Caligula Club couldn't satisfy them. What the hell could William Griffin be into that he couldn't find it in a place like this? I was still considering that when a final party-goer emerged from the far door and came over to join me at the desk. William's wife Gloria was dressed in a blood-red basque studded with razor blades, thigh-length boots of tanned human hide, and a black choker round her slender neck bristling with steel spikes. An unusually large snake coiled around her shoulders and draped down one long dark arm. As she came to a halt before me, the snake raised its head and looked at me knowingly. I gave the head a brief pat. I like snakes.

"Forgive the outfit," said Gloria, in a calm husky voice. "It's my turn to play Queen of Sin again, and when you're Mistress of the Revels they expect you to dress the part. I blame Diana Rigg; I swear there are whole generations who never got over seeing her in that episode of *The Avengers*. I've been looking for a chance to speak with you, Mr. Taylor."

"Really?" I said. "How nice."

"I knew you'd find your way here, looking for William. I think we could have . . . useful things to say to each other."

"Wouldn't surprise me," I said. "You first."

"Not here," said Gloria. She glared at the teenage receptionist. "You can't trust the staff. They sell stories to the media."

"Then you should pay us better," said the receptionist, and disappeared behind her tabloid again. Gloria ignored her and led me across the lobby to a side door, which was almost invisible until you were right on top of it. She opened the door, and ushered me into what looked very much like a dentist's surgery from hell. There were nasty-looking steel instruments all over the place, and half a dozen drills hung over a reclining chair fitted with heavy leather restraining straps. There was a strong smell of antiseptic and recent fear. *Takes all sorts, I suppose.* Gloria shut the door firmly, then put her back against it.

"Security will know you're here by now. I've paid off the right people so we can have some time together, but I can't guarantee how long we've got."

"Tell me about William," I said. "And why he came here."

"He brought me here right after we were married. My membership was his wedding gift to me. It wasn't exactly a surprise. I knew all about his *tastes* before we were married. I didn't care. I've always been more interested in power. And William didn't care who knew. He'd been everywhere and done everyone, in his search for . . . well, pleasure, I suppose. Though perhaps satisfaction would be a better word. He came here to be on the receiving end of very heavy S&M sessions. Bondage and discipline, whippings and brandings, that sort of thing. It's amazing how much punishment an immortal body can soak up. He never got that much out of it that I could see, but he felt a need to be punished. I never did understand why. He could be very private about some things. Eventually they couldn't do enough for him here, and he left. I stayed." She smiled slowly. "I like it."

"You didn't share William's tastes?" I said.

"I told you, it's all about power for me. And there's never any shortage of men here for me to order around, to abuse and mistreat as I wish. Men of substance and standing, begging to satisfy my every whim, eager to suffer and bleed for my slightest nod of approval. To worship me as the goddess I am. Such a pleasant change from the way they treat me at Griffin Hall. As far as

Jeremiah and Mariah are concerned, I'm just William's latest. Even the servants can't be bothered to remember my name. No-one expected me to last this long."

"But you're immortal now," I said. "You're part of the family."

"You'd think so, wouldn't you? But you'd be wrong. I've never been allowed to be part of the family business, even though I'd be far better at it than William, because family business is only for those of Griffin blood. And even more than that, I'm not allowed to do anything, or have anything of my own, that might possibly interfere or compete with Griffin business or interests. And that covers pretty much everything in the Nightside. So I shop till I drop, and when I get tired of that, I come here to play at being . . . what I thought I'd be when I married William."

"Did you ever love him?" I said bluntly.

"He chose me. Wanted me. Made me immortal and very rich. I was very grateful. Still am, I suppose. But love . . . I don't know. It's hard to get to know William. He doesn't let anyone in. He never once opened up to me about anything that mattered, not even in our most private moments. I married him because . . . he was good company, and generous, and because I was getting a little old for the catwalk. Supermodels have a very limited shelf life. I might have loved him, if I'd ever thought for one moment that he loved me."

"How about your daughter, Melissa?"

"I would have loved her, given the chance. But Jeremiah took her away the day William and I presented her to him. We didn't get a say in the matter. I couldn't stop him. William did try, bless him—actually raised his voice to his father and called him every name under the sun. Only time I ever saw William talk back to his father.

But of course, he couldn't do anything . . . so it didn't do him any good. No-one says no to Jeremiah Griffin."

"Can you tell me anything about Melissa's disappearance?" I said. "I can be discreet. The Griffin doesn't have to know everything I discover in my investigation."

"He'd find out," Gloria said flatly. "He always finds out. I'm amazed we were able to keep Melissa's existence a secret for as long as we did. He probably couldn't bring himself to believe his own son could defy him so completely . . . Ask me anything you want, Mr. Taylor, and I'll tell you what I can. Because . . . I just don't care anymore. William doesn't seem to care whether I'm around or not, so I'm probably on the way out anyway. And it's not as if I know anything that matters. My daughter's disappearance is as much a mystery to me as anyone else."

"I have to say, you don't seem very upset that she's missing, perhaps kidnapped, perhaps even murdered," I said. "Don't you care what's happened to her?"

"Don't think too harshly of me, Mr. Taylor. Melissa is my daughter in name only. Jeremiah reared her and made sure I was kept very much at arm's length. Melissa hasn't wanted anything to do with me in years. And now . . . it seems she stands ready to steal William's inheritance. And mine, of course."

"There are those who believe," I said carefully, "that an adult grand-child could mean the death of the Griffin."

"If only," said Gloria. "It's just another story. There have always been stories about the Griffin, but no-one knows anything for sure."

"Does William believe it?"

"He did once. That's why he wanted a child. To use as a weapon against his father."

"William wanted his father dead?"

"Dead and gone, because that was the only way William could ever be his own man. Free at last . . . though free to do what, I couldn't tell you. Perhaps even he doesn't know."

"Do you want me to find your daughter?" I said. "Given that if I do bring her back, safe and well, she could disinherit William and you?"

"Find her," said Gloria, fixing me with her calm dark gaze. "It's all right that she never loved me. You can't love a stranger. But I gave birth to her, nursed her, held her in my arms . . . Find her, Mr. Taylor. And if anyone has dared to hurt her . . . kill them slowly."

"Any idea where I should look for William?" I said.

Gloria smiled. "And just like that, you're finished with me. I told you all I knew, and you told me nothing. What a marvellous private investigator you are, Mr. Taylor."

"You didn't ask me anything," I said.

"No," said Gloria. "I didn't, did I? If you want to find William . . . try the Arcadian Project."

And the snake draped across her shoulders looked at me and seemed to laugh silently, as though it knew something I didn't.

Like the Caligula Club, I knew the Arcadian Project by reputation; but whereas everyone talked about what went on at the Caligula, no-one knew anything about the inner workings of the Arcadian Project. *The most private place in the Nightside*, some said. *A lot of people go in, but not all of them come out again*, others said. Its very location was a secret, known only to the trusted few, and this in a place where the secrets of the universe are sold openly on street corners. But I can find anything. That's my job.

I fired up my gift and looked out over the Nightside through my third eye, my private eye. Great forces were abroad in the night, ancient and awful Powers walking unseen and unsuspected, but they were too big to notice something as small as me. I concentrated on the single thing I was looking for, and my Sight rocketed through the streets and alleys of the Nightside, before finally ze- roing in on a narrow dark alley, where most people only went to dump their garbage or the occasional body.

It wasn't all that far from Uptown, but it might as well have been another world. No private clubs and restau- rants here, just paint-peeling doors and fly-specked win- dows, guttering neon signs with half the lettering burnt out, and sloe-eyed cold-eyed daughters of the twilight on every corner, selling their shop-soiled wares. The kind of place where there's nothing for sale that didn't originally belong to someone else, where the pleasures and pursuits on offer leave a nasty taste in the mouth, and even the muggers go around in pairs, for safety.

I found the alley easily enough and looked down it from the relative safety of the brighter-lit street. The light didn't penetrate far into the hot sweaty shadows, and I was pretty sure I could hear things scrabbling about in the darkness beyond. The air smelled close and moist and ripe. Ripe for an ambush, certainly. I reached into my coat-pocket and brought out a dead salamander in a plas- tic globe. I shook it hard, and a fierce silver glow burst from the globe, illuminating the alley ahead of me. Things scuttled away from the sudden new light, hurry- ing off to hide in darker, safer places. I made my way slowly and cautiously down the alleyway, being very careful where I put my feet, and finally came to a simple green door set into the grimy stone of the left-hand wall. There was no sign over the door, not even a handle on the door, but this was it. The one and only access point to the Arcadian Project. I studied the door carefully, not touching it, but it seemed like simply another door. It wasn't locked or booby-trapped or cursed—my gift would have told me. So I just shrugged, placed one hand against it, and gave it a good push.

The door swung easily open and I almost cried out as a blindingly bright light spilled into the alleyway. I tensed, ready for anything, but nothing happened. There was only the golden sunlight, warm and fresh and sweet as a summer's day, heavy with the scents of woods and fields and meadows. I realised I was still holding the salamander globe, with its sickly inferior light, and put it back in my coat-pocket. And then I walked forward into daylight, and the green door swung slowly shut behind me.

I was standing on the side of a great grassy hill, looking out over a view of open countryside that took my breath away. Fields and meadows stretched away before me for as far as I could see, and perhaps forever. To one side were sprawling woods with tall dark trees, and down below a stream of clear and sparkling water ran happily on its way, crossed here and there by simple old-fashioned stone bridges. A dream of old England, as it never was but should have been, happy and content under the bright blue sky of a perfect summer's day. A soft gusting breeze brought me scents rich as perfume, of flowers and grass and growing things. Birds sang, and there was a gentle buzz of insects, and it was good, so good, just to stand in daylight again after so very long away.

This was the great secret, never to be shared with the unworthy for fear it would be spoiled—Arcadia.

A single pathway meandered away before me, starting at my feet. A series of square stone slabs resting on the grass, leading down the hillside. I set off, stepping carefully from slab to slab, like stepping-stones on a great green sea. The path curved around the side of the hill, then led me along a river-bank, while I watched birds swoop and soar, and butterflies drift this way and that, and smiled to see small woodland creatures scurry all around me, undisturbed by human presence. Pure white swans sailed majestically down the stream, bowing their heads to me as I passed.

Finally I rounded a corner, and there on a river-bank before me were my father and my mother, reclining at their ease on the grassy bank, with the contents of a wicker picnic basket spread out on a checked tablecloth. My father Charles was lying stretched out, in a white suit, smiling as my mother Lilith, in a white dress, threw pieces of bread to the ducks. I made some kind of sound, and my mother looked round and smiled dazzlingly at me.

"Oh, Charles, see who's here! John has come to join us!"

My father raised himself up on one elbow and looked round, and his smile widened as he saw me. "Good of you to join us, son. We're having a picnic. There's ham and cheese, and scotch eggs and sausage rolls, and all your favourites."

"Come and join us, darling," said my mother. "We've been waiting for you."

I stumbled forward and sat down between my mother and my father. He squeezed my shoulder in a reassuring way, and my mother passed me a fresh cup of tea. I knew it would be milk and two sugars, just the way I liked it. I sat there for a while, enjoying the moment, and there was a part of me that would have liked to stay for the rest of my life. But I've never been any good at listening to that part of me.

"There are so many things I meant to say to you, Dad," I said finally. "But there wasn't time."

"You have all the time in the world here," said my father, lying on his back again and staring up into the summer sky.

"And despite everything that happened, I would have liked to get to know you, Mother," I said to Lilith.

"Then stay here with us," she said. "And we can be together, forever and ever and ever."

"No," I said regretfully. "Because you'd only ever say what I wanted you to say. Because this isn't real, and neither are you. My parents are gone, and lost to me forever. This is Arcadia, the Summerland where dreams can come true, and everyone is happy, and good things happen every day. But I have things to do, and people to meet, because that's what I do and who I am. And besides, my Suzie will be waiting for me when I get home. She might be a psycho gun nut, but she's *my* psycho gun nut. So, I have to be going now. My life might not be perfect, like this, but at least it's real.

"And I've never let down a client yet."

I got up and walked away, following the stepping-stone path again. I didn't look back to see my father and my mother fade away and disappear. Perhaps because I liked to think of them there together, picnicking on a river-bank forever and a day, happy at last.

The path led me along beside the river-bank for a while, then turned abruptly to take me up a grassy hillside towards a stretch of woodland, standing tall and proud against the sky. I could hear voices up ahead now, loud and happy and occasionally bursting into laughter. It sounded like children. When I got close enough, I could see William Griffin, lying at his ease on the grassy slope, looking out over the magnificent view, while all around him his childhood friends laughed and played and ran in the never-ending sunshine of Summerland.

I knew some of them, because they'd been my childhood friends, too. Bruin Bear, a four-foot-tall teddy bear in his famous red tunic and trousers and his bright blue scarf, every young boy's good friend and brave companion. And there beside the Bear, his friend the Sea Goat in a long blue-grey trench coat, human-sized but with a large blocky goat's head and long, curling horns. Everyone had those books when I was a kid, and we all went on marvellous adventures with the Bear and the Goat in our imaginations . . . There was Tufty-Tailed Squirrel, and Barney the Battery Boy, and even Beep and Buster, one boy and his alien. There were others, too— child-sized toys and anthropomorphic animals in cut-down human clothes, and happy smiling creatures of the kind we all forget as we grow up and move on. Except we never do forget them, not deep down, where it really matters. They played together all around William Griffin, squabbling cheerfully, laughing and chattering and chasing each other back and forth. Old companions, and sometimes the only real friends a child ever had.

They all stopped abruptly and looked round as I approached. They didn't look scared, just curious. William sat up slowly and looked at me. I held up my hands to show they were empty, and that I came in peace. William hugged his knees to his chest and looked at me over them, and finally sighed tiredly.

"You'd better go," he said to the toys and animals. "This is going to be grown-up talk. You'd only be bored."

They all nodded and faded away, like the dreams they were. Except for Bruin Bear and the Sea Goat, who stood their ground and studied me thoughtfully with calm, knowing eyes. The Sea Goat pulled a bottle of vodka from his coat pocket and took a long pull.

"That's right," he said thickly. "We're real. Sort of. Get used to it."

"Not many remember us anymore," said the Bear. "We're legends now, so we live in Shadows Fall, where all stories have their ending. We commute into the Nightside now and again, to be here for those who still have a need for us."

"Yeah, right," said the Sea Goat, belching loudly. "I just come here for the view and a bit of peace and quiet. And the free food. You're John Taylor, aren't you? You'll probably end up a legend yourself, after you've been dead long enough for people to forget the real you. Then it's Shadows Fall for you, whether you like it or not. I'll tell you now, you won't like it. And don't you mess with William. He's with us. You spoil his day, and I'll shove this bottle so far up you, you'll need a trained proctologist with spelunking gear to get it out again."

"Don't mind him," Bruin Bear said fondly. "He's just being himself."

They moved off into the dark wood, still arguing companionably. They didn't seem quite as I remembered them. I moved forward and sat down beside William.

"So this is the Arcadian Project," I said. "Nice. I really like the view."

"What do you want, Taylor?" said William. "And how did you know to find me here anyway? This was supposed to be the one place where no-one could bother me."

"It's a gift," I said. "Gloria pointed me in the right direction. I think she's worried about you."

William snorted briefly. "That would be a first."

"What are you doing here?" I said, honestly curious. "Why . . . this?"

"Because I never had a childhood," said William. He wasn't looking at me. He was staring out over the view, or perhaps seeing something else in his head, in his past. "For as far back as I can remember, my father's only interest in me was to groom me as his heir and successor. So he could be sure everything he built would still continue, even without him. He wanted me to be just like him. It wasn't my fault that I wasn't, and never would be. There's only one Jeremiah Griffin, which is probably for the best. But even as a small child, I was never allowed much time to play, to be myself. Never allowed to have any real friends because they couldn't be trusted. They might be spies for my father's many enemies. It was always work, work, work. Endless lessons, on family business and family duty. My only means of escape was into books and comics. I lived in my dreams then, whenever I could, in the simpler happier realms of my imagination.

The only place that was truly mine, that my father couldn't reach and spoil or take away."

I couldn't have stopped him talking if I'd tried. He'd held this bottled up inside him for years, and he would have told it to anyone who found him here. Because he had a terrible need to tell it to someone . . .

"That's why I started body-building as a teenager," said William Griffin, still not looking at me. "So I could have some control over some part of my life, even if it was only the shape of my body. By then I knew I wasn't up to running the family business. I knew that long before my father did. I liked to think . . . I might have managed some smaller triumph if I'd been left to myself. If I'd been left to choose my own way, follow my own interests. But the Griffin couldn't bear to have a son who was anything less than great.

"These days, I'm just a glorified gopher, there to deal with all the things my father can't trust to anyone who isn't family. We both pretend I'm someone important, but everyone knows . . . I carry out the policy he sets, but God help me if I should ever dare to make even the smallest decision on my own. I move papers from one place to another, talk to people with my father's voice, and every day I die a little more. Do you have any idea what that's like, for an immortal? To die by inches, forever and ever . . .

"For a while I filled my time by indulging my senses and my pleasures . . . I must have belonged to every private club in the Nightside, at one time or another. Tried everything they had to offer . . . and everyone. But while that distracted, it never satisfied."

He turned suddenly to look at me, and his eyes were dark and angry and dangerous. "You can't tell anyone about this, Taylor. About me, being here. With my friends. People wouldn't understand. They'd think me weak, and try to take advantage. And my father . . . really wouldn't understand. I don't think he ever *needed* anything in his life. In fact, it's hard to think of the mighty and powerful Jeremiah Griffin ever having had anything as normal and vulnerable as a childhood. This is the only thing I have that he isn't a part of. The only place I can be free of him."

"Don't worry," I said. "Your father doesn't need to know about this. He hired me to investigate Melissa, not you. I'm only interested in what you can tell me about your daughter and her disappearance."

"I wanted to be a father to her," said William, his eyes lost and far away again. "A good father, not like Jeremiah. I wanted her to have the childhood I never had. But he took her away, and after that I was only allowed to see her when Jeremiah said so. I think Melissa sees him as her real father. Her daddy. I spent years trying to reach out to her . . . but even when I timed my visits so Jeremiah wasn't there, somehow Melissa was never there either. She'd always just gone out . . . Hobbes is my father's man, body and soul. He runs the Hall, and no-one gets past him. In the end . . . I just stopped trying."

He looked at me, and there was something beaten, and broken, in his face. "I don't hate my father, you know. Don't ever think that. He only ever wanted what he thought was best for me. And for so long . . . all I wanted was for my father to be proud of me."

"All sons do," I said.

"What about your father? Was he proud of you?"

"At the end," I said. "I think so, yes. When it was too

late for either of us to do anything about it. You know about my mother . . ."

William smiled for the first time. "Everyone in the Nightside knows about your mother. We all lost someone in the Lilith War."

"Do you believe Melissa was kidnapped?" I said bluntly.

He shook his head immediately. He didn't even have to think about it. "How could she have been, from inside Griffin Hall, with all our security? But she couldn't have run away, either. There was no way she could have got out of the Hall without someone noticing. And where could she have run to, where could she go, where they wouldn't know who she was? Someone would have been bound to turn her in, either for the reward or to our enemies, as a way of getting back at Father."

"Unless someone else in the family was involved," I said carefully. "Either to help her escape or to override the security so she could be taken . . ."

William was shaking his head again. "She has no friends in the family, except perhaps Paul. And nobody would risk interfering with the security that protects us."

"Who would dare kidnap Melissa Griffin?"

"I don't know. But I'll tell you this, John Taylor; I'd kill anyone who hurt her. So would the Griffin."

"Even though he could stand to lose . . . everything when she turns eighteen?"

William laughed briefly, though there wasn't much humour in the sound. "Oh, you've heard that story, have you? Forget it. It's bullshit. Urban legend. If it was true, my father would have killed Melissa and Paul the moment he learned of their existence. He's always been able to do the hard, necessary, vicious things, no matter who it hurt. Even him. A very practical man, my father. I didn't have Melissa to threaten him, no matter what anyone says. I just wanted something that was mine. I should have known he'd never allow that."

"Then why did your immortal father make a will?" I said.

"Good question," said William. "I didn't even know about the first will, never mind the second. My father can't die. He'd never do anything so ordinary, so weak." He looked straight at me again. "Find my daughter, Mr. Taylor. Whatever it takes, whatever it costs."

"Whoever it hurts?" I said. "Even if it's family?"

"Especially if it's family," said William Griffin.

"Aren't you two finished yet?" the Sea Goat said loudly. "Me and the Bear have some important lounging about we should be getting on with."

William Griffin smiled fondly at his two friends, and for a moment he looked like someone else entirely. Bruin Bear gave him a big hug, and the Sea Goat passed over his bottle of vodka. William took a long drink, passed the bottle back, and sighed deeply.

"It's hard to tell which of the two comforts me more," he said sadly.

"You just need a good crap, clear the system out," the Sea Goat said wisely. "Everything looks better after a good crap."

"Can't take you anywhere," said Bruin Bear.

# SIX

# It's All About Reputations

I was learning a lot about the inner secrets of the Nightside's most mysterious family, but I wasn't getting any closer to finding Melissa, or what had happened to her. No-one wanted to talk about her; they just wanted to talk about themselves. I hadn't realised how much I'd come to depend on my gift for finding things to help get me through cases. It had been a long time since I'd had to investigate the hard and honest way, by asking questions and following up on the answers. But I could tell I was narrowing in on something, even if I wasn't sure what. All I could do was keep digging and hope that if I asked enough awkward questions, someone would tell me something I wasn't supposed to know. I asked William where I could find his sister Eleanor, and he shrugged and said *Try Hecate's Tea Room*. I should have known.

Hecate's Tea Room was the premiere watering hole for all the Nightside's Ladies Who Lunch.

I walked back out of the long, green dream of the Arcadian Project and back into the more comfortable nightmare of neonlit streets and hospitable shadows. Not all of us thrive in sunlight. Hecate's Tea Room is one of the most expensive, exclusive, and extravagant bistros in the Nightside, set right in the heart of Uptown. A refined and resplendent setting where the better halves of rich and famous men could come together to chat and gossip and practice character assassination on those of their kind unfortunate enough not to have made the scene that day. There was a long waiting list to get in, and you could be barred for the slightest lapse in etiquette. But no-one ever complained because it was so very much the In place, to see and be seen. And there never was a faux pas so bad that a big enough cheque couldn't put right.

I studied the place from a safe distance, watching from the shadows of an alley mouth as a steady stream of chauffeur-driven limousines glided down the street to pull up outside the heavily guarded front door and drop off famous faces from the society pages and the gossip rags. The sweet and elite of the Nightside, in stunning gowns and understated makeup, weighed down with enough jewellery to make even the smallest gesture an effort.

The neon sign above the door spelt out *Hecate's Tea Room* in stylings so rococo it was almost impossible to read, and the whole place reeked of art deco redux. There's nothing more fashionable than an old style come round again. I used my Sight to check out the security, and sure enough the whole building was surrounded by layer upon layer of defensive magics, everything from shaped curses to Go Straight to Hell spells. There were all kinds of guards, tactfully hidden behind camouflage magics, and the two large gentlemen standing by the front door might be dressed in elegant tuxedos, but they both had tattoos on their foreheads that marked them as combat magicians. Ex-SAS, from the look of them. Even the paparazzi maintained a very discreet distance.

So, fighting or intimidating my way in wasn't going to work here. That just left bluff and fast talking, which fortunately I've always been very good at. My reputation's always been more impressive than me, and that's because I put a lot of work into it. I left the alley-way and sauntered up to the front door. The two gentlemen in tuxedos saw me coming, recognised me immediately, and moved to stand in front of the door, blocking my way. A bouncer is a bouncer, no matter how smartly you dress him. I stopped before them and smiled easily, like I didn't have a care in the world.

"Hi guys. I'm here representing the Griffin, to speak with his daughter Eleanor."

They weren't expecting that. They looked at each other, communicating in that silent way of bouncers everywhere, then they looked back at me.

"Do you have any proof of that, sir?"

"Would even I claim the Griffin's support if I didn't have it?" I countered.

They considered that, nodded, and stepped aside. My reputation might be unsettling, but the Griffin's was downright scary. I strolled through the door and into the Tea Room as though I was slumming just by being there. When it comes to looking down the nose at someone, it pays to get your retaliation in first. The cloakroom girl was a friendly looking zombie dressed in a black bustier and fishnet stockings to set off her dead white skin. The dead make the best servants—so much less back-talk. She asked very nicely if she could take my trench coat, and I said I thought not.

I got her phone number, though. For Dead Boy.

I stepped through a hanging bead curtain into the main Tea Room, and the loud babble of conversation didn't even dip for a moment. The Ladies Who Lunch saw scarier and more important people than me every day. I wandered slowly between the crowded tables, taking my time. A few people got up and left, heading discreetly but speedily for the rear exit. I was used to that. The Tea Room was all steel and glass and art deco stylings, with one entire wall dominated by a long row of high-tech coffee machines, the kind that labour mightily for ages that little bit longer than you can actually stand, in order to finally provide you with a cup full of flavoured froth. I've always preferred tea to coffee myself, and preferably in a brew so strong that when you've finished stirring it, the spoon has stress marks on it.

The staff darted gracefully back and forth among the tables, pretty young boys and girls dressed in nothing but collars and cuffs, which presumably made them very careful not to spill anything. The rich and therefore very important women sat huddled around their tables, ignoring everything except their own conversation, laughing and shrieking loudly and throwing their hands about to make it clear they were having a much better time than everyone else. There were a few private booths at the back, for assignations of a more personal nature, but not many used them. The whole point of being at Hecate's Tea Room was to prove that you were rich and important enough to be allowed into such a prestigious gathering.

(But just try and get in after you'd been divorced or dumped or disinherited, and see how fast they slam the door in your face.)

All the women were dressed to the nines, chattering raucously like so many gorgeous creatures of the urban jungle as they drank their tea and coffee with their little fingers carefully extended. They all felt free to stroke and caress the staff's bare flesh as they came and went with fresh cups of tea and coffee, and the pretty young things smiled mechanically and never lingered. They all knew a caress could turn into a slap or a blow for any reason or none, and that the customer was always right. Every table was full, the ladies crowded together under conditions they would never have tolerated anywhere else. These were the fabled Ladies Who Lunch, though there didn't seem to be any actual lunching going on anywhere. You didn't get to look that good and that svelte by eating when you felt like it. There was civilised music playing in the background, but I could barely make it out through the din of the raised voices.

I soon spotted Eleanor Griffin, seated at a table right in the middle of the room, (of course), where everyone could get a good look at her. She wore a long, elegant gown of emerald green, set off with flawless diamonds, and a black silk choker with a single polished emerald at her throat. Even in this gathering of professionally beautiful women, there was something about her that stood out. Not just style and grace, because they all had that, or something like it. Perhaps it was that Eleanor seemed to have made less of an effort than everyone else, because she didn't have to. Eleanor Griffin was the real thing; and there's nothing more threatening than that to women who had to work hard to be what they were. She was beautiful, poised, and effortlessly aristocratic. Three good reasons to hate anyone in this circle. But her table was larger than most and surrounded by women who had clearly made a considerable effort to appear half as impressive as Eleanor. A circle of "friends" who got together regularly to chat and gossip and practice one-upwomanship on each other. Ladies who had nothing in common except the circles they moved in, who clung together only because it was expected of them.

It's hard to be friends with anyone when they can disappear at a moment's notice through divorce or disapproval, and never be seen or spoken of again. And when they vanish from your circle, all you feel is the relief that the bullet missed you, this time . . .

I knew some of the faces at Eleanor's table. There was Jezebel Rackham, wife of Big Jake Rackham. Jezebel was tall and blonde and magnificently bosomed, with a face like a somewhat vacant child. Big Jake took his cut from every sex business that operated in the Nightside, big or small. Word is Jezebel used to be one of his main money earners before he married her, but of course noone says that out loud anymore. Not if they like having knee-caps. Jezebel sat at the table like a child among grown-ups, following the conversation without ever joining in, and watching the others carefully so she'd know when to laugh.

Then there was Lucy Lewis, sweet and petite and exotically oriental, splendidly outfitted in a midnight dark gown to match her hair and eyes. Wife to Uptown Taffy Lewis, so called because he owned most of the land that Uptown stood on. Which meant all the famous clubs and bars and restaurants relied on his good will to stay in business. Taffy never leased anywhere for more than twelve months at a time, and he'd never even heard of rent control. Lucy was famous for always having the best gossip, and never caring who it hurt. Even if they were sitting right next to her.

Sally DeVore was married to Marty DeVore, mostly called Devour, though never to his face. No-one has ever been able to prove what it is that Marty does for a living, but if anyone ever does there'll be a general rush to hang him from the nearest lamp-post. Sally was big and brassy, with a loud voice and a louder laugh. People always talk louder when they're afraid. Sally was the fourth Mrs. DeVore, and no-one was betting she'd be the last.

And these were the kind of women Eleanor lunched with. Personally, I'd rather go swimming with sharks with a dead cow tied round my neck.

None of these women had come here alone, of course. Their other halves would never let them out on their own; something might happen to them. They must be protected from everything, including having too much of the wrong kind of fun. Ownership must be shown at all times. So all the ladies' bodyguards and chaperones sat together on their own at a row of tables set carefully to one side. They didn't drink or eat anything, but sat there blank-faced and empty-eyed, waiting for something to happen to give them an excuse to hurt somebody. They talked to each other now and then, in a quiet, desultory way, to pass the time. Interestingly enough, it seemed Eleanor had come here accompanied by her latest toy boy, a gorgeous young man called Ramon. Ramon was always in the tabloids, photographed on the arm of some rich woman or other. None of the bodyguards or chaperones were talking to him. They were professionals. But then, in his own way, so was Ramon. He sat perfectly casually, staring off into the distance, perhaps already considering where in the Tea Room his next meal ticket was coming from. I felt obscurely disappointed. Eleanor could have done better than Ramon.

I headed straight for Eleanor's table, and at every table I passed the conversation quieted and stopped, as the women looked to see where I was going and who I was going to talk to. By the time I got to Eleanor the whole Tea Room had gone quiet, with heads everywhere turning and craning to see what would happen. All the body-guards had gone tense. For the first time I could clearly hear the classical music playing in the background. A string quartet was committing Mozart with malice afore-thought. I stopped behind Eleanor, said her name, and she took her time turning round to look at me.

"Oh," she said. "It's you, Taylor." The careless bore-dom in her voice was a work of art. The infamous John Taylor. Again. How very dull . . .

"We need to talk," I said, playing it brusque and mys-terious, not to be outdone.

"I don't think so," said Eleanor, calmly and dismis-sively. "I'm busy. Some other time, perhaps."

The Tea Room loved that. The other women at Eleanor's table were all but wetting themselves, silent and goggle-eyed, wriggling with excitement to see her so casually brushing off the disreputable and deliciously dangerous John Taylor. She couldn't have impressed them more if she'd shat rubies.

"There are things you know that I need to know," I said, playing my role to the hilt.

"What a shame," said Eleanor. And she turned her back on me.

"Your father had some very interesting things to say

about you," I said to her turned back, and smiled slightly as I saw it stiffen. "Talk to me, Eleanor. Or I'll tell everyone here."

She turned around again and considered me coldly. I was bluffing, and she had to be pretty sure I was, but she couldn't take the risk. The Ladies Who Lunch thrive on weaknesses exposed, like piranha thrown raw meat. And besides, I had to be more interesting than her present company. So she'd talk to me and try to find out exactly what I knew, while telling me as little as possible in return.. I could see all of that in her face . . . because she let me.

"If I must, I must," she said, an aristocrat being gracious to an underling. She smiled sweetly at the women sitting all agog around her table. "Forgive me, darlings. Family business. You know how it is."

The women smiled and nodded and said all the right things in return, but it was clear they couldn't wait for us to leave so they could start gossiping about us. All across the room, every eye watched as I led Eleanor to a private booth at the back and settled her in. Conversations rose slowly in the Tea Room again. The bodyguards relaxed at their tables, no doubt relieved they weren't going to have to take me on after all. Ramon watched me with his cold, dark eyes, and his face showed nothing at all. I sat down in the booth opposite Eleanor.

"Well," I said, "fancy meeting you here."

"We do need to talk," she said, leaning forward earnestly. "But you understand I couldn't make it easy for you."

"Oh, of course," I said, and wondered where this was going.

"I wouldn't want you to think I talk freely to just any-one."

"Perish the thought."

"Look at them," she said, gesturing at her table. "Chattering like birds because I dared talk back to the in-famous John Taylor. If I hadn't, the gossip sheets would have had us in bed together by tomorrow. Some of them will anyway just because it's such a good story."

"Perish the thought," I said again, and she looked at me sharply. I grinned, and she smiled suddenly in return. She relaxed a little and sat back in her chair. "You're eas-ier to talk to than I'd thought, Mr. Taylor. And I could use someone to talk to."

I gestured at Ramon, sitting alone at his table. "Don't you have him to talk to?"

"I don't underwrite Ramon's considerable upkeep for his conversation," she said dryly. "In many ways, he's still a boy. Pretty enough, and fun to play with, but there's not a lot going on in his head. I prefer my sweeties that way. The whole point of toy boys is that you play with them for a while, and when you get tired of them you move on to the next toy."

"And your husband doesn't care?" I said.

"I didn't marry Marcel for *that*," Eleanor said, matter-of-factly. "Daddy wants me to be married, because he can still be very old-fashioned about some things. Hardly sur-prising, I suppose, for someone born as long ago as he was. You can take the immortal out of the past, but . . . Daddy believes a woman should always be guided by a man. First her father, then a husband. And since Daddy Dearest has more important things to concern himself with these days, it has to be the husband. It never seems to have occurred to him that I only ever marry men who have the good sense to do as they're told, away from Griffin Hall. I wouldn't marry at all if it weren't necessary to stay on Daddy's good side ...

"I married Marcel because he makes me laugh. He's charming and civilised and good company ... and he doesn't make demands. He has his life, and I have mine, and never the twain shall meet. In the old days, Daddy's formative days, they would have called it a marriage of convenience. But since this is the modern age, it's my convenience that matters. What did you want to talk to me about, Mr. Taylor? Daddy didn't tell you anything interesting about me because I've gone to great pains to make sure he doesn't know anything interesting about me."

"You'd be surprised what I know," I said, because you have to say something. "I'm still trying to get a handle on everyone in the Griffin family, so I can work up some theories about who might have kidnapped Melissa, and why."

Eleanor shrugged. "We're really not all that complicated. Daddy has his business, Mummy lives to be Queen of High Society, William runs away and hides whenever Daddy isn't looking, Melissa is a sanctimonious pain in the arse, and my dear little pride and joy Paul won't come out of his bedroom. And there you have the Griffins in a nutshell."

"What about you?" I said. "Who are you, Eleanor Griffin?"

Like her brother, once Eleanor started talking she couldn't stop. It all came tumbling out. Perhaps because it had been such a long time since she could talk to anyone honestly, to someone she could trust to keep a secret

SIMON R. GREEN

and not pass it on . . . because they honestly didn't give a damn.

"Daddy never had much time for me," she said, and though she was looking at me, her gaze was far away, in the past. "He's very old-fashioned. His son could be an heir, and part of the family business, but not a daughter. So I was left much more to my own devices than William ever was. Mummy didn't care, either. She only had me and William to be fashionable. So I was brought up by a succession of nannies, tutors, and paid companions, all of whom reported back to Daddy. I couldn't trust any of them. I grew up to rely on no-one but myself, and to look out for myself first and foremost. Just like Daddy.

"Down the years I've tried to interest myself in lots of things to pass the time . . . There's so much time to fill when you're immortal. I've tried politics, religion, shopping . . . but none of them ever satisfied for long. For the moment I have decided simply to enjoy my money and position and be a happy little lotus eater. Does that make me sound terribly shallow?"

"Why toy boys?" I said, carefully avoiding a question that had no good answer. "Word is none of them ever seem to last long . . ."

"As the years go by, and I get no older, I'm drawn more and more to youth," said Eleanor. "Real youth, as opposed to this splendid body of mine that never ages. Despite all the things I've done to it. I dread growing old and crotchety, and stuck in my ways . . . Constant exposure to young thoughts and opinions and fashions helps to keep me young at heart. I'll never be like Daddy; for all his years and experience he's still really no different from the medieval trader he originally was. Business is business, no matter what century you're in. He may have assumed aristocratic airs and graces, but he's still stuck in his old ways. Inflexible in his values, even though they were formed centuries ago . . . I don't ever want to be like that."

"What do you want?" I said.

She smiled briefly. "Damned if I know, Mr. Taylor. I'd quite like to inherit Daddy's money, but not his business. I'll sell my share in a shot, first chance I get. And I don't want to end up like William, lost in his own indulgences. He thinks I don't know what he gets up to at the Caligula Club, but everyone knows . . . I want to do something that matters, be someone who matters. But no-one will ever see me as anything more than the Griffin's daughter. You have no idea how limiting extreme wealth and power can be."

"Poor little rich girl," I said solemnly. "Got everything but happiness and peace of mind."

She glared at me. "You're mocking me, Mr. Taylor. And anyone here could tell you that's a very dangerous thing to do."

I smiled. "Danger is my business."

"Oh please . . . What do you want, Mr. Taylor?"

"Well, to start with, I want you to call me John. After that . . . I want to find Melissa. Make sure she's safe."

"And take her home again? Back to Griffin Hall?"

"If that's what she wants," I said carefully.

Eleanor studied me for a moment. "You don't think she was kidnapped, do you? You think she's a runaway. I have to say, it wouldn't surprise me. But, as and when you do find her, you won't take her back against her will because that would be against your principles, right?"

"Right," I said.

She smiled at me dazzlingly. "I like you rather better

for that, John. You're actually ready to defy the Griffin himself, to his face? He's had people killed for less. Perhaps you really are everything they say you are."

"No," I said. "No-one could be everything they say I am."

She laughed briefly again. "You have no idea how refreshing it is to talk to someone . . . real. You don't give a damn that I'm a Griffin, do you?"

"No," I said honestly. "I've fought worse, in my time."

"Yes . . . you probably have. You didn't take this case for the money, either, did you? You actually do want to find Melissa."

"Well," I said honestly, "the money helped."

And then we both looked round as Ramon appeared at the entrance to our private booth. He was tall and well built inside his expensive suit, and he held himself like he might have been a fighter at some time. He glared at me coldly, ignoring Eleanor.

"Who do you think you are, Taylor? Walking in here like you have a right to be here and ordering your betters about? Eleanor, you don't have to say anything to him. I know his kind—all bluff and reputation."

"Like you want to be?" I said. "Before you realised how much hard work was involved and how much easier it was to use your pretty face and manners to trade up for a better life? Go and sit at your table again, like a good boy. Eleanor will come and collect you when she's ready."

"That's right, Ramon," said Eleanor. "No-one's forcing me to do anything. It's sweet of you to be concerned, but . . ."

"Shut up," said Ramon, and Eleanor stared blankly at him as though he'd just slapped her. Ramon turned his glare on her. "This isn't about you, for once. It's about me. How do you think it makes me look when you ignore me to smile and simper with street scum like him?"

"Ramon," I said, and something in my voice jerked his attention back to me. "I understand the need to make a good showing in front of your woman and your . . . peers, but really, don't push your luck."

He snarled at me, and suddenly a long stiletto blade shone brightly in his hand. It had the look of a professional weapon, probably hidden in a forearm sheath. He held the blade like he knew what to do with it, and I sat very still. Eleanor stared at Ramon as though she'd never seen him before.

"What the hell do you think you're doing, Ramon? Don't be stupid! Put that thing away immediately!"

He ignored her, caught up in his anger and the drama of the moment. The whole Tea Room had gone quiet, everyone looking at us, at him, and he knew it and loved it. He sniggered loudly.

"They say you have werewolf blood in you, Taylor. Let's see how well you do against a silver blade. My guess is you'll bleed just like anyone else when I cut your nuts off and make you eat them."

I stood up, and he fell back in spite of himself. I fixed him with my gaze, holding his eyes with mine, despite everything he could do to look away. I stepped out of the booth, and he stumbled backwards, still unable to wrench his gaze away. He was whimpering now, as slow bloody tears began to ooze out from under his eyelids. The silver stiletto slipped from his numbing fingers as I stared him down. And then one of the bodyguards appeared out of nowhere from my blind side and threw his cup of coffee right into my face. I cried out as the scalding liquid burned my face and temporarily blinded me. I scrabbled frantically at my face with my hands, trying to clear my sight. I could hear other footsteps approaching.

Eleanor brushed past me as she launched herself out of the booth and put herself between me and Ramon. I heard her yelling at him and at others I couldn't see yet. The accustomed authority in her voice was holding them back, but I didn't know for how long. I knuckled savagely at my tearing eyes, and finally my sight returned. My face still stung painfully, but I ignored it. All the bodyguards had left their tables to form a pack behind Ramon. They scented blood in the water and a chance to bring down the infamous John Taylor. And, of course, a chance to look like real men in front of their women. If they could take down John Taylor, they could name their own prices in the future.

They were jostling each other uneasily for position, all eager for the chance to get a crack at me, but not that eager to be the first. They had no weapons, but they all looked happy at the chance of a little excitement, of handing out a vicious beating to an upstart who didn't know his place. I straightened up and glared at them, and a few actually fell back rather than face my gaze. Ramon flinched, bloody tear marks still drying on his face. Then he quickly got his confidence back as he realised I couldn't stare him down again. Eleanor was still standing between me and the pack, hands on hips and head held high as she berated them all impartially.

"This man is my guest! He has my protection and my father's! And I will talk with whoever I damn well feel like, Ramon!"

"He shouldn't be here," said Ramon, his voice thick

with the anticipation of violence. "He doesn't belong here."

"Neither do you," Eleanor said coldly. "But I brought you in anyway. Though God knows what I ever thought I saw in you. Get out, Ramon. It's over. And don't you dare make a fuss, or I won't write you a reference."

"Just like that?" said Ramon. "Just like all the others? No . . . I don't think so. I think I'll leave you a little something to remember me by." He slapped her hard across the face. Eleanor stumbled backwards, one hand pressed to her reddened cheek. Ramon smiled. "You have no idea how long I've wanted to do that. Now stay out of my way. You don't want to get blood on your new dress." He turned his cold gaze back to me. "Come on, boys, it's fun time."

While he was still talking, I stepped forward and kneed him in the groin. He made a sick, breathless sound and folded over, so I rabbit-punched him on the back of the neck to help him on his way to the floor. The pack of bodyguards surged forward, shouting angrily, and they were all over me. Punches came at me from every direction at once, and I all I could do was get my head down and my shoulders up and take it, riding out the blows as best I could and concentrating on staying on my feet. If I went down, they'd all take turns putting the boot in, and I wouldn't get up from that. I didn't think they'd deliberately kill me, for fear of incurring the Griffin's anger, but accidents have been known to happen when the blood's up.

Luckily they weren't used to fighting in a group. Body-guarding is more about protecting the client, and one-on-one intimidation. They got in each other's way in their eagerness to get at me, and they were too eager to get their own blows in to think of co-operating. I concentrated on getting my hands into my coat-pockets. I keep all kinds of useful things there. The bodyguards hit and kicked me, but I didn't go down. People (and others) have been trying to kill me ever since I was a child, and I'm still here.

I pulled a whizz-bang out of my left pocket and threw it onto the floor. It exploded in a burst of brilliant light, and the bodyguards fell back, cursing and blinking furiously. Which gave me all the time I needed to draw a small brown human bone out of my right pocket and show it to the bodyguards. They all stood very still, and I grinned nastily.

"That's right, boys. This is a pointing bone. All I have to do is point and say the Word, and whoever I'm pointing it at will be going home in a coffin. So pick up what's left of Ramon, and get the hell out of my sight."

"You're bluffing," said one of the bodyguards, but he didn't sound as though he meant it.

"Don't be an idiot," said the man beside him. "That's John bloody Taylor. He doesn't need to bluff."

They picked up Ramon and hauled him out of the Tea Room. All the ladies watched in silence, then looked back at me. A few looked like they would have liked to applaud. I turned my back on the room, and Eleanor helped me sit down in the private booth again. I sat down hard, breathing heavily. I hurt pretty much everywhere. Taking a beating gets harder as you get older. At least I hadn't lost any teeth this time. I hate that. I put the bone away and looked at Eleanor.

"Thanks for standing up for me."

"I absolutely hate and loathe machismo," she said. "But you were pretty impressive there. Was that a genuine aboriginal pointing bone? I always understood the real thing is pretty hard to find."

"They are," I said.

"Then you were bluffing?"

"Maybe," I said. "I'll never tell."

"Your face was badly burned," she said, studying me closely. "I saw it. But now all the burns are gone. And anyone else would have needed an ambulance after a beating like that. But not you. Do you really have were-wolf blood in you, Mr. Taylor?"

"Something like that," I said. "And it's John, remember? Now, where were we . . . Ah yes, Melissa. Tell me about Melissa, Eleanor."

I'll never know what she might have said then, because we were interrupted again. This time by an over-sized goon squeezed into a bright red messenger's outfit, complete with gold braid. He didn't look at all comfortable in it and squirmed surreptitiously as he bowed jerkily to Eleanor, ignoring me. He then made a big deal of presenting her with a sealed envelope on a silver platter. There was no name on the envelope. Eleanor picked it up and looked at the messenger.

"Bearer waits," he said, in a rough and distinctly unmessenger-like tone. "There's a car outside."

Eleanor ripped open the envelope and studied the single sheet of paper within. I leaned forward, but all I could make out was a handwritten message by someone who had clearly never even heard of penmanship.

"Oh how dreary," she said, dropping the message onto the table like a dead fish. "It seems my dear Marcel has got himself in trouble again. You know he gambles? Of course you do. Everybody knows. I don't know why he's so keen on it; he's never been any good. All the reputable houses won't let him through their doors these days, not since Daddy made it very clear that he wouldn't underwrite Marcel's debts anymore. I really thought that might knock some sense into him, but I should have known better. It seems Marcel has been sneaking off to some of the nastier little clubs, where they'll let absolutely anybody in, and running up his debts there. And while these . . . people are smart enough to realise they can't dun my father for Marcel's losses, they do seem to think they can pressure me."

"What do they want?" I said, ignoring the messenger goon.

"Apparently, if I don't go with the messenger right now, in his no-doubt-pokey little car, to discuss the repayment of Marcel's debts, they'll send my husband back to me one small piece at a time until I do. He won't die. He's immortal now, like me, but that just means his suffering could be infinitely extended . . . It's such a bother, but I'd better go."

"That might not be entirely wise," I said carefully. "Then they'd have two hostages with which to extort money from your father. And while he wouldn't pay up for Marcel, he would for you."

"They wouldn't dare threaten me! Would they?"

"Look at the state of the thing they sent as a messenger," I said. "These people don't impress me as being a particularly up-market operation."

"I have to go," said Eleanor. "He's my husband."

"Then I'd better go with you," I said. "I have some experience in dealing with these sorts of people."

"Of course," said Eleanor. "They're from your world, aren't they? Very well. Stick around and look menacing, and try not to get in my way while I negotiate."

"Perish the thought," I said. I turned my gaze on the messenger, and he shuffled his feet uneasily. "Talk to me," I said. "Who do you work for?"

"I'm not supposed to answer questions," the goon said unhappily. "Bearer waits. Car outside. That's all I'm supposed to say."

"But I'm John Taylor, and I want to know. So tell me, or I'll turn you into something small and squishy and jump up and down on you."

The messenger swallowed hard and didn't know what to do with his hands. "I work for Herbert Libby," he said hoarsely. "At the Roll a Dice club, casino, and bar. It's a high-class place. Real cuisine and no spitting on the floor."

"Never heard of it," I said to Eleanor. "And I've heard of everywhere that matters. So, let's go and talk with Mr. Libby and explain to him what a really bad idea this was." I glared at the messenger. "Lead the way. And don't try anything funny. We won't laugh."

We left Hecate's Tea Room, accompanied by many gossiping voices. The bodyguards were back at their tables and sulking quietly, but the Ladies Who Lunched were ecstatic. They hadn't known this much excitement in their lives in years. There was indeed a car waiting outside. Small, black, and anonymous, it stood out awkwardly among the shimmering stretch limousines waiting patiently for the ladies inside. The uniformed chauffeurs stopped talking together over a passed round hand-rolled, and looked down their noses at the goon in the messenger suit. Eleanor's chauffeur actually stepped forward and raised an eyebrow inquiringly, but Eleanor told him to take the limousine back to Griffin Hall. She'd find her own way home. The chauffeur looked at the messenger, then at me, and I could see he didn't like it, but, as always, he did what he was told. Eleanor stalked over to the small black car, stood by the back door, and glared at the messenger until he hurried forward to open it for her. She slipped elegantly into the back of the car, and I got in after her. The messenger eased his feelings by slamming the door shut behind me, and clambered in behind the wheel.

"The Roll a Dice," Eleanor said coldly, "and step on it. I have things to be about."

The messenger made a low, unhappy sound, and we pulled out into the traffic.

"I know it's going to be one of those pokey little places, with sawdust on the floor and back rooms full of cigar smoke, where the cards are so crooked it's a wonder the dealer can shuffle them," said Eleanor. "Marcel must really be running out of bolt-holes if he's been reduced to the likes of the Roll a Dice."

"Hey," protested the messenger, "it's a good club. Got acoustics and everything."

"Watch the road," I said. "And anyway, it should be the Roll a Die. *Dice* is plural, *die* is singular."

"What?"

"Oh shut up and drive," I said.

The Nightside traffic flowed past us, including a lot of things that weren't really traffic, driven by things that didn't even look like people. There are no traffic lights in the Nightside and no speed limits. As a result, driving isn't so much a journey as evolution in action. The bigger prey on the smaller, and only the strongest survive to reach their destination. Significantly, no-one bothered us.

Which meant someone must have lashed out a fair amount of money for some decent protection magics for the car. The goon undid the collar and first few buttons of his messenger suit so he could concentrate better as he drove.

We soon left Uptown behind and quickly turned off into the darker, lesser-used streets, where sleaze and decay weren't so much a style as a way of life. The Nightside has its own bottom feeders, and they're nastier than most. The neon signs fell away because this wasn't the kind of area where you wanted to advertise your presence. People might be looking for you. These were the kinds of clubs and bars you heard about by word of mouth, where everything was permitted because nobody cared. Enter at your own risk, mind your own business, and think yourself lucky if you came out even at the end of the game.

The car finally lurched to a halt before a row of dingy joints that were only a step up from hole-in-the-wall merchants. Blank doors and painted-out windows, with nothing to recommend them but the gaudy names they gave themselves. Rosie's Repose, the Pink Pelican, the Roll a Dice. The messenger goon got out of the car, started towards the club, then remembered. He hurried back to open the back door for Eleanor. He wouldn't have done it for me. Eleanor stalked past him to the club, not even deigning to look about her. The messenger hurried to get to the club door ahead of her, leaving me to get out of the car and close the door behind me. The goon made a real production out of his secret knock, and the door swung open to reveal a gorilla in a huge tuxedo. It was a real mountain gorilla, a silverback, with a long, pink scar across his forehead to show where the brain implants had gone in. It nodded familiarly to the messenger, looked Eleanor and me over carefully, and gave us both a sniff for good measure before turning abruptly to lead us into the club. The door slammed shut behind us with nobody touching it, but that probably came as standard in an area like this.

The room before us was silent and gloomy, closed down. Chairs had been put up on the tables, and the roulette wheel was covered with a cloth. The bar was sealed off behind a heavy metal grille. The floor was bare wood, no sawdust. The room stank of sweat and smoke and desperation. This wasn't the kind of place where people gambled for pleasure. This was a place for addicts and junkies, for whom every card, every roll of the dice or spin of the wheel was a matter of life and death.

There weren't any staff around. Not even a cleaner. The owner must have sent everybody home. Presumably Mr. Herbert Libby didn't want any witnesses for whatever might happen now the Griffin's daughter had arrived to join her erring husband. The gorilla led us through the room, out the back, and down a steep set of stairs. The messenger goon brought up the rear. We emerged into a bare stone cellar, a brightly lit space with bare walls, piles of crates and stacked boxes, and a handful of men standing around one man tied to a chair. The stone floor around the chair was splashed with blood. The man in the chair was, of course, Marcel, or what was left of him.

He raised his head slowly to look at Eleanor and me. He might have been glad to see us, but it was hard to tell past the mess they'd made of his face. His eyes were swollen shut, his nose had been broken and bent to one side, and his lips were cracked and bloody. They'd cut off his left ear. Blood soaked his left shoulder and all down the front of his shirt. Marcel's breathing was slow and heavy, interspersed with low moans of pain and half-snoring noises through his ruined nose. Eleanor made a low, shocked noise and started forward, but I grabbed her arm and held her still. No point in giving these scumbags what they wanted this early in the game.

One of the thugs standing in the semicircle beyond the chair stepped forward, and it was easy to identify him as the boss, Herbert Libby. He was large and blocky, fat over muscle, with a square, brutal face and a shaven skull to hide the fact that he was going bald. He wore an expensive suit as though he'd just thrown it on, and his large hands were heavy with gold and silver rings. He had the look of a man who liked to indulge himself, preferably at someone else's expense. There was blood on his hands, and his cuffs were soaked red. He smiled easily at Eleanor, but it was a cold thing that didn't touch his eyes. He ignored me to glare at the goon in the messenger suit.

"Charlie, I told you to bring back Eleanor Griffin. What is John Taylor doing here? Did I ask you to bring back John Taylor?"

The messenger squirmed unhappily under his boss's gaze. "Well, no, Mr. Libby, but . . ."

"Then what is he doing here, Charlie?"

"I don't know, Mr. Libby! He sort of . . . invited himself."

"We'll talk about this later, Charlie." Libby finally deigned to notice me. He nodded briefly, but didn't smile. "Mr. John Taylor. Well, we are honoured. Welcome to my very own little den of iniquity. I'm afraid you're not seeing us at our best, at the present. Me and the boys got a little carried away, expressing our displeasure with Marcel. I do like to think of myself as a hands-on kind of manager . . . And since I'm the owner of the Roll a Dice, I take it very personally when some aristocratic nonce comes strolling in here with the express purpose of cheating me out of my hard-earned . . ."

"My husband doesn't cheat," Eleanor said flatly. "He may be the worst gambler that ever lived, but he doesn't cheat."

"He came in here to play without the money to cover his bets, or the means to pay off his debts," said Libby. "I call that cheating. And no-one cheats me and lives to boast of it. I do like to think of myself as a reasonable and understanding sort, but I can't let anyone get away with cheating me. That would be bad for business and my reputation. Which is why we are using Marcel here to send a message to any and all who might think they can welch on a debt and get away with it. What are you doing here, Mr. Taylor, exactly?"

"I'm with Eleanor," I said. "Her father asked me to see that she got home safely."

"The Griffin himself! What a thrill it must be, to move in such exalted circles!" Libby smiled again, like a shark showing its teeth. "You and he have both made a name for yourself in the Nightside, as people it is very dangerous to cross. But you know what, Mr. Taylor? Uptown reputations don't mean anything down here. Down here you can do anything you want if you can get away with it. It's a dog-eat-dog world, and I am top dog."

"If I'd known, I'd have brought you some biscuits," I said brightly. "I could throw something for you to fetch if you want."

The other thugs stared blankly. People didn't talk like that to Mr. Libby.

"Funny man," Libby said dispassionately. "We get a

lot of those in here. But I'm the one who ends up laughing."

He grabbed Marcel's bloody chin and forced the battered face up so I could see it more clearly. Marcel moaned softly, but didn't struggle. All the resistance had been beaten out of him.

"We get all sorts in here," said Libby, turning Marcel's face back and forth so he could admire his handiwork. "They come into my club, big and bold and full of themselves, and they throw all their money away at cards or dice or at the wheel, and when the time comes to make good, surprise surprise, they haven't got the money on them. And they expect me to be reasonable. Well, reasonable is as reasonable does, Mr. Taylor. I extended Marcel here a longer-than-usual run of credit because he assured me his father-in-law would be good for his debts. However, when I take the quite reasonable precaution of contacting Mr. Griffin about this, he denies this. He is, in fact, quite rude to me. So, if Marcel can't pay, and the Griffin won't . . . where am I going to get my money?"

"Don't tell me," I said. "You have a plan."

"Of course. I always have a plan. That's why I'm top dog of this particular dung heap. I was going to show Eleanor what I'd done to her deadbeat husband, then send her home to Daddy with her husband's ear in a box so she could plead for enough money to save him further pain. Fathers are often more indulgent with their daughters than they are with their sons-in-law; especially when the daughters are crying."

"My father will have you skinned for this," Eleanor said firmly. "Marcel is family."

Libby just shrugged. "Let him send his heavies down here if he likes, and we'll send them back to him in pieces. No-one bothers us on our own territory. Now where was I . . . Oh yes, the change in plans. I will keep you and Marcel here, while Mr. Taylor goes back to Griffin Hall to beg your father for enough money to ransom your miserable lives. And Mr. Taylor had better be very persuasive, because I'm pretty sure even an immortal will die if you cut them into enough small pieces . . ."

"You really think you can take on the Griffin?" I said. "He could send a whole army in here."

"Let him," said Libby. "Him and his kind, they know nothing about life down here. We stand together, down here. It's dog-eat-dog, but every man against the outsider. If the Griffin turns up here mob-handed, he'll find a real army waiting to meet him. And no-one fights dirtier than us. I guarantee you, Mr. Taylor; if the Griffin makes a fight of this, I will take out my displeasure on Eleanor and Marcel, and he'll be able to hear their screams all the way up on Griffin Hall. And what I'll leave of them he wouldn't want back. So, he'll pay up, to save the expense of a war he can't win. He is, after all, a businessman. Just like me."

"My father is nothing like you," said Eleanor, and her voice cut at him like a knife. "Marcel, can you hear me, darling?"

Somehow Marcel found the strength to jerk his chin out of Libby's hand and turn his bloody face to look at Eleanor. His voice was slow and slurred and painful.

"You shouldn't have come here, Eleanor. The service is terrible."

"Why did you come here?"

"They wouldn't take my bets anywhere else. Your father saw to that. So this is all his fault, really."

"Hush, dear," said Eleanor. "Mr. Taylor and I will get you out of here."

"Good," said Marcel. "The place really has gone to the dogs."

Libby back-handed him across the face, hard enough to send fresh blood flying through the air. Eleanor made a shocked sound. She wasn't used to such casual brutality. I looked at Libby.

"Don't do that again."

Libby automatically lifted his hand to hit Marcel again, only to hesitate as something in my gaze got through to him. He flushed briefly, lowering his hand. He wasn't used to having his wishes thwarted. He looked at the messenger goon.

"Charlie, bring the lady over here so she can get a close-up look at what we've done to her better half."

The messenger grabbed Eleanor's arm. She produced a small silver canister from somewhere and sprayed its contents in the goon's face. He howled horribly and crashed to the floor, clawing at his eyes with both hands. I looked at Eleanor, and she smiled sweetly.

"Mace, with added holy water. Mummy gave it to me. A girl should always be prepared, she said. After all, there are times when a girl just doesn't feel like being molested."

"Quite right," I said.

Libby actually growled at us, like a dog before regaining his composure. "I saw you in action, Mr. Taylor, during the Lilith War. Most impressive. But that was then, and this is now, and this is my place. Due to the nature of my business, I have found it necessary to install all kinds of protective magics here. The best money can buy.

Nothing happens here that I don't want to. Down here, in my place, there's no-one bigger than me."

"A gambling den, soaked in hidden magics?" I said. "I am shocked, I tell you, shocked. You'll be telling me next your games of chance aren't entirely on the up and up."

"Gamblers only come here when they've been thrown out of everywhere else," said Libby. "They know the odds are bent in my favour, but they can't afford to care. And there never was a gambler who didn't know he was good enough to beat even a rigged game. But enough of this pleasant chit-chat, Mr. Taylor. It's time to get down to business. You keep Eleanor under control while I carve a decent-sized piece off Marcel for you to take back to the Griffin. What do you think he'd be most easily able to identify, a finger or an eye?"

"Don't touch him," I said. "Or there will be . . . consequences."

"You're nothing down here," Libby said savagely. "And just for that, I think I'll cut something off Eleanor, too, for you to take back to her father."

He raised his right hand to show me the scalpel in it, and smiled. The other thugs grinned and elbowed each other, anticipating a show. And I raised my hand to show them the piece of human bone I'd shown in Hecate's Tea Room. Everyone stood very still.

"This," I said, "is an aboriginal pointing bone. Very old, very basic magic. I point, and you die. So, who goes first?"

"This is my place," said Libby, still smiling. "I'm protected, and you're bluffing, Taylor."

I stabbed the bone at Libby and muttered the Words, and he fell dead to the floor.

"Not always," I said.

The remaining thugs looked at the dead body of their erstwhile boss, looked at me, then looked at each other. One of them knelt beside Libby and tried to find a pulse. He looked up and shook his head, and the other thugs immediately knelt and started going through Libby's pockets. They weren't interested in us anymore. I still covered them with the pointing bone while Eleanor produced a delicate little ladies' knife from somewhere and cut the ropes holding Marcel to his chair. He tried to stand up and fell forward into Eleanor's waiting arms as his legs failed him. She held him up long enough for me to get there, and together we half led, half carried him out of the cellar and up into the main room of the Roll a Dice. No-one tried to follow us.

"So you weren't bluffing in the Tea Room," Eleanor said as we headed for the door.

"Sort of," I said. "I've never actually used the bone before. I wasn't entirely sure it was what I thought it was. I stole it from old blind Pew, years ago."

Eleanor looked at me. "What would you have done if it hadn't worked?"

"Improvised," I said.

Eleanor drove the goon's car back to Hecate's Tea Room, where she called for a limousine to take Marcel back to Griffin Hall. I did suggest an ambulance might be more appropriate, but Eleanor wouldn't hear of it. He'd be safer at the Hall, and that was all that mattered. Marcel was an immortal, so he couldn't die, and he'd heal quicker in familiar surroundings.

"And besides," said Eleanor, "the Griffin family keeps its secrets to itself."

The limousine arrived in a few minutes and took Marcel away. The liveried chauffeur didn't even raise an eyebrow at Marcel's condition. Eleanor and I went back into the Tea Room and sat down again in our private booth. The storm of gossip over our reappearance was practically deafening.

"Thanks for the help," said Eleanor. "I could have called Daddy, but he always favours the scorched earth policy when it comes to threats against the family. And I'm not ready to lose Marcel, just yet."

"So," I said, "tell me about Melissa."

Eleanor pulled a face. "You are persistent, aren't you? I suppose I do owe you something . . . and unlike my dear husband, I always pay my debts. So, Melissa . . . I can't tell you much about her because I don't know much. I'm not sure anyone does, really. Melissa . . . is a very private, very quiet person. The kind who spends a lot of time living inside her own head. Reads a lot, studies . . . She does talk to Jeremiah, though don't ask me about what. They spend a lot of time together, in private.

"I never cared much about her, to be honest. I was always more concerned with my Paul. I moved back into the Hall so I could be close to him. I wasn't going to lose my son to the Griffin. What little I do know of Melissa is only because she and Paul have always been close. They spend a lot of time in each other's rooms . . . Because they grew up together in the Hall, they see themselves as brother and sister. Though my Paul never took to Jeremiah the way Melissa did. I saw to that. I didn't give up on my child, like William did." She smiled wistfully. "Paul and I were very close when he was small. Now that he's a teenager it's all I can do to get him to come out of his room."

"I didn't get to meet him," I said. "But I talked to him, through his bedroom door. He seemed . . . highly strung."

Eleanor shrugged angrily. "He's a teenager. For me, that's so long ago I can barely remember what it was like. I try to be understanding, but . . . he'll get over it. I raised Paul to be his own man, not Jeremiah's. I just wish he'd talk to me more . . ."

"Do you believe Melissa was kidnapped?" I said bluntly.

"Oh yes," said Eleanor, not hesitating for a moment. "But it must have been done with inside help to get past all the security. Not anyone in the family. I'd know. More likely one of the servants."

"How about Hobbes?" I said. "He seems to know everything there is to know about the Hall's security. And he is a bit . . ."

"Creepy?" said Eleanor. "Damned right. Can't stand the fellow, myself. He sneaks around, and you never hear him coming. Gives himself airs and graces, just because he's the butler. But no . . . Hobbes is Jeremiah's man, body and soul. Always has been. What bothers me is that there hasn't been any ransom demand yet."

"Maybe they're still working out how much to ask for," I said.

"Maybe. Or perhaps they believe they can find the secret of Griffin immortality by interrogating her. Or dissecting her. The fools." She looked at me appealingly and put her hand on top of mine. "John, I might not be as close to Melissa as I should, but I still wouldn't want anything like that to happen to her. You rescued Marcel for me. Rescue my niece. Whatever it takes."

"Even though her return could disinherit you?" I said.

"That's only a whim on Daddy's part," Eleanor said

flatly. She drew her hand back from mine, but her gaze was just as steady. "He's testing William and me, to see how we'll react. He'll change his mind. Or I'll change it for him." She smiled suddenly, like a mischievous child. "William never did understand how to work our father. He always had to go head to head, and you never get anywhere with Daddy like that. He's had centuries to build up his stubbornness. And William . . . has never been strong. I know how to get Daddy to do what I want, without him ever realising that it's my idea and not his. Which is why I have a life of my own, away from the family and the family business, and a child of my own, and poor William doesn't."

"There is a story," I said carefully, "about an adult grand-child leading to the Griffin's death . . ."

"No-one believes that old story!" said Eleanor, not even bothering to hide her scorn. "Or at least, no-one who matters. Do you think for one moment I'd let my Paul live in the Hall with the Griffin if I thought he was in any danger? No, that story is one of the many legends that have grown up around my family and my father, down the centuries. Most of them contradictory. I think Daddy encourages them. The more stories there are, the less chance there is that someone might discover the truth. Whatever it might be. I don't know. I don't think anyone does anymore, except Daddy."

She paused, and looked at me in a thoughtful, considering way. "I find myself . . . drawn to you, John Taylor. You're the first man I've met in a long time who genuinely doesn't seem to give a damn about my family's wealth, or power. Who isn't scared shitless of my father. Do you have any idea how rare that is? Every one of my husbands all but fainted the first time I dragged them into the great man's presence. Could it be that I've finally found a real man, after so many boys . . . ?"

"I'm hard to impress," I said. "You never met my mother . . . And you should remember that I'm only passing through your life, Eleanor. I have no intention of staying. I have my own life and a woman I share it with. I'm just here to do a job."

Eleanor put her hand on top of mine again. There was a sense of pressure, not unpleasant, as though she could hold me there by force. "Are you sure I can't tempt you, John?"

I gently but firmly pulled my hand out from under hers. "You haven't met my Suzie. Has it ever occurred to you, Eleanor, that what you're looking for isn't a man, but another Daddy?"

"I am never that obvious," said Eleanor, not insulted. "Or that shallow."

"I don't have time for this," I said, not unkindly. "I have to find Melissa, and I'm on a very tight deadline. I can't help feeling I'm missing something . . . I've talked to everyone in your family now, except Paul. You said he and Melissa were very close. If I were to go back to the Hall, would you happen to have a spare key to his bedroom?"

"He isn't there right now," said Eleanor, looking away for the first time. "He has . . . friends he goes to see. At this club . . . He thinks I don't know. If I tell you where to find him, John, you have to promise me you'll be gentle with him. Treat him kindly. He is very precious to me."

"I shall be politeness itself," I said. "I can be civilised, when I have to be. There just isn't much call for it, in my line of business."

"You have to promise me you won't tell anyone else," Eleanor insisted. "People wouldn't understand."

I put on my most trustworthy face. Eleanor didn't look entirely convinced, but she finally told me the name of the club, and at once I understood a lot more about Paul Griffin. I knew the club. I'd been there before.

"It's so good to have had a real conversation, for a change," said Eleanor, a little wistfully. "To actually talk about something that matters . . ." She looked out of our booth at the Ladies Who Lunch, and her gaze was not kind. "You have no idea how lonely you can feel, in the middle of a crowd, when you know you have nothing in common with any of them. Some days, I could turn my back on the family and walk away from it all. Make a new life for myself. But I couldn't leave Paul to my father's mercies . . . and besides, I don't know how to do poor. So I guess I'll go on being a goldfish in a bowl, swimming round and round, forever. I enjoyed meeting you, John Taylor. You're . . . different."

"Oh yes," I said. "Really. You have no idea."

# SEVEN

# Divas! Las vegas!

There are all kinds of clubs in Uptown, and Divas! is perhaps the most famous. Certainly the most glamorous, Divas! is where men go to get in touch with their feminine side by dressing up in drag as their favourite female singing sensations. They then channel their idols' talents so they can get up on the big raised stage and sing their little hearts out. At Divas! girls just want to have fun.

I'd been to the club once before, during the Nightingale case, but I was hoping the management had forgotten about that by now. It wasn't my fault all the trannies got possessed by outside forces, attacked me and my friends, and we were forced to trash the place. Well, technically, yes it was my fault; but for once I was pretty sure I had the moral high ground as I did save the day,

SIMON R. GREEN

eventually. It really wasn't my fault that the club had to
be practically rebuilt from the ground up afterwards.

I stood outside Divas! and looked the place over. It
looked as I remembered it—loud, overstated, and tacky
as all hell. That much flashing neon in one place should
be declared illegal on mental health grounds. You
couldn't criticise the club's taste because it gloried in the
fact that it didn't have any, but I still felt the neon figures
over the door engaged in what I'd thought at first was a
sword-swallowing act was way over the top.

Bright young things and gorgeous young creatures
sauntered and sashayed through the main entrance. They
came in groups and cliques, in ones and twos, laughing
and chattering and arm in arm, their heads held high. This
was their place, their dream, their heaven on earth. And
this . . . was Paul Griffin's club. I wondered what (or
who) he'd look like when I finally tracked him down.

I strolled casually towards the main entrance, feeling
positively dingy in my plain white trench coat, hoping
against hope that I wouldn't run into anyone who was
involved in the previous . . . unpleasantness. The big and
burly bouncer at the door was Ann-Margaret, in a leopard-
skin print leotard, a flaming red wig, and surprisingly
understated makeup. The illusion was fairly convincing,
until you got close enough to spot the over-developed
biceps. He moved quickly to block my way, a distinctly
unfeminine scowl darkening his face.

"You are not coming in," the Ann-Margaret said flatly.
"You are banned, John Taylor, banned and barred and
banished from this club for the rest of your unnatural life.
We'd excommunicate you and burn you in effigy if we
thought you'd care. You are never setting foot in Divas!
ever again, not even if you get reincarnated. We've only

just got the place looking nice again. And even you can't force your way in now, not with all the really neat new protections we've had installed since you were here last. I have new and important weapons to use against you! Mighty weapons! Powerful weapons!"

"Then why aren't you using them?" I asked, reasonably.

The Ann-Margaret shifted uneasily on his high-heeled feet. "Because there are a lot of really nasty rumours going around just now as to how you really won the Lilith War. They say you did some really awful things, even for you. They say you burned down the Street of the Gods and ate Merlin's heart."

"Does that really sound like something you think I'd do?" I said.

"Hell, yes! Whatever happened to Sister Morphine? What happened to Tommy Oblivion? Why have their bodies never been found?"

"Trust me," I said calmly, "you really don't want to know. I did what I had to, but I couldn't save everyone. Now let me in, or I'll set fire to your wig."

"Beast!" hissed the Ann-Margaret. "Bully." But he still stepped aside to let me pass. The painted and powdered peacocks waiting to get in watched in disapproving silence as I entered the club, but I didn't look back. They can sense fear. The hatcheck girl in her little art deco cubicle was a 1960s Cilla Black in a tight leather bustier. He clearly remembered me from last time because he took one look and immediately dived beneath his counter to hide until I was gone. Lot of people feel that way about me. I could sense all kinds of weapon systems tracking and targeting me as I strolled through the lobby towards the club proper, but none of them locked on. Sometimes my reputation is more use to me than a twenty-third-century force field.

I pushed open the gold-leaf-decorated double doors and stepped through into the huge ballroom that was the true heart of Divas! I stopped just inside the doors, stunned by the make-over they'd given the old place. The club had gone seventies. Las Vegas seventies, with a huge glittering disco ball rotating and sparkling overhead. Bright lights and brighter colours blazed all around, gaudy and tacky by turns, with rows of slot machines down one wall, a mirrored bar, and a row of long-legged, high-kicking chorus girls slamming their way through a traditional routine up on the raised stage. It was as though the seventies had never ended, a Saturday Night Feverdream where the dancing never stopped.

Gorgeous butterflies in knock-off designer frocks fluttered around the crowded tables on the ballroom floor, crying out loud in excited voices, catcalling and laughing and shrieking with joy. It was all almost too glamorous to bear. The chorus line trotted off-stage to thunderous applause, replaced by a Dolly Parton in hooker chic hand-me-downs, who sang a medley with more enthusiasm than style. I wandered through the tables, nodding appreciatively at some of the more famous façades, but no-one ever smiled back. They all knew me and what had happened here before, and they wanted to make it very clear I was not at all welcome. I get a lot of that. Up on the raised stage, the Dolly gave way to a Madonna and a Britney, duetting on "I Got You Babe."

I was still looking for Paul Griffin, or somebody like him. Eleanor had given me a rough description of her son and what he might be wearing, but all I knew of him for sure was a frightened voice on the other side of a locked bedroom door. I was going to have to ask someone; and getting answers here wasn't going to be easy. As in Hecate's Tea Room, the girls at every table grew silent as I approached, glared at me as I passed, and gossiped loudly about me after I'd moved on.

And then I caught a glimpse of Shotgun Suzie, moving among the tables on the other side of the room. My Suzie, in her black motorcycle leathers, with a shotgun holstered on her back and two bandoliers of bullets crossed over her chest. What the hell was she doing here? She was supposed to be hunting down a bounty out on Desolation Row. I pushed my way through the tables and the crowds, but even before I could call out her name she turned to look at me, and I saw at once that it wasn't my Suzie at all. He stood and waited as I went over to him. People scattered in all directions, fearing a confrontation, but the Suzie look-alike stood his ground, calm and cold and unconcerned. Or perhaps he was just staying in character. Up close I could see all the differences. Still looked pretty dangerous, though.

"Why?" I said.

"I'm a tribute Suzie Shooter." The voice was low and husky, and not that far off the real thing. "Shotgun Suzie is my heroine."

I nodded slowly. "I still wouldn't let her catch you looking like that," I said, not unkindly. "Suzie tends to shoot first and not ask questions afterwards."

"I know," said the tribute Suzie. "Isn't she wonderful?"

I let him go. I sort of wondered if perhaps there was a tribute John Taylor out there somewhere, too, but I didn't like to ask. With my luck, it would probably be a drag king. While I was still considering that, I was approached by a towering Angelina Jolie, dressed in shiny black plastic from head to toe, along with an absolute proliferation of straps and buckles and studs. She crashed to a halt before me, stuck her hands on her shiny hips, pursed her amazing lips, and looked down her nose at me. It was a hell of a performance. I felt like applauding.

"I am the Management," the Angelina said flatly. "What the hell are you doing here, Taylor? Wasn't the contract we put out on you enough of a hint? Haven't you caused us enough trouble?"

"You'd be surprised how often I get asked that," I said calmly. "Relax, I'm just here looking for someone." I paused, looking thoughtfully down at the Angelina's impressive exposed cleavage. "You know, those breasts look awfully real."

"They are real," she said frostily. "Don't show your ignorance, Taylor. Divas! doesn't exist only for men who like to dress up pretty. I am a pre-op transsexual. Chick with a dick, if you must. Divas! caters to transvestites, transsexuals, and supersexuals. All those who through an unkind twist of fate were born into the wrong bodies. Divas! is for everyone who ever felt alienated by the sexual identity they were thrust into at birth, and have since found the courage to make new lives for themselves. To make ourselves over into what we should have been all along. Tell me who you're looking for, and I'll point you in the right direction. The sooner I can get you out of here, the happier we'll all be."

"I'm looking for Paul Griffin," I said.

"Who?"

"Don't give me that. Everyone in the Nightside's heard of the Griffin's grandson."

The Angelina shrugged, unmoved. "Can't blame a girl

for trying. Paul comes here for privacy, like so many others. And he has more reasons than most for not wanting to be found or identified. The paparazzi always ask our permission before they take a photograph, ever since we impaled one on a parking meter, but even so . . . I suppose if I don't tell you, you'll just use your gift anyway . . . See that table over there? Ask for Polly."

"You're very kind," I said.

"Don't you believe it, cowboy." The Angelina sniffed briefly. "You know, we tried to claim on our insurance after you happened here, but they wouldn't pay out. Apparently you're classified along with natural disasters and Acts of Gods."

"I am deeply flattered," I said.

I headed for the table the Angelina had pointed out. All the bright young things crowded around it were dressed up as Bond girls—female villains and lust interests from the James Bond movies. There was an Ursula Andress in the iconic white bikini, a gold-plated Margaret Nolan from *Goldfinger*'s opening credits, and of course a haughty-looking Pussy Galore. They all turned and started to smile as they saw someone approaching, then their painted smiles and eyes went cold when they saw who it was. But I'm used to that. I was more interested in the happy, laughing, blonde-haired teenager who sat among them. She wasn't any Bond girl I recognised. In fact, she looked subtly out of place in this glamorous company, just by looking more like a real, everyday girl. She finally turned to look at me, and I stopped in my tracks. I knew that face from the photograph Jeremiah Griffin had given me at the start of this case. It was Melissa Griffin.

Except, of course, it wasn't. Small subtle things told

me immediately that this wasn't a teenage girl at all, and I knew who it was, who it had to be. Paul Griffin, dressed up all pretty, and the very image of his missing cousin. I moved slowly towards him, not wanting to scare him off, and he stood up to face me.

"Hi," I said carefully. Paul, or Polly? Polly would seem more friendly. "I'm John Taylor. I need to talk to you, Polly."

"You don't have to say anything to him, honey," the Pussy Galore said immediately. "Say the word and we'll . . ."

"It's all right," Polly said, in a soft and very feminine voice.

"We can protect you!"

"No you can't," Polly said sadly. "No-one can. But it's all right. I don't think Mr. Taylor came here to hurt me. I'll have a quick word with him, then I'll come right back, I promise. And don't you dare finish that story without me. I want to hear all the horrid, intimate details."

We moved away to a small empty table at the very edge of the dance floor. Polly moved gracefully, in a fashionable off-the-shoulder pale blue gown. The long blonde hair looked very natural. A dozen assorted Spice Girls sat at the next table, and after a few quick glances, made a point of ostentatiously ignoring us. I had a sneaking suspicion that one of them might be the real thing. Polly and I sat down, facing each other.

"We all have secrets," he said softly. "And Griffin family members have more than most. It's as though we're born with lies in our blood. This is my secret, Mr. Taylor. I want to be a woman. Always have. Even as a small child, I knew some terrible mistake had been made. My body was a foreign country to me. I grew up knowing that while I was Paul outside, I was Polly inside. And Polly was the real me. I had to keep it secret from the rest of the family, as well as the outside world.

"Grandfather in particular would never understand. Could never understand . . . He can be very old-fashioned, sometimes. For him, a man must always be strong, aggressive, masculine in all things. He'd see . . . this as a weakness. So would everyone else. If our family's enemies ever found out, they'd seize the opportunity to make me a laughing-stock, and through me, my grandfather. And I won't have that. I won't be used as a weapon against my family."

"There are any number of advanced sciences and sorceries in the Nightside," I said, "that could change a man into a woman, or indeed, anything else."

"I know," said Polly. "I've tried them all. Every difficult, painful, and degrading process I could track down . . . and not one of them would work on me. Even temporarily. The magic that makes me immortal is so powerful it overrides any other change spell or scientific procedure. Even simple surgery. I'm stuck like this, forever and ever and ever. The best I can manage is Paul dressed up as Polly. The only time I feel even half-real."

"I'm sorry," I said. "There's nothing I can do to help you. But I'm hoping there's still time to help your cousin. I need you to tell me all you know about Melissa and her kidnapping."

For the first time Polly looked away from me, his whole body language changing, becoming tense, stubborn, evasive. "She was kidnapped. Never doubt that, Mr. Taylor. But I can't help you."

"Don't you have any idea who might have taken her, or why?"

"I can't talk to you about that. I just can't."

"Can you at least tell me why they went after her and not any other member of the family?"

Polly looked back at me, and his eyes were desperate, pleading. As though begging me to come up with the answers myself so he wouldn't have to tell me. He knew something, but it was up to me to trick or force it out of him.

"Melissa had a secret," Polly said finally. "Just like me. Something about herself, her real self, that she kept from the rest of the family, and the rest of the world. Because they could never understand. And no, I won't tell you what it is."

"Is it anything to do with the story about your grandfather selling his soul to the Devil?" I said.

Polly just smiled sadly. "Melissa is the only one in our family who hasn't sold their soul to the Devil, one way or another. Out of all of us, she alone is good and true and pure. You'd never know she was a Griffin at all."

"And how did she manage that?" I said, honestly curious.

"She has the strength of ten because her heart is pure," said Polly. "She always was the most strong-willed and stubborn member of our family. I think that's why Grandfather always liked her best. Because in her own way, she was the most like him."

I thought about that. Paul clearly idolized his cousin. Perhaps because she was the woman he could never be.

"Why do you lock yourself in your bedroom?" I said finally. "So you can dress up as Polly?"

"No," he said immediately. "I'm only Polly when I'm here, or among friends I know I can trust. I'm Paul at the Hall. I wouldn't dare dress up there. It isn't safe, there. It always feels like I'm being watched. Hobbes seems to know everything. He always did, even when I was a child. You couldn't get away with anything, when he was around . . . Nasty, creepy old man. Always watching and spying and reporting back to Grandfather. We all hate Hobbes, except for Grandfather . . .

"I lock myself in my room because my life is in danger, Mr. Taylor. You have to believe me! I haven't dared sleep in my room for weeks, but I can't stay away too much or it would look suspicious . . . They'd know for sure that I know . . . They have to kill me because I know the truth!"

"Which truth?" I said. "About Melissa? About the kidnapping?"

"No! The truth about Jeremiah Griffin! About what he did to become what he is!" Polly leaned forward across the table and grabbed my hand with masculine strength. "Ask Jeremiah. Ask him why no-one is ever allowed to go down into the cellar under Griffin Hall. Ask him what he keeps down there. Ask him why the only door to that cellar is locked and protected by the most powerful magics in the Hall!"

Polly let go of my hand and sat back in his chair, breathing hard. There was something about him of a small animal in the wild, hunted and harried by wolves.

"Talk to me," I said, as gently as I could. "Tell me what you know, and I'll protect you. I'm John Taylor, remember? The scariest man in the Nightside?"

Polly smiled at me sadly, almost pityingly. "You can't help me. No-one can. I should never have been born. I'm only safe here because I'm Polly, and no-one here would ever tell. Sisterhood is a wonderful thing." She looked at me with sudden intensity. "You mustn't tell either! You can't tell anyone! How did you find me here?"

"Relax. I'm John Taylor, remember? Finding things and people is what I do." It was a lie, but he didn't need to know that. He didn't need to know that his mother knew about Polly. "My only interest in you is what you can tell me about Melissa."

Polly smiled, a little shamefacedly. "Sorry. When your whole life is a secret and a lie, you tend to forget the whole world doesn't revolve around you. Grandfather tried to make me his heir, you know; when I was younger. He'd given up on Uncle William. But I was stubborn, even then. I never wanted anything to do with the family business. That's why Grandfather finally turned to Melissa, because he saw so much more of himself in her. And because she was the only one left. All I ever wanted was to be me, and to sing every night at Divas!"

He stood up suddenly and strode away from the table, heading for the raised stage. He took the microphone from the departing Mary Hopkin, and there he was, standing tall and proud in the spotlight, singing "For Today I Am A Boy," by Anthony and the Johnsons. He put his whole heart into the song, and it seemed like the whole room stopped to listen. He was good, he really was, and I have heard the Nightingale sing and lived to tell of it.

I sat and listened to Polly sing, and it occurred to me that Paul had found his own safe artificial world to hide away in, just like his Uncle William. All the Griffins had their own worlds, their own secrets . . . and it seemed to me that if I could only discover Melissa's, I'd know the who and how and why of everything that had happened.

That was when a small army of heavily armed women

in combat fatigues came abseiling down from the high ceiling, a dozen of them, firing short machine pistol bursts over the heads of the crowd below. The glittering disco ball exploded, and everyone on the ballroom floor jumped to their feet and ran screaming in all directions, like so many panicked birds of paradise. Some ducked down behind hastily overturned tabletops, while others scrambled for the nearest exit. Alone on the stage, Polly stood frozen where he was, staring in horror at the assault force that had invaded his private world. *You can't protect me,* he'd said. *No-one can.* I plunged towards the stage, ignoring the flying bullets, fighting my way through the screaming crowd.

I vaulted up onto the stage, grabbed Polly, and threw him to the floor, covering him with my own body. I glanced out across the ballroom floor. The women in army fatigues were all touching down now, still firing their short, controlled bursts into the air at regular intervals. As far as I could see, they hadn't actually hit anyone yet, but several bright young things had fallen and been trampled underfoot in the panic. The pattern for fire being laid down seemed designed to intimidate, for the moment. Which had to mean they'd come here with some definite purpose in mind.

By now the army women had moved to block all the exits and were herding the club members back into the middle of the ballroom floor. A lot of the trannies had got over their first fear and were glaring fiercely at their captors. Some were clearly bracing themselves to do something. One of the army women stepped forward. Her hair was cropped brutally short, right back to the skull, and her face was plain and harsh and determined. When she spoke, her voice was flat and controlled, without a trace of mercy or compassion in it.

"Stay where you are and we won't have to hurt you. We're here for one man, and when we've got him, we'll leave. We won't leave without him. Anyone gives us any trouble, we'll make an example of him. So, who's in charge of this den of iniquity?"

The Angelina Jolie moved cautiously forward. Half a dozen guns moved to track her. She stopped before the army leader. "I'm the Management. How dare you do this? How dare you burst in here and . . ."

The army leader punched the Angelina in the mouth, and he staggered backwards under the force of the blow. Blood spilled down his chin from his ruined mouth. The army leader snarled at him.

"Shut your painted mouth, creature. Unnatural thing. If it was up to me, I'd have you all killed. Your very existence offends me. But I have my orders. I am here for the man. Give him to me. Show me where he is."

"It's John Taylor, isn't it?" said the Angelina, spitting blood onto the floor at the army woman's feet. "You want him, you can have him."

"John Taylor is here?" The army leader looked quickly around, then took control of herself again. "No. Not him. We want Paul Griffin."

A low, angry murmur spread quickly through the crowd. The army women raised their machine pistols threateningly, but the murmur got louder, if anything. I searched desperately through my coat-pockets. I had a whole bunch of things I could use to turn events in my favour, but the trick was to find something that wouldn't get a whole lot of innocent victims killed. When I looked up again, the Angelina was glaring right into the face of the army leader.

"Paul Griffin is one of us. We don't betray our own."

"Give him to us," the army woman said coldly. "Or we'll start killing you freaks until you do."

"Paul is family," said the Angelina. "And you can't have him. Take these ugly cows down, girls!"

Suddenly, every transvestite, transsexual, and supersexual had some kind of weapon in their hand. Guns and knives, weapons scientific and magical because you can buy anything in the Nightside, all trained on the surprised women in their army fatigues. The girls all opened fire at once, with savage force and merciless eyes, cutting down their enemies with overwhelming firepower. Most of the army women were so startled they hardly had time to get a shot off. They fell screaming, in shock and pain and fury. The girls kept firing, the army women dying hard and bloody, until none of the attackers were moving anymore. The girls slowly lowered their weapons, and a slow silence fell as thick pools of blood spread slowly across the ballroom floor. And then the girls were laughing and cheering, hugging and high-fiving each other.

I helped Polly to his feet, and together we got down from the stage and made our way through the jumping, excited crowd. They had the smell of blood and death in their nostrils, and some of them had found they liked it. Others were crying quietly, from shock or relief, and were being comforted on the edges of the crowd. I came to a halt before the Angelina, and we both looked down at the army leader. She'd died with a snarl on her face, her gun still in her hand. The Angelina had cut the leader's throat with one fast sweep from a vicious-looking knife. Though God alone knew where he'd hidden it in an outfit like that. The Angelina looked at me sourly, hefting the bloody knife thoughtfully.

"I knew you were trouble. After what followed you here last time, we all decided we needed to be able to defend ourselves, in future. The girls might have panicked a bit at first, but all it took was a threat against one of us to bring them all together again. We look after our own. We have to, no-one else will. Do you have any idea who these stupid cows were?"

I knelt beside the body of the army leader and checked her over thoroughly. "These combat fatigues are interesting . . . No identification anywhere, and the cloth feels stiff and new. Maybe bought just for this job. And she didn't sound like a soldier doing a job. She made it sound personal . . . Short-cropped hair, no makeup, no colour or manicure on the fingernails, but she does have a gold wedding ring. Check and see if the others are the same." While I waited for the girls to confirm that all the other bodies were identical, I opened the combat jacket. "Silver crucifix on a chain round the neck? Yes, I thought so."

I stood up and looked at the Angelina. "Nuns. They're all nuns. Hair cropped short to fit under a wimple, no feminine touches, wedding ring because they're all Brides of Christ. And from the insults they used, I think we're safe in supposing they're Christian terrorists, of one stamp or another."

"But what were they doing here, dressed up as soldiers?" said the Angelina. "I mean, I think we can safely assume they weren't drag kings . . . A disguise? And why did they want Polly?"

"They wanted Paul Griffin," I said. "I don't think they knew about Polly."

"Nobody knows Polly is Paul. We guard our secrets here."

"Somebody knew. Somebody talked. Someone always does." I considered the situation thoughtfully. "Maybe if we knew which kind of nun . . . Salvation Army Sisterhood? Little Sisters of the Immaculate Chain-saw? Order of the Hungry Stigmata? There's never any shortage of fanatics on the Street of the Gods. Maybe they hired out . . . I'd better take Paul out of here, get him back to the Hall where he'll be safe."

But when I looked around, he was already gone. I should have known he wouldn't trust the Hall to keep him safe. And it was clear from the angry eyes all around me that no-one here would tell me where he might have gone. Even if they knew, which most of them probably didn't. So I just nodded politely to them and to the Angelina, and walked out of Divas! If I hung around, they might expect me to help clean up the mess.

EIGHT

# Truths and Consequences

Live in the Nightside long enough, and you're bound to start hearing voices in your head. It can be anything from godly visitations to Voices from Beyond to interdimensional admail. You have to learn to block it out or you'll go crazy and start hearing voices. Cheap mental spam-blockers are available from every corner shop, but when you operate in the darker areas of the Twilight Zone, as I mostly do, you can't afford to settle for anything but the very best. My current shields could block out the Sirens' call, a banshee's wail, or the Last Trump, and yet somehow Jeremiah Griffin's peremptory voice ended up inside my head again without even setting off a warning alarm.

*John Taylor, I have need of you.*

"Bloody hell, Jeremiah, turn the volume down! You're frying my neurons! Couldn't you at least give me some

advance notice, ring a little bell in my ear, or something?"

*I could have Hobbes bang a gong if you like . . .*

"What do you want, Griffin? If it's a progress update,
you're out of luck. I've been following promising leads
into dead ends for hours, and I still don't have a single
clue as to what happened to your grand-daughter. For all
I know, she was abducted by pixies."

*Don't bring them into it. If the job was easy, I
wouldn't have needed to hire you. Right now, I need you
to return to Griffin Hall. Now. My wife Mariah is throwing a party, and all kinds of important and influential
people will be attending. You could learn much from talking to them.*

"A party? With Melissa still missing? Why?"

*To show I'm still strong. That I'm not cracking or
falling apart under the pressure. The right people need to
see I'm still in control. And, I need to see who my real
friends and allies are. Any fair-weather friends who
choose not to attend will be noted, for future retribution.
I need you to be here, Taylor. I need everyone to see you
at my side, to know you're working for me. Let my enemies know that the infamous John Taylor is on their trail,
and hopefully shock some fresh information out of them.*

"You expect your enemies to show up at this party?"

*Of course. I've invited them. They won't miss a chance
to see how I'm really coping, and delight in my misery,
and I'll get a chance to see who looks shiftier than usual.
All of my family will be present. I insisted.*

"All right," I said. "I'll be there. When does this party
start?"

*It's started. Get here soon, before the canapés run out.*

Just like that, his presence was gone from my head.

Luckily for me, he had no idea that I'd entirely run out of leads and that he'd just thrown me a major life-line. Or he might have asked for some of his advance money back. All I had to do now was get back to the Hall, and that meant transport. I got out my mobile phone and called Dead Boy.

"All right, Taylor, what do you want this time? My lovely car came back with bits of dead plant stuck in all its crevices and half its defences exhausted. Also, I think it's grinning more than usual. See if I ever lend you anything again."

"Put your glad rags on, Dead Boy, and bring your car over to Divas! We're going to a party at Griffin Hall."

"How in hell did you wrangle an invitation to a top-rank gathering like that? Mariah Griffin's society bashes are even more notorious than you! Good food, excellent booze, and more unattached aristocratic tottie than you can shake a bread-stick at. I'll be with you in five minutes or less."

Unlike most people who say that, Dead Boy actually meant it. The shimmering silver car glided to a halt in front of me in well under five minutes, having no doubt broken all the speed restrictions and several laws of reality in the process. The door opened, I got in, and we were off and moving even before the seat belt could snap into place around me. Dead Boy toasted me with his whiskey bottle and knocked back a handful of purple pills from a little silver case. He swallowed hard, giggled like a schoolgirl, and beat out a rapid tattoo on the steering wheel with both hands. The car ignored him and concentrated on bullying its way through the teeming traffic.

Dead Boy looked seventeen, and had done for some thirty years now, ever since he was mugged and murdered in the Nightside. He was tall and adolescent-thin, wearing a long, purple greatcoat over black leather trousers, and tall calf-skin boots. He wore a black rose in one lapel. His long, bony face was so pale as to be almost colourless, though he'd brightened it up for the party with a touch of mascara and some deep purple lipstick. His coat hung open at the front, revealing a dead white torso covered in scars and bullet-holes, held together with stitches, staples, and the occasional stretch of duct tape. I glanced at his forehead, but the bullet-hole I knew was there couldn't be seen, thanks to some builder's putty and careful makeup.

For all his finery, his features had a weary, debauched, Pre-Raphaelite look, with burning fever-bright eyes and a sullen, pouting mouth. Rossetti would have killed to paint him. Dead Boy wore a large floppy hat pressed down over long, dark, curly hair, and a pearl-headed tie-pin in his bare throat. Show-off. I couldn't help noticing that his car wouldn't let him drive either. He dropped the whiskey bottle carelessly between his feet and fished about in the glove compartment before coming up with a packet of chocolate biscuits. He ripped the packet open and popped one in his mouth. He offered me the packet, but I declined. He shrugged easily and crunched happily on a second biscuit. Dead Boy didn't need to eat or drink anymore, but he enjoyed the sensations. Though being dead, he had to work harder at it than most.

You don't even want to hear the rumours about his sex life.

"So," he said, somewhat indistinctly, spraying crumbs, "are you sure you can get me in? I mean, I'm persona non grata in so many places they have a preprinted form waiting, these days. It's not my fault I haven't got any manners. I'm dead. They should cut me some slack."

"I'm invited," I said, "so you can be my plus one. Please don't piss in the potted plants, try to hump the hostess, or kill anyone unless you absolutely have to. But, you're an immortal, sort of, so the Griffins will just love to meet you. They collect celebrity immortals, eager as they are for hints and tips on how to get the most out of their long lives, and perhaps a few clues on how to get out of the deal that made the Griffin immortal in the first place." I looked thoughtfully at Dead Boy. "There are those who say the Griffin made a bargain with the Devil, though I'm starting to wonder. You made a bargain . . ."

"But not with the Devil," said Dead Boy, staring straight ahead. "I would have got a better deal with the Devil."

The futuristic car slammed through the packed traffic, leaving weeping and mayhem in its wake, and got us back to Griffin Hall in record time. Sometimes I think the car takes short cuts through adjoining realities when it's in a hurry. We tore through the tall gates, barely giving them enough time to get out of our way, and rocketed up the long, winding road to Griffin Hall. This time the surrounding jungle all but fell over itself cringing back on all sides as we passed. I'd never seen trees twitch nervously before. Dead Boy opened a silver snuff-box and snorted something that glowed fluorescent green. I think you have to be dead to be able to tolerate stuff like that.

The silver car swung smoothly around into the great enclosed courtyard outside the Hall and slammed on the brakes. The courtyard was packed full, with every kind of vehicle under the moon. All kinds of cars, from every time and culture, including one that floated smugly several inches above the ground. A Delorean was still spitting discharging tachyons, right next to a pumpkin coach with tomato trimmings, drawn by a really disgruntled-looking unicorn giving everyone the evil eye. Beside it was a large hut standing on tall chicken legs. That Baba Yaga can be a real party animal when she's got a few drinks inside her. Dead Boy's car made some room for itself by forcibly shunting some of the weaker-looking cars out of the way, then waited impatiently for Dead Boy and me to disembark, before slamming its doors shut after us and engaging all its security systems. I could hear all its guns powering up. I was also pretty sure I could hear it giggling.

Griffin Hall was alive with light, every window blazing fiercely, and hundreds of paper lanterns glowed in perfect rows all across the courtyard to guide guests to the front door. Happy sounds blasted out of the door every time it opened, spilling a warm golden glow into the night. I waited patiently while Dead Boy checked he was looking his best and took a quick snort on an inhaler, then we headed for the door. If nothing else, Dead Boy was going to make a great distraction while I circulated quietly, asking pointed questions . . . Over to one side, a small crowd of uniformed chauffeurs were huddled together against the evening chill, sipping hot soup from a thermos. One of them wandered over to pet the unicorn, and the beast nearly took all his fingers off.

It took Dead Boy and I some time to cross the packed courtyard, and I watched with interest as a silver Rolls Royce opened its doors to drop off a Marie Antoinette, complete with a huge hooped skirt and a towering powdered white wig, a very large Henry VIII, and a pinch-faced Pope Joan. They sailed towards the front door, chattering brightly, and the butler Hobbes was there to greet them with a smile and a formal bow. He passed them in, then turned back to see me approaching with Dead Boy, and the smile disappeared. At least he held the door open for us.

"Back again so soon, Mr. Taylor?" Hobbes murmured suavely. "Imagine my delight. Should I arrange for servants to throw rose petals in your path, or is Miss Melissa still at large?"

"Getting closer to the truth all the time," I said easily. "Hobbes, this is a costume party, isn't it, and not some Time-travellers' ball?"

"It is indeed a costume party, sir. The Time-Travellers' Ball is next week. We're sacrificing a Morlock for charity. Since a costume of some kind is required at this gathering, might I inquire what you have come as, sir?"

"A private eye," I said.

"Of course you have, sir. And very convincing, too. Might I also inquire what your disturbing companion is supposed to be?"

"I'm the Ghost of Christmas Past," Dead Boy growled. "Now get your scrawny arse out of my way, flunky, or I'll show you something deeply embarrassing from your childhood. Are those your own ears?"

He slouched past the butler and sauntered off down the hall, and I hurried after him. It's never wise to let Dead Boy out of your sight for long. A servant came hurrying forwards to lead us to the party, being careful to walk a safe distance ahead of us. I'd brought Dead Boy along to be the centre of attention, and already he was doing a fine job. I hoped he wouldn't defenestrate anyone important this time. I could hear the party long before we got there—a raised babble of many voices, all determined to have a good time whatever it cost. The Griffin's parties were reported on all the society pages and most of the gossip rags, and no-one wanted to be described as a wall-flower or a wet blanket.

The party itself was being held in a great ballroom in the West Wing, and Mariah Griffin herself was there at the door to greet us. She was magnificently attired as Queen Elizabeth I, in all the period finery, right down to a red wig over an artificially high forehead. The heavy white makeup and shaved eyebrows, however, only added to the pretty vacuity of her face. She extended an expen-sively beringed hand for us to kiss. I shook it politely, and Dead Boy dropped her a sporty wink.

"Well now, we are honoured, aren't we?" she said, fanning herself with a delicate paper fan I didn't have the heart to tell her was way out of period. "Not only the in-famous John Taylor, but also a fellow immortal, the leg-endary Dead Boy himself! Come to join my little gathering! How sweet."

I looked at Dead Boy. "How come I'm infamous, but you're legendary?"

"Charm," said Dead Boy. "Solid charm."

"The tales you must have to tell," said Mariah, tapping Dead Boy playfully on the arm with her fan. "Of all your many exploits and adventures! We would of course have invited you here long ago, but you do seem to move around a lot . . ."

"Got to keep the creditors on their toes," Dead Boy

said cheerfully. "And a moving target is always the hardest to hit."

"Well, yes," said Mariah, a little vaguely. "Quite! Do come in. I think you're one of the very few long-lived we haven't actually had the pleasure of meeting yet."

"Have you met the Lord of Thorns?" I said, just a little mischievously. "Or Old Father Time? Or Razor Eddie? Fascinating characters, you know. I could arrange introductions if you like."

She glared at me briefly, then turned her full attention back to charming Dead Boy. He gave her back his best darkly smouldering look, and she simpered happily, not realising he was sending her up. I grabbed Dead Boy firmly by the arm and steered him through the door before he could do or say anything that would require Jeremiah to have him reduced to his component parts and disposed of in a trash compactor. Dead Boy has remarkable appetites and absolutely no inhibitions. He says he finds being dead very liberating.

The huge ballroom had been elaborately and expensively transformed into a massive old-fashioned rose garden. Low hedges and blossoming rose-bushes and creeping ivy trailing up the walls. Artificial sunlight poured through the magnificent stained-glass windows, and the air was full of sweet summer scents, along with the happy trills of bird-song and the quiet buzz of insects. There were wooden chairs and benches, love-seats and sun-dials, and even a gently gusting summer breeze, to cool an overheated brow. Neatly cropped grass underfoot, and the illusion of a cloudless summer sky above. No expense spared for the Griffin's guests.

I hoped none of the flowers had been brought in from the outside jungle.

A uniformed and bewigged servant came forward with a silver platter bearing various drinks and beverages. I took a flute of champagne, just to be polite. Dead Boy took two. I glared at him, but it was a waste of time. He knocked back both glasses, belched loudly, and advanced determinedly on another servant carrying a tray full of party snacks. I let him go and looked around the crowded garden. There had to be at least a hundred people come to attend Mariah's little do, all dressed up in the most outlandish and expensive costumes possible. They were here to see and be seen, and most importantly, talked about. All the usual celebrities and famous faces had turned up, along with all the most aristocratic members of High Society, and a small group of men keeping conspicuously to themselves, immediately recognisable as Jeremiah Griffin's most prominent business enemies.

Big Jake Rackham, Uptown Taffy Lewis, both in formal tuxedos, because their dignity wouldn't allow them to be seen in anything less in the presence of their enemy. Max Maxwell, the Voodoo King, so big they named him twice, dressed up as Baron Samedi, and next to him, somewhat to my surprise, General Condor. I'd never met the man, but I knew his reputation. Everyone did. The General had been a starship commander in some future time, before he fell into the Nightside through a passing Timeslip. A very strong-minded, moral, and upright man, he disapproved of pretty much everything and everyone in the Nightside, and had made it his mission to change the Nightside for the better. He disapproved of the Griffin and his business practices most of all. But enough to ally himself with these men? A straight-backed, strait-laced military man, working with the Griffin's enemies? Presumably because the enemy of my enemy is my ally, if not my friend. I just hoped he knew any one of them would stab him in the back first chance they got. The General really should have known better. He might have been a hero in the future he came from, but the Nightside does so love to break a hero . . .

The businessmen kept a careful and discreet distance from the ongoing festivities, and from each other. They were only here to check out the Griffin, and for all General Condor's attempts to find some common ground, they had nothing to say to each other. All they had in common was their hatred and fear of a shared enemy. I looked round sharply as the party's noise level dropped abruptly, in time to see the crowd part respectfully to allow Jeremiah Griffin to approach me. He ignored everyone else, his attention focused solely on me, his expression ostentatiously calm and unconcerned. Dead Boy wandered back to join me, stuffing his face with a handful of assorted snacks and spilling crumbs down the front of his coat. He moved into position beside me, facing Jeremiah, so everyone would know where he stood. The Griffin crashed to a halt in front of us.

"John Taylor!" he said, in a loud and carrying voice, so everyone present would be in no doubt of who I was. "So good of you to come at such short notice. I'm sure we have lots to talk about." It wasn't exactly subtle, but it made the required impression. People were already muttering and whispering together about what I was doing here and what I might have to tell. The Griffin looked dubiously at Dead Boy. "And you've brought a friend, John. How nice."

"I'm Dead Boy, and you're very pleased to meet me," Dead Boy said indistinctly, through a mouthful of food. "Yes, I am immortal, sort of, but no, there's nothing I can do to help you with any deal you may or may not have made. Good food. You got any more?"

The Griffin summoned a servant with a fresh tray of party nibbles, watched with a somewhat pained expression as Dead Boy grabbed the lot, then turned his attention back to me. "I see you've spotted my business rivals, cowering together," he said, in a somewhat lower voice. "Afraid to circulate, for fear they'll hear bad things about themselves. But I knew they couldn't stay away. They had to see for themselves how I was coping. Well, let them look. Let them see how calm and controlled I am. Let them see who I have hired to deal with this threat to me and my family."

"So business is still good?" I said. "The city still has confidence in you?"

"Hell, no. All this uncertainty is ruining me financially. But I've made arrangements, and you can be sure that if I go down, I'll take them all with me." The Griffin fixed me with a fierce stare. "You let me worry about the finances, Taylor. You concentrate on finding Melissa. Time is running out. Once she is returned to me, everything will be well again."

He then made a deliberate effort to change the subject by pointing out several other immortals who had come to grace his party with their presence. The vampire Count Stobolzny had come as a white-faced clown, in a white clown suit set off with a row of blood-red bobbles down the front. To match his eyes, presumably. But for all the Count's airs and graces, there was nothing human about him. You only had to look at him to see him for what he really was—a slowly rotting corpse that had dug itself up out of its own grave to feast on the living. Behind the ragged lips were animals' teeth, made for rending and tearing. I've never understood why some people see leeches as romantic.

Then there were two elves in full Elizabethan dress, probably because that was the height of fashion the last time they'd shared the world with us. The elves walked sideways from the sun centuries ago, disappearing into their own private dimension once it became clear they were losing their long war with Humanity. They only come back now to mess with us and screw us over. It's all they have left. Both elves were supernaturally tall and slender and elegant, holding themselves ostentatiously apart from the vulgar displays of human enjoyment, while never missing a chance to look down their arrogant noses at anyone who got too close. So why invite them? Because they were immortal, and knew many things, and magic moved in them like breath and blood. It is possible to make a deal with an elf, if you have something they want badly enough. But you'd be well advised to count your testicles afterwards. And those of anyone close to you. The Griffin named these elves as Cobweb and Moth, which rang a faint bell in my memory. I knew that would bug me all evening till I got it.

Not that far away, two godlings were chatting easily together. The huge Hell's Angel in big black motorcycle leathers was apparently Jimmy Thunder, God for Hire, descended from the Norse God Thor and current holder of the mystic hammer Mjolnir. He was a happy, burly sort, with a long mane of flame red hair and a great bushy beard. He looked like he could bench-press a steam engine if he felt like it, and also like he wouldn't stop boasting about it for weeks afterwards. His companion was Mistress Mayhem, a tall blue-skinned beauty with midnight-dark hair down to her slender waist. She was descended (at many removes, one hopes) from the Indian death goddess Kali. She'd come dressed as Elvira, Mistress of the Dark, her form-fitting black silk dress cut away to show as much blue skin as possible. Jeremiah insisted on walking me over and introducing me, and they both smiled politely.

"Just passing through," Jimmy Thunder boomed. "I was over in Shadows Fall, consulting with the Norns, and I had to stop over here to refuel my bike. You wouldn't believe how much they wanted to charge me for a few gallons of virgin's blood! I mean, I know there's a shortage these days, but . . . Anyway, Mayhem told me about this party, and I never miss a chance for a good knees up at someone else's expense." He prodded me cheerfully in the chest with one oversized finger. "So, you're Lilith's son. Not sure if that makes you a godling or not. Either way, don't let anyone start a religion over you. They get so damned needy, and they never stop bothering you. These days I limit my worshippers to setting up tribute sites on the Net."

"Which you are always visiting," said Mistress Mayhem.

I studied her thoughtfully. "Are you really descended from a death goddess?"

"Oh yes. Would you like to see me wither a flower?"

"Maybe later," I said politely.

Jimmy Thunder put a huge arm companionably across Mistress Mayhem's shoulders. "Hey sweetie, want to hold my hammer?"

Perhaps fortunately, at that point someone grabbed me firmly by the arm and steered me over to the nearest wall for a private chat. I don't normally let people do that, but for Larry Oblivion I made an exception. We'd fought side by side in the Lilith War, but I wouldn't call us friends. Especially after what happened to his brother Tommy. Larry Oblivion, the deceased detective, the post-mortem private eye. Murdered by his own partner, he survives now as some kind of zombie. No-one knows the details, because he doesn't like to talk about it. You wouldn't know he was dead till you got up close and smelled the formaldehyde. He was dressed in the very best Armani, tall and well built, with straw-coloured hair over a pale, stubborn face. But you only had to look into his eyes to know what he was. Meeting Larry Oblivion's gaze was like leaning over an open grave. I stared right back at him, giving him gaze for gaze. You can't show weakness in the Nightside, or they'll walk right over you.

"Looking good, Larry," I said. "And what have you come as? A fashion model?"

"I came as me," he said, in his dry flat voice. He only breathed when he needed air to speak, which became disturbing after a while. "I'm only here because you're here. We need to talk, Taylor."

"We've already talked," I said, just a little tiredly. "I told you what happened to your brother. He went down fighting during the War."

"Then why has his body never been found?" said Larry, pushing his face right into mine. "My brother trusted you. I trusted you to look after him. But here you are, alive and well, and Tommy is missing, presumed dead."

"He died a hero, saving the Nightside," I said evenly. "Isn't that enough?"

"No," said Larry. "Not if you let him die to save yourself."

"Back off, Larry."

"And if I don't?"

"I'll rip your soul right out of your dead body."

He hesitated. He wasn't sure I could do that, but he wasn't sure I couldn't, either. There are a lot of stories about me in the Nightside, and I never confirm or deny any of them. They all help build a reputation. And I have done some really bad things in my time.

Dead Boy came over to join us. He'd found a large piece of gateau and was licking the chocolate off his fingers. He nodded familiarly to Larry, who glared back at him with disdain. They might both be dead, but they moved in very different circles.

"Not drinking, Larry?" said Dead Boy. "You should try the Port. And the Brandy. Get them to spike it with a little strychnine. Gives the booze some bite. And there's some quail's eggs over there that are quite passable . . ."

"I don't need to eat or drink," said Larry. "I'm dead."

"Well, I don't need to either," Dead Boy said reasonably. "But I do anyway. It's all part of remembering what it felt like, to be alive. Just because you're dead it doesn't mean you can't indulge yourself, or get bombed out of your head. We just have to try that little bit harder, that's all. I've got some pills that can really perk you up, if you'd care to try some. This little old Obeah woman knocks them out for me . . ."

"You're a degenerate," Larry said flatly. "You and I have nothing in common."

"But you are both zombies, aren't you?" I said, honestly curious.

"I'm a lot more than that," Dead Boy said immediately. "I am a returned spirit, possessing my murdered body. I'm a revenant."

"You chose to be what you are," Larry said coldly.

"This was done to me against my will. But at least I've gone on to make something of myself. I now run the biggest private detective agency in the Nightside. I am a respected businessman."

"You're a corpse with delusions of grandeur," said Dead Boy. "And a crashing bore. John was the first private investigator in the Nightside. You and the rest are all pale imitations."

"Better than being the bouncer at a ghost-dancing bar!" snapped Larry. "Or hiring out as muscle to keep the dead in their graves at the Necropolis. And at least I know how to dress properly. I wouldn't be seen dead wearing an outfit like that!"

He turned his back on us and stalked away, and people hurried to get out of his path. Dead Boy looked at me.

"That last bit was a joke, wasn't it?"

"Hard to say," I said honestly. "With anyone else, yes, but Larry was never known for his sense of humour even when he was alive."

"What's wrong with the way I dress?" said Dead Boy, looking down at himself, honestly baffled.

"Not a thing," I said quickly. "It's just that we haven't all got your colourful personality."

The Lady Orlando swayed over to join us, every movement of her luscious body a joy to behold. One of Jeremiah's celebrity immortals, and the darling of the gossip rags, the Lady Orlando claimed to have been around since Roman times, moving on from one identity to another, and she had an endless series of stories about all the famous people she'd met, and bedded, if you believed her. In the Nightside she drifted from party to party, living off whoever would have her, telling her stories to anyone who'd stand still long enough. She'd come to the party dressed as the Sally Bowles character from *Cabaret*, all fishnet stockings, bowler hat, and too much eye makeup. Bit of a sad case, all told, but we can't all be legends. She came to a halt before Dead Boy and me, and stretched languorously to give us both a good look at what was on offer.

"Have you seen poor old Georgie, darlings, dressed up as Henry VIII?" she purred, peering owlishly at us over her glass of bubbly. "Doesn't look a bit like the real thing. I met King Henry in his glory days at Hampton Court, and I am here to tell you, he wasn't nearly as *big* as he liked to make out. You boys and your toys . . . Have you seen our resident alien, positively lording it over his loopy admirers? Klatu, the Alien from Dimension X . . . Thinks he's so big time, just because he's downloading his consciousness from another reality . . . I could tell you a few things about that pokey little body he's chosen to inhabit . . ."

I tuned her out so I could concentrate on Klatu, who was holding forth before a whole throng of respectful listeners. He was always offering to explain the mysteries of the universe, or the secrets of existence, until you threatened to pin him down or back him into a corner, then he suddenly tended to get all vague and remember a previous appointment. Klatu was only another con man at heart, though his background made him more glamorous than most. There's never been any shortage of aliens in the Nightside, whether the interstellar equivalent of the remittance men, paid not to go home again, or those just passing through on their way to somewhere more interesting. Klatu claimed to be an extension of a larger personality in the Fifth Dimension, and the body he inhabited just a glorified glove puppet manipulated from afar. And you could believe that or not, as you chose. Certainly for an extradimensional alien, he did seem to enjoy his creature comforts, as long as someone else paid for them . . .

I had to remind myself I was here for a purpose. I needed new leads on where to look for Melissa and some fresh ideas on what might have happened to her. So I nodded a brisk farewell to Dead Boy and the Lady Orlando, and wandered off through the party, smiling and nodding and being agreeable to anyone who looked like they might know something. I learned a lot of new gossip, picked up some useful business tips, and turned down a few offers of a more personal nature; but while everyone was only too willing to talk about the missing Melissa, and theorize wildly about the circumstances of her dramatic disappearance . . . no-one really knew anything. So I went looking for other members of the Griffin family to see if I could charm or intimidate any more out of them.

I found William dressed as Captain Hook, complete with a three-cornered hat and a metal hook he was using to open a stubborn wine bottle. He'd also brought along Bruin Bear and the Sea Goat as his guests. Apparently everyone else thought they were simply wearing costumes. We had a pleasant little chat, during which the Sea Goat poured half a dozen different drinks into a flower vase he'd emptied for the purpose, and drank the lot in a series of greedy gulps. Surrounding guests didn't know whether to be impressed or appalled, and settled for muttering *I say!* to each other from a safe distance. The Sea Goat belched loudly, ripped half a dozen roses from a nearby bush, and stuffed them into his mouth, chewing thoughtfully, petals and thorns and all.

"Not bad," he said. "Could use a little something. A few caterpillars, perhaps."

"What?" said William.

"Full of protein," said the Goat.

"Now you're just showing off," said Bruin Bear.

"This is the best kind of food and drink," insisted the Sea Goat. "It's free. I'm filling all my pockets before I leave."

"I really must introduce you to Dead Boy," I said. "You have so much in common. How are you enjoying the party, Bruin?"

"I only came along to keep William company," said the Bear. "I am, after all, every boy's friend and companion. And for all his many years William is still a boy in many ways. Besides, I do like to get away from Shadows Fall now and again. Our home-town has legends and wonders like a dog has fleas, and they can really get on your nerves, after a while. If everyone's special, then no-one is, really. The Nightside makes a pleasant change, for short periods. Because for all its sleazy nature, there are still many people here in need of a Bear's friendship and comfort . . ."

The Sea Goat made a loud rude noise, and we all looked round to see him glaring at the elves Cobweb and Moth as they passed by.

They must have heard the Goat but chose not to acknowledge his presence. The Sea Goat ground his large blocky teeth together noisily.

"Bloody elves," he growled. "So up themselves they're practically staring out their own nostrils. Giving me the cold shoulder because I used to be fictional. I was a much-loved children's character! Until the Bear and I went out of fashion, and our books disappeared from the shelves. No-one wants good old traditional, glad-hearted adventure anymore. I was so much happier and contented when I wasn't real."

"You never were happy and contented," Bruin Bear said cheerfully. "That was part of your charm."

"You were charming," the Goat said testily. "I was a character."

"And beloved by my generation," said William, putting an arm across both their shoulders. "I had all your books when I was a boy. You helped make my childhood bearable, because your Golden Lands were one of the few places I could escape to that my father couldn't follow."

"Elves," growled the Sea Goat. "Wankers!"

Cobweb and Moth turned suddenly and headed straight for us. Up close, they were suddenly and strikingly alien, not human in the least, their glamour falling away to reveal dangerous, predatory creatures. Elves have no souls, so they feel no mercy and no compassion. They can do any terrible thing that crosses their mind, and mostly they do, for any reason or none. William actually fell back a pace under the pressure of their inhuman gaze. Bruin Bear and the Sea Goat moved quickly forward to stand between William and the advancing elves. So of course I had to stand my ground, too. Even though the best way to win a fight with an elf is to run like fun the moment it notices you.

The two elves came to a halt before us, casually elegant and deadly. Their faces were identical—same cat's eyes, same pointed ears, same cold, cold smile. Cobweb wore grey, Moth wore blue. Up close, they smelled of musk and sulphur.

"Watch your manners, little fiction," said Moth. "Or we'll teach you some."

The Sea Goat reached out with an overlong arm, grabbed the front of the elf's tunic, picked him up, and threw him the length of the ballroom. The elf went flying over everyone's heads, tumbling head over heels, making plaintive noises of distress. Cobweb watched his fellow elf disappear into the distance, then looked back at the Sea Goat, who smiled nastily at the elf, showing his large blocky teeth.

"Hey, elf," said the Goat. "Fetch."

There was the sound of something heavy hitting the far wall, then the floor, some considerable distance away, followed by pained moans. Cobweb turned his back on us and stalked away into the crowd, who were all chattering loudly. They hadn't had this much fun at a party in years. It helped that absolutely no-one liked elves. Bruin Bear shook his head sadly.

"Can't take you anywhere . . ."

William couldn't speak for laughing. I hadn't seen him laugh before. It looked good on him.

"I should never have let you mix your drinks," Bruin Bear scolded the Sea Goat. "You get nasty when you've been drinking."

"Elves," growled the Goat. "And those two think they're so big time, just because they got name-checked in a Shakespeare play. Have you ever seen *A Midsummer Night's Dream*? Romantic twaddle! Don't think the man ever met an elf in his life. One play . . . the Bear and me starred in thirty-six books! Even if no-one reads them anymore . . ." He sniffed loudly, a single large tear running down the side of his long, grey muzzle. "We used to be big, you know. Big! It's the books that got small . . ."

I excused myself and went to see if the elf was feeling okay after his forced landing. Not that I gave a damn, of course, but I could use a contact at the Faerie Court. And while an elf would know better than to respond to an offer of friendship, he might well respond to a decent-sized bribe. By the time I got to the other end of the ball-room, Moth was back on his feet and looking none the worse for his sudden enforced exit. It's not easy to kill an elf, though it's often worth the effort. Cobweb and Moth were currently doing their best to stare down Larry Oblivion, who was quietly but firmly refusing to be out-stared.

"Queen Mab wants her wand back," Cobweb said bluntly.

"She sent us to tell you this," said Moth. "Don't make us tell you twice."

"Tough," said Larry, entirely unmoved. "She wants it back, tell her to come herself."

"We could take it from you," said Cobweb.

"We'd like that," said Moth.

Larry laughed in their faces. "What are you going to do, kill me? Bit late for that. Queen Mab gave me her wand, for services rendered. You tell her . . . if she ever tries to pressure me again, I'll tell everyone exactly what I did for her and why. Now push off, or I'll set the Sea Goat on you."

"Queen Mab will not forget this slight," said Cobweb.

Larry Oblivion grinned. "Like I give a Puck."

The elves stalked away, not looking back. I studied Larry Oblivion thoughtfully, from a distance. I was seri-ously interested. Larry Oblivion had an elven weapon? That was worth knowing . . . The elves only unlocked their Armoury when they were preparing to go to war.

And since I hadn't seen Four Horsemen trotting through the Nightside recently, it seemed a few of the ancient elvish weapons were running around loose . . . I was still considering the implications of that when the Lady Orlando turned up again and backed me into a corner before I could escape. She was in full flirt mode, and I had to wonder why she'd targeted me, when there were so many richer men in the room. Maybe she'd heard how much Griffin was paying me for this case . . .

"John, darling," she said, smiling dazzlingly, her eyes wide and hungry. "You must be the only real Nightside celebrity I haven't had. I really must add you to my collection."

"Back off," I said, not unkindly. "I'm spoken for."

"I just want your body," said the Lady Orlando, wrinkling her perfect nose. "Not your love. I'm sure Suzie would understand."

"I'm pretty sure she wouldn't," I said. "Now be a good girl and go point those bosoms at someone else."

Luckily, at that point Eleanor Griffin turned up to rescue me. She breezed right past the Lady Orlando, slipped her arm through mine, and led me away in one smooth movement, before the Lady could object, chattering loudly non-stop so the Lady couldn't even get an innuendo in. I didn't dare look back. Hell hath no fury like a woman outscored.

Eleanor was currently dressed as Madonna, from her John-Paul Gautier period, complete with black corset and brass breast cones. I looked them over and winced just a little.

"Aren't those cold?"

Eleanor laughed briefly. "I'm wearing them for Marcel, to cheer him up. He's fully recovered now, thanks to some heavy duty fast-acting healing spells, but he's still a bit down in the dumps, because I've had him electronically tagged. If he tries to leave the Hall again to sneak off gambling, the tag will bite his leg off. He's around here somewhere, sulking, dressed as Sky Masterson from *Guys and Dolls*. A bit predictable, I suppose, but he's a big Marlon Brando fan. But never mind him. I need to talk to you, John. Am I correct in assuming that Daddy summoned you here to fill him in personally on your search for Melissa? Thought so. He's always found it hard to delegate and depend on other people. Are you any nearer tracking her down?"

"No," I said, glad to be talking to someone I could be straight with. "I've talked to every member of your family, and if anyone knows anything, they're doing a really good job of keeping it to themselves."

"Couldn't you try asking, well, underground people you know? I mean, criminals and informers, that sort of person?"

"The kind I know wouldn't dare touch a Griffin," I said. "No, the only people big and bad enough to try something like that are mostly right here in this room."

"Have you talked with Paul?" said Eleanor, not looking at me.

"I spoke with Polly," I said carefully. "I heard her sing. She's got a really good voice."

"I've never heard Polly sing," said Eleanor. "I can't go to the club. Paul mustn't know . . . that I know about Polly."

She led me back to William, who was standing alone now. The Sea Goat and Bruin Bear were presumably off getting into trouble somewhere else. William scowled ungraciously at Eleanor as we came to a halt before him. All the old sullenness was back in his face.

"Whatever she's been telling you about me, don't believe a word of it," he snapped. "Hell, don't believe anything she tells you. Dear Eleanor always has her own agenda."

Eleanor smiled sweetly at him. "Name one person in our family who doesn't, brother dear. Even sweet saintly Melissa had her own life, kept strictly separate from the rest of us."

"A secret life?" I said. "You mean like Paul?"

"No-one knows," said Eleanor. "She always was a very private little girl."

"Best way, in this family," growled William. "People find out your secrets in this place, they use them against you."

They fell to squabbling then, rehearsing old hurts and grievances and wounds that had never been allowed to heal, and I just tuned them out. So Melissa had a secret life, so private that none of them had even thought to mention it before. Perhaps because no-one in this family liked to admit to not knowing something.

I looked round the ballroom. The party seemed to be going well enough, but I was interested in the other Griffins. Jeremiah was right at the centre of things, of course, holding court before a large group who gave every indication of hanging on his every word. Mariah paraded back and forth through her artificial rose garden, accepting and bestowing compliments, in her element at last. I couldn't see Marcel or Gloria anywhere, but it was a really big garden. So if I wanted to learn any more about Melissa's secret life, I was going to have to dig it out of Eleanor and William.

"Have you told him yet?" said William, in a very pointed way, and I started paying attention again.

"I was working up to it," said Eleanor. "It's not the sort of thing you can just spring on someone, is it?" She turned to me, forcing the anger out of her face through sheer force of will, and in a moment she was all smiles and charm again. "John, we need you to do something for us."

"Set up the security field first," William interrupted.

"No-one can hear us in all this babble," said Eleanor. "And a privacy shield might be noticed."

"This isn't the sort of thing we can afford to have overheard," said William. "Better for someone to be suspicious than for anyone to *know*."

"All right, all right!"

She glanced unobtrusively around her and produced a small charm of carved bone from a concealed pocket. She clutched it in her fist, muttered an activating spell, and the background noise faded quickly away to nothing. I could see lips moving all around me, but not a whisper got through the shield; or, presumably, out. Our privacy was ensured. Until somebody noticed. I looked curiously at William and Eleanor, and they looked back at me with a kind of stubborn desperation in their faces. And I suddenly knew that whatever they were going to ask me, it had nothing at all to do with Melissa.

"What would it take," Eleanor said carefully, "for you to kill our father for us?"

I looked at them both in silence for a long moment. Whatever I'd expected them to say, that wasn't it.

"You're the only man who might stand a chance," said William. "You can get close to him, where no-one else could."

195

"We've heard about some of the things you did," said Eleanor. "During the Lilith War."

"Everyone says you did things no-one else could," said William. "In the War."

"You want me to murder Jeremiah?" I said. "Why exactly would you want me to do that?"

"To be free," said William, and his gaze was so intense it seemed to bore right through me. "You have no idea what it's like, having lived in his shadow for so long. My whole life controlled, and ruined, by him. You've seen the lengths I have to go to simply to feel free for a time."

"With him gone, we could live our own lives, at last," said Eleanor. "It's not like he ever loved either of us."

"This isn't about money, or business, or power," said William. "I'd give them all up to be free of him."

"Do it for us, John," said Eleanor. "Do it for me."

"I'm a private eye," I said. "Not an assassin."

"You don't understand," William said urgently. "We've talked this over. We believe our father is behind Melissa's disappearance. We think he arranged to have her taken against her will from the Hall. Nothing happens here without his knowing, without his permission. Only he could have bypassed the Hall's extensive security and made sure all the servants were in areas of the Hall where they wouldn't see anything. He wants my daughter dead, with someone else set up to take the blame. I believe my daughter is dead, John, and I want that murder avenged."

"If he's had Melissa killed," said Eleanor, "my Paul could be next. I can't let that happen. He's all I've got that's really mine. You have to help us, John. Our father is capable of anything to get what he wants."

"Then why did he hire me?" I said.

"What better way publicly to display his grief and

anger?" said William. "Our father's always understood the need for good publicity."

"And if he does need someone to fix the blame on," said Eleanor, "what better choice than the infamous John Taylor?"

"The best way I can help you," I said carefully, "is by finding Melissa and bringing her back, safe and well. I'll go this far: whoever is behind her disappearance will get what's coming to them. Whoever it turns out to be."

I walked away from them, bursting through the privacy field and back into the raucous clamour of the party. I had some thinking to do. I couldn't say it surprised me that Jeremiah's children would turn out to be as ruthless as him, but I was still disappointed in them. I'd started to like William and Eleanor. Still, could Jeremiah have brought me in to be his very visible fall guy? Someone to blame when Melissa never turned up? It wouldn't be the first time a client had been less than honest with me. And as though just the thought was enough to conjure him up, Jeremiah appeared abruptly out of the crowd before me.

"Not drinking?" he said cheerfully. "This is a party!"

"Someone here needs to keep a clear head," I said.

Jeremiah nodded vaguely. "You haven't seen Paul around anywhere, have you? I had one of the servants shout through his door that I expected him to make an appearance along with the rest of the family, but that's Paul for you. Probably still sulking in his room, with his music turned up loud. Unless he's sneaked out again." Jeremiah laughed briefly. It had a sour sound. "He thinks I don't know . . . Nothing goes on in this house that I don't know about. I had some of my people follow him at first, from a discreet distance . . . turns out the boy's a shirtlifter. Spends all his time at gay clubs . . . After everything I did to try and make a man out of him. Damned shame, but what can you do?"

I nodded. It was clear Jeremiah didn't know about Polly, and I wasn't about to tell him.

"Why didn't you tell me this was a costume party?" I said. "I feel rather out of place. It might even have been embarrassing if I was the kind who got embarrassed."

"But you're not," said Jeremiah. "I needed you to come as you are so everyone would be sure to recognise you. I want them all to know you're working for me. First, it makes it clear that I'm doing something about Melissa's kidnapping. Second, the fact that I'm able to hire you, the infamous John Taylor, helps make me look strong and in command. Perception is everything, in business. And third, maybe your presence will be enough to provoke Melissa's captors into making a move, at last. Have you found out anything yet?"

"Only that someone is really determined to keep me from finding out what's going on," I said. "And you already knew that."

"Ah. Yes. That business in the conference room." Jeremiah scowled at me. "You must hurry, Taylor. Time is running out."

"For her?" I said. "Or for you?"

"Both."

Suddenly, the doors to the ballroom slammed open with a deafening crash. Everyone turned to look, and a sudden hush fell across the party because there in the doorway, standing perfectly poised and at ease, was Walker. The man who currently ran the Nightside, inasmuch as anyone did, or could, because everyone else was too scared to challenge him. In the old days he was the voice of the Authorities, those grey shadowy men behind the scenes, but now they were dead and gone, and Walker was . . . The Man.

As always, he looked every inch the smart city gent, in his expensively cut suit, old school tie, and bowler hat. Calm, relaxed, and always very, very dangerous. He had to be in his sixties now, his trim figure yielding just a little to gravity and good living, but he still radiated confidence and quiet power. His face seemed younger, but his eyes were old. Walker represented authority now, if not actually law and order; and he did so love to make an entrance.

He looked round the ballroom, smiling politely, taking his time. Letting everyone get a good look at him. He had come alone into the lair of his enemies, and I had to wonder whom he could call on for support, now. There was a time when he could have summoned armies to back him up, from the military and the church, courtesy of the Authorities. But would those armies still come now if he called? They might—this was Walker, after all. A man who knew many things, not all of them good or lawful or healthy.

The crowd fell back to allow Jeremiah to walk unhurriedly through it to confront Walker. Walker smiled easily and let the most powerful businessman in the Nightside come to him. I moved quickly after Jeremiah. I wasn't going to miss this. Jeremiah came to a stop before Walker, looked him up and down, and snorted dismissively. Walker nodded politely.

"You've got a nerve coming here, Walker," said Jeremiah. "Into my house, my home, uninvited!"

"I go where I'm needed, Jeremiah," said Walker, his calm voice carrying clearly on the quiet. "You know that. Nice place you've got here. Good security systems, too.

State-of-the-art. But you should have known even they wouldn't be enough to keep me out when I want in. Still, not to worry; I haven't come to haul you away in chains. Not this time. I've come to take someone else away, to answer for their crimes."

"Everyone present in this room is a guest of mine," Jeremiah said immediately. "And therefore under my personal protection. You can't lay a finger on any of them."

"Oh, I think you'll want me to take this person away," said Walker, still smiling, entirely unmoved by the Griffin's open defiance. "They really have been very naughty."

He looked round the ballroom, and any number of people quailed under his glance; because after all . . . this was Walker, and they all had something to feel guilty about.

Jeremiah snapped a Word of Power, and his security came bursting right out of the ballroom walls—huge grey golems twice the size of a man, with fists like mauls. There was a great commotion among the guests as they scrambled to get out of the golems' way. The ugly grey things crashed through the artificial rose garden, destroying the hedges and the bushes, intent on their prey. One guest didn't get out of their way fast enough, and the golems trampled him underfoot, ignoring his screams. The floor shook under their heavy tread as they closed in on Walker.

He stood his ground, entirely casual and at his ease. He waited till they were almost upon him, and then he used his Voice on them. The Voice that cannot be disobeyed.

"*Go away,*" Walker said to the golems. "*Go back where you came from, and don't bother me again.*"

The golems stopped as one in a great crash of heavy feet, then they all turned and walked back through the party and disappeared into the ballroom walls again. Jeremiah called desperately after them, using increasingly powerful Words, but they ignored him. They still had Walker's Voice echoing in their heads, and there wasn't room for anything else. They disappeared one by one until they were all gone, and none of the guests said anything. They watched until all the golems had disappeared, then they looked at Jeremiah, then they looked at Walker. And everyone in the ballroom knew where the real power lay. Jeremiah glared at Walker, his hands clenched into fists, actually trembling with rage.

"You'll never get out of here alive, Walker. Everything in this house is a weapon I can use against you."

"Oh hush, Jeremiah, there's a good fellow; petulance is so unbecoming in a man of your age and standing. I told you I'm not here for you. Believe me, you want this person out of here as much as I do. Because one of your guests isn't who you think they are."

That got everyone's attention. They all started looking around them, some actually backing away from each other. Where once they might have united against Walker, now they were all looking out for themselves. Walker strode past Jeremiah, nodding to me in an affable, urbane, and totally dismissive way, and walked into the crowd as though he was a favourite uncle come to bestow gifts. The thoroughly unnerved guests scattered before him, but he only had eyes for one very well known personage. He came to a halt before her and shook his head, seemingly more in sorrow than in anger.

"But . . . that's the Lady Orlando!" protested Jeremiah.

"Not as such," said Walker, studying the Lady Orlando thoughtfully while she stared coldly back at him. "Actually, this is the Charnel Chimera—shapeshifter, soul eater, identity thief. Not the Lady Orlando at all. So, *show yourself. Show us your true face.*"

His Voice beat upon the air, as unrelenting as fate, as unavoidable as death. The Lady Orlando opened her mouth, then kept on opening it, stretching her features unnaturally, and the sound that came out of the ugly gaping maw was in nó way human. Impelled by Walker's Voice, the creature before us dropped the shape it had adapted and showed us what it really was. The Lady Orlando melted away, revealing a horrid patchwork thing, like pieces of raw meat slapped together in a roughly human shape. It was all red-and-purple flesh, wet and glistening, marked with dark traceries of pulsing veins. The lumpy head was featureless, save for a circular mouth filled with needle teeth. The thing stank of filth and decay, sulphur and ammonia like all the bodies in a charnel house far gone in rot and suppuration. All around the thing people were stumbling backwards, coughing and choking at the smell, horrified at the awful creature that had walked unsuspected among them. Nightmares like this belonged in the streets of the Nightside, not in the safer and protected houses of the rich. The Charnel Chimera stood its ground, brought to bay, and turned its terribly unfinished face on Walker, who stared calmly back at it. When the creature finally spoke, its voice sounded more like an insect's buzz than anything else.

"Even your Voice can't hold me for long, Walker. It was never designed to work on such as me. There are far too many people in me for you to control us all."

"What the hell is that thing?" I said. I'd come forward

to join Walker, thinking he might need some kind of backup.

"The Charnel Chimera collects DNA through casual contact," said Walker, not taking his eyes off the creature. "Handshakes, and the like. And then it stores the epithelial cells in its internal database. It's always adding new people to its collection. It only needs a few cells to be able to duplicate anyone, right down to the last hair on their head. But to hold on to a single shape for long, it needs to kidnap the victim, imprison them somewhere safe, and . . . feed off them. Some kind of psychic transference . . . Until the original is all used up and rots away to nothing. And then the Charnel Chimera has to move on to a new form.

"One of my agents tracked down the creature's lair and found the real Lady Orlando chained to a wall in a rather nasty little oubliette under an abandoned warehouse out on Desolation Row. Along with the rotting remains of over a dozen previous victims." Walker shook his head sadly at the creature before him. "You really shouldn't have taken such a well-known personage. You're not that good an actor. But it got you in here, didn't it? Among all the rich, important people. You must have been spoilt for choice for your next identity. How many hands did you shake? How many cheeks did you kiss?"

Shocked and disgusted noises came from all across the ballroom, as people remembered greeting or being greeted by the Lady Orlando, who was always so very popular, and so very touchy-feely . . . A few actually vomited. I remembered being backed into a corner, and the Lady saying to me, *I want your body . . . I really must add you to my collection.* And how badly I had misunderstood.

Jimmy Thunder, his face bright crimson with outrage, came roaring up behind the Charnel Chimera and hit it over the head with his hammer. The blunt meaty head collapsed under the impact and crashed down between its shoulder-blades, scattering bits of flesh like shrapnel, only to rise back up again with a soft wet sucking sound. The creature whirled round unnaturally fast and hit Thunder hard with an oversized arm. The Norse godling flew through the air and crashed into the wall behind him so hard he cracked the wooden panelling from top to bottom. The creature swung back to lash out at Walker, but he'd already stepped back out of reach. I saw Dead Boy eagerly pushing his way forward through the panicking crowd and yelled to him.

"Keep it busy! I've got an idea!"

Dead Boy came charging out of the crowd and threw himself at the Charnel Chimera. He waded right in, grabbing meaty chunks of the creature's body with his bare hands, tearing them free by brute force, and throwing them aside. The creature didn't bleed, but it howled with rage and hit Dead Boy square in the face with a hand like a fleshy club. Dead Boy's head snapped all the way round under the terrible force of the blow, and people gasped as they heard his neck break. Dead Boy stood for a moment with his face staring right at me, twisted so far round it was practically on back to front. Then he winked at me and slowly turned his head back into its proper position. In the shocked silence we could all hear his neck bones grinding as they realigned themselves. Dead Boy grinned nastily at the Charnel Chimera.

"That the best you've got? I'm dead, remember? Come on, give me your best shot! I can take it!"

The two of them slammed together, tearing at each other with unnatural strength, while everyone around them cried out in shock and horror at the awful things they were doing to each other. And while all this was going on I concentrated on slowly and cautiously raising my gift, opening my inner eye, my third eye, a fraction at a time. Previously, when I'd tried to use my gift in this house, Someone had shut me down, hard. But nothing happened this time, and I was able to use my gift to find the old and very nasty magic that held the various parts of the Charnel Chimera together, in defiance of all natural laws. And it was the easiest thing in the world for me to rip that magic away.

The creature just fell apart. It screamed like a soul newly damned to Hell as all the separate pieces of meat dropped to the floor, already rotting, the last dying remnants of people the creature had been before. The Charnel Chimera collapsed, its scream choking off as it sagged to the floor, losing all shape and running like filthy liquids, until nothing was left but a quietly steaming stain on the floor and the last, lingering traces of its charnel house stench.

Walker nodded pleasantly to me. "Thank you, John. I could have handled it myself. In fact, I would have liked to take it back in one piece for questioning and study . . . but then, you can't have everything."

"Indeed," I said. "Where would you put it all?"

Jeremiah came over to join us and looked down at the stain on the floor. "First you, Walker, and now this. It's getting so anyone can walk into my house. I'm going to have to upgrade my security again. What am I supposed to do with this mess? Look, there are still bits of meat scattered everywhere."

"Tasty," said Dead Boy, chewing on something. "Why not jam them on cocktail sticks and hand them round as party snacks? People could take them home in doggy bags, as party favours."

More people vomited, and there was general backing away from Dead Boy. I looked apologetically at Jeremiah.

"Sorry about that. Being dead hasn't mellowed him at all. He doesn't get invited out much, you know."

"Really?" said Jeremiah. "You do surprise me."

"Nice use of the Voice," I said to Walker. "But I have to wonder, with the Authorities dead and gone now, who's powering it? Or should that be What, rather than Who?"

"Life goes on," Walker said easily. "And I'm still in charge. Because somebody has to be. Certainly I don't see anyone suitable coming forward to replace me."

"You've always hated the Nightside," I said. "You told me it was your dearest wish to wipe out the whole damned freak show, before it spilled out over its boundaries to infect the rest of the world."

"Perhaps I'm mellowing in my old age," said Walker. "All that matters is that I am still here, preserving order in the Nightside, and with the Authorities gone, I have a much freer hand to go after those who threaten the way things are."

"I see," I said. "And would that include people like me?"

"Probably," said Walker.

"You kidnapped my grand-daughter!" Jeremiah said abruptly, his face ablaze with the power of a new idea, glaring right into Walker's face. "You walked right past my security and used your Voice to make Melissa leave with you! What is she? Your hostage, your insurance to stop me from taking my rightful place as ruler of the Nightside?"

"That certainly sounds like something I might do," murmured Walker. "But I don't need to stop you from taking over. You're not up to it. And I wouldn't take your grand-daughter because we both know I'd be the first person you would come after. And I don't want another war in the Nightside, just yet."

"You think I'd take your word for it?" snorted the Griffin. "I'll tear this whole city down to find where you've hidden her!"

"Would you swear to me that you had nothing to do with Melissa's disappearance?" I said quickly to Walker. "Would you swear it, on my father's name?"

"Yes, John," said Walker. "I'll swear to that, on your father's name."

I looked at Jeremiah. "He hasn't got her."

"How can you be so sure?" Jeremiah said suspiciously. "Exactly how closely are you two connected?"

"Long story," I said. "Let's just say . . . he knows better than to lie to me."

Walker nodded politely to Jeremiah, tipped his bowler hat briefly to me, and walked unhurriedly out of the ballroom. No-one said anything, or tried to stop him, not even Jeremiah. Shortly after Walker left, the butler Hobbes arrived with a small army of servants to clean up the mess and restore order to the demolished hedges and rosebushes trampled by the golems. The party slowly resumed, with much animated chatter over what had just happened. They'd be telling stories about it for years.

• • •

Surprisingly, the Griffin didn't seem at all put out. Once Walker was gone, Jeremiah calmed right down and even started smiling again. "Nothing like a little excitement to get your party talked about," he said cheerfully. "Look at Mariah, surrounded by all her friends and hangers-on, all of them comforting her and offering to bring her food or drink or anything else she might desire . . . and she's loving it. She's the centre of attention now, and that's all she ever wanted. Behind the tears and the swoons, she knows all this excitement guarantees her party will be written up in all the right places, and anyone who wasn't here will be killingly jealous of everyone who was."

He looked at me thoughtfully. "One of the problems with living as long as we have is that you've seen it all, done it all. Boredom is the enemy, and anything new is welcomed, good or bad. Everyone in my family is preoccupied with finding new things to distract and entertain them. I've spent centuries fighting and intriguing to gain control of the Nightside, because . . . it was there. The most difficult task I could set myself, and the biggest prize. Anything less . . . would have been unworthy of me. And now it infuriates me! That I'm so close to winning it all, and perhaps a bit too late!"

"Because you're expecting to die soon?" I said bluntly.

"There's a way out of every bargain," said Jeremiah, not looking at me. "And a way to break every deal. You only have to be smart enough to find it."

"Even if it means killing your own grand-children to stay alive?"

He finally looked at me, and surprised me by laughing, painfully. "No. I couldn't do that. Not even if I wanted to."

"You have to tell me the truth," I said. "The whole truth, or I'm never going to get anywhere with this case. Talk to me, Jeremiah. Tell me what I need to know. Tell me about the cellar under this house, for instance, and why no-one but yourself is ever allowed to go down there."

"You have been digging, haven't you?" said Jeremiah.

"You do want me to find Melissa, don't you?"

"Yes. I do. Above everything else, I want that."

"Then either take me down to the cellar and show me what you've got hidden there, or tell me the truth about how you became immortal."

The Griffin sighed but didn't seem too displeased by my insistence. "Very well," he said finally. "Come with me, and we'll discuss this in private."

I was half-expecting another privacy field, but the Griffin led me over to a corner of the ballroom, produced a small golden key on a length of gold chain, and fitted the key carefully into a small lock hidden inside a particularly rococo piece of scroll-work. The key turned, and a whole section of the wall swung open, revealing a room beyond. Jeremiah ushered me in, then shut and locked the door behind us. The room was empty, the walls bare, dimly lit by a single light that came on as we entered.

"I keep this room for private business conferences," said Jeremiah. "It's specially shielded against all eavesdroppers. You'd be surprised how much business gets done at parties. Hobbes will stand guard outside, to see that we're not disturbed. So . . . here I am at last, finally about to tell someone the true story of my beginnings as an immortal. I always thought I'd find it difficult, but now

209

that the moment has arrived I find myself almost eager to unburden myself. Secrets weigh you down; and I have carried this one for so many years . . .

"Yes, John. I really did make a deal with the Devil, back when I was nothing more than a simple mendicant in twelfth-century London. It wasn't even particularly difficult. Heaven and Hell were a lot closer to people in those days. I took an old parchment scroll I'd acquired in part payment of an old debt and used it to summon up the Prince of Darkness himself." He stopped abruptly, looking at his hands as they shook, remembering the moment. "I abjured and bound him to appear in a form bearable to human eyes, but even so, what I saw . . . But I was so very ambitious in my young days, and I thought I was so clever. I should have read the contract I signed in my own blood more carefully. The Devil is always in the details . . .

"There is a clause, you see, in that original infernal document, which states that any grand-child of my line, once safely born, cannot be killed by me. Neither can I have them killed, or through inaction allow them to come to harm. On pain of forfeiture of soul. So once I discovered their existence and had them brought before me, all that was left . . . was to embrace them. In a way I never did, or could, with William and Eleanor. Two grand-children were my death sentence, the sign of my inevitable damnation, but I couldn't say their existence came as much of a surprise. I did everything I could to ensure I'd never father children, but they came anyway. I could have had them killed, but . . . a man wants his line to continue, even if he knows it means his end. I'm a ruthless man, John. I've destroyed many men in my time. But I never once harmed a child.

"I tried my best with Paul, but it soon became clear he could never lead the family, any more than William could. Not their fault—they were born to wealth and luxury. Made them soft. But Melissa . . . turned out to be the best of all of us. The only uncorrupted Griffin."

"And the cellar?" I said. "What have you got down there?"

"The contract I signed, locked away and hidden, and protected by very powerful defences. I came to the Nightside because I'd heard that Heaven and Hell couldn't interfere directly, but of course, they both had their agents here. And while the contract cannot be destroyed, someone with the right connections to Heaven or Hell could rewrite its terms. I couldn't risk that. I have paid so very much for my immortality."

"Why the sudden change in your will?" I said. "Why risk alienating your whole family by leaving everything to Melissa?"

"Because she's the only one fit to run the empire I built. Her intelligence, her drive, her strength of character . . . made me see how limited the others are. What could I leave to my wife that others wouldn't take from her? Mariah couldn't hang on to anything I gave her. She'd throw my empire away, or let others take control of it through impulsive marriages or bad business deals. And it's not like she'll be left impoverished. She has her own money, invested in properties all over the Nightside. She thinks I don't know! She never could hide anything from me, least of all the identities of her many lovers, men and women. I don't begrudge her, not really. All my family has a desperate need for novelty in all things, to divert us from the endless stream of similar days . . . And William and Eleanor are just too damned weak."

"Oh, I don't know," I said. "They might surprise you."

"No," Jeremiah said firmly. "They wouldn't. They couldn't hold on to my business. If I left it to one, the other would try and take it, and they'd destroy my empire fighting over it, like two dogs with one bone. If I left the business to both of them, they'd destroy it fighting for control. They're both Griffins enough that neither would settle for second best. And Paul . . . has made it very clear he's not interested. My empire must survive, John. It's all I have to leave behind . . . my footprints on the world. A business is perhaps the only thing in this world that can be truly immortal . . . I can't let it be destroyed. Or everything I've done has been for nothing."

"You're sure there's nothing you can do?" I said. "You're sure that you're . . . damned?"

He smiled briefly. "Everything I've created and everything I own, I'd give it all up in a heart's beat to avoid what's coming . . . but there's no way out. Even apart from the deal I made, I've damned myself to the Pit a thousand times over by the things I've done to make myself rich and powerful. I was immortal, you see, so what did sin matter to such as I? I was never going to have to pay the price for all the terrible things I did . . ."

"But . . . all the years you've lived," I said. "All the things you've seen and done, aren't they enough?"

"No! Not nearly enough! Life is still sweet, even after all these centuries."

"All the things you could have achieved," I said slowly. "With your centuries of wealth and power. You could have been someone. Someone who mattered."

"Do you think I don't know that?" said the Griffin. "I know that. But all I've ever been any good at is business.

I sold my soul away to eternal punishment, and all I have to show for it is . . . things."

There was a sudden, though very polite, knock at the door. Jeremiah opened it with his golden key, and Hobbes came in, bearing a folded letter on a silver tray. Next to the letter was a knife.

"Forgive the interruption, sir, but it seems we have a ransom note at last."

Jeremiah snatched the letter from the tray, opened it, and read it quickly. I looked at Hobbes, then at the knife still on the tray.

"The letter was pinned to the front door with the knife, sir," said Hobbes.

I took the knife and examined it while Jeremiah scowled over the letter. There wouldn't be any physical evidence. These people were professionals, but there might still be some psychic traces I could pick up. I started to raise my gift, and once again a force from Outside slammed my inner eye shut. I tensed and stared quickly about me, but nothing appeared to attack me this time. I scowled, and studied the knife again. Just an ordinary, everyday knife with nothing unusual or distinctive about it. No doubt the paper and ink used in the letter would prove just as commonplace. Nice touch with pinning the letter to the front door. Traditional. Symbolic. And meaningful, saying *We can come and go as we please, and you'll never see us.* Jeremiah handed me the letter, and I put the knife back on the tray so I could study the note thoroughly. It was typed, in a standard font.

"We demand that Jeremiah Griffin put up all his holdings, business and personal, at public auction and dispose of everything he owns, within the next twelve hours. All monies gained are then to be given away to established charities. Only then will the Griffin see his grand-daughter Melissa alive and well. If the Griffin agrees, he is to go to the address below, in person and alone, within the next hour, and give evidence that the process has begun. Should the Griffin fail to do so, he will never see his grand-daughter again."

I checked the address at the bottom of the letter. I knew it. An underground parking area, in the heart of the business district. I looked at Jeremiah.

"Interesting," I said. "That they should demand from you the one thing you'd never give up, even for Melissa."

"I can't let her die," said the Griffin. "She's the only good thing that ever came out of my life."

"But if you give up your business, then it's all been for nothing."

"I know!" Jeremiah looked at me, his face torn with anguish. "I can't let these bastards win! Destroy everything I've created! John, there must be some way to save Melissa without having to give the kidnappers what they want. Can't you do anything?"

"You can't go to this meeting," I said firmly. "Then they'd have you and Melissa, and no guarantee they'd ever release either of you. Even if they got what they wanted. They could just kill you both right there, on the spot. For all we know, that could be what this has all been about—to get you so rattled you'd leave your security and walk into an obvious trap. No, I'll go. See if I can negotiate a better deal."

"They might kill Melissa immediately once they see you coming, instead of me!"

"No," I said. "These are professionals. They'd know better than to get me angry at them."

NINE

# one Dead
# griffin

Everyone knows that the traffic in the Nightside never
stops. That all the cars and trucks and vehicles, some of
which are so much more than they appear, are only passing through on their way to somewhere more interesting.
But like most of the things that everyone knows, it's only
partly true. Some of these anonymous vehicles ferry important people to important places in the Nightside, and
there has to be somewhere for these very important people to leave their very dangerous cars while they attend
their extremely private meetings. So there are car-parks
in the Nightside, but they're limited to the business area
so that when, rather than if, things go horribly wrong . . .
the damage and loss of life can be restricted to one con-
fined area.

I persuaded Dead Boy to drive me over to the business

area. I couldn't tell him why I needed to get there so urgently, but he was used to that from me. And he must have seen something in my face because for once he didn't give me a hard time about it. We drove in silence through the busy Nightside streets, and all the other hungry and dangerous vehicles recognised the futuristic car and took great pains to maintain a safe and respectful distance. I was still trying to decide what to do for the best. This could all go terribly wrong, in any number of distressing ways, but . . . it wasn't like I had any other leads. All this time I'd spent looking for Melissa, and now I was handed her location on a plate. Had to be a trap. And the kidnappers had to know that I'd know . . . So either they had something really nasty lined up and waiting for me, or . . . I was missing something, and the situation wasn't at all what I thought it was. It didn't matter. If there was even the smallest chance of rescuing Melissa from her captors, I had to take it, no matter what the risk.

That was what I signed on for.

There was always a chance the kidnappers would shoot me on sight for not being the Griffin, but I was counting on my reputation to make them hesitate long enough for me to get the first word in. There are lots of stories floating around the Nightside of really nasty things that have happened to people who pulled guns on me. Most of these stories aren't true, or at least greatly exaggerated, but I make a point of encouraging them. It helps to keep the flies off. Sometimes a scary rep can be better protection than triple-weave Kevlar. If I could just get them talking, I was pretty sure I could get them to negotiate. I can talk most people into anything, if I can just get them to stop trying to kill me long enough to listen.

Dead Boy found the address easily enough, in spite of

my directions, and brought his marvellous car gliding to a halt a sensible distance away. We looked the place over from the safety of the car. Business operations and warehouses with steel-shuttered windows and reinforced doors, guarded by heavily armed security men and magical protections so powerful they all but shimmered on the air, filled the area. Not many people on the streets. People only come here to do business, and they wouldn't be seen dead just walking. No hot neon here, none of the usual come-ons. This was where sober people met to make sober deals, and money changed hands so often it wore the serial numbers off. Tourists were firmly discouraged from lingering, and you could be shot on sight for looking scruffy.

The underground parking area looked like all the others—a single entrance, a long, sloping ramp down to an underground concrete bunker, and lots of heavily armed rent-a-cops in gaudy uniforms hanging around trying to look tough. Dead Boy stirred uncomfortably beside me.

"I could come with you," he said. "I could help. With whatever this is. No-one would have to know I was there. I could hide in the shadows. I'm really good at hiding in shadows. It's all part of being dead."

"No," I said. "Too many things could go wrong. They're going to be upset enough at seeing me instead of the Griffin. So I think we'll keep the shocks to a minimum. Thanks for offering, though."

"Hell," said Dead Boy, "if I let you get killed on my watch, Suzie Shooter will blow away both my knee-caps, then rip all my bones out. One at a time. You want me to wait for you?"

"Better not," I said. "There's no telling how long this

could take, and your car is already drawing glances. You go on. I'll see you later."

"I've got a whole lot of guns stacked away in this car," said Dead Boy, "and quite a few things that go Bang! in a loud and unfriendly manner."

I gave him a look, and he had the grace to look embarrassed. "When have I ever needed a gun?" I said.

I got out of the car and strolled down the street, not looking at anything in particular. Dead Boy drove off, slipping easily into the sparse traffic of the business area. The entrance to the car-park didn't seem to be protected by anything serious; presumably the need for constant easy access made that impractical. And once inside, the only security I'd have to face would be the rent-a-cops. The vehicles were expected to be able to look after themselves.

Some cars specialise in looking helpless, so they can sucker another vehicle into getting too close; and then out come the teeth and claws, and the suckered car moves down one place on the food chain. Survival of the fittest doesn't only apply to the living in the Nightside. And any human thief foolish enough to try it on with the cars in a place like this deserves every appalling thing that happens to him. The cars here are death on wheels, monsters in living steel.

The rent-a-cops were only around to keep out the uninvited and to try and persuade the various vehicles to play nicely with each other. Mostly they shot at anyone who wasn't them and hid behind anything solid when the cars started getting frisky. Rocket scientists need not apply. I found an air vent round a corner, pried it open, and peered down into the underground parking area. No-one saw me, no-one challenged me. One good thing about a night that never ends—there's never any shortage of shadows to hide in.

Though you have to be careful something isn't already in there.

Some twenty or so assorted vehicles lay spread out across the concrete, with plenty of space between them to avoid territory disputes. Lots of open space, lots of shadows despite the bright electric lighting, and only a handful of rent-a-cops on the ground. Melissa's captors must have chosen this place and time carefully, to limit the number of men and cars present. So, first things first. Get rid of the guards. I took half a dozen marbles from my coat-pocket and tossed them carefully down through the open air vent, one at a time. Each marble hit a parked car, and six different alarms went off at once. More alarms joined in, as other vehicles snapped awake, angry and suspicious and prepared to defend against any attack.

Horns sounded, Klaxons blared, and two cars lashed out at everything around them, thinking they'd been sneaked up on while they were dozing. Vehicles swelled in size, bonnets opening to reveal bright red maws lined with rows of grinding steel teeth. Machine guns extended from unlikely locations, along with chain-saws, energy weapons, and even a few missile launchers. Cars barked challenges at each other, radiators drooled acid that ate into the ground, and there was a terrible revving of engines. The rent-a-cops ran for their lives, not looking back. And all I had to do was walk round to the undefended entrance and stroll casually down the long, curving ramp into the parking area.

The vehicles detected my presence long before I could see them, and one by one they quieted down, settling back into watchful readiness. They recognised me. By the time I reached the bottom of the slope, everything was calm and quiet again. I made my way slowly and carefully between the parked cars, careful not to get too close to any of them. The cars watched me pass in silence, their headlamps blinking on and off to keep track of me. A few pretended to be sleeping, but I wasn't fooled. Get too close, and pride would demand they at least take a snap at me. A radiator grille stretched slowly as I approached, separating into metal teeth. A long pink tongue emerged, slowly licked the teeth, then disappeared again. I kept walking. A few cars edged away, to give me more room, and one actually disappeared.

Reputations are great. As long as you don't start believing them yourself.

I left the parked vehicles behind, to our mutual relief, and headed for the far end of the parking area, where Melissa's captors were supposed to be waiting. I still couldn't see anyone. I was leaving the lighted area behind, and the shadows were getting darker and deeper. My footsteps sounded very loud on the quiet surface. I tried firing up my gift, to search out any hidden traps or nasty surprises, but although nothing interfered to stop me this time, the aether in the car-park was so suffused with protection magics I couldn't See a thing. It was like peering through fog.

A single bright light snapped on over a doorway at the back I hadn't noticed before. A dozen dark figures stood close together, staring silently at me. Set against the bright light they were just silhouettes. Could have been anybody. I stopped and looked at them. They had to know by know that I wasn't Jeremiah Griffin.

"Over here, Mr. Taylor," said a harsh female voice. "We've been waiting for you."

A trap. Just as I'd thought. I straightened my back, put on my most confident smile, and sauntered unhurriedly over to join them. Never let them see they've got you worried. Someone at Griffin Hall must have told them I was coming in the Griffin's place. Could the kidnappers have had someone operating inside the Hall all along? My first thought had been that it was an inside job . . .

I was soon close enough to see them clearly, and the only reason I didn't blurt out something in surprise was because I was shocked silent. Nuns. They were all nuns, in full habit and wimple, and all of them carrying guns. Really serious guns. And they all looked like they knew how to use them. Nuns? Melissa Griffin had been kidnapped by nuns? Actually . . . an awful lot of things were starting to make sense now. I came to a halt before them and nodded politely to the one nun standing a little forward, at their head.

"So," I said, keeping my voice carefully calm and casual. "How did the Salvation Army Sisterhood get involved in kidnapping?"

The nuns stirred uneasily. They clearly hadn't expected to be identified so easily. The head nun glared at me. She was tall and blocky, with a blunt, plain face and fierce dark eyes. She looked like she meant business.

"Your reputation as a detective goes before you, Mr. Taylor," she said. "Indulge me. How did you identify our order so quickly?"

"My attackers at Divas! were all nuns," I said easily. "And the woman who attacked me with Kayleigh's Eye at Strangefellows did so right after some of your Sisters had given me the evil eye. For no reason I could understand. Of course, now it's obvious—once you knew I was on the case you were hoping a pre-emptive strike would keep me from interfering. But I'm still baffled as to why you should want to kidnap a teenaged girl. That's a bit low-rent for such infamous Christian terrorists as yourselves, isn't it?"

"We are not terrorists!" snapped the head nun. "We are Warriors of the Lord! We act in His name. And we go where we are needed."

"Lot of people claim to act in God's name," I said. "Did you ask His permission first?"

"We have sworn our lives and our sacred honour to God," the nun said proudly.

"What about the innocent victims who died at Divas!" I said.

"Things got out of hand there," said the nun, meeting my gaze steadily. "Mistakes were made. You made us pay a heavy price for those mistakes. So many good and noble Sisters dead. How is your conscience, Mr. Taylor?"

I studied her thoughtfully. "Are you the one who's been interfering with my gift, just lately?"

"No. We would if we could, but we don't have that kind of power."

"Damn," I said. "That means I've got another enemy out there somewhere . . ."

The nun sniffed impatiently. "Let your mind wander on your own time. I am Sister Josephine. I will speak for the Salvation Army Sisterhood."

"I want to see Melissa," I said immediately. "I need to know she's still alive and well, or there'll be no negotiations."

"Of course," said Sister Josephine, and she turned and gestured briefly to the nuns behind her. Those at the back parted for a moment to give me a quick glimpse of Melissa Griffin, huddled up against the rear door. She looked exactly as she had in the photograph, right down to the same dress. She started to say something to me, but the nuns closed in before her again. She didn't seem to be tied up or restrained in any magical way. If I could get close enough, getting her out might be easier than I'd thought. It was good to see her at last. I'd told myself all along that she had to be alive, but I'd never been entirely sure. The Nightside isn't known for its happy endings.

"Stay where you are, Melissa." I said loudly, keeping my voice bright and assured. "Your father sent me to take you home." I looked at Sister Josephine. "You wanted to talk, so let's talk. What are the grounds for negotiation?"

"There aren't any," the Sister said calmly. "There will be no negotiations. This isn't about Melissa. It's about you, Mr. Taylor. We knew you'd insist on coming here in the Griffin's place, once you got the note. We had to bring you here, to talk to you directly. You must stop interfering, Mr. Taylor. You don't know what's really going on. And this is far too important for you to be allowed to meddle anymore. There's too much at stake. Souls are at stake."

"So what are you going to do, if I don't stop?" I said. "Shoot me?"

"Not unless we have to." Sister Josephine's voice didn't waver at all.

All the time we'd been talking, I was unobtrusively trying to work an old magic trick of mine—taking the bullets out of guns without their owners realising. Unfortunately, there was already a magic in place, specifically designed to stop mine from operating. I was forced to admit that I might have let myself become too dependent on that particular trick. Too many people had seen me use it. I returned my full attention to Sister Josephine, who was watching me carefully.

"We don't want to have to kill you, Mr. Taylor. Despite our reputation, we only ever kill where necessary. To prevent further suffering. But we will use whatever force is necessary to bend you to our will in this matter."

"What do you have in mind?" I said, letting my hands drift a little closer to my coat-pockets.

"Come with us now. We'll imprison you somewhere safe until this is all over. Don't resist us unless you want Melissa to suffer for your disobedience."

"Melissa needs to go home," I said. "That's what I'm here for. And you'll have to kill me to stop me. I really don't like people who kidnap children. So what do you say, Sister Josephine? Are you really ready to murder me in cold blood to get your own way? A cardinal sin, surely, even for a Warrior of the Lord?"

"We do God's will," Sister Josephine said flatly. "It's not a sin if you do it for God."

I had to smile. "Now that really is bullshit."

"Don't you laugh at us! Don't you dare laugh at us!" She stepped forward, her face red with rage. "We have dedicated our lives, our very souls, to the good work! We're not doing this for money, not like you!"

"I'm not doing it just for the money," I said. "I'm doing it for Melissa. And I really think it's time we were going."

I forced my inner eye open, peered through the mystic fog, and found the sprinkler system overhead. I turned them all on at once. Water slammed down all across the car-park, thick as pouring rain, laced with holy water to deal with magical fires. All the parked vehicles went crazy. Thinking they were under attack, cars smashed together head to head, like rutting deer. Other vehicles swelled up and engulfed smaller vehicles beside them. Some changed their shapes completely, revealing their true nature as they became suddenly strange, alien, other . . . Shapes that made no sense at all in merely three dimensions. Something that now looked a hell of a lot like a giant black spider jumped out of the shadows onto a nun who'd strayed a little too far from the group. It brought her down in a moment, sucking the blood out of her as she screamed helplessly. More cars surged forward, excited by the smell of blood. Several nuns opened fire, shooting indiscriminately at the vehicles around them with machine pistols and automatic weapons.

The pouring water had shorted out most of the lights. There were shapes and figures moving everywhere in the gloom. I edged cautiously through the chaos, crouched to avoid the bullets flying everywhere. I slipped easily between the scattered nuns, dodging the frenzied vehicles as they roared back and forth, concentrating all my attention on getting to Melissa. I could see her clearly in the light by the end door, still huddled against it in terror, her arms wrapped around her head to keep out the noise.

A car behind me took half a dozen bullets in its fuel tank and exploded in a fireball that shook the whole carpark. All kinds of alarms were going off now, though I could hardly hear them through the ringing in my ears. The burning wreckage cast a flickering hell-fire glare across the scene, the transformed cars rearing up like demons. The surviving nuns were standing back-to-back now, firing at anything that moved. I dodged through the smoke from the burning car and headed for Melissa. I yelled her name, but she didn't look up. The uproar was almost painfully loud. I ran towards her, crossing the last of the distance as quickly as I could. A nun came at me out of nowhere, her gun pointing straight at me. I threw myself to one side, but the gun barrel turned to follow me. The nun opened fire. And Melissa ran forward to stop the nun.

The nun caught a glimpse of something coming at her, and spun round. The gun was already firing. The bullets slammed into Melissa, stitching a line of bullet-holes across her chest. The impact picked her up and threw her backwards, smashing her against the far wall. She slid slowly down the concrete wall, leaving a bloody trail behind her. She sat down hard, her chin on her chest. The whole of her front was soaked in blood. The nun screamed in shock and horror, threw her gun away, and ran for the exit. A car got her before she made a dozen steps. I ran forward and took Melissa in my arms, cradling her against my chest, but I was already too late. I'd failed her. I'd promised her father I'd find her and bring her safely back, and all I'd done was get her killed.

Melissa slowly raised her head to look at me, and the long blonde wig slipped sideways. It wasn't Melissa. It was Paul, made up as Polly, dressed like his beloved cousin. He tried to say something to me, but all that came out of his mouth was a bloody froth. He raised a shaking hand, and pushed something into my hand. I looked at it. A simple golden key. When I looked back at Paul, he was dead.

I sat there for a while, holding him in my arms, more numb than anything. There was blood and screams and gunfire all around me, but none of that mattered. A car came roaring out of the driving rain, headed right at me. I looked at it, and all my rage and horror and frustration came together in me, and I threw it at the approaching car. It stopped dead in its tracks and exploded, showering fiery debris over a wide area. It screamed as it died, and I smiled.

One by one, the surviving vehicles fled the car-park, butting and snapping at each other all the way. The pouring rain from the sprinklers shut off abruptly, as someone finally hit the override, even though half a dozen vehicles were still burning fiercely. The alarms shut down, too, and suddenly it was all very quiet. As though nothing had happened at all. There were bodies sprawled on the ground all around me, but I couldn't seem to make myself care. I heard footsteps approaching, splashing across the water-soaked floor. I slowly raised my head to look, and there was Sister Josephine, looming over me. Her gun hung forgotten at her side. She looked at Paul, lying dead and bloody in my arms, and her face was full of a terrible sadness.

"This wasn't supposed to happen," she said. "It's all been a ghastly mistake. Paul shouldn't even have been here, but he wanted so badly to be involved, to help, to support his cousin. And she didn't have the heart to tell him no."

I put Paul's body gently to one side and stood up to face Sister Josephine. "Tell me. Tell me what's really going on. Tell me everything."

"We didn't kidnap Melissa Griffin," said Sister Josephine. "Melissa came to us of her own free will."

# TEN

# That Old - Time Religion

"We can't stay here," Sister Josephine said urgently. "The car's owners will be here soon to see what set off all the alarms. They aren't going to be at all happy. There will almost certainly be harsh language and threats of violence. Even worse, they might want us to fill out insurance forms. Mr. Taylor . . . John . . . Can you hear me? We have to go now!"

I could hear her trying to reach me, but I couldn't seem to make myself care. I knelt beside Paul's body, hoping that if I stared at it long enough, it would start to make some kind of sense. He seemed like such a small and delicate thing in his blood-stained dress, like a flower someone had carelessly crushed and thrown aside. I'd told him I could protect him. I should have known better. The Nightside does so love to make a man break a promise. I slowly became aware of the sound of running feet approaching fast from all sides, along with the barking of orders. With all the maddened cars finally gone, the rent-a-cops had rediscovered their courage. They'd probably come in shooting. I smiled slowly, and I could feel it was the wrong kind of smile. Let them come. Let them all come. I was in the mood to kill a whole bunch of people.

"You can't kill them all," said Sister Josephine, reading my mood accurately.

"Watch me," I said, but it didn't sound like me. Already my dark mood was passing. I sighed heavily, picked up Paul's body, and stood facing Sister Josephine. "Tell me you know of a secret way out of here."

"I have an old Christian charm," the nun said quickly. "Through which any door made be made over into any other door, leading anywhere. It's how we were able to arrive here unobserved, despite all the protections. Come with me, Mr. Taylor. And I'll take you to Melissa."

I looked around. "Where are the rest of your Sisters?"

"They're all gone," Sister Josephine said steadily. "All dead. It seems the stories about you are true after all, that death follows you around like a dog because you feed it so well."

"Open the door," I said, and something in my voice made her hurry to obey.

Sister Josephine reached inside her habit and took out a Hand of Glory, and distracted as I was, I still felt a jolt of surprise. A Hand of Glory is pagan magic, not Christian. A mummified human hand, cut off a hanged man in the last moments of his dying, the fingers soaked in wax to make them into candles. With the candles lit and the proper Words spoken over them, a Hand of Glory can open any door, reveal any secret, show the way to hidden treasures. Simply owning one was a stain on the soul. Sister Josephine caught me looking at her.

"This is the Hand of a Saint," she said, not quite defiantly. "Donated with her consent, prior to her martyring. It is a blessed thing, and a Christian weapon in the fight against Evil."

"If you say so," I said. "Which Saint?"

"Saint Alicia the Unknown. As if you'd know which Saint was which, you heathen."

She muttered over the mummified thing, and the wicks set into the end of each bloated finger burst simultaneously into flames. The light was warm and golden, and I could feel a new presence on the air, of something or someone else joining us. It was a . . . comfortable feeling. Sister Josephine thrust the Hand of Glory at the rear door, and the door shuddered in its frame, as though crying out at what was being done to it. Sister Josephine gestured sharply with the Hand, and the door swung inwards, as though forced open against its will by some unimaginable pressure. Bright light spilled into the underground car-park, and with it the scent of incense. Harsh voices cried out behind us. There was the sound of gunfire, but the bullets came nowhere near us. Rent-a-cops couldn't hit a cow on the arse with a banjo. Sister Josephine walked forward into the light, and I followed after, carrying Paul's body in my arms.

And found myself in the Street of the Gods. Where all the gods that ever were or are or may be are worshipped, feared, and adored. All the Forces and Powers and Beings too powerful to be allowed to run free in the Nightside. Churches and temples line both sides of the Street, up and down and for as far as anyone has ever dared to walk; though only the most popular and powerful religions hold the best territory, near the centre. All the other gods and congregations have to fight it out for position and status, competing for worshippers and collection moneys in a positively Darwinian battle for survival. You can find anything on the Street of the Gods, if it doesn't find you first.

Sister Josephine blew out the candles on her Hand of Glory and put it away. A door shut solidly behind us, cutting off the sound of running feet and increasing gunfire. I looked behind us and discovered the Sister and I had apparently emerged from the Temple of Saint Einstein. The credo over the door said simply: *It's all relative.*

People were calling out my name, and not in a good way. I turned to look. People had good cause to remember me after I went head to head with my mother here, during the Lilith War. A lot of people died up and down the Street on that awful night, and a lot of gods, too. Being a god isn't necessarily forever, not in the Nightside. Worshippers up and down the Street took one look at me and started running, just in case. I smiled briefly at Sister Josephine, a little embarrassed, and she shook her head before setting off down the Street. I followed after her, hugging Paul to me like a sleeping child.

A lot of the Street was still rebuilding itself after the War. I remembered Lilith, wrapped in all her terrible glory and majesty, walking unhurriedly down the Street while churches and temples and meeting places blew apart or burst into flames or shuddered down into the earth, under the pressure of her implacable will. Many of the old landmarks were gone, ancient structures so beautiful they soared up into the night sky like works of art.

Only rubble now, or burnt-out blackened shells. Some of the destroyed churches and their gods had snapped back into being later, a tribute to the faith of their congregations; but all too many worshippers had their faith shattered by Lilith's calm, happy destruction of everything they'd ever believed in. Because, after all, if a god can be destroyed, then he isn't really a god, is he?

Lilith murdered many of the oldest Names on the Street, out of anger or petulance or because they got in her way. Or just because she could. Some she killed because they were her children, and she was so disappointed in them. The Carrion in Tears was gone, and The Thin White Prince, and Bloody Blades. And others who had lasted for centuries uncounted. All gone now, unmade, uncreated.

Sister Josephine and I made our way down the Street, and people hurried to get out of our way and give us plenty of room. A few zealots shouted threats and curses from the safety of their church doors, ready to duck back inside if I looked like I was noticing them. There were great holes between the standing churches, dark and bloody like pulled teeth. Ancient places of worship were smoking pits now, and in the years to follow the very names of their gods would be forgotten. Would a murdered god still haunt the place where its church used to be? And what kind of ghost would a god make? You can find yourself thinking the damnedest things, in the Nightside.

On the other hand, new churches were springing up here and there like spring flowers after the rain, as lesser gods and beliefs arrived to stake a claim after being squeezed out in the past by more powerful religions. They sprouted from the rubble, proud structures traced in delicate lines of pure light or gleaming marble or solid stone, standing stoutly against the night sky. Some of these gods were new, some were unknown, and some were older than old . . . ancient and terrible Names whose time had, perhaps, come round again. Baal and Moloch and Ahriman. Hell, even the Temple of Dagon was making a comeback.

Gargoyles scurried along the guttering in high places, keeping a careful watch on me as I passed. Something with too many bright eyes sniggered to itself in the dark shadows of an alley-way, its many legs weaving a shimmering cocoon around something that still shrieked and struggled. And a human skeleton, its bones yellowed with age and held together with copper wire, smashed its face against a stone wall, over and over again. Business as usual, on the Street of the Gods.

I had heard of some easily impressed types who kept trying to raise churches to worship me—proof if proof were needed that most of the people operating on the Street of the Gods weren't too tightly wrapped. I'd made it clear I disapproved in every possible way, if only because I didn't believe in tempting fate. My good sometime friend Razor Eddie, Punk God of the Straight Razor, had taken it upon himself to burn down these churches as fast as they appeared, but the damned things kept springing up like weeds. Hope springs eternal among the seriously deluded.

One of the new gods came swaggering out of his splendid new church to greet me and Sister Josephine. To be honest, he planted himself right in front of us, blocking our way, so we had to stop and talk to him or walk right over him. I was tempted, but . . . The new god was a big brawny type, with a smooth pink face and a smile with far too many perfect teeth, all wrapped up in a pristine white suit. He looked more like a used-car salesman than a god, but it takes all sorts . . . His church looked a lot like a supermarket, where prayers could buy you the very best divine intervention money could buy, at knockdown prices. The guy's halo looked fake, too, more like a CGI effect.' And the jaunty angle was particularly offputting. In my experience, the real thing tends to be much more impressive, and downright disturbing to be around. Pure good and pure evil are equally unsettling and unfathomable to the everyday human mind.

"Hi there, sir and Sister! Good to meet you both! I am Chuck Adamson, the god of Creationism. Blessed be!"

I hefted Paul's body into a more comfortable position and considered Chuck thoughtfully. "Creationism has its own god now?"

The new god smiled easily and struck an impressive pose. "Hey, if enough people believe in a thing . . . sooner or later, it will appear somewhere on the Street of the Gods. Though I have to say, if I see one more Church of Elvis materialise from the aether, complete with blazing neon and stereophonic cherubs, I may puke. A great singer, to be sure, but a fornicator and drug abuser nonetheless. We are a proudly old-fashioned, traditional Church, sir, and there's no room in it for a sinner, no matter how talented."

"Cut to the chase, Chuck," I said, and something in my voice made his big wide smile waver just a little.

"Well, sir, it seems to me that I am in a position to do you some good. I see that you carry in your arms the mortal remains of a dear departed friend. Cute little thing, wasn't she? You mourn her loss, sir. I see it clearly, but I am here to tell you that I can raise her from the dead! I can raise her up, make her walk and talk and praise Creationism in a loud and carrying voice. Yes, sir! All you have to do in return . . . is bear witness. Tell everyone you meet who did this wonderful thing, and then send them here to learn the glory of Creationism! Oh yeah! Can I hear a Halleluiah?"

"Probably not," I said.

Chuck stepped in a little closer, and lowered his voice confidentially. "Come now, sir, you must understand that every new church needs a few good old-fashioned miracles to get it off the ground? You just spread the word, and the worshippers will come running like there's a sale on. And before you know it, my humble establishment will be leap-frogging up this Street to better and better positions. Praise Creationism!"

"You can bring my friend back from the dead?" I said, fixing him with my coldest stare. "You can repair Paul's body and return his soul to the vale of the living?"

"Ah," said Chuck. "Repair the body, yes. The soul . . . is a different matter. A bit out of my reach, you might say."

"So what you're proposing," I said," is to turn Paul into a zombie and have him lurch about shouting *Brains! Brains!* while he slowly but inevitably decays?"

"Well, not as such . . . Look, I'm new," said Chuck, a little desperately. "We've all got to start somewhere!"

"You don't even know who I am, do you?" I said. "I'm John Taylor."

"Oh Christ."

"Bit late to be invoking him, Chuck. You're the god of Creationism . . . That means you don't believe in evolution, right?"

"Yes, but . . ."

"Your belief started out as Creationism, but has now become Intelligent Design, right?"

"Yes, but . . ."

"So your argument has evolved, thus disproving your own argument."

"Oh bugger," said Chuck, as he disappeared in a puff of logic.

"Nice one," said Sister Josephine. "I would have just shoved a holy hand-grenade up his arse and pulled the pin. Heretics! Worse than fleas on a dog. His church has disappeared, too, and I have to say I find the pile of rubble that has replaced it rather more aesthetically satisfying."

"He'll be back," I said. "Or something like him. If enough people believe in a thing . . ."

"If a million people believe a stupid thing, it is still a stupid thing," Sister Josephine said firmly. "I am getting really tired of having to explain that a parable is just a parable."

We walked on, down the Street of the Gods. Past the Churches of Tesla and Crowley and Clapton, and an odd silvery structure that apparently represented a strange faith that originated in the small town of Roswell. Big-eyed Grey aliens lurked around the ever-open door, watching the people go by. They were the only church that didn't bother trying to attract worshippers; they simply abducted them right off the Street. Luckily, they mostly stuck to picking on the tourists, so no-one else gave a damn. There's never any shortage of tourists on the Street of the Gods.

In fact, a large crowd of them had gathered before an old-style Prophet in filthy rags and filthier skin, who harangued the crowd with practiced skill.

"Money is the source of all evil!" he yelled, his dark eyes fierce and demanding. "Wealth is a burden on the soul! So save yourself from its taint by giving it all to me! I am strong; I can bear the burden! Look, hand over all your wallets right now, or I'll bludgeon you severely about the head and shoulders with this dead badger I just happen to have about my person for perfectly good reasons."

The tourists hurried to hand over all their possessions to the Prophet, laughing and chattering. I looked at Sister Josephine.

"Local character," she said. "He adds colour to the Street. The tourists love him. They line up to be mugged, then have their photographs taken with him."

"This place is going to the gods," I said.

It took us a while, but we came at last to the headquarters of the Salvation Army Sisterhood, a small modest church in the low-rent part of the Street. No neon, no advertising, just a simple building with strained-glass windows. The front door was guarded by a pair of very large nuns with no obvious weapons. They tensed as I approached, but Sister Josephine settled them with a few quiet words. They both looked sadly at Paul's body in my arms as I followed Sister Josephine through into the church, and I heard them muttering prayers for the soul of the dead before the door closed firmly behind me. More nuns came forward, and I reluctantly handed Paul over into their care. They carried him away into the brightly lit interior of their church, quietly singing a hymn for the departed.

"They'll look after him," said Sister Josephine. "Paul was well liked among us, though he was never a believer.

He can lie in our chapel of rest until his family decides what provisions they wish to make for his final interment."

"Nice church you've got here," I said. I needed something to distract me. Humour could only do so much. I don't know why Paul's death affected me so much. Perhaps because he was the only true innocent in the case. "I like what you've done with the place. Candles and fresh flowers and incense. I was expecting something with barbed wire and gun emplacements."

"This is a church," Sister Josephine said sternly. "Though it functions more as a convent, or retreat. We worship here, but our true place is out in the world, smiting the evil-doer. We believe in doing unto others, and we're very good at it. We only come back here to rest and rededicate our faith. Our sustained belief maintains our presence on the Street of the Gods; but we make no effort to attract new worshippers. We're just here for people who need us."

"Like Melissa?"

"Yes. Like Melissa Griffin."

"And Paul?"

"No. Paul never expressed any interest in our religion, or our cause. I don't think he ever really believed in anything, except Melissa. But he was a happy soul, a bright and colourful bird of paradise in our grey and cloistered world. He was always welcome here, as Paul or Polly, and I like to think he found some peace within these walls. There weren't many places he could go that would accept him as he was and not just as the Griffin's grandson. We will clean and redress his body, and send him back to the Hall as Paul, with no trace of Polly on him. She was his secret. The world doesn't need to know."

"I'll take him home, when he's ready," I said.

"The Griffin will ask questions."

"And I'll tell him what he needs to know, and no more."

"You're probably one of the few people who could get away with that," said Sister Josephine. "But you know he's going to insist on knowing who's responsible for his grandson's death."

"That's easy," I said. "I'm responsible. Paul is dead because of me."

Sister Josephine started to say something, then stopped and shook her head. "You're very hard on yourself, John."

"Someone has to be."

"Not even the great John Taylor can protect everyone."

"I know," I said. "But knowing doesn't help."


She led me through the narrow corridors of her church. There were flowers everywhere, perfuming the air with their scent, mixed with sandalwood and beeswax and incense from the slow-burning candles. It was all so quiet and peaceful, the brightly lit rooms suffused with a real sense of calm and compassion, and grace. Out in the world the Sisters might be Warriors of the Lord, and steadfast in their violent cause, but here they were simply secure in their faith, however contradictory that might seem to outsiders. Sister Josephine took me into her study, a simple room with book-lined walls, a single stained-glass window, and two comfortable chairs on either side of a banked open fire. We sat down, facing each other, and I looked steadily at Sister Josephine.

"It's time for the truth. Tell me about Melissa Griffin. Tell me everything."

"It's really very simple," said Sister Josephine, settling back into her chair, her hands clasped loosely in her lap. "What kind of rebellion and defiance is there left to a teenager when your parents and grandparents have already done everything, broken every law and committed every sin, and gotten away with it? And even made a deal with the Devil himself? What was there left to Melissa to demonstrate her independence except to become devoutly religious, take holy orders, and go into seclusion in a convent? Melissa wanted to become a nun. It probably started out as an act of teenage defiance, but the more she studied religion, and Christianity in particular because of her grandfather, the more she realised she'd found her true calling. And since Jeremiah had sold his soul to the Devil, it's hardly surprising that Melissa would end up choosing the most extreme, hard-core Christian church she could find. Us. The Salvation Army Sisterhood. She first made contact through Paul, because he'd do anything for her. He was the only one in the family who could come and go undisturbed, because his grandfather had already given up on him."

Sister Josephine smiled briefly. "We took some convincing, at first. We couldn't believe that any member of the notorious Griffin family could be seriously devout, let alone wish to join our order. And not even as a Warrior, but as a solitary contemplative. But, finally, she slipped her bodyguards and escorts, with Paul's help, and came here to us, to listen and to learn. We were all impressed, despite ourselves. She truly believed, a pure and simple faith that actually shamed some of us. It's sometimes too easy for us to forget that we act to protect the innocent, not punish the guilty. Melissa is a gentle soul, with not a spark of violence in her. Hard to believe she's really a Griffin . . . I suppose it just goes to show that miracles can happen anywhere."

"Melissa wanted to be a nun," I said slowly. "Didn't see that one coming. But . . . you must have been very eager to sign her up. Having a Griffin on your books would be a real catch."

"I told you," Sister Josephine said steadily, "we don't seek to convert anyone. They come to us, for their own reasons, and only the most sincere are ever allowed to stay. Melissa . . . is the real thing."

"Hold it," I said. "Melissa already knew her grandfather made a deal with the Devil, for immortality? You didn't tell her?"

"No. He told her. The single greatest secret of his life. I think . . . he wanted to show her he was sincere about making her his heir."

"Did she also know that Jeremiah could still save his life, and hang on to his soul, if she and Paul were to die?"

"Oh yes. He told her everything. And then he took her up onto a mountaintop and showed her all the kingdoms of the world, and said, *All this can be yours if you will just accept my legacy and continue it.* But she was stronger than even she suspected and would not be tempted. She didn't want anything that came from a deal with the Devil. She knew it was tainted, and would inevitably corrupt her. So she determined to leave the family while she still could. She tried to persuade Paul to leave with her, but he already had his other life as Polly."

"I have to say," I said carefully, "I'm more than a bit surprised that an old-fashioned and strait-laced church like yours would approve of Paul, and Polly."

"We are a truly fundamentalist Christian church," Sister Josephine said sternly. "We follow Jesus' teachings of tolerance and compassion. We only vent our wrath on those who have proven themselves beyond any hope of redemption. Those who only exist to lead the innocent into darkness and damnation. We know what real evil is. We see it every day. Paul, either as himself or as Polly, served the light in his own way. He delighted in making people happy. Just a happy little songbird . . . a butterfly, crushed on the wheel of a small-minded world."

"So . . . Melissa asked you to help her fake a kidnapping?" I said.

"Yes. She had it all worked out and arranged down to the last detail." Sister Josephine paused and looked at me steadily. "You mustn't see her as a selfish girl, Mr. Taylor. She still loved her family, and hoped through her religious studies to find some way of saving them all from the consequences of their sins . . . even her grandfather. She truly believed that a sincere enough faith could break even a compact with the Devil. You might call her naïve. We see in her a pure and true faith that has humbled all of us. We would do anything for her. So when she begged and pleaded with us to help her escape her family home, we went along with it.

"She made it possible for four of us to approach the Hall unobserved and enter through the front door without setting off any of the alarms. Her grandfather had shared all his secrets with her, including Hall security, because he still believed he could talk her into taking control of the family empire. For such an experienced man, he could be very blind where his family was concerned. Melissa sent the servants away into other parts of the Hall, and even persuaded the Griffin to send Hobbes down into the city for the evening, on some spurious but plausible errand. She was always scared of Hobbes and the way he seemed to know everything that was going on . . ."

I nodded. I'd always known it had to be some kind of inside job. "Why did she need the four of you there? Why not just walk out?"

"We were there to leave specific evidence of our presence," said Sister Josephine. "A footprint here, a handprint there, that sort of thing. I told you Melissa thought of everything. It was all misdirection, you see. And . . . there was always the chance of someone seeing something they shouldn't, then we might have to fight our way out. I thought of that even if Melissa didn't."

"But why was she so keen to be thought of as a kidnap victim rather than just another teenage runaway?"

"To confuse the issue. So the Griffin would be forced to spread his forces thinly, chasing every possibility."

"All right," I said. "I'll buy that. But I'm still having trouble understanding why such a gentle, meek, and mild little soul like Melissa would want to join an order that specialises in destruction and bloody vengeance."

"Think it through," said Sister Josephine. "Melissa did. She needed an order strong enough to protect her from her grandfather's wrath if he should ever find out where she was hiding. She hoped her grandfather would understand her rejection of his empire, and accept it, but the Griffin . . . has always been a very proud and vindictive man. Melissa knew there was no point in entering a convent if her grandfather could simply send his people in to drag her out again. She knew our reputation and hoped that would be enough to give even the Griffin pause."

"You have to be straight with me here," I said. "How sincere are you, in accepting meek and mild Melissa into your order? Are you just using her to strike a blow at her grandfather?"

"No," Sister Josephine said immediately. "Melissa's faith is real and that is the only reason we ever accept anyone into our church."

"I need to talk to her," I said. "In person. To validate your story and to discuss with her what the hell I'm going to do next. I said right from the beginning I wouldn't drag her back home against her will . . . but Paul's death changes everything. Jeremiah will never stop looking for Melissa now. She's the only grand-child he's got. Either he'll want to bring her back into the family, or if he believes she's completely lost to him . . . he might decide she'd be better off dead, so he can go on living."

"That's why we're keeping Melissa in a safe house, for the time being," said Sister Josephine. "Connected to, but quite separate from, this church. Security begins at home. In case anyone came here looking for her."

"Someone like me?" I said.

"Of course. We were all very . . . concerned when we heard the Griffin had hired you to find his grand-daughter. Your gift's reputation goes before you. So we chose a pocket dimension for Melissa's temporary bolt-hole. Even you couldn't find her there."

"Don't be so sure of that," I growled. I wasn't sure at all, but in my job it's important to keep up appearances.

Sister Josephine stood up abruptly, so I did, too. She drew the Hand of Glory from inside her habit and lit the candles on the fingers with a quick gesture. She smiled at me suddenly, and it was a warm and even kindly smile.

"Come with me, John. It's time for you to meet Melissa Griffin. The most Christian soul I have ever met."

She used the Hand of Glory on her study door, and it groaned loudly in its frame, as though protesting. The door swung open before us, and we stepped through, and immediately we were in another place. The ground shook briefly under my feet, as though settling into place, and the air was suddenly hot and humid. Sweat sprang out on my bare face and hands, and I had to struggle to get my breath in the thick moist air. It stank of brimstone and foulness and blood. We were standing in a simple chapel, with rows of basic wooden pews and a bare functional altar at the far end. The crucifix above the altar had been turned upside down.

The pews were full of nuns, but they were all dead. There might have been a dozen or more. It was hard to tell now. They'd all been murdered, savagely, inhumanly. Torn quite literally limb from limb, gutted, beheaded. Blood soaked the pews and the floor, and body parts lay scattered everywhere. The stench grew worse, the more I breathed it.

I moved slowly down the central aisle, heading for the altar, and Sister Josephine was right there at my side. I glanced at her, to see how she was holding together. Her face was terribly cold with a controlled fury, and she had a machine pistol in each hand now. Fourteen severed heads had been impaled on the carved wooden guard before the altar, still wearing their wimples, their faces stretched and contorted by their final horrified screams. The altar itself had been thickly smeared with blood and shit.

"Do you see Melissa here anywhere?" I said, keeping my voice low.

"No. She's not here." Sister Josephine looked quickly back and forth, her machine pistols tracking with her, desperate for a target.

"Who else could get in here?"

"No-one. Just me. That's the point." Sister Josephine made a visible effort to calm herself. "Only I know how to operate the Hand of Glory, to open the door between dimensions."

"So, to track Melissa here, and then force a way in and do . . . all this, means whoever beat us here has to be someone of considerable power." I thought about that, and the more I considered it the less I liked it. If this was the same Someone who'd been interfering with my gift, that meant they'd been one step ahead of me right from the beginning.

"If all they wanted was Melissa, why take the time to do this?" said Sister Josephine, her voice tight and strained. "Why mutilate these Sisters and desecrate the altar?"

"Has to be someone who takes the Christian faith seriously, to hate it this much," I said.

Sister Josephine looked at me seriously. "I smell brimstone."

"So do I."

"Do you think Melissa is dead?"

"No," I said immediately. "Or they'd have left her body here for us to find, looking like the rest. No, she was taken away from here so I couldn't have her. Someone who didn't want me involved from the very beginning. I hate to say it, but all of this could be Jeremiah's work. If he didn't trust me to bring his grand-daughter back to him. The man made a deal with the Devil, and this looks like the Devil's work to me."

I broke off as something in the chapel changed. The stench was suddenly almost overpowering, and I could hear the buzzing of flies. All the flowers in the chapel burst into flames, burning fiercely in their vases. It felt like there was Someone else in the place with us . . . and then Sister Josephine and I moved quickly to stand back-to-back, as one by one the dead nuns in the pews came slowly, horribly, to life again. Limbless torsos lurched out into the aisle, while hands pulled severed arms along the floor towards us. Lengths of purple intestines curled slowly on the floor like meaty snakes. Blood pattered down from the ceiling. And all the severed heads spiked on the wooden guard began to speak as one.

*Sister Josephine, John Taylor. Come on down! There's a special place in Hell reserved just for you, and all the heroes who failed to protect those they swore to save! You'll like it in Hell, John. All your friends and family are here . . .*

I laughed right back in their faces. "Save your mind games for someone who gives a damn. What were you planning to do with all these bits and pieces? Nudge us to death?" I looked at Sister Josephine. "Don't let the bastard get to you. He's only messing with us, hoping to break our spirit. I can deal with this."

I fired up my gift, and straightaway found the very basic magic that was reanimating the dead nuns. We'd triggered the spell by entering the chapel, and it was the easiest thing in the world to push the switch back into the off position. The spell shut itself down, and the dead bits and pieces were still again, their dignity restored. Sister

Josephine put her machine pistols away. She was breathing hard, but otherwise seemed unmoved.

"Who could have done this?" she said, sounding very dangerous indeed. "And where do I have to go to find him and make him pay?"

"Griffin Hall's probably your best bet," I said. "But since my gift seems to operate fine here, why don't I make sure?"

I forced my inner eye all the way open, and my Sight showed me a vision of the recent past. I saw who it was who had come here, and done all this, and taken Melissa Griffin away . . . and just like that, a whole lot of things suddenly made sense.

# ELEVEN

# Hell to pay

It's never easy arguing with a nun, but it's harder than usual when she's waving a machine pistol around to emphasize her point. Sister Josephine was mad as hell because I wouldn't tell her what I'd seen in my Vision, but I couldn't tell her. Not until I had proof to back it up. Some things are just too weird to say out loud, even for the Nightside. Sister Josephine finally settled for insisting on coming back to Griffin Hall with me, and I couldn't find it in me to say no. Not while we were surrounded by the dismembered bodies of her fellow Sisters. Besides, she had the Hand of Glory, the only way of getting us all the way across the Nightside to Griffin Hall in a single moment. So I agreed, and Sister Josephine made me wait while she loaded herself up with extra guns, grenades, and incendiaries, just in case. I had to smile.

"I really must introduce you to my girl-friend. You have so much in common."

The nun snorted loudly. "I seriously doubt it. Right, that's it. I'm ready. Time to go."

She looked around the deserted chapel one last time, making herself look at every dead and mutilated body so that she'd be in a proper frame of mind when she arrived at Griffin Hall. And then she lit the candles on the Hand's waxy fingers, and stabbed them at the door before her. The heavy wood bulged and rippled, shaking in its frame as though scared of what was being asked of it, and it swung open abruptly, revealing only darkness beyond. I walked through with Sister Josephine close on my heels.

But when I reappeared, I was still a long way short of Griffin Hall. I was right in the middle of the jungle surrounding the Hall, and there was no sign of Sister Josephine anywhere. My first instinct was to retreat back through the door, but when I looked behind me it was gone, too. Thin shafts of shimmering moonlight drifted down through the thick overhead canopy, painting silvery highlights on the trembling leaves and slowly stirring vegetation. There were strange lights in between the trees, and slow, heavy sounds deep in the earth. And all around me, slow, malevolent movement in the jungle, as it realised who it had at its mercy.

The Hall's defences must be working overtime. They couldn't stop a powerful working like the Hand of Glory, but they could keep me out of the Hall itself, by dumping me here. In the jungle. Where the plants are always hungry . . .

The vegetation was rising up all around me now, flowers opening out to reveal sharp teeth and spiny maws, barbed branches reaching towards me, lianas uncurling like strangling ropes. Even the trees were wrenching their roots up out of the wet earth in their eagerness to get at me. The jungle remembered me and hated me with all of its parts in a slow, cold rage.

I was surrounded by enemies and a long way from help. Situation normal in my line of business. I fished a couple of basic incendiaries out of my coat-pockets, primed them quickly, and tossed them where I thought they'd do the most good. Explosions rocked the jungle and lit up the night, and rustling vegetation everywhere flared up into wildly burning shapes. They shook back and forth, trying to throw off the flames that were consuming them, but only succeeded in spreading the fires further. The rising light pushed back the night, giving me a better look at my surroundings. Griffin Hall was just visible through the trees, right up at the top of the hill. It wasn't that far. I could make it.

The jungle heaved all around me, the trees beating at the flames with heavy branches, while everything else withdrew out of the fire's reach. Thin reedy screams filled the night as unnatural plants were consumed by artificial fires. But the flames were already dying down, and soon there would be nothing left to keep the jungle at bay. Except . . . the plants seemed as much afraid of the fire's light as the heat. I raised my gift and found a place outside the Nightside where the sun was shining bright; and I reached out and brought the sunlight to me. A great circle of blindingly bright light stabbed down from above, surrounding me with warm, healthy daylight.

The jungle hated it. Even as I screwed up my eyes against the unaccustomed glare, the night-dwelling plants shrivelled and shrank back from the daylight, shrinking in upon themselves. Flower petals darkened and fell away, tree trunks blistered, and branches hauled themselves back out of the scorching light. Leaves curled up, lianas retreated back into the shadows, and some of the trees actually groaned under the impact of the daylight.

"Listen up!" I said loudly. "I don't have time for this shit. I am going to Griffin Hall, and if anything at all gets in my way, I will make it a bright summer's day here for weeks on end!"

I was bluffing, but the jungle didn't know that. I strode purposefully forward, the circle of light moving with me, and all the plants in my way shrank back to give me plenty of room. I ran through the jungle, pushing the pace as much as I dared. Melissa was back in the Hall and in deadly danger, and probably the rest of the family, too. Time was running out for all the Griffins. The Devil would be here soon to claim his due, and then there'd be Hell to pay.

I finally lurched out of the jungle, exhausted and wringing with sweat, shaking in every limb and fighting for breath. I'm built for stamina, not speed. The daylight snapped off the moment I left the jungle and stepped into the courtyard, as though healthy natural light was not permitted in this place. I leaned against the open metal gates while I got my breath back and checked out the situation. I actually felt better without the light. Maintaining it for so long really had taken it out of me. I wiped the sweat from my face with my coat-sleeve and looked around me.

The first thing I noticed was that there weren't any

cars parked in the courtyard. All the guests had been sent home. Lights were burning in every window of Griffin Hall, but there was something . . . wrong about those lights. They were too bright, too fierce, and unnaturally piercing. And the whole place was deathly silent. Looking at Griffin Hall now felt like looking into an open grave. I took one final deep breath, to steady me, and headed straight for the front door. Nothing and no-one appeared to stop me. When I got to the door, it was locked. And when the Hall's defences blocked Sister Josephine, they also kept out her Hand of Glory.

I shook the handle hard, just in case, but the door was very big and very heavy, and it hardly moved in its frame. I didn't even bother trying my shoulder against it. I checked the lock; it was large and blocky and very solid-looking. I knew a few unofficial ways to open stubborn locks but nothing that would get past the Hall's powerful defences. I suddenly remembered the golden key Paul had pressed on me as he was dying. He must have known it would come to this. I fished the key out of my coat-pocket and tried it in the door lock, but it didn't fit. Not even close. I put the key away again and scowled at the closed door. I hadn't come this far, got this close, to be stopped by a simple locked door. So when in doubt, think laterally.

I ran quickly through a mental list of what I had on me, searching for anything useful, then smiled suddenly and took out the aboriginal pointing bone. I stabbed the bone at the door, saying all the right Words, and the heavy wood of the door heaved and buckled as though trying to flinch away from the awful thing that was killing it. The wood cracked and blackened, rotting and decaying in moments, and great holes opened up in the spongy dead matter. I put the bone away and thrust both hands into the sagging holes, tearing at them until I finally had a gap big enough to force my way through.

I strode forward, expecting to be confronted by an army of heavily armed guards and even some shocked servants, but the great echoing lobby was empty. Deserted. And still the Hall was eerily silent, with not a sound or sign of life anywhere. I couldn't allow myself to believe I'd arrived too late. There was still time. I could feel it. I raised my gift to find where the Griffin family was, and once again Something from outside forced my inner eye shut with brutal strength. I cried out from the horrid pain that filled my head. I staggered back and forth, forcing down the pain through sheer force of will. The effort left me panting and shaken. It felt like a bomb had just exploded inside my head.

And it seemed to me that not all that far away, I could hear Something laughing, taunting me.

I stood up straight, pulling the last of my strength around me like armour. I didn't need my gift. I knew where the Griffin family was, where they had to be. In the one place forbidden to everyone but the Griffin himself—the old cellar underneath the Hall. I moved quickly through the ground floor, looking for a way down. And I discovered what had happened to all the guards and servants. They were dead, every one of them, mutilated and murdered like the nuns in the chapel. Torn apart, gutted, dismembered, and disfigured. But at least these bodies still had their heads. Every face was stretched and distorted with the agony and horror of their final moments. I would have liked to stop and close all the staring eyes, but there wasn't time.

Because the bodies had been laid out in a single

line . . . carefully arranged to lead me on, to the door that led down to the cellar. Servants in their old-fashioned uniforms, guards in their body armour; they'd all died just as easily and as horribly. Blood pooled everywhere, most of it still sticky to the touch, and long, crimson streaks trailed across the walls in arterial spatter. The air was thick with the stench of it, and when I breathed through my mouth I could still taste the copper. I finally reached the end of the line and stood before the door that had helpfully been left just a little ajar, inviting me to go on down to the cellar . . . I knew what was waiting for me down there, eager to show me what he'd done with the Griffin family, and Melissa.

I pushed the door all the way open with one hand. A long line of stone steps fell away into the earth, the way brightly lit with paper lanterns. And sitting slumped against the bare stone wall on every other step was a dead servant or guard, carefully propped up to stare down the steps with dead eyes. I prodded the nearest one with a cautious finger. The dead body rocked slightly but showed no signs of rising to attack me. I started down the steps, sticking carefully to the middle, and as I passed by the dead men, now and again one would slowly lift his head and look at me and whisper secrets in a lost, far-away voice.

*"The fires burn so hot here. Even the birds burn here."*

*"Something's holding my hand and it won't let go."*

*"They drink our tears like wine."*

*"We don't like being dead. It's not what they told us it would be like. You won't like it either."*

I did my best not to listen to them. Hell's business is despair, and it always lies. Except when the truth can hurt you more.

• • •

I finally came to the bottom of the steps. It took a long time. I had no idea how far down I'd come, but I had to be deep under the Hall by now, maybe right at the heart of the hill upon which Griffin Hall sat. (*They say he raised up the hill and the Hall in a single night . . .*) The door to the cellar was a perfectly ordinary-looking door, again standing slightly ajar, inviting me in. I kicked it open and strode into the stone chamber beyond as though I had an army at my back. And sure enough, there they all were—the Griffin family. Jeremiah and Mariah, William and Gloria, Eleanor and Marcel, all of them crucified, nailed to the cold stone walls. Blood still dripped from the cruel wounds at their pierced wrists and ankles. They looked at me silently, with wide, pleading eyes, afraid to say anything. Melissa Griffin sat alone in the middle of the stone floor, inside a pentacle whose lines had been laid out in her family's blood. She was still wearing the tattered remains of her black-and-white novice's habit, though the wimple had been torn away. Someone had beaten the crap out of her, probably just because they could. Blood had dried on her bruised and swollen face, but there was still a calm, stubborn grace in her eyes when she looked at me.

I nodded and smiled reassuringly, as much for me as for her. My first thought was how much she looked like Paul as Polly, but there was an inner light and peace in Melissa that Paul had never found. I walked carefully forward and knelt before Melissa, careful not to touch any of the lines of the pentacle.

"Hello, Melissa. I'm John Taylor. I've been looking for you. It's good to meet you at last. Don't worry. I'll get you out of here."

"And my family?" said Melissa.

"I'll do what I can," I said. "It might be too late for some of them, but I specialise in lost causes."

"Of course you do, Mr. Taylor," said a calm, hateful, familiar voice. "After all, you're the greatest lost cause of all."

I looked around and there he was, leaning against the far wall with his arms casually folded across his chest, smiling like he had all the answers and several aces tucked up his sleeve. The man behind it all, right from the beginning. The man I'd Seen slaughter all those nuns in the chapel.

The butler, Hobbes.

I rose slowly to my feet and turned to look at him. "I knew there was something wrong about you from the start, but I just couldn't bring myself to believe the butler did it."

"Welcome to the real heart and soul of Griffin Hall, Mr. Taylor. So glad you could attend. The floor show will begin soon."

"The devil you say." I started towards him, but stopped as he pushed himself away from the wall. Without actually doing anything, he was suddenly very dangerous and not at all human. I adopted a casual stance and gave him my best sneer. "I should have known it was you the moment I heard your name. Hob is an old name for the Devil. Your name isn't Hobbes, it's Hob's—belonging to the Devil."

"Exactly," said Hobbes. "It's amazing how many people miss the most obvious things even when you thrust them right under their stupid mortal noses."

"Enough," I said. "We're well past the time for civilised

conversation. Show me your real face. Show me what you really are."

He laughed at me. "Your limited human mind couldn't cope with all the awful things I am. Just one glimpse of my true nature would blow your little mind apart. But there is a shape I like to use, when I am summoned to this dreary mortal plane . . ."

He stretched and twisted in a way that had nothing to do with the geometries of the material world, and in a moment Hobbes was gone and something else was standing in his place. Something that had never been, never could be, merely human. It was huge, almost twelve feet tall, bent over to fit into the stone-walled cellar, its horned head scraping against the ceiling. It had blood-red skin covered in seeping plague sores and great membranous batwings that stretched around it like a ribbed crimson cloak. It had cloven hoofs and clawed hands. It was hermaphrodite, with grossly swollen male and female parts. It stank of sulphur and suffering. And its face . . . I had to look away for a moment. Its face was full of all the evil and pain and horror in the world.

The Griffin family all cried out at the first sight of the demon in its true form, and I think I did, too.

"A bit medieval, I know," said Hobbes, in a soft, purring voice like spoiled meat and babies crying and the growl of a hungry wolf. "But I always was a traditionalist. If a thing works, stick with it, that's what I say."

"Fight him, Taylor!" said Jeremiah Griffin. And even crucified to a wall in his own cellar, some of the Griffin's strength and arrogance still came through. "Stop him before he destroys us all!"

Hobbes looked at me interestedly, a long red hairless tail slithering round its hoofs. I stood very still. I was thinking hard. I didn't dare rush into anything. In this place we were all in danger, not just of our lives, but of our souls as well. This wasn't one of the minor demons, like those I'd bluffed successfully in the past—this was the real deal. A Duke of Hell, and Hell was very near now, getting closer by the moment. I had to find a way out of this mess and be long gone before the Devil arrived to claim what was owed him. Hobbes said it was a traditional sort, so . . . I pulled a silver crucifix out of my coat-pocket, pre-blessed with holy water, and thrust it at Hobbes. The crucifix exploded in my hand, and I cried out in agony as silver fragments were thrust deep into my palm and inner fingers. Hobbes laughed, and the sound of it made me shudder.

"This is Hell's territory," it said calmly. "A shape is only a shape unless you have the faith to back it up. Have you ever had faith in anything, Mr. Taylor?"

*Don't try and argue with it. They always lie. Except when the truth can hurt you more . . .*

"How long?" I said, cradling my injured hand against my chest. "How long have you been masquerading as the Griffin's butler?"

"I've always been the Griffin's butler," said Hobbes. "Right from the very beginning. But I changed my face and form down the centuries, disappearing as one man and reappearing as another, and no-one ever noticed, least of all the Griffin. No-one notices servants. I stayed very close to him as he built his precious empire on the blood and suffering and wasted lives of others, dropping the odd word of advice here, a suggestion there, to see my master's work done. My true master . . . For I was always my master's servant, and never Jeremiah's . . ."

"How did you get into the Nightside?" I said. "This

place was designed to be free from the direct interventions of Heaven or Hell."

"I was invited," said Hobbes. "And Above and Below have always had their agents in the Nightside. You know that better than most. I'm so glad you found your way here, John. It wouldn't be the same without you here, watching helplessly as I win at last."

"You can save that crap," I said. "I'm here because you couldn't keep me out, despite all your efforts. You were the one who kept interfering with my gift. I should have spotted it only ever happened when you were around. And now you're scared shitless I'll find some way to stop you, after all your hard work, and cheat the Devil of his prize. Your master can be very hard on those who fail him . . ."

"I led you here," said Hobbes. "I laid out the dead, to bring you down . . ."

"You put them there to frighten me off," I said. "But I don't frighten that easy."

"Even you can't break a compact willingly entered into with Hell!"

I had to smile. "I've been breaking the rules all my life."

"My master will be here very soon," said Hobbes. "And if you are here when he rises through that pentacle to claim his own, he will drag you down into Hell along with the others."

"Answer me this," I said. I was playing for time, and Hobbes had to know it, but its kind love to boast. "Why should the Devil grant a man such a long life if not actual immortality?"

"Because it corrupts," Hobbes said easily. "Knowing that you can get away with anything. Jeremiah has done such terrible things, in his many years, and never once been punished for any of it. He made himself rich and powerful in awful ways, and so, through example, led many others into temptation and corruption. This one man has brought about the downfall of thousands, even hundreds of thousands, directly and indirectly. Spreading evil down the centuries as his business grew and spread. Based on evil, infecting others with its evil. We're all very pleased with what Jeremiah has achieved, doing Hell's work for so long . . . You won't believe the welcome we've got planned for him and his family, in the very hottest flames of the Inferno."

"Not Melissa," I said.

Hobbes snorted loudly. "Who could have foreseen that such a man, steeped in centuries of evil, would go soft over a pretty face? But as time runs out, the damned often search for a way to wriggle out of the deal they made, to undo the evil they've done. All they really have to do is repent, honestly and truly, and Hell couldn't touch them. But of course, if they were the kind who could repent, they wouldn't make a deal with the Devil in the first place. Jeremiah, at least, was less hypocritical than most. He thought by leaving his empire to a pure soul, she could at least redeem his legacy. But that couldn't be allowed. I've put too much work into ensuring that Jeremiah's evil will live on after him, corrupting others for years to come, because only a business can be truly immortal."

"Look, I shouldn't even be here," Gloria said frantically. "I never made any deal! I'm not even really a Griffin! I just married into the family!"

"Right!" said Marcel. "None of this is any of my business! Please, let me go. I won't say anything . . ."

"You became immortal because of the deal Jeremiah made," said Hobbes. "You profited from it, that makes you culpable. Now stop whining, both of you, or I'll rip your tongues out. Soon enough it will be time for all Griffins to go down . . . All the way down . . ."

I still hadn't thought of anything, and I was getting desperate. "Tell me about Melissa," I said. "Why are you keeping her separate? Isn't she damned, too, as a Griffin?"

"She has sworn her soul to Heaven," said Hobbes. "And so has put it beyond Hell's reach. So I'll simply kill her, slowly and horribly, in the time remaining. And see if perhaps agony and horror and despair will lead her to renounce her faith. And then she will be Hell's property again and join her family, forever. Oh little Sister, meek and mild, hope you're feeling strong, my child."

"Don't you dare touch her!" yelled Jeremiah, straining against the iron nails that pinned him to the wall. "Taylor, do something! I don't matter, but my family can still be saved! Do whatever you have to, but save my children and Melissa!"

"You bastard!" screeched Mariah. "All our years together, and you don't even think of me?"

Jeremiah turned his head painfully to look at her. "I would save you if I could, my love, but after all the things we've done . . . Do you really think Heaven would take us now? We gloried in our crimes and our sins, and now we have to pay the price. Show some backbone, woman." He looked at me again. "Save them, Taylor. Nothing else matters."

"Who cares about the bloody children?" wailed Mariah. "I never wanted them! I don't want to die! You promised me we would live forever and never have to die!"

Jeremiah smiled. "What man doesn't lie to a woman to get what he wants?"

I looked at Melissa, crouched, shocked, and hurt but somehow still unbowed in the middle of the bloody pentacle. It was still hard for me to look at her and not think of Polly . . . Which made me think again of the golden key Paul had pressed on me so desperately as he was dying. It had to open something important, but what? A small golden key . . . like the one Jeremiah used to open a hidden door in the ballroom. Could there be another hidden space, down here in the cellar? And if so, what could it hold? And then I remembered Jeremiah telling me that the original document of his compact with the Devil was kept down here in the cellar, under lock and key, because although the document couldn't be destroyed, the terms could still be rewritten . . . by someone with the right connections to Heaven or Hell . . .

I fired up my gift, my inner eye started to open, and then it slammed shut again as Hobbes closed it down. I fought the demon, using all my strength, but it was a demon and I was only mortal . . . I looked desperately at Melissa.

"Help me, Melissa! I can help you and your family, but you have to help me! That pentacle can't hold you, a Bride of Christ! It is a thing of Hell, and you are sworn to Heaven! Fight it!"

As exhausted and battered and beaten down as she was, Melissa nodded and threw herself against the invisible wall of the pentacle. In her own very different way, Melissa could be as strong and determined as her grandfather. She slammed against the invisible wall again and again, even though it hurt her, chanting prayers aloud, while her grandfather laughed and cheered her on. Mariah was crying hysterically, William and Eleanor encouraged Melissa as best they could, and Gloria and Marcel watched silently, not quite daring to hope . . . And while the demon Hobbes looked this way and that, thrown for the moment by this sudden rebellion from those it had thought cowed and broken, I concentrated on my gift . . . and forced my inner eye open in spite of him.

My Sight showed me a secret space behind the wall to my left, and a concealed lock hidden in the stonework. I lurched over to it, jammed the golden key into the lock, and opened it. A section of the wall slid back, revealing an old roll of parchment tucked into a crevice in the stone. I pulled the parchment out and unrolled it. I know a little Latin, just enough to recognise the real thing when I saw it. A contract with Hell, signed by Jeremiah Griffin in his own blood.

I took out a biro and quickly crossed out the clauses applying to Jeremiah's descendants. And prayed that the remains of the blessed crucifix still embedded in my writing hand would add enough sanctity to make the change binding.

The demon Hobbes gave up concentrating on keeping Melissa inside her pentacle and turned on me, howling with rage. Fire blazed at me from an outstretched hand, but I held the parchment up before me, the contract that could not be destroyed by anything . . . and the fire couldn't reach me. And then the nails holding William and Eleanor and Gloria and Marcel to the wall jerked out of their pierced flesh and disappeared, and the four of them fell helplessly onto the cold stone floor. They struggled to get up onto their feet, while Hobbes stood frozen in shock and surprise.

"Get me down!" shrieked Mariah. "You can't leave me here!"

"Of course they can," said Jeremiah. "We are where we belong, darling. Taylor, get my family out of here!"

Melissa burst through the barrier of the pentacle and fell sprawling at my feet. I hauled her up.

"No!" roared Hobbes, in a voice too loud and too awful to be borne. "I'll see you all dead before I let you go!"

And I used my gift to find the sunlight again, and bring it to me, right there in the cellar deep under Griffin Hall. Brilliant sunshine smashed down on Hobbes, holding it in a bright circle like a bug transfixed on a pin. Hobbes screamed, and Jeremiah laughed. Melissa grabbed my arm.

"Please, can't you help him . . . ?"

"No," I said. "He sealed his fate long ago. He is where he's supposed to be. But you're not, and neither are the others. There's still hope for them. Help me get them out of here."

"*Hurry!*" howled Jeremiah, fighting to be heard over Hobbes's screams. "*He's coming!*"

I could feel it. Something huge and unspeakable was rising inexorably from the place beneath all places, come to claim what was his. We had to get out while we still could. Between us, Melissa and I got the others moving. The stone floor was rocking and breaking apart under our feet. A terrible presence was beating on the air, and none of us dared look back. Jeremiah was still laughing, and Mariah was screaming in horror. I pushed the Griffin family through the cellar door. And suddenly we were standing in the courtyard, outside the front door of Griffin Hall, and there was Sister Josephine with the Hand of Glory held out before her.

"I told you they couldn't keep me out!" she said, and hurried forward to help with the walking wounded. We made our way as quickly as we could across the empty courtyard, then we stopped and looked back as all the lights in the Hall suddenly went out. With a long, loud groan like a dying beast, the great building slowly collapsed in on itself, crumbling and decaying, and finally disappeared into a huge sucking pit at the top of the hill.

We all stood together, thinking our own thoughts and holding each other up, and watched the fall of the house of Griffin.

# EPILOGUE

I don't do funerals. I don't like the settings or the services, and I know far too much about Heaven and Hell to take much comfort from the rituals. I don't visit people's graves to say good-bye, because I know they're not there. We only bury what gets left behind. And besides, most of the time I'm glad the people concerned are dead and not bothering me anymore.

The only ghosts that haunt me are memories.

So I didn't go to Paul Griffin's funeral. But I did go to visit his grave a few weeks later. Just to pay my respects. Suzie Shooter came along, to keep me company. Paul was buried in the Necropolis graveyard, in its own very private and separate dimension. It was cold and dark and silent, with a low ground mist curling slowly around the endless rows of headstones, statues, and mausoleums. I stood before Paul's grave, and Suzie slipped her arm lightly through mine.

"Do you still feel guilty about his death?" she said after a while.

"I always feel guilty about the ones I can't save," I said.

The simple marble headstone said PAUL AND POLLY GRIFFIN; BELOVED SON AND DAUGHTER. I was pretty sure I detected Eleanor's way with words there. Paul would have smiled. The mound of earth hadn't settled yet. The large wreath from all the girls at Divas! was made up entirely of plastic flowers, bright and colourful and artificial. Just like Polly.

Not that far away stood a huge stone mausoleum, in the old Victorian style, with exaggerated pillars and cornices and altogether too many carved stone cherubs. The oversized brass plaque on the front door proudly declared to one and all that the mausoleum was the last resting place of Jeremiah and Mariah Griffin. Only the names; no dates and no words. Jeremiah paid for the ugly thing ages ago, not because he thought he'd ever need it, but because such things were the fashion, and Mariah had to have everything that was in fashion. And of course her mausoleum had to be bigger and more ornate than everyone else's. I was surprised she hadn't had the stone cherubs carved thumbing their turned-up noses at everyone else.

Of course, Jeremiah and Mariah weren't in there. Their bodies were never recovered.

"I hear Melissa joined a convent after all," Suzie said finally.

"Yeah, a contemplative order, tucked away from the world, like she wanted. Attached to, though not really a part of, the Salvation Army Sisterhood. So she should be safe enough."

"She's the richest nun in the Nightside."

"Actually, no. She did inherit everything, according to the terms of the final will, but she gave most of it away. William and Eleanor were guaranteed very generous life-

SIMON R. GREEN

time stipends, via a trust, in return for not contesting the
will, and everything else went to the Sisterhood. Who are
currently rebuilding their church and fast becoming one
of the main movers and shakers on the Street of the Gods.
Evil-doers beware. God alone knows what kind of armaments the SAS could buy with an unlimited budget . . ."

"And William and Eleanor?"

"Both getting used to being only mortal, now that
Jeremiah is gone. Since they're not immortal or inheritors
anymore, Society and business and politics have pretty much
turned their backs on the pair of them, which is probably a
good thing. Give them a chance to make their own lives, at
last. William's off visiting Shadows Fall, with Bruin Bear
and the Sea Goat. They're the only real friends he ever had.
Eleanor's gone into seclusion, still mourning her child. But
she'll be back. She's tougher than anyone thinks. Even her."

"You think their spouses will stick around?"

"Probably not," I said. "But you never know. People
can surprise you."

Suzie snorted loudly. "Not if you keep your guard up
and a shell in the chamber." She looked around her.
"Depressing bloody place, this. All the ambience of an
armpit. Promise me you'll never let me end up here, John."

I smiled and hugged her arm briefly against my side.
"I do know of a place, called Arcadia. Where it's calm
and peaceful and the sun always shine, and only good
things happen. We could lie side by side on a grassy
bank, beside a flowing river . . ."

Suzie laughed raucously, shaking her head. "You
soppy sentimental old thing. I was thinking more along
the lines of being buried under a bar, so there'd always be
music and laughter, and people could pour their drinks on
the floor as a libation to us."

"That does sound more like you," I admitted. "But the kind of bars we frequent, someone would be bound to dig us up for a laugh."

"Anyone disturbs my rest, I'll disturb them right back," Suzie said firmly. "It's in my will that I'm to be buried with my shotgun and a good supply of ammunition."

I nodded solemnly. "I thought I'd have my coffin booby-trapped. Just in case. Maybe something nuclear."

Suddenly Suzie pulled away from me and drew her shotgun from its rear holster in one smooth movement. I followed her gaze, and there was Walker, standing calmly at the other end of Paul's grave. I hadn't heard him approach, but then I never did. He smiled easily at Suzie and me.

"Such a dramatic reaction," he murmured. "Anyone would think I wasn't welcome."

"Anyone would be right," I said. "How did you know we'd be here?"

"I know everything," said Walker. "That's my job."

"Come to check that the Griffins are really dead?" said Suzie, not lowering her shotgun.

"Simply paying my respects," said Walker. "One must observe the proprieties."

"Anyone interesting turn up at the funerals?" I said.

"Oh, only the usual suspects. Friends and enemies, and rather a lot of interested observers. Nothing like a dead celebrity to bring out the crowds and the paparazzi. It was quite a social gathering. Mariah will be furious she missed it."

Suzie snorted loudly. "Half of them probably turned up to dance before the Griffin's mausoleum, or piss on it."

"There was quite a queue," Walker admitted. "Some people waited for hours. And yet, a lot of the people who matter aren't convinced the Griffin is really dead. They think that this is another of his intricate and underhanded schemes, and he's still out there somewhere, plotting . . ."

"No," I said. "He's gone."

Walker shrugged. "Even being dead doesn't necessarily mean departed. Not in the Nightside. So everyone's being very cautious."

"What did you think of him?" I said, honestly curious. "The Griffin?"

"A man whose reach exceeded his grasp," said Walker. "A lesson there for all of us, perhaps."

"Why are you here, Walker?" said Suzie. Her shotgun was still trained on his face, but he didn't even look at it.

"I'm here for you, John," said Walker. "Suzie already works for me as one of my field operatives."

"Only when I feel like it," Suzie growled. Walker ignored her, his calm gaze fixed on me.

"I want you to work for me, John, full-time. Help me keep the peace in this ungodly cesspit, and ease the transition of power that will inevitably follow the Griffin's death."

"No," I said.

"Well, thank you for thinking about it," said Walker.

"I don't have to think about it." I met his gaze steadily and did everything I could to make my voice as cold as the cemetery we were standing in. "You're a political animal, Walker, always have been. You will do whatever you feel is necessary, or expedient, to maintain order and the status quo. And to hell with whoever might get hurt or killed in the process."

Walker smiled. "How well you know me, John. And

that's why I want you. Because like me, you'll do whatever it takes to get the job done."

"I'm nothing like you, Walker."

"Well, if you ever change your mind, you know where to find me." He started to turn away, then looked back at me. "Change is coming, John. Choose a side. While you still can."

He tipped his bowler hat to us and walked away, disappearing into the mists and the shadows. Suzie finally lowered her shotgun and put it away.

"That man is such a drama queen . . ."

"That man worries me," I said. "He's still running things in the Nightside, inasmuch as anyone does, or can, even though the Authorities are all dead and gone. So who's backing him now? Where is he getting his power from? What kind of deal did he make to stay in charge?"

"There are lots of other people who'd like to run things," Suzie said carelessly. "He won't have it all his own way."

"When the lions die, the jackals gather to feast," I said. "I guess we're in for some interesting times in the Nightside."

"Best kind," said Suzie.

We laughed, and arm in arm we walked out of the cemetery.

"Not the most successful case I ever worked on," I said.

"You found the missing girl. That's all that matters. Hey, you never did tell me how much the Griffin paid you?"

I smiled.

# The
# unnatural
# enquirer

# ONE

# The wrath of the Loa

One of the many problems with working as a private eye, not counting all the many people who want to kill you, often for perfectly good reasons, is that you have to wait for the work to come to you. And since I refuse to sit around my office, on the grounds that all the high tech my secretary, Cathy, has installed intimidates the hell out of me, I seem to spend most of my time sitting around in bars, waiting for something to happen. Not a bad way to spend your life, all told. But in the end, cases are a lot like buses; you wait around for ages, then three come along at once.

I'm a private eye of the old school, right down to the long white trench coat, the less-than-traditional good looks, and the roguish air of mystery that I go to great lengths to maintain. Always keep them guessing. A good, or more properly bad, reputation can protect you from more things than a Kevlar jump-suit. I investigate cases of the weird and uncanny, the sins and problems too dark and too nasty even for the Nightside. I don't do divorce work, and I don't carry a gun. I've never felt the need.

I'd just finished a fairly straightforward case, when trouble came looking for me. I'd been called in by the slightly hysterical manager of one of the Nightside's most prominent libraries, the H P Lovecraft Memorial Library. Their proud boast: more forbidden tomes under one roof than anywhere else. I'd leafed through some of their proud exhibits in the past and hadn't been impressed. Of course they had the *Necronomicon*, in forty-eight languages, including Braille, and one of the few unexpurgated texts of *The Gospel According to Pontius Pilate*. They even had *Satan's Last Testament*, originally tattooed on the inside of the womb of the Fallen Nun of Lourdes. But a lot of it was strictly tourist stuff. *The Book of Unpronounceable Cults*, *Satanism for Dummies*, and *Coarse Fishing on the River Styx*. Nothing there to expand your mind or endanger your soul.

I'd been called in because twenty-seven of the Library's patrons had been discovered wandering through the stacks wide-eyed and mind-wiped. Not a trace of personality or conscious thought left in them. Which was unusually high for a Monday morning, even in the H P Lovecraft Memorial Library. Using my gift, it didn't take me long to discover that a recently acquired treatise had been reading people . . . I persuaded the book to put the minds back, mostly in the right bodies, and introduced it to the wonders of the Internet. Which should keep it occupied until the Library could send it somewhere else.

So, happy smiles all round, a wallet full of cash (I don't take cheques or plastic, don't ask for credit, as a refusal might involve a back elbow between the eyes), and all in all I was feeling quite pleased with myself . . . until I left the Library and looked down the steps to find Walker and Suzie Shooter waiting for me at the bottom. Probably two of the most dangerous people in the Nightside.

Suzie Shooter, also known as Shotgun Suzie, and *Oh Christ It's Her Run*, is the Nightside's leading bounty hunter. Have shotgun and grenades, will travel. A tall blonde Valkyrie in black motor-cycle leathers, with two bandoliers of bullets criss-crossing over her ample bosom, steel-toed boots, and the coldest gaze in the world. The whole left side of her face was covered in ridged scar tissue, sealing shut one eye and twisting up one side of her mouth in a constant caustic smile. She could have had it fixed easily, but she chose not to. She said it was good for business. It did give her a grim, wounded glamour.

Suzie and I are an item. Safe to say neither of us saw that one coming. We love each other, as best we can.

Walker is even more dangerous to be around, though in more subtle and indirect ways. He looks very much like your average city gent; pin-striped suit, bowler hat, calm air of authority. Someone in the City, you might think, or perhaps a Permanent Under-Secretary to some Minister you never heard of. But Walker polices the Nightside, inasmuch as anyone does, or can. In a place where everything is permitted, and sin and temptation are the order of every day, there are still lines that must not be crossed. For those who do, Walker is waiting.

He used to represent the Authorities, those grey faceless men who owned everything that mattered and took a profit from every dirty and dangerous transaction in the Nightside. Walker spoke in their name, with the Voice they gave him that could not be disobeyed, and he could call in the Army or the Church to back him up, as necessary. But since all the Authorities were killed and eaten during the Lilith War, lots of people had been wondering just where Walker drew his authority from these days. He still had his Voice, and his backup, so everyone went along.

But an awful lot of people were waiting for the other shoe to drop.

He smiled and nodded at me politely, but I ignored him on principle and gave my full attention to Suzie.

"Hello, sweetie. I haven't seen you for a few days."

"I've been working," she said, in her cold, steady voice. "Chasing down a bounty."

"For Walker?" I said, raising an eyebrow.

She shrugged easily, the butt of the shotgun holstered on her back rising briefly behind her head. "His money is as good as anyone else's. And you know I need to keep busy. I only really feel alive when it's death or glory time. You finished with your case?"

"Yes," I said, glancing reluctantly at Walker.

"Then walk with me, John," he said. "I could use your assistance on a rather urgent case."

I went down the steps to join him, taking my time. I'd worked with Walker before, on occasion, though rarely happily. He paid well enough, but he only ever used me for those cases where he didn't want to risk his own people. The kind of cases where he needed someone potentially deniable and utterly expendable. We strode together through the Nightside, Walker on my left and Suzie on my right, and everyone else made sure to give us plenty of room.

"I hired Suzie because someone big and important had gone missing," Walker said easily. "And I needed him found, fast. Nothing unusual there. But unfortunately, Suzie has proven entirely unable to locate the target."

"Not my fault," Suzie said immediately. "I've been through all my usual contacts, and none of them could tell me anything. Even after all the usual bribes and beatings. The man's just vanished. Jumped into a deep hole and pulled it in after him. I'm not even sure he's still in the Nightside."

"Oh, he's still here," said Walker. "I'd know if he'd left."

"Who exactly are we talking about?" I said.

"Max Maxwell," said Walker. "Ah; I take it from your expression that you have at least heard of him."

"Who hasn't?" I said. "Max Maxwell; so big they named him twice. Night-club owner, gang boss, fence, and fixer. Also known as the Voodoo Apostate, though I couldn't tell you why."

"The very man," said Walker. "A well-established, very well-connected individual. He tried to have me killed twice, but I'm not one to bear grudges. Anyway, it would appear dear Max came into possession of something rather special, something he should have had more sense than to get involved with. To be exact, the Aquarius Key."

"I know the name," I said, frowning. "Some artifact from the sixties, isn't it? Back when every Major Player had to have their very own Object of Power to be taken seriously. I've never trusted the things. You can never tell when the cosmic batteries are suddenly going to run out of juice, and you're left standing there with a silly-looking lump of art deco in your hand."

"Quite," said Walker. "Still, a very useful tool, the Aquarius Key. Part scientific, part magical, it was created to open and close dimensional doors. This was after the Babalon Working fiasco, you understand."

"Why . . . Aquarius?" I said.

Walker shrugged. "It was the Age. Word is, the Collector had it for a time, which was how he was able to start his marvellous collection of rare and fashionable items. Then he lost it in a card game to old blind Pew, and after that the Key went wandering through many hands, causing mischief and mayhem as it went, until finally it ended up in the possession of Max Maxwell. Where it apparently gave him ideas above his station."

"And that's how he became the Voodoo Apostate?" I said.

"Unfortunately, yes," said Walker. "Voodoo is, first and foremost, a religion in its own right. Its followers worship a wide pantheon of gods, or loas: Papa Legba, Baron Samedi, Erzulie, and Damballa. These personages can be summoned, or invited, into our world, where they possess willing worshippers. Max made himself Apostate by using the power of the Key to drag the loa into this world, whether they wanted to come or not, then thrust them into his own people. Who could then be commanded to serve him in all kinds of useful ways. Inhumanly strong, utterly unfeeling, and almost impossible to kill, they made formidable shock troops."

I winced. "Messing with gods. Always a bad idea."

"Always," said Walker. "Max used his new shock troops to enlarge his territory, with much slaughter and terror; which brought him to my attention. Inevitably, Max became greedy and overstretched himself, spread his control too thin; and the loa broke loose. Max didn't wait for them to come looking for him. He went on the run, taking the Key with him, and none of my people have been able to find him. So I turned to Suzie, with her excellent reputation for finding people who don't want to be found."

Suzie growled something indistinct. I wouldn't want

to be Max Maxwell when she finally got to him. She took a target's attempts to escape capture as a personal insult.

"What makes this case so urgent that you need me?" I said. "Suzie will find him. Eventually."

"The loa have come to the Nightside," said Walker. "And they are not in a good mood. They have possessed a whole crowd of the very best bounty hunters and are currently rampaging through the Nightside, on the trail of Max Maxwell."

"Let them have him," I said. "The man is scum. A jumped-up leg-breaker, who used his voodoo to run protection rackets. Pay up, or he'd turn you into a zombie. You, or someone in your family. Nasty man. Let the loa tear him apart. The Nightside will smell better when he's gone."

"Right," said Suzie. "Wait a minute; if the loa have been possessing all the best bounty hunters . . . why didn't they choose me? I'm the best there is, and I'll shoot the kneecaps off anyone who says otherwise. Why didn't the loa come after me?"

"They wouldn't dare," I said, gallantly.

"Well, there is that, yes," said Suzie. "And unlike some, I'm always careful to keep my protections up to date. A girl can't be too careful."

I pitied anyone or anything dumb enough to dive into Suzie's steel-trap mind, but I wasn't dumb enough to say so out loud. Besides, a new idea had just occurred to me. I looked at Walker.

"Max still has the Aquarius Key. And you want me to get it back for you."

"I knew you'd get there eventually," said Walker. "I want you to find Max and take the Key away from him. Then bring it back to me, so I can stow it away somewhere safe and see Max locked safely away in Shadow Deep."

I would have shuddered, but it was never wise to show weakness in front of Walker. Shadow Deep is the worst prison in the world, carved out of the bedrock deep under the Nightside. It's where we put the really bad ones; or at least the ones we can't just execute and be done with, for one reason or another. Forever dark, never a glimmer of light, once they've sealed you up in your cell, you never leave again. You stay there in your cell, till the day you die. However long it takes.

"Might be kinder to just let the loa have him," I said. "We could always take the Key off whatever's left of his body afterwards."

"No," Walker said immediately. "Partly because the loa will cause havoc looking for him. Like most gods, they can be very single-minded when it comes to revenge. It's already become clear they aren't following standard bounty hunter etiquette and allowing informers to live after they've informed. But mostly I want Max back in my hands because the Nightside takes care of its own problems. Can't let outsiders think they can just walk in here and throw their weight around."

He stopped abruptly, and Suzie and I stopped with

him. He took an old-fashioned gold repeater watch from his waistcoat-pocket, checked the time, put it away, and gave me a measuring look.

"Don't screw this up, John. I'm under a lot of pressure to get this done quickly, efficiently, and with no loose ends. That's why I'm handing this case over to you instead of just flooding the Nightside with my own people. If you can't locate Max, and the Key, within the next three hours, I'll have no choice but to unleash my dogs of war, which will make me very unpopular in all sorts of areas. So don't let me down, John, or I shall be sure to blame it all on you."

Suzie looked at him steadily, and give the man credit, Walker didn't flinch.

"You come for him," Suzie said coldly, "you come for me."

"Sooner or later, I come for everyone," said Walker.

"Under pressure?" I said thoughtfully, and he looked back at me. I grinned right into his calm, collected face. "From whom, precisely? Whom do you serve, now the Authorities are all dead and gone?"

But he just smiled briefly, nodded to me, and tipped his bowler hat to Suzie, then turned and walked away, disappearing unhurriedly back into the night.


Suzie Shooter and I went to the Spider's Web. A sort of up-market cocktail bar, owned by Max Maxwell ever since he had its previous owner killed, stuffed, mounted, and put on display; it was widely known as his seat of power, where he did business with the poor unfortunates who came before him. By the time we got there, the place had already been very thoroughly trashed. Bits of it were still smouldering. Suzie drew her pump-action shotgun from its rear holster with one easy movement and led the way as we entered through the kicked-in front door.

The lobby was wrecked, with bodies everywhere. None of them had died easily. Blood had soaked into the carpet, splashed up the walls, and even stained the ceiling. Severed hands had been piled up in one corner, and all the heads were missing their faces. Suzie and I moved slowly and cautiously between the bodies, but nothing moved. The furniture looked like it had exploded.

Max Maxwell's inner office at the back of the club didn't look much better. No blood or bodies, though, which suggested Max had got out in time. A pack of tarot cards had been left scattered across the top of a huge mahogany desk, which had been cracked casually in half. Thick mats of ivy crawled across all four walls, reportedly part of Max's early-warning system; but every bit of it was dead, withered away as though blasted by a terrible frost. Here and there, something had gouged deep claw-marks through the ivy and into the wood beneath. The bare floor was covered with cabalistic symbols, a whole series of overlapping defence systems.

A lot of good they'd done.

"This man had to be seriously worried to have so many protections in one place," said Suzie.

"He had good reason," I said. "Gods really don't like it when worshippers start forgetting their place and flexing their muscles."

I fired up my gift, and the world changed around me. I couldn't use my gift to pin down Max's current location; I need a specific question to get a specific answer. But there's more than one way to find someone who doesn't want to be found. I opened up my inner eye, my third eye, and Saw the world as it really is. There's a lot going on around us that most people aren't aware of, and it's probably just as well. If they knew who and what we share this world with, an awful lot of them would probably rip their own heads off rather than see it.

There were things in the office with us, drifting on currents unknown to mortal men, filling the aether like the tiny creatures that swarm and multiply in a drop of water. And just as ugly. I focused my gift, concentrating on Max Maxwell, and his ghost image appeared before me—his past, imprinted on Time.

Max was just as big as everyone said he was. A giant of a man, huge and looming even in this semi-transparent state. Eight feet tall, and impressively broad across the chest and shoulders, he wore an impeccably cut cream-coloured suit, presumably chosen to contrast with the deep black of his harsh, craggy face. He looked like he'd been carved out of stone, a great brooding gargoyle in a Saville Row suit. He was scowling fiercely, his huge dark hands clenched into fists.

He stamped silently around his office, as though look-

ing for something. He didn't seem scared, or even concerned. Simply angry. He unlocked a drawer in his desk
and brought out something wrapped in a blood-red cloth.
He made a series of signs over the bundle and then un-
wrapped it, revealing a bulky square contraption made up
of dully shining metal pieces joined together in a way
that made my eyes hurt to look at it. The Aquarius Key,
presumably. It looked like a prototype, something that
hadn't had all the bugs hammered out of it yet.

Max weighed the thing thoughtfully in one oversized
hand, then looked round sharply, as though he'd heard
something he didn't like. He gestured grandly with his
free hand, and all the cabalistic signs on the floor burst
into light. The ivy on the walls writhed and twisted, as
though in pain. One by one, the lines on the floor began
to gutter and go out. Max headed for the door.

I went after him, Suzie right there at my side. She
couldn't see what I was Seeing, but she trusted me.

In as much as she trusted anyone.


We tracked Max Maxwell's ghost half-way across the
Nightside. I had to fight to concentrate on his past
image. When my inner eye is cranked all the way open, I
can See all there is to See in the Nightside, and a lot of it
the human mind just isn't equipped to deal with. The
endlessly full moon hung low in the star-speckled sky,
twenty times the size it should have been. Something
with vast membranous wings sailed across the face of the

moon, almost eclipsing it. The buildings around us blazed with protective signs, magical defences, and shaped curses scrawled across the storefronts like so much spitting and crackling graffiti. A thousand other ghosts stamped and raged and howled silently all around me, memories trapped in repeating loops of Time, like insects in amber.

Dimensional travellers flashed and flared in and out of existence, just passing through on their way to somewhere more interesting. Demons rode the backs of unsuspecting souls, their claws dug deep into back and shoulder muscles, whispering in their host's ear. You could always tell which ones had been listening; their demons were particularly fat and bloated. Wee winged sprites, pulsing with light, shot up and down the street, fierce as fireworks, buzzing around and above each other in intricate patterns too complex for human eyes. And the Awful Ones, huge and ancient, moved through our streets and buildings as though they weren't even there, about their unguessable business.

I kept my head down, focused on Max Maxwell, and Suzie saw to it that no-one bothered me or got in our way. She had her shotgun out and at the ready, and no-one ever doubted that she'd use it. Suzie had always been a great believer in the scorched-earth solution for all problems, great and small.

Max led us right through the centre of the Nightside, and out the other side, and I had a bad feeling I knew where he was headed. Bad as the Nightside undoubtedly is, even it has its recognised Bad Places, places you simply don't go if you've got any sense. One of these is Fun Faire. It was supposed to be the Nightside's very first amusement park, for adults. Someone's Big Idea; but it never caught on. The people who come to the Nightside aren't interested in artificial thrills; not when there are so many of the real thing available on every street corner. Fun Faire was shut down years ago, and the only reason it's still taking up valuable space is because the various creditors are still arguing over who owns what. Now, it's just a collection of huge rusting rides, great hulking structures left to rot in the cold, uncaring night.

Last I'd heard, they'd run through fourteen major league exorcists, merely trying to keep the place quiet.

Max had chosen Fun Faire as his bolt-hole precisely because so many bad things had happened there. So much death and suffering, so much cheerful slaughter and infernal malice, had turned the Fun Faire grounds into one big psychic null spot. The genius loci had become so awful, so soaked in blood and terror, that no-one could See into it. Which made it a really good place to hide out, for as long as you could stand it.

Suzie and I stopped at the amusement park entrance, and stood there, looking in. Max's ghost image had snapped off the moment he walked through the main archway. I shut down my Sight. The great multi-coloured arch loomed above us, paint peeling and speckled with rust. The old neon letters along the top that had once blazed the words FUN FAIRE! to an unsuspecting public were now cracked and dusty and lifeless. Someone had spray-painted over them ABANDON HOPE ALL YE WHO ENTER HERE. Graveyard humour, but I had to admire their nerve. Beyond the archway it was all dark shapes and darker shadows, the metal bones of old rides standing out in stark silhouettes against the night sky. No lights, anywhere in Fun Faire. Only the uneasy shimmering blue-white glare of the full moon, marking out the paths between the rides. A glowing maze, where the monster wasn't trapped in the centre any more. A slow breeze issued out of the arch, pressing against my face, cold as the grave.

Bad things had happened here, and perhaps were still happening, on some level. You can't kill that many people, spill that much blood, delight in that much suffering and slaughter, and not leave a stain on Time itself.

It all started out so well. The Fun Faire did have its share of unusual, high-risk, high-excitement attractions. Just the thing to tempt the jaded palates of Nightside aesthetes. Or perhaps even the worst of us need to play at being children again, just for a while. So, the Dodgems of Doom could hit Mach 2 and came equipped with mounted machine-guns. The planes on the Tilt-A-Wheel had heat-seeking missiles and ejector seats. The Ghost Train was operated by real ghosts, the Tunnel of Love by a real succubus. The roller coaster guaranteed to rotate you through at last five different spatial dimensions or your money back. And the candy floss came treated with a hundred and one different psychotropic drugs.

But eventually someone noticed that though an awful lot of people were going into Fun Faire, a significant percentage weren't coming out again.

And then it all went to Hell.

No-one's too sure what started it. Best guess is someone put a curse on the place, for whatever reason. The first clue that something was severely wrong came when the wooden horses on the Merry-Go-Round became possessed by demons and started eating their riders. The Tilt-A-Wheel speeded itself up and sent its mock planes shooting off into space. They didn't fly far. The roller coaster disappeared into another dimension, taking its passengers with it, and never returned. Distorted reflections burst out of the distorting mirrors and ran amok, killing everyone they could get their hands on.

Screams came out of the Ghost Train, and even worse screams out of the Tunnel of Love. The I-Speak-Your-Weight machines shouted out people's most terrible inner secrets. The Clown that never stopped laughing escaped from his booth and strode through Fun Faire, ripping off people's heads and hanging them from his belt. Still laughing. The customers ran for the exit. Some made it out.

The Authorities sealed off Fun Faire, so nothing inside could get out, and soon the whole place was dark and still and silent. No-one volunteered to go in and check for survivors, or bring out the dead. The Nightside isn't big on compassion.

The owners, and then their creditors, turned to priests

and exorcists, air strikes and high explosives, and none of it did any good. Fun Faire had become a Bad Place, and most people had enough sense to stay well clear of it. But, this being the Nightside, there were always those brave enough or stupid enough to use it as a hiding place, secure in the knowledge that only the most desperate pursuers would even think of coming in after them.

I looked at Suzie. "Fancy a stroll around? Check out all the fun of the fair?"

"Why not?" said Suzie.

We strode through the archway, shoulder to shoulder, into the face of the gusting breeze. It was bitterly cold inside the Faire, and the silence had a flat, oppressive presence. Our footsteps didn't echo at all. The rides and attractions loomed up around us, dark skeletal structures, and the rounded, almost organic shapes of the tattered tents and concession stands. We stuck to the middle of the moonlit paths. The shimmering light couldn't seem to penetrate the shadows. Here and there, things moved, always on the edge of my vision. Perhaps moved by the gusting wind, which seemed to be growing in strength. Suzie glared about her, shotgun at the ready. It might have been the oppressive nature of the place getting to her, or it might not. Suzie always believed in getting her retaliation in first.

We passed an old-fashioned I-Speak-Your-Weight machine, and I stopped and regarded it thoughtfully.

"I know a guy who collects these," I said, deliberately

casual. "He's trying to teach them to sing the 'Halleluiah Chorus.'"

"Why?" said Suzie.

"I'm not sure he's thought that far ahead," I admitted.

And then we broke off, as the machine stirred slowly into life before us. Parts moved inside it, grinding against each other, even though neither of us had stepped on it; and the voice-box made a low, groaning sound, as though it was in pain. The flat painted face lit up, sparking fitfully. And in a voice utterly devoid of humanity, or any human feeling, the machine spoke to us.

"John Taylor. No father, no mother. No family, no friends, no future. Hated and feared, never loved, or even appreciated. Why don't you just die and get it over with?"

"Not even close," I said calmly. "You'd probably get my weight wrong, too."

"Susan Shooter," said the voice. "Always the celibate, never the bride. No-one to touch you, ever. Not your breast, or your heart. You miss your brother, even though he sexually abused you as a child. Sometimes you dream of how it felt, when he touched you. No love for you, Susan. Not any kind of love, now or ever."

Suzie raised her shotgun and blew the painted face apart. The machine screamed once, and then was still. Suzie pumped another shell into the magazine. "Machines should know their place," she said.

"You can't trust anything you hear in Fun Faire," I said carefully. "The Devil always lies."

"Except when a truth can hurt you more."

"He doesn't know you like I do," I said. "I love you, Suzie."

"Why?"

"Somebody has to. There's a man for every woman, and a woman for every man. Just be glad we found each other."

"I am," said Suzie. And that was as far as she would go.

She spun round suddenly, her gun trained on one particular shadow. "Come out. Come out into the light where I can see you."

Max Maxwell emerged slowly and cautiously, even bigger in life than his ghost image had suggested. He held his huge hands up to show us they were empty, and then he smiled slowly, grey lips pulling back to show grey teeth.

"You're good, Suzie," he said, in a low, deep voice like stones grinding together. "No-one else would have known I was there."

"No-one sneaks up on me," said Suzie, her shotgun trained unwaveringly on his barrel chest. His cream suit looked somehow off in the moonlight, as though it had gone sour.

"I might have known they'd send you two," he said, apparently unmoved by the threat of the shotgun. "But I'm afraid you got here just a little too late. I didn't come here to hide; this whole place is a sink of other-dimensional energies, and the Aquarius Key has been soaking them up for hours. Soon the Key will be strong enough to open a door into the world of the loa; and then I will go through into that world . . . and the power stored in the Key will make me their master. A god of gods, lord of the loa."

"Really bad idea, Max," I said. "Messing with gods on their own territory. They'll eat your soul, one little bit at a time. What did you think you were doing, bringing them here and humiliating them?"

"It's wrong that we should be at their beck and call," said Max Maxwell, the Voodoo Apostate. "My people have worshipped them for centuries, and still the most we can hope for is that they will deign to ride us as their mounts. This is the Nightside. We have a Street full of gods, and we have taught them to know their place. As I will teach the loa."

He held out one hand towards me, and just like that, the Aquarius Key appeared upon it. The metal box looked like a toy on his huge pale palm. Its steel parts moved slowly against each other, sliding around and above each other, and I tried to look away, but I couldn't. The Key was becoming something actually uncomfortable to look at, as though it was rotating itself through strange, unfamiliar spatial dimensions, in search of the doorway into the world of the loa. It burst open, blossoming like a metal flower, and a wide split opened up in mid air, like a wound in reality.

A great sound filled the air, echoing through the silent forms of Fun Faire, like a cry of outrage. A bright light blasted out of the opening hanging on the air, so sharp and fierce I had to look away, and just like that the spell of the Key was broken. I fell back a pace, raising one arm to shield my watering eyes against the fierce light. The split in the night widened inexorably, sucking the air into itself. It tugged at me, and at Suzie. I grabbed her waist, as much to steady myself as hold her in place, and she was steady as a rock, as always. Suzie grabbed on to the side of the nearest ride, and I held on to Suzie as the pull increased. Max Maxwell stood unaffected, protected by the Aquarius Key, shuddering and twitching on the palm of his hand. The rushing air shrieked as it was pulled into the growing split in the air, along with everything else loose. All kinds of junk flew through the air, tumbling end over end. I was holding Suzie so tightly it must have hurt her, but she never made a sound, and her white-knuckled grip on the ride never faltered. She raised her free hand, aimed the shotgun with one casual movement, and shot the Aquarius Key right out of Max's hand.

He cried out in rage as much as pain, as his hand exploded in a flurry of flying blood and blown-away fingers. The Key flew undamaged through the air, hit the ground, and rolled away into the shadows. The long split in the air slammed shut, and, just like that, the howling wind died away to nothing. Max fell on all fours, ignoring the blood that still spurted from his maimed hand, scrambling in the shadows for the Key. I let go of Suzie's waist, and we walked purposefully forward. Suzie chambered another round, and Max rose suddenly, the Key raised triumphantly in his good hand. He snarled at me, and I leaned forward and threw a handful of black pepper right into his face.

I never travel anywhere without condiments.

The pepper filled Max's eyes and nose, and he fell backwards, sneezing so hard it shook his whole body, while his eyes screwed shut around streaming tears. He couldn't even hold on to the Aquarius Key, let alone concentrate enough to operate it, and the metal box fell to the ground before him. So I just stooped down and took it away from him. Suzie nodded respectfully to me.

"You always did know the best ways to fight dirty."

She kicked Max briskly in the ribs with her steel-toed boot, just enough to take the fight out of him. He grunted once, and then glared up at us from his knees, forcing his watering eyes open. He was squeezing his injured hand with the other so tightly the bleeding had almost stopped. There were no signs of pain or weakness or even defeat in his dark face; only an implacable hatred, while he waited for his chance to come round again. Suzie shoved the barrel of her shotgun into his face.

"I get paid the same whether I bring you in dead or alive," she said, her voice cold and calm as always. "On the whole, I tend to prefer dead. Less paper-work."

"I am not carrying anyone that large out of here," I said firmly. "Unless I absolutely have to. So let's all play nice, then we can all walk out."

But Max wasn't listening to either of us. He was staring at something behind me, and even before he said anything, I could feel all the hackles on my neck rising.

"Ah, hell," said Max Maxwell. "Just when I thought things couldn't get any worse . . ."

Suzie and I turned to look, and there standing in rows behind us was a small army of the Nightside's very best bounty hunters. Heavily armed and armoured, they stood unnaturally still, all of them grinning unpleasantly, while their eyes glowed golden in the gloom, like so many candle-flames in the depths of Hell. Their wide grins showed teeth, like hunting dogs who'd brought their game to ground at last.

The loa had found us.

Max laughed suddenly, a flat, breathy sound. "Protect me, Suzie, Taylor. If you want your bounty money."

I looked at Suzie. "Do we really need the money that badly?"

"Always," said Suzie. "It isn't the principle of the thing, it's the money. No-one takes a bounty away from me."

"Maybe we could split him down the middle," I said.

"Tempting, but messy. And I don't share."

I sighed. "Things are in a bad way if I have to be the voice of reason . . ."

I stepped forward, conspicuously putting myself between the loa's hosts and their prey, and they all fixed their glowing unblinking eyes on me.

"We know you, John Taylor." It was hard to tell where the voice came from. It could have been any of them, or all of them. It sounded almost . . . amused. "We know who and what you are, probably better than you do yourself. But do not presume to stand between us and what is rightfully ours."

"And I know you, lords of the loa," I said, keeping my voice reasonably polite and respectful. "But this is my world, not yours, and Max is mine. He will be punished severely, I promise you."

"Not good enough," said the voice, and the whole possessed army surged forward as one.

Max reared up suddenly, catching me off guard. He snatched the Aquarius Key away from me with his one good hand and twisted it savagely, shouting Words of Power. And all the bounty hunters screamed, as the possessing loa were forced out of them. Dozens of men and women crumpled to the ground, twitching and shuddering and crying hot tears of relief. For a moment, I actually thought the threat was over. I should have known better.

All around me, all the old rides and machinery creaked slowly back into life, wheels turning, machinery stirring, while the wooden Merry-Go-Round horses slowly turned their heads to look at us. The loa had found new hosts. A slow, awful life moved through Fun Faire, burning fiercely inside cold metal and painted wood, and out of the mouths of oversized clowns and Tunnels of Love and Horror came the outraged screams of the defied loa.

Max was hunched over, struggling to manipulate the Aquarius Key with just the one good hand, trying to open a door that would take him away. Suzie clubbed him in the side of his head with the butt of her shotgun, and he hardly felt it. She hit him again, and while he was distracted I moved in and snatched the Key away. Max glared at me, grey lips pulling back to show grey teeth.

"I will kill you for this, Taylor. Make you crawl first; make her crawl. I'll let you watch helplessly as I violate your woman. Do her and do her till she bleeds, until her throat rips from screaming. Tear her apart, body and soul. I'll send her to Hell . . . and then it'll be your turn."

I looked at Suzie. "Kneecap him."

She blew off his left kneecap with her shotgun. His leg burst apart, blood spurting, and Max collapsed, crying out in agony as he clutched at his leg. I looked down at him.

"Shouldn't have threatened Suzie, Max. No-one messes with me and mine."

I turned my attention back to Fun Faire, coming slowly alive like a great beast stretching after a long sleep. Lights were snapping on all around us, flaring blue and green and pink in the dark. The huge rides creaked and groaned as rusting metal stirred to life again. Suzie moved in beside me, swinging her shotgun back and forth, restless for a target.

"John, what's happening?"

"The loa have possessed the whole damned fairground," I said. "All those exorcisms must have left it wide open . . ."

"Can't we get Max to throw them out again?"

"Possibly," I said. "If he wasn't currently preoccupied with holding his shattered leg together."

"It was your idea."

"I know, I know!"

The dodgem cars came first, smashing through the reinforced sides of their stand and heading straight for us at impossible speed. They hammered through the shadows, their wooden sides already splitting as they struggled to contain the terrible energies that were animating them. Suzie stood her ground and blasted the first car at pointblank range. It exploded in a shower of wooden spikes and splinters, some of which pattered harmlessly against the front of Suzie's motorcycle jacket. The rest of the dodgem cars were already upon us, so Suzie and I threw ourselves in opposite directions, out of their way. The cars swung round and over each other to come after us, their garishly painted faces grinning the same grin I'd seen on the faces of the possessed bounty hunters. The loa were having fun. The loa were playing with us.

I ran down the moonlit paths between the slowly stirring stands, and the cars came after me, calling out now in terrible voices. I could hear Suzie running, not far away, and yelled for her to intersect with me at the next crossing of the paths. We both arrived at the intersection at the same time, and I grabbed Suzie by the hand and pulled her to the ground. The cars came up on us too fast to stop, and flew right over our heads to slam into each other head-on. There was an explosion of splintered wood and released uncanny energies, and when Suzie and I scrambled to our feet again, their was nothing left of the dodgem cars but gaily painted wreckage.

"We need to get back to Max," said Suzie. She'd already pulled her hand out of mine, the moment we were safe. She couldn't bear to be touched for long, even when I was saving her.

"Max isn't going anywhere on that leg," I said.

"He could crawl," said Suzie.

So back we went, to face the loa again. I sometimes wonder which of us is crazier—Suzie for suggesting these things or me for going along with them.

She was right. We found Max at the end of a long bloody trail, crawling for the exit, dragging his useless leg behind him. We'd just caught up with him when the snub-nosed planes came flying down at us from the Tilt-A-Whirl. They'd broken free of their supporting struts and shot through the air towards us on stubby wooden wings. I just hoped someone had got around to removing the heat-seeking missiles. Suzie shot them out of the air, one by one, just like pigeon shooting. (There are no pigeons in the Nightside, and people like Suzie are the reason why. Sometimes you can't even find a dove to sacrifice when you're in a hurry.) The last plane crashed to the ground not five feet away from us and gave up its ghost. Suzie looked at me as she reloaded her shotgun.

"So? Do I win a prize?"

"Depends," I said. "You shoot horses, don't you?"

Suzie looked where I was looking and hurried her reloading. The carved wooden horses had dragged themselves free from the Merry-Go-Round and were heading our way. They were big and nasty and brightly coloured in places where paint still clung to the diseased wood. They had snarling rusty teeth in their grinning mouths, the hinged jaws working hungrily. Their eyes gleamed gold, just like the bounty hunters', and they stamped their heavy hoofs deep into the ground. And for all their rusty hinged joints, they moved very much like living things, driven by the wrath of the loa.

The old stories said the horses ate their riders; and right then I believed it.

"Now this is what I call a Fun Faire," said Suzie, and she opened fire with her shotgun.

The noise was deafening as she fired shell after shell, but though she hit every horse she aimed at, blowing huge chunks of wood out of them, they just kept coming. Suzie emptied her shotgun in under a minute and swore harshly as she scrambled at the bandoliers over her chest for reloads. The horses were very close now, but she still held her ground. The first wooden head lunged forward, and rusting teeth snapped shut on her black leather sleeve.

Which meant it was down to me, and one last desperate idea. I raised my gift and used it to find the last traces of the old magic that had once run the Faire, when it was still just an amusement park. Some last vestiges of that old innocent magic still remained, untouched by all the prayers and exorcisms, the evil and the horror, and I found it and put it back in touch with the wooden horses.

They stumbled to a halt, one by one, as the old magic stubbornly reinstated the terms of the original compact.

And one by one the horses were dragged back to the Merry-Go-Round. They fought it all the way, shaking their heads and stamping their heavy feet, but back they went. And as they stepped backwards up onto the Merry-Go-Round, the old steel poles slammed down again, piercing their wooden bodies through and holding them mercilessly in place.

I looked round at Suzie. She'd finished reloading her shotgun and was standing with one foot in the small of Max's back, to keep track of him. I nodded to her, and she took her boot away. I knelt down beside Max and helped him roll over onto his back. He was breathing hard, sweat beading all over his face, but he still glared unwaveringly up at me. I showed him the Aquarius Key in my hand.

"You know how to operate this, and I don't," I said carefully. "Use it and drive the loa out of Fun Faire. Use it for anything else, and Suzie will do to your head what she's already done to your knee."

He glared silently at me, but held out his good hand for the Key. I helped him sit up, then gave him the metal box. Suzie moved quickly forward to press the barrel of her shotgun against the back of his skull. He had to use what was left of his shattered hand in the end, despite the blood and the pain, but he made the Key do what he wanted, and a great cry went up all through Fun Faire as the loa were forced out. I quickly took the Key back again.

"John . . ." said Suzie. "Was this what you meant to happen?"

I looked where she was looking. The bounty hunters were back on their feet again, smiling their awful smiles, watching us with their glowing golden eyes. I had to sigh. Sometimes things wouldn't go right even if you bribed St. Peter. I moved forward to confront the bounty hunters, holding up the Aquarius Key so they could all see it. They stood very still, their glowing eyes fixed on me.

"When you were forced out of the rides, you were supposed to take the hint and go back where you came from," I said reproachfully.

"We won't go," they said, in their creepy single voice. "We can't go until we have satisfaction. And if you stand between us and our rightful vengeance, we will be at your back and at your throat for as long as you live."

I considered the problem. I could probably get Max to use the Key to send the loa home; but they'd just come back again, and again, till they got what they wanted. Max had hurt their pride, undermined their status as gods, and posed a threat to their whole religion. Hard to argue with that. It was an intriguing stand-off, and there was no telling which way it might have gone if Walker hadn't arrived. As usual he appeared out of nowhere, strolling casually out of the shadows as though he happened to be passing and thought he'd drop in for a chat. He came and stood beside me, and Suzie immediately moved to stand on my other side. Walker smiled easily at the ranks of possessed bounty hunters.

"Well, well, the gang's all here. But I think we've had

DAMNED IF YOU DO IN THE NIGHTSIDE

enough fun and games for one night. Max Maxwell is in my custody, and therefore under my protection. I can give you my word that he will be severely punished. I have a nice little cell just waiting for him, in Shadow Deep. And you know what we do to prisoners there."

"Not enough." One of the bounty hunters stepped forward to confront Walker. "Revenge, to be properly savoured, has to be personal. Has to be . . . hands-on."

"Not this time," said Walker. "This is the Nightside, and we deal with our own problems. *Go home.*"

He used the Voice on them. The Voice that cannot be disobeyed or opposed. It hammered on the air, so loud and forceful that even I winced. But the loa wouldn't budge. Until I raised my voice.

"Go home," I said. "Or I'll be very upset with you."

Perhaps I was bluffing. Perhaps not. I'll never tell. But it tipped the balance. They might have defied the powerful Walker or the infamous John Taylor, but not both of us at once. The bounty hunters collapsed again as the loa left them, returning at last to their own world. And that . . . was that. For now.

I looked at Walker. "You do know they'll be back, sometime. We hurt their feelings."

"Let them," said Walker. "They should have accepted a place on the Street of the Gods, when I offered it to them. There's no room for independent operators any more."

"Like me?" I said.

"Exactly."

I considered him thoughtfully. "Your Voice was impressive as always; but I can't help remembering it was granted to you by the Authorities. Who are all now extremely dead. So who powers your Voice these days?"

Walker smiled briefly. "I'm sure you'll find out, John. One of these days." He looked at Max Maxwell. *"Come with me."*

And shattered leg notwithstanding, Max Maxwell rose up and followed Walker out of Fun Faire, limping heavily all the way. The bounty hunters moved off after them, talking rather confusedly amongst themselves. Until only Suzie and I were left. She looked at me with her cold, utterly contained face.

"You saved my life, John. Again."

"And you saved mine," I said easily. "It's what we do. All part of being in a relationship."

"I know . . . it's not easy, for you," she said. "That close as we are, we still can't be . . . close. You've been so patient with me."

She reached out and touched my face gently with her fingertips. I stood very still and let her do it. I could feel the effort it took, for her to do that much. She trailed a fingertip across my lips—the closest we could come to a kiss. Suzie Shooter, Shotgun Suzie, who took no shit from me, or gods, or anyone in the Nightside, was still mostly helpless in the face of her own inner demons.

I would have killed the brother who'd done this to her if she hadn't already killed him years ago.

"I love you, Suzie," I said. "If you never believe anything else, believe that."

"I love you, John. As much as I can."

"That's what matters. That's all that matters."

"No it isn't!"

She made herself hug me, holding me tight. Her bandoliers of bracelets pressed against my chest. She was breathing hard, from the effort of what this cost her. Her whole body was stiff and tense. I didn't know whether to put my own arms around her or not, but in the end I held her as gently as I could.

"Love you, John," she said, her chin on my shoulder. I couldn't see her face. "Die for you. Kill for you. Love you till the world ends."

"I know," I said. "It's all right. Really."

But we both knew it wasn't.

TWO

# Demon Girl Re-
# porter

Some days they won't even give you a chance to catch
your breath. Suzie and I were just walking out of Fun
Faire when my mobile phone rang. (The ring tone is the
theme from *The Twilight Zone*. When I find a joke I like,
I tend to stick with it.) An unctuous voice murmured in
my ear.

"You have one phone call and one important message.
Which would you like to hear first?"

"The call," I said determinedly.

"I'm sorry," said the voice. "I'm afraid I have been paid
to insist you listen to the important message first. Have
you ever considered the importance of good Afterlife insurance?"

I sighed, hit the exorcism function on the phone, and was gratified to hear the voice howl in pain as it was forced out of my phone. Admail . . . You'll never convince me it isn't a plot by demons from Hell to make life not worth living. With the admail banished, my call came through clearly. It was my teenage secretary, Cathy, calling from my office. (I'd rescued her from a house that ate people, and she adopted me. I didn't get a say in the matter. I let her run my office to keep her out of my hair. Worryingly, she's far better at it than I ever was.)

"Got a case for you, boss," she said cheerfully.

"I've just completed two in a row," I said plaintively. "I was looking forward to some serious quality time, with a nice hot bath and my rubber ducky. Rubber ducky is my friend."

"Oh, you'll want to take this one," said Cathy. "The offices of the one and only *Unnatural Inquirer* called. They need your services desperately, not to mention very urgently."

"What on earth does that appalling rag want with me? Or have they finally decided to hire someone to try to find their long-missing ethics and good taste?"

"Rather doubt it, boss. They wouldn't go into details over an open line, but they sounded pretty upset. And the money offered really is very good."

"How good?" I said immediately.

"Really quite staggeringly good," said Cathy. "Which means that not only are they pants-wettingly desperate, but there has to be one hell of a catch hidden away in it somewhere. Go on, boss, take the case. I'd love to hear what goes on in that place. They have all the best stories; I never miss an issue."

"The *Unnatural Inquirer* is a squalid, scabrous, tabloid disgrace," I said sternly. "And the truth is not in it."

"Who cares about truth, as long as they have all the latest gossip and embarrassing celebrity photos? Oh please please please . . ."

I looked at Suzie. "Do you need me to . . . ?"

"Go," she said. "I have to claim my bounty money."

She strode off, not looking back. Suzie's never been big on good-byes.

"All right," I said into the phone. "Give me the details."

"There aren't many. They want you to visit their editorial offices to discuss the matter."

"Why can't they come to my office?"

"Because you're never here. You have to come in soon, boss; I have a pile of paper-work that needs your signature."

"Go ahead and forge it for me," I said. "Like you did when you acquired those seven extra credit cards in my name."

"I said I was sorry!"

"Where do they want to meet?"

"They'll send someone to bring you to them. Employees of the *Unnatural Inquirer* don't like to be caught out in public. People throw things."

"Understandable," I said. "Where am I supposed to go, to be met?"

Cathy gave me directions to a particular street corner, in a not-too-sleazy area of the Nightside. I knew it: a busy place, with lots of people always passing through. A casual meeting stood a good chance of going unnoticed, lost in the crowd. I said good-bye to Cathy and shut down the phone before she could nag me about the paper-work again. If I'd wanted to shuffle papers for a living, I'd have shot myself in the head repeatedly.

Didn't take me long to get to the corner of Cheyne Walk and Wine Street, and I lurked as unobtrusively as possible in front of a trepanation franchise—Let Some Light In, Inc. Personally, I've always felt I needed trepanation like a hole in the head. Still, it made more sense than smart drinks ever did. People and others came and went, carefully minding their own business. Some stood out; a knight in shining armour with a miniature dragon perched on his steel shoulder, hissing at the passers-by; a fluorescent Muse, with Catherine-wheel eyes; and a sulky-looking Suicide Girl with a noose round her neck. But most were just people, familiar faces you wouldn't look twice at, come to the Nightside for the forbidden pleasures, secret knowledge, and terrible satisfactions they couldn't find anywhere else. The Nightside has always been something of a tourist trap.

I don't like standing around in the open. It makes me

feel vulnerable, an easy target. When I have to do surveillance, I always take pains to do it from somewhere dark and shadowy. People were starting to recognise me. Most gave me plenty of room; some nudged each other and stared curiously. One couple asked if they could take my photo. I gave them a look, and they hurried away.

To keep myself occupied, I went over what I knew about the *Unnatural Inquirer*. I'd read the odd copy; everyone has. People do like gossip, in the way we always like things that are bad for us. The Nightside has its own newspaper of record; that's the *Night Times*. The *Unnatural Inquirer*, on the other hand, has never allowed itself to be inhibited by mere facts. For them, the story is everything.

All the news that can be made to fit.

The *Unnatural Inquirer* has been around, in various formats, for over a hundred years, despite increasingly violent attempts to shut it down. These days Editorial, Publishing, and Printing all operate out of a separate and very private pocket dimension, hidden away behind layer upon layer of seriously heavy-duty protections. You can get cursed down to the seventh generation just for trying to find it. The paper's defences are constantly being upgraded, because they have very powerful enemies. Partly because they print exaggerations, gossip, and outright lies about very important people, and partly because every now and again they tell the truth when no-one else will dare. The paper has no fear and shows no favour.

Only properly accredited staff can even approach the paper's offices. They're given special dimensional keys, bonded directly to the owner's soul, to prevent theft. The offices still get attacked on a daily basis. The paper prints details of every failed assault, just to rub it in. Despite everything the *Unnatural Inquirer* appears every day, full of things the rich and powerful would rather you didn't know about. There are no delivery trucks any more; they kept getting fire-bombed. New editions of the paper just appear out of nowhere, materialising right next to the news-stands all across the Nightside, direct from the printing presses. No-one ever interferes with the news-sellers; for fear of being lynched on the spot by the paper's fanatical audience.

And when you've finished reading the *Unnatural Inquirer*, just throw it away. It automatically disappears, returning to the printing presses to be recycled for the next edition. Even the *Night Times* can't match that. No-one has ever wrapped fish and chips in the *Unnatural Inquirer*.

On the other hand, the *Night Times*'s reporters and staff are on the whole well-known, respected, and admired. The *Unnatural Inquirer*'s people are often shot at on sight (especially the paparazzi), though if you survive long enough, you can end up as a (minor) celebrity. There's a high burn-out rate amongst the staff, but surprisingly there are always more, waiting in the wings to take their place. If you don't have it in you to be someone important or significant, or a celebrity, the next best thing is being someone who knows all about them and can crash all their parties.

"Hello, hello, John Taylor! Good to see you again, old thing! Still busy being infamous and enigmatic?"

I winced internally even as I turned to face the man who'd hailed me so cheerfully. I should have known who they'd send. Harry Fabulous was a fence and a fixer, and the best Go To man in the Nightside—for all those little and very expensive things that make life worth living. You want to smoke some prime Martian red weed, mainline some Hyde, or score someone else's childhood (innocence always goes down big in the Nightside), then Harry Fabulous is your man, always ready to take your last penny with a big smile and a hearty handshake.

Or at least he used to be. Apparently he'd had one of those life-changing experiences in the back room of a members-only club, and now he was more interested in doing Good Deeds. Before it was too late. There's nothing like a glimpse of Hell to jump-start a man's conscience.

Harry was dressed to kill, as always, looking slick and polished. He wore a long coat whose inside pockets were practically crammed with all sorts of things you might or might not want to spend too much money on. He had a long, thin face, a lean and hungry look, and dark, somewhat haunted, eyes. He smiled easily at me, a very practised smile, and I gave him something very similar in return.

We were both, after all, professionals.

"Didn't know you worked for the *Unnatural Inquirer*, Harry," I said.

"Oh, I'm just a stringer," he said vaguely. "I do get

around, and I have been known to hear things, so . . . I've been sent to bring you to their main offices, old thing. Sorry to keep you waiting, but I had to be sure you hadn't been followed."

"Harry," I said. "Remember who you're talking to."

"Oh, quite! Yes, indeed! Just a formality, really."

He fished inside his long coat and produced a very ordinary-looking key. He glanced round briefly, turned to face me to cover his movements, and pushed the key into an invisible lock, apparently floating in mid air between us. The key disappeared even as Harry turned it, and just like that the world seemed to drop away under my feet. There was a brief sensation of falling, and we left the Nightside behind us.

We reappeared in a Reception office that looked just like any other Reception office. Luxurious enough to impress on you how important the operation was, but not comfortable enough to encourage you to stick around any longer than was absolutely necessary. A cool blonde Receptionist sat behind a desk behind a layer of bullet-proof glass. Manning the phones, doing maintenance on her fingernails, and dealing with visitors when she absolutely had to. Harry went to take my arm to usher me into the waiting area. I looked at him, and he quickly withdrew the hand. You can't let people like Harry Fabulous get too chummy; they take advantage. I strolled forward, looking curiously about me, and all the bells in the world went off at once.

"It's all right! It's all right!" yelled Harry, waving his arms and practically jumping up and down on the spot. "It's just John Taylor! He's expected!"

The bells shut off, and the Receptionist reappeared from underneath her desk, glaring venomously at Harry. I looked at him.

"Security scan," he said quickly. "Purely routine. Nothing to worry about. It's supposed to detect dangerous objects, and people, and you . . . set off every alarm they have. I did warn them to dial down the settings while you were here . . . Would you like me to take your coat?"

"Wouldn't be wise," I said. "I haven't fed it recently."

Harry looked at me for some clue as to whether he was supposed to laugh, but I just looked right back at him. Harry swallowed hard, took a step back, and looked at the Receptionist.

"Contact Security, there's a dear, and tell them to make an exception for John Taylor."

"Make lots of them," I said. "I'm a very complicated person."

"I won't hang around," Harry decided. "I'm almost sure I'm urgently needed somewhere else."

He did the business with the key again and disappeared. That's Harry Fabulous for you. Always on the go.

The Receptionist and I looked at each other. Somehow I just knew we weren't going to get along. She was a small petite platinum blonde with sultry eyes, a mouth made for sin, and a general air of barely suppressed rage and violence. I didn't know whether that was a result of working here, or why they hired her in the first place. She was the first line of defence against anyone who turned up, and I had no doubt she had all kinds of interesting weapons and devices somewhere close at hand . . . I decided to be polite, for the moment, and gave her my best professional smile.

"My name is John Taylor. The Editor wants to see me."

She sniffed loudly and gave me a pitying smile. Her voice came clearly through the narrow grille in the bullet-proof glass. "No-one ever sees the Editor. In fact, no-one's seen Mr. du Rois in the flesh for years. Safer that way. Your appointment will be with the Sub-Editor, Scoop Malloy."

"Scoop?" I said. "Was he one of your best reporters?"

"No; he used to work with animals. Take a seat."

I took a seat. I know when I'm outclassed. The long red leather couch was hard and unyielding. There was no-one else waiting in Reception. An assortment of old magazines were laid out on a low table. I leafed through them, but there was nothing particularly interesting. *Which Religion*'s cover boasted the start of a new series: *We road test ten new gods!* The Nightside edition of *Guns & Ammo* had Suzie Shooter on the cover again. They think she adds a touch of glamour. *What's on in the Nightside* was the size of a telephone directory. It's cover boasted *101 Things You Need to Know About Members Only Clubs! Including How to*

*Get In, and How to Get Out Alive Again.* I quite like *What's On*; it's constantly updating itself as people and places change and disappear. Sometimes the page will rewrite itself even as you're reading it. They stopped having an index because it kept whimpering.

I gave up on the magazines, leaned back on the rock-hard sofa, and thought some more about what I knew about the *Unnatural Inquirer*'s legendary Editor, Owner, and Publisher, Gaylord du Rois. Everyone was pretty sure that wasn't his real name, but it had been right there at the top of the masthead of every issue for years now, right from the days when the photos were grainy black and white, the type-face was tiny, and they printed the whole thing on toilet paper. Gaylord might be a man, or a woman, or a committee. Might even have been several people in a row. No-one knew for sure, and it wasn't for want of trying to find out. Certainly the aggressive tone of the paper hadn't changed in over a hundred years; it was just as blunt and brash and obnoxious now as it had always been.

I sat more or less patiently on the couch, idly considering the possibilities of redecorating the Reception area with a couple of incendiaries, while a handful of people drifted in and out. Reporters and office functionaries wandered past, caught up in their own business and paying no attention at all to me. Paparazzi teleported in just long enough to drop off their latest snatched photos of celebrities doing things they shouldn't, and then disappeared again. There are cannibal demons on the Street of the Gods less hated and despised than the *Unnatural Inquirer*'s paparazzi. Suzie shoots at them on sight, but so far she's only managed to wing a couple. We stopped them hanging about our house by planting disguised man-traps. Nothing like the occasional scream of a wounded paparazzi in the early hours of the morning to help you sleep peacefully.

A few of the paparazzi looked at me thoughtfully but were careful not even to point their cameras in my direction. It's all in the reputation.

"You're sure the Sub-Editor knows I'm waiting?" I said to the Receptionist. "I was told this was urgent."

"He knows," she said. "Or maybe he doesn't. Embrace the possibilities!"

I walked over to her and gave her one of my best hard looks. "I'll bet this place would burn up nicely if I put my mind to it."

"Go ahead. See if I care. The only time this place gets a makeover is after a good fire. Sometimes they just scrub down the walls."

I gave up. "Distract me. Talk to me. Tell me things."

"What sort of things?"

"Well, how big is the paper's circulation these days?"

She shrugged. "Don't think anyone knows for sure. The print run's been rising steadily for thirty years now, and it was huge before that. Sales aren't limited to the Nightside, you know. It goes out to all kinds of other worlds and dimensions. Because everyone's interested in what's happening in the Nightside. We get letters from all over. We got one from Mars."

"Really? What did it say?"

"No-one knows. It was in Martian."

I decided I didn't want to talk to her any more. I sat down on the couch again and looked at the framed front pages on the walls, showcasing the paper's long history.

*Elvis Really Is Dead! We Have Proof! Honeymoon Over; Giant Ape Admits Size Isn't Everything! Hitler Burns in Hell! Official! Orson Welles Was Really a Martian! We Have X-Rays! Our Greatest Ever Psychic Channels New Songs from Elvis, John Lennon, Marc Bolan, and Buddy Holly! All Available on a CD You Can Buy Exclusively from the* Unnatural Inquirer*!*

Proof, if proof were needed, that not only is there one born every second, but that they grow up to read the tabloids.

Still, if nothing else, the *Unnatural Inquirer* had style. It got your attention. For want of anything better to do, I picked up a copy of the latest edition from the low table. The front-page headline was *Tribute Four Horsemen of the Apocalypse to Tour Nightside! Over Their Dead Bodies, Says Walker!* I leafed through the paper, grimacing as the cheap print came off on my fingers.

Apparently the Holy Order of Saint Strontium had been forcibly evicted from the Street of the Gods after it was discovered that their Church had a radioactive half-life of two million years. "Bunch of pussies," said Saint Strontium. He had a lot more to say, but none of the reporters present wanted to hang around long enough to find out what . . . There were some intriguing Before and After photos of Jacqueline Hyde, poor soul. Jacqueline and Hyde were in love, but doomed never to meet save for the most fleeting of moments . . . Another story insisted that the Moon really was made of green cheese, and that the big black monoliths were just oversized alien crackers . . . And right at the bottom of an inner page, in very small type: *Old Ones Fail to Rise Yet Again.*

Most of the rest of the pages were filled with excited puff pieces about various Nightside celebrities I either hadn't heard of, or didn't give a damn about, including two whole pages given over to photos of young women getting out of limousines and taxis, just so the paparazzi could get a quick photo of their underwear, or lack of it. As far as the *Unnatural Inquirer* is concerned, taste is something you find in the restaurant guides.

I skipped through to the personal ads and announcements in the back pages; all human life is there, and a whole lot more besides.

Soul-swapping parties; just show up and throw your karma keys into the circle. Bodies for rent. Sex change while you wait. Go deep-sea diving in sunken R'lyeh; no noise-makers allowed. A whole bunch of pyramid schemes, some involving real pyramids. Remote viewing into the bedrooms and bathrooms of the rich and famous; highlights available on VHS or DVD. Time-share schemes, involving real time travel. (Though those tended to be stamped on pretty quick by Old Father Time, especially if they weren't cons.) And, of course, a million different drugs from thousands of dimensions; buyer very much beware. The paper felt obliged to add its own warning here; apparently some intelligent plant civilisations had been attempting to stealthily invade our world by selling their seeds and cuttings as drugs. Sort of a Trojan horse invasion . . .

And then, of course, there were the personal messages . . . *Lassie come home, or the kid gets it. Boopsie loves Moopsie; Moopsie loves Boopsie?* (Oh, I could see tears before bedtime in the offing there . . . ) *Dagon shall rise again! All donations welcome. Desperately Seeking Elvira . . . Mad scientist who digs up graves, steals the bodies, and sews the bits together to create a new living supercreature seeks similar . . . GSOH essential.*

The *Unnatural Inquirer* has the only crossword puzzles that insult you if you take too long at guessing the clues—very cross word puzzles. And they had to cancel the kakuro because the numbers kept adding up to 666.

I dropped the paper back onto the table, went to wipe my inky fingers on my coat, and then realised that's not a good idea when you're wearing a white trench coat. I took out a handkerchief and rubbed briskly at my fingers. I hadn't realised how much I knew about the paper. The tabloid had insinuated itself into the Nightside so thoroughly that pretty much anything you saw or thought of reminded you of something that had appeared in the *Unnatural Inquirer*. For a while there was even a rumour going around that the Editor had a precog on staff, who could see just far enough into the future to view the next day's edition of the *Night Times*, so that the *Unnatural Inquirer* could run all their best stories in advance. I had trouble believing that. First, I knew the Editor of the *Night Times*, and he wouldn't sit still for something like that for one moment, and second, the *Unnatural Inquirer* had never been that interested in news stories anyway. Not when there's important gossip and tittle-tattle to spread.

Not that the *Unnatural Inquirer* gets everything its own way. The Editor once sent a reporter into Rats' Alley, where the homeless and down-and-outs gather, to dig up some juicy stories on rich and famous people who'd been brought low by misfortune and disaster. Razor Eddie, Punk God of the Straight Razor, and defenders of street people everywhere, rather took exception to such hard-heartedness. He sent the reporter back to the Editor in forty-seven separate parcels. With postage owing.

"The Sub-Editor is ready to see you now," said the Receptionist. "He's sending a copy-boy to escort you in."

"Does he think I'll get lost?" I said.

She smiled coldly. "We don't like people wandering around. Personally, I think all visitors should be electronically tagged and stamped with time codes so they'd know exactly when their welcome was wearing out."

The door to the inner offices opened, and out shambled a hunched and scowling adolescent in a grubby T-shirt and jeans. His T-shirt bore the legend FUCK THEM ALL AND LET THE DOCTORS SORT THEM OUT. He flicked his long, lank hair back out of his sullen face, looked me over, grunted once, and gestured for me to follow him inside. I felt like giving him a good slap, on general principles.

"Let me guess," I said. "Everything's rotten and nothing's fair."

"I'm nineteen!" he said, glaring at me dangerously. "Nineteen, and still a copy-boy! And I've got qualifications . . . I'm being held back. You just wait; there'll be some changes made around here once they finally see sense and put me in charge . . ."

"What's your name?" I said.

"I'm beginning to think it's *Hey you!* That's all I ever hear in this place. Like it would kill the old farts that work here to remember my name. Which is Jimmy, if you really care, which you probably don't."

"And what do you want to be when you grow up?" I said kindly.

His glare actually intensified, and veins stood out in his neck. "To be a reporter, of course! So I can dig up the secrets of the rich and powerful, and then blackmail them." He looked at me slyly. "I could always start with you. Get a good story on the infamous and mysterious John Taylor, and they'd have to give me my own by-line. Go on; tell me something really shocking and sordid about you and Shotgun Suzie. Does she really take the gun to bed with her? Do you sometimes swap clothes? You'd better give me something, or I'll just make up something really juicy and extra nasty anyway. I'll say you said it, and it'll be just your word against mine."

I looked at him thoughtfully, and he fell back a step. "Jimmy," I said, "if I see one word about Suzie or me in this rag with your name on it, I will use my gift to find you. And then I'll send Suzie to you, who will no doubt wish to demonstrate her extreme displeasure. Suddenly and violently and all over the place."

He sniffed dismally. "Worth a try. Follow me. Sir."

He led me into the inner offices of the *Unnatural Inquirer*. The air was thick with cigarette smoke, incense, sweat, and tension. People bustled importantly back and forth around the various reporters, who were all working with furious concentration at their desks, hammering their computer keys like their lives depended on it. They kept calling out to each other, mostly without looking up from what they were doing, demanding information, opinions, and the very latest gossip, like so many ravenous baby birds in a nest. They all sounded cheerful enough, but there was a definite undercurrent of malice and cut-throat competition. The general noise level was appalling, the air was almost unbreathable, and the whole place seethed with talent and ambition.

It was everything I'd hoped it would be.

The copy-boy slouched down the main central aisle with me in tow, and everyone ostentatiously ignored me. There was a definite bunker atmosphere to the inner offices; probably because most people really were out to get them, for one reason or another. The industrious men and women of the *Unnatural Inquirer* drank and smoked like it was their last day on Earth, because it just might be.

Their readers might love them, but nobody else did. For the staff here it was always going to be Us versus Them, with everything and everyone fair game. There were always lawsuits, but the Editor & Publisher could afford the very best lawyers and took pride in keeping cases in court forever and a day. The paper might never have won a case, but it had never lost one either, mostly because the paper outspent or outlived the litigants. The *Unnatural Inquirer* had never once apologised, never printed a retraction, and never paid a penny in compensation. And was proud of it. Which was why the staff had to hide away in a bunker and take out special insurance against assassination attempts.

There was a prominent sign on one wall. YOU DON'T HAVE TO BE VICIOUS, PETTY-MINDED, AND MEAN-SPIRITED TO WORK HERE; BUT IT HELPS. Anywhere else, this would have been a joke.

Jimmy the copy-boy finally brought me to the Sub-Editor's office, knocked on the door like he was announcing the imminent arrival of the barbarian hordes, and pushed the door open without waiting for a reply. I followed him in, shutting the door carefully behind me, and Scoop Malloy himself stood up from behind his paper-scattered desk to greet me. He was a short, dumpy figure, with a sad face and a prematurely bald head, wearing a pullover with the phrase SMILE WHEN YOU CALL ME THAT embroidered over his chest. He popped a handful of little purple pills from a handy bottle, dry-swallowed them in one, and came out from behind his desk to give me a limp, almost apologetic handshake. I shook his hand gingerly. Partly because I was remembering where his nickname came from, and partly because his hand felt like it might come off in mine.

He glared at the copy-boy. "What are you still doing here? Isn't there some important tea you should be making?"

"Fascist!" Jimmy hissed, slamming the door behind him on his way out. Then he opened it again, shouted, "I'm nineteen! Nineteen!" and disappeared again.

Scoop Malloy sighed deeply, sat down behind his desk, and gestured for me to take the visitor's chair. Which was, of course, hard and uncomfortable, as visitor's chairs always are. I think it's supposed to imply you're only there on sufferance.

"Puberty's a terrible thing," said Scoop. "Particularly for other people. I'd fire him if he wasn't someone's nephew . . . Wish I knew whose . . . Welcome to the salt mines, Mr. Taylor. Sorry to drag you all the way in here, but you see how it is. The price of freedom of the Press is eternal vigilance and constant access to heavy-duty armaments."

"I was given to understand that the matter was urgent," I said. "And that the pay would be quite staggeringly good."

"Oh, quite," said Scoop. "Quite." He looked at me searchingly. "I understand you've done some work for Julien Advent, at the *Night Times*."

"On occasion," I said. "I approve of Julien."

Scoop smirked unpleasantly. "I could tell you some things about him . . ."

"Don't," I said firmly. "First, I wouldn't believe them; and second, if you were to insult my good friend Julien Advent, I would then find it necessary to beat you severely about the head and shoulders. Quite probably until your head came off, after which I would play football with it up and down the inner offices."

"I never believed those stories anyway," Scoop said firmly. He leaned forward across his desk, trying hard to look business-like. "Mr. Taylor, here at the *Unnatural Inquirer* we are not in the news business, as such. No. We print stories, entertainment, a moment's diversion. We employ a manic depressive to write the Horoscopes; to keep our readers on their toes, we run competitions with really big prizes, like *Guess where the next Timeslip's going to appear*; and we're always first with news about what the rich and famous are up to. Even if that news isn't exactly accurate. We print the stories people want to read."

"And to Hell with whether they're true?" I said.

Scoop shrugged, smiling his unpleasant smile again. "Oh, you'd be surprised how close to the truth we get, even if it is by accident."

There was a knock at the door. Scoop looked up with a certain amount of relief that he wouldn't have to face me alone any more. He called for the new arrival to enter, the door opened, and both Scoop and I stood up to greet the newcomer. She was tall and athletic-looking, and drop-dead gorgeous. Long jet-black hair framed a heart-shaped face, with high cheek-bones, sparkling eyes, and one of those old-fashioned pouting rosebud mouths. She wore a smart polka-dot dress, carefully cut to show off as much of her excellent body and magnificent bosom as possible.

She also had two cute little horns curling up from her forehead, poking out of her Bettie-Page-style bangs.

"This is one of our most promising young journalists," Scoop said proudly. "John Taylor, may I present to you Bettie Divine. And vice versa, of course. She'll be partnering you on this case."

I'd been reaching out to shake Bettie's hand, but immediately withdrew it. I glared at Scoop.

"I don't think so. I choose my own partners on cases, people I know can keep up with me and look after themselves. I can't guarantee you results if I have to drag a passenger around with me. No offence, Bettie."

"None taken," she said cheerfully in a rich husky voice. "But I work for the *Unnatural Inquirer*. Let's see if you can keep up with me."

She sat on the edge of the Sub-Editor's desk, crossing her legs to show off an awful lot of thigh, and leaning back so she could arch her back and point her breasts at me. Good tactics. Good legs. Really good breasts.

"Hey," she said, amused. "My face is up here."

"So it is," I said. "What exactly is it you do here, Bettie?"

"I am a demon girl reporter, darling. And I do mean demon. Daddy was a Rolling Stone, on one of their Nightside tours, Mummy was a slut lust demon groupie.

Somebody ought to have known better, but here I am. Large as life, and twice as talented. I really am a first-class journalist, and you're going to need me on this case, darling. So, just lie back and enjoy it."

"She's right," Scoop said heavily. He sat down behind his desk again, and I lowered myself back onto the unwelcoming visitor's chair. Scoop laced his fingers together and looked at me steadily. "Bettie's accompanying you is part of the deal, Mr. Taylor. If we've got to spend the kind of money it's going to take to get you to do this for us, we are determined to get our money's worth. And the best way to recoup some of the expense is by running our very own exclusive story of how you did it."

"*On the case with John Taylor!*" said Bettie. "*An intimate account of our time together, traversing the darkest depths of the Nightside!* Honestly, sweetie, we won't be able to print copies fast enough. The bouncer might as well be outside throwing them in. No-one's ever had a story like this."

"No," I said.

She slid forward off the desk and leaned over me, so close I could feel her breath on my face. "You're going to need me on this case, darling. Really you are. And I can be very helpful."

I stood up, and she retreated a little. "Put the brakes on, *darling*," I said. "I'm spoken for."

"Ah, yes!" said Bettie, clapping her dainty little hands together and giving me a knowing look. "We know all about that! The infamous John Taylor and the sexy psycho killer Shotgun Suzie! We're already taking odds as to which of you will end up killing the other. Do tell us all about her, John; what's Suzie really like? Is she still sexy when the bedroom door is shut? What do you talk about in those special little moments? Inquiring minds are positively panting to know all the sordid little details!"

"Let them pant," I said, and something in my voice made her fall back a step. "Suzie is a very private, very dangerous person."

"Why don't I explain exactly what the case entails," Scoop said quickly. I sat down in my chair again, and Bettie leaned against the side of the desk, facing me, her arms folded under her impressive bosom. I concentrated on Scoop.

"There has been a broadcast from the Afterlife," Scoop said bluntly. "And the broadcast has been intercepted. It turned up on someone's television set, quite out of the blue with no warning; and the possessor of that television set, one Pen Donavon, was sharp enough to record it, and burn it onto a DVD. He then approached us, offering the Afterlife Recording for sale; and we bought exclusive rights to it for one hell of a lot of money."

"An intercepted broadcast?" I said. "From Heaven, or Hell?"

"Who knows?" said Scoop. "For that matter, who cares? This is actual information, from the Great Beyond! Our readers will eat this up with spoons."

"Am I to understand you haven't actually seen what's on this DVD yet?" I said.

"Not a glimpse," Scoop said cheerfully.

"It could be a fake," I said. "Or it could be a broadcast from some other world or dimension."

"Doesn't matter," said Scoop. "We own it. We want it. But unfortunately, Donavon has disappeared. He was on his way to us, with the DVD, in return for the very generous cheque we had waiting, but he never got here. We want you to find it, and him, for us. We have to have that Recording! We've been trailing it all week, for its appearance in the Sunday edition! If someone else gets their hands on it, and pips us to the post . . . And it's not just the story; do you have any idea how much we could make selling copies of the DVD?"

I was still unconvinced, despite his enthusiasm. "This isn't going to be like that transmission from the future that someone taped off their television back in the nineties, is it? Suzie bought a copy of the tape off eBay, and when we played it, it was only a guy in a futuristic outfit, showing his bare arse to the camera and giggling a lot."

Scoop leaned forward over his desk, doing his best to fix me with his watery eyes. "The *Unnatural Inquirer* authorises you to find and recover this Afterlife Recording, and its owner, by any and all means you deem necessary. Bring the DVD to us, preferably with the owner but not necessarily, and the *Unnatural Inquirer* will pay you one million pounds. In cash, gold, diamonds, or postage stamps; whatever you prefer. We'll also pay you a bonus of another fifty thousand pounds, if you will agree to watch the Recording and give us your expert opinion as to whether or not it's the real thing. The word is, you are qualified to know."

I nodded, neither confirming nor denying. "And if I say it's a fake?"

Scoop shrugged. "We'll put it out anyway. We can always spice it up with some specially shot extra footage. We can use the same people we've got working on Lilith's diaries."

"Wait just a minute!" I said. "I know for a fact that my mother never left any diaries!"

"We know!" said Scoop. "That's why we've got three of our best people writing them now, in the next room. They're going to be big, I can tell you! Not as big as the Afterlife Recording, of course, which will be a license to print money . . . Not that we'd do that, of course. Not after the last time . . . You have to find this DVD for us!"

"And I go along with you to tell the story of how you tracked it down!" said Bettie.

I thought about it. A million pounds was an awful lot of money . . . "All right," I said. "Partner."

Bettie Divine jumped up and down, and did a little dance of joy, which did very interesting things to her breasts. I looked back at Scoop.

"If this Afterlife Recording should turn out to be the real thing," I said, "I'm not sure anyone should be allowed to see it. Real proof of Heaven or Hell? I don't think we're ready for that."

"It's the headline that's important," said Scoop. "That's

what will sell lots and lots of papers. The DVD . . . can be fixed, one way or the other. It's the concept we're selling."

"But if it is real," I said. "If it is hard evidence of what happens after we die . . . the whole Nightside could go crazy."

"I know!" said Bettie Divine. "A real story at last! Who would have thought it! Isn't it simply too wonderful, darling!"

# THREE

# Faith, Hope and Merchandising

Bettie and I stepped out of the *Unnatural Inquirer*'s offices and shot straight back to the same street corner I'd left, appearing abruptly out of nowhere thanks to Bettie's dimensional key. No-one paid us any attention. People appearing out of nowhere is business as usual in the Nightside. It's when people start disappearing suddenly that everyone tends to start screaming and taking to their heels, and usually with good reason. I realised Bettie was looking at me expectantly, and I sighed inwardly. I knew that look.

"I know that look," I said to her sternly. "You've heard all the stories, studied up on the legend, and now you expect me to solve the whole case with one snap of my fingers. Probably while smiling sardonically and saying something wickedly witty and quotable. Sorry, but it doesn't work that way."

"But . . . everyone knows you have a gift!" said Bettie, fixing me with her big dark eyes like a disappointed puppy. "You can find anyone, or anything. Can't you?"

"You of all people should know better than to believe in legends," I said. "Reality is always far more complicated. Case in point: yes, I do have a gift for finding things, and people, but I can't just use it to pinpoint the exact location of Pen Donavon or his DVD. I need a specific question to get a specific answer. But with the information I've got, I should be able to get a rough sense of where to start looking . . ."

I concentrated, waking my third eye, my private eye, and the world started to open up and reveal its secrets to me . . . and then I cried out in shock and pain as a sudden harsh pressure shot through my head, slamming my inner eye shut. Some great force from Outside had shut down my gift as quickly and casually as a dog shrugging off a bothersome flea. I swore harshly, and Bettie actually retreated a couple of steps.

"Sorry," I said, trying to ease the scowl I could feel darkening my face. "Something just happened. It would appear that Someone or Something big and nasty doesn't want me using my gift. They've shut me down. I can't See a damned thing."

"I didn't know anyone could do that," said Bettie.

"It's not something I'm keen to advertise," I said. "Has

to be a Major Player of some kind. I hope it's not the Devil again . . ."

"*Again?*" said Bettie delightedly. "Oh, John, you do lead such a fascinating life! Tell me all about it!"

"Not a chance in Hell," I said. "I don't discuss other client's cases. Anyway, it's not like I'm helpless without my gift. We'll have to do this the old-fashioned way: asking questions, following leads, and tracking down clues."

"But . . . if a Major Player is involved, doesn't that mean the Afterlife Recording must be the real deal?" said Bettie. "Or else, why would they get involved?"

"They're involved for the same reason we are," I said. "Because they want to discover whether the Recording is the real deal, or not. Or . . . because Someone wants us to think it's real . . . Nothing's ever simple in the Nightside."

And then I stopped and looked thoughtfully at Bettie Divine. There was something subtly different about her. Some small but definite change in her appearance since we'd left the *Unnatural Inquirer* offices. It took me a moment to realise she was now wearing a large floppy hat.

"Ah," said Bettie. "You've noticed. The details of my appearance are always changing. Part of my natural glamour, as the daughter of a succubus. Don't let it throw you, dear; I'm always the same underneath."

"How very reassuring," I said. "We need somewhere quiet, to think and talk this through . . . somewhere no-one will bother us. Got it. The Hawk's Wind Bar and Grille isn't far from here."

"I know it!" said Bettie, clapping her little hands together delightedly. "The spirit of the sixties! Groovy, baby!"

"You're like this all the time, aren't you?" I said.

"Of course!"

"I will make your Editor pay for this . . ."

"Lot of people say that," said Bettie Divine.

The Hawk's Wind Bar & Grille started out as a swinging café and social watering hole for all the brightest lights of the 1960s. Everyone who was anyone made the scene at the Hawk's Wind, to plot and deal and spread the latest gossip. It was wild and fabulous, and almost too influential for its own good. It burned down in 1970, possibly self-immolation in protest at the splitting up of the Beatles, but it was too loved and revered to stay dead for long. It came back as a ghost, the spirit of a building haunting its own location. People's belief keeps it real and solid, and these days it serves as a repository for all that was best of the sixties.

You can get brands of drink and food and music that haven't existed for forty years in the rest of the world at the Hawk's Wind Bar & Grille, and famous people from the sixties are always dropping in, through various forms of Time travel, and other less straightforward means. It's not for everyone, but then, what is?

I pushed open the Hindu latticed front door and led the way in. Bettie gasped and oohed at the psychedelic patterns on the walls, the rococo Day-Glo neon signs, and the Pop Art posters of Jimi, Che, and Timothy Leary. The air was thick with the scents of jasmine, joss sticks, and what used to be called jazz cigarettes. A complicated steel contraption hissed loudly in one corner as it pumped out several different colours of steam and dispensed brands of coffee with enough caffeine to blow the top of your head clean off. Hawk's Wind coffee could wake the dead, or at least keep them dancing for hours. I sat Bettie down at one of the Formica-covered tables and lowered myself cautiously onto the rickety plastic chair.

Revolving coloured lights made pretty patterns across walls daubed in swirls of primary colours, while a jukebox the size of a Tardis pumped out one groovy hit after another, currently the Four Tops' "Reach Out, I'll Be There." Which has always sounded just a bit sinister to me, for a love song. All around us sat famous faces from the Past, Present, and Futures, most there to just dig the scene. Bettie swivelled back and forth in her chair, trying to take it all in at once.

"Don't stare," I said. "People will think you're a reporter."

"But this is so *amazing*!" said Bettie, all but bouncing up and down in her chair. "I've never been here before. Heard about it, of course, but . . . people like me never get to come to places like this. We only get to write about them. Didn't I hear this place had been destroyed?"

"Oh, yes," I said. "Several times. But it always comes

back. You can't keep a good ghost down, not when so many people believe in it."

The juke-box's music changed to Manfred Mann's "Ha! Ha! Said the Clown." Go-Go girls, wearing only handfuls of glued-on sequins, danced wildly in golden cages suspended from the ceiling. At a nearby table, a collection of secret agents exchanged passwords and cheerful tall tales, while playing ostentatiously casual one-upmanship with their latest gadgets—pens and shoes that were communication devices, watches that held strangling wires and lasers, umbrellas that were also sword-sticks. One agent actually blinked on and off as he demonstrated his invisibility bracelet. Not far away, the Travelling Doctor, the Strange Doctor, and the Druid Doctor were deep in conference. Presumably some Cosmic Maguffin had gone missing again. And there were the King and Queen of America, smiling and waving, as they passed through.

A tall and splendid waitress dressed in a collection of pink plastic straps and thigh-high white plastic boots strode over to our table to take our order. Her impressive bust bore a name badge with the initials EV. She leaned forward over the table, the better to show off her amazing cleavage.

"Save it for the tourists, Phred," I said kindly. "What are you doing working here? The monster-hunting business gone slack?"

She shrugged prettily. "You know how it is, John. My work is always seasonal, and a girl has to eat. You wait till the trolls start swarming again in the Underground and see how fast they remember my phone number. Now, what can I do you for? We've got this amazing green tea in from Tibet, though it's a bit greasy; or we've got some freshly baked fudge brownies that will not only open your doors of perception, but blow the bloody things right off their hinges."

"Just two Cokes," I said firmly.

"You want curly-wurly straws with that?"

"Of course," I said. "It's all part of the experience."

"Excuse me," said Bettie, "but why does he call you Phred, when your initials are EV? What does the EV stand for?"

"Ex-Virgin," said Phred. "And I stand for pretty much anything."

And off she went to get our order, swaying her hips through the packed tables perhaps just a little more than was strictly necessary.

"You know the most interesting people, John," said Bettie.

I grinned. "Let us concentrate on the matter at hand. What can you tell me about the guy who originally offered to sell you the Afterlife Recording?"

"All anyone knows is the name, Pen Donavon," said Bettie, frowning prettily as she concentrated. "No-one in the offices has ever met him; our only contact has been by phone. He called out of the blue and almost got turned away. We get a lot of crank calls. But he was very insistent, and once we realised he was serious, he got bumped up to Scoop, who in turn passed him on to the Editor, who made the deal for exclusive rights."

"For a whole lot of money," I said. "Doesn't that strike you as odd, given that no-one ever met Donavon, or even glimpsed what was on the DVD?"

"We had to pin the rights down before he went somewhere else! Trust me, the paper will make more money out of this story than Donavon will ever see."

"Do you at least have his address?"

"Of course!" Bettie said indignantly. "We've already checked; he isn't there. Skipped yesterday, owing two weeks' rent."

"We need to go there anyway," I said patiently. "There may be clues."

"Ooh, *clues*!" Bettie said delightedly. "Goody! I've never seen a clue."

She opened up a large leather purse, which I would have sworn she wasn't carrying before, and rummaged around in it for her address book. The purse seemed to be very full and packed with all kinds of interesting things. Bettie caught me looking, and grinned.

"Mace spray, with added holy water. Skeleton keys, including some made from real bones. And a couple of smoke grenades, to cover a quick exit. A demon girl reporter has to be prepared for all kinds of things, sweetie."

We went to Pen Donavon's place. It wasn't far. Bettie stuck close beside me. She wasn't too keen on appearing in public, given some of the stories she'd written. Apparently while celebrities tended to take such things in their stride, their fans could be downright dangerous.

"Relax," I said. "No-one's going to look at you while I'm here."

"You do seem to attract a lot of attention," Bettie agreed, peering out from under her large floppy hat, which was now a completely different colour. "It's really fascinating, the way people react to your presence. I mean, there's fear, obviously, and even an element of panic; but some people look at you in awe, as though you were a king, or a god. You really have done most of the things people say, haven't you?"

"I shall neither confirm nor deny," I said. "Let's just say I get around, and leave it at that."

"And you and Shotgun Suzie . . . ?"

"Are off-limits. Don't go there."

She smiled at me dazzlingly. "Can't blame a girl for trying, darling."

It turned out Pen Donavon had a small apartment over a pokey little junk shop, one more in a row of shabby, grubby establishments offering the usual dreams and damnations at knocked-down prices. The kind of area where the potential customers scurry along with their heads bowed, so they won't have to make eye contact with anyone. Pen Donavon's establishment boasted the grandiose name *Objets du Temps Perdu*, a literary allusion that was no doubt wasted on most of his clientele. I wasn't entirely sure I got it myself.

Bettie and I peered through the streaky, fly-specked window. It appeared that Donavon specialised in the kind of weird shit that turns up in the Nightside, through the various Timeslips that are always opening and closing. Lost objects and strange artifacts, from other times and dimensions. All the obviously useful, valuable, or powerful things are snapped up the moment they appear; in fact, there are those who make a good living scavenging the Timeslips. (Though they have to be quick on their feet; there's never any telling how long a Timeslip will last, and you don't want to be caught inside it when it disappears.) But a lot of what appears often defies easy description, or analysis, and such things tend to trickle down through the mercantile community, the price dropping at every stage, until it ends up in shops like these. Things too intricate, too futuristic, or just too damned weird to be categorised, even by all the many learned authorities that the Nightside attracts like a dog gets fleas. Great discoveries, and fortunes, have been made in places like this. But not many.

I rubbed the sleeve of my trench coat against the window. It didn't help.

"Well," I said. "Nothing here to give the Collector any sleepless nights. Only the usual junk and debris from the various time-lines. I wouldn't give you tuppence for any of it."

"Wait a minute," said Bettie. "You know the Collector? Personally? Wow . . . I keep forgetting, you know all the legends of the Nightside. What's he like?"

"Vain, obsessive, and very dangerous," I said.

"Oh, that is so cool. I never get to meet any legends. I just write about them."

"Best way," I said. "They'd only disappoint you in person."

"Like you?" said Bettie.

"Exactly."

The window display did its best to show off odd bits of future technology, most of which might or might not have been entirely complete, along with oddly shaped things that might have been Objects of Power, alien artifacts or relics of lost histories. Carpets that might fly, eggs that might hatch, puzzle-boxes that might open if only you could find the right operating Words. No price tags on anything, of course. Bargaining was everything, in a place like this.

The sign on the door said CLOSED. I tried the door, and it opened easily. No bell rang as we entered. There was no sign of any shop assistant, or customers, and the state of the place suggested there hadn't been any for some time. The gloomy interior was so still and silent you could practically hear the dust falling. I called out, in case anyone might still be skulking somewhere, but no-one answered. My voice sounded flat in the quiet, as though the nature of the place discouraged loud noises. Bettie dubiously studied some of the things set out on glass shelves, wrinkling her perfect nose at some of the more organic specimens, while I went behind the counter to check out the till. It was the old-fashioned type, with heavy brass push keys, and pop-up prices. It opened easily, revealing drawers empty save for a handful of change. Beside the till was a letter spike with piled-up bills. I checked through them quickly; they weren't so much bills as final demands, complete with threats and menaces. Clearly the shop had not been doing well.

A man with this kind of economic pressure hanging over him might well see a way out through fabricating an Afterlife Recording, and then lose his nerve when the time came to actually present it to the *Unnatural Inquirer*.

I found a set of stairs at the back, leading up to the overhead apartment. I insisted on going first, just in case, and Bettie crowded my back all the way up. The bare wooden steps creaked loudly, giving plenty of advance warning, but when we got to the apartment the door was already slightly ajar. I made Bettie stand back and pushed the door open with one hand. The room beyond was silent and empty of life. I stepped inside and stood by the door, looking around thoughtfully. Bettie pushed straight past me and darted round the place, checking all the rooms. No-one was home. Pen Donavon's apartment was a dump, with the various sad pieces of his life scattered everywhere. There were no obvious signs that the place had already been searched. It would have been hard to tell.

The furniture was cheap and nasty, the carpet was threadbare, and the single electric light bulb didn't even have a shade. And yet the main room was dominated by a huge wide-screen television, to which had been bolted a whole bunch of assorted unfamiliar technology. The additions stood out awkwardly, with trailing wires and spiky antennae. Some of it looked like future tech, some of it alien. Lights glowed here and there, to no apparent purpose or function. Presumably it had all been brought up from the shop downstairs. I approached the television and knelt before it, careful to maintain a safe distance. Metal and mirrors, crystal and glass, and a few oily shapes that looked disturbingly organic. Up close, the stuff smelled . . . bad. Corrupt.

Bettie produced a camera from her embroidered purse and took a whole bunch of photos. She wanted to photograph me, too, and I let her. I was busy thinking. She finally ended up bending down beside me, sniffing disparagingly.

"Isn't this an absolutely awful place? There's underwear soaking in the bath, and no-one's cleaned up in here for months. Some men shouldn't be allowed to live on their own. You don't even want to know what I found in the toilet. This television is very impressive, though. Have you ever seen anything like it?"

"No," I said. "But then future and alien technology isn't my speciality. This could be genius, or it could be junk."

"Could it have enabled the television to look in on a broadcast from the Afterlife?"

"Who knows? But I wouldn't touch any of it, if I were you. It looks . . . unhealthy."

"Trust me, darling. I wouldn't touch *that* if it offered to buy me champagne."

I straightened up, and she straightened up with me. Her knees didn't creak. I looked round the apartment again. For all the clutter, the room was still basically characterless. No paintings or posters on the walls, no personal touches like photos or prized possessions, nothing to show Donavon had ever thought of this place as home. No; it was more like a place to stay while he was passing through on his way to better things. Once he got his lucky break . . . I was beginning to get an idea of who Pen Donavon might be, one of those desperate dreamers, always chasing that big break, that lucky find that would make him rich and famous and change his life forever. And maybe, this time he had . . .

I tried my gift again, hoping to pick up a ghost image of Pen Donavon's past, so I could follow it as he left . . . but once again the force from Outside slammed my inner eye shut the moment it started to open. I grimaced and shook my head slowly, waiting for the pain to settle. I was going to find out who was behind this, then do something about it. Something really nasty and violent.

"So, what do we do now?" said Bettie, who, despite everything I'd said, persisted on looking at me like I had all the answers.

"When faced with serious questions of a religious nature, there's only one place to go," I said. "And that is the Street of the Gods. If only because they always have the best gossip."

•   •   •

We took the Underground train. There are other ways of getting to the Street of the Gods, but the train is by far the safest. Bettie and I descended into the Underground system and strode through the cream-tiled tunnels covered in the usual graffiti, not all of it in human languages. CTHULHU DOES IT IN HIS SLEEP, was a new addition, along with THE EYES OF WALKER ARE UPON YOU. Bettie went to pay for our tickets, and I stopped her.

"It's all right, darling!" she said. "When you work for the *Unnatural Inquirer*, we pay for everything!"

"I don't pay," I said. I gestured at the ticket machine, and it opened obediently to let us pass. I smiled just a little smugly at Bettie. "Payment for an old case. One of the trains had gone rogue; people got on and then it wouldn't let them get off again. You could hear the trapped passengers beating helplessly on the walls, screaming for help."

"What happened?" said Bettie, her eyes wide. "What did you do?"

"I frightened the train," I said. "And it let everyone go."

"I shall never look at a train in the same way again," said Bettie.

We went down to the platform, giving the various buskers a wide berth. Especially the one singing four part harmonies with himself. It's one thing to drop a few coins in a hat, because the wheel turns for all of us, but it isn't always wise to listen to the music they play. Music really can have charms in the Nightside.

The platform was crowded, as usual. Half a dozen members of the Tribe of Gay Barbarians, standing around looking tough with their leathers and long swords, complete with shaved legs, pierced nipples, and heavy face make-up. A silverback gorilla wore an exquisitely cut formal suit, complete with top hat, cane, and a monocle screwed firmly into one eye. A Grey alien wearing fishnet stockings and suspenders, passing out tracts. And a very polite Chinese demon, sipping hot steaming blood from a thermos. The usual crowd.

The destination board offered the usual possibilities: SHADOWS FALL, HACELDAMA, STREET OF THE GODS. There are other destinations, other possibilities, but you have to go down into the deeper tunnels for those; and not everyone who goes down that far comes back up again.

A train roared in, right on time. A long, silvery bullet, preceded by a blast of approaching air that smelled of other places. The carriages were solid steel tubes, with only the heavily reinforced doors standing out. No windows. To get to its various destinations, the train had to travel through certain intervening dimensions; and none of them were the kinds of places where you'd want to see what was outside. The door hissed open, and Bettie and I stepped into the nearest carriage. The seats were green leather, and the steel walls were reassuringly thick and heavy. No-one else wanted to get into our carriage, despite the crowd on the platform.

The trip to the Street of the Gods was mostly uneventful. The few things that attacked us couldn't get in, and the dents in the steel walls had mostly smoothed themselves out again by the time the train pulled into the station. Bettie was still laughing and chattering as we made our way up the elevators to the Street of the Gods. You learn to take such things in your stride in the Nightside.

On the Street of the Gods, you can find a Church to pretty much anything that anyone has ever believed in. They stretched away forever, two long rows of organised worship, where the gods are always at home to callers. Prayers are heard here, and answered, so it pays to be careful what you say. You never know who might be listening. The most important Beings get the best spots, while everyone else fights it out for location in a Darwinian struggle for survival. Sometimes I think the whole Nightside runs on irony.

Most of the Beings on the Street of the Gods didn't want to talk to me. In fact, most of them hid inside their churches behind locked and bolted doors and refused to come out until I'd gone. Understandable; they were still rebuilding parts of the Street from the last time I'd been here. But there are always some determined to show those watching that they aren't afraid of anyone, so a few of the more up-and-coming Beings sauntered casually over to chat with me. A fairly ordinary-looking priest who said he was the newly risen Dagon. Stack! The Magnificient; a more or less humanoid alien who claimed to be slumming it from a higher dimension. And the Elegant Profundity, a guitar-carrying avatar from the Church of Clapton, who was so laid-back he was practically horizontal. The small and shifty God of Lost Things hung around, evasive as always. None of them professed to know anything about a broadcast from the Afterlife, let alone a DVD recording. Most of them were quite intrigued by the thought.

"It can't be authentic," said Dagon. "I mean, we're in the business of faith, not hard evidence. And if there had ever been a broadcast from the Hereafter, we'd have heard about it long before this."

"And just the idea of recording one is so . . . tacky," Stack! said, folding his four green arms across his sunken chest.

"But it could be very good for business," said the Elegant Profundity, strumming a minor chord on his Rickenbacker.

The group went very thoughtful.

"There's money to be made here," said Dagon. "Serious money. And there's nothing like business success to bring in bigger congregations. Everyone loves a winner."

"But . . . if this recording should prove real, and accurate, it would provide proof of What Comes After," Stack! said. "And the last thing anyone here wants is hard evidence of that. We derive our power from faith and worship. A true and actual Afterlife Recording could drive a lot of us out of business. Besides, most of Humanity isn't ready for the truth."

I regarded him thoughtfully. "Are you saying you know What Comes Next?"

Stack! squirmed uncomfortably, which given his rather fluid shape was a somewhat disturbing sight. "Well, no, not as such. I may be from a higher dimension, but not that high."

"You have to have faith," said the Elegant Profundity. "Solid evidence of the true nature of Heaven or Hell would only screw up everyone's life. It's one thing to suppose, quite another to know."

"This whole situation raises more questions than I'm comfortable with," I said. "What exactly is the DVD a recording of? Have there always been broadcasts from Heaven and Hell, and we never knew? And who were the broadcasts aimed at?"

"Each other?" said Bettie. "Maybe they just like to . . . keep in touch."

"But then why has no-one ever intercepted one of these broadcasts before?" I said. "Why should it suddenly turn up on someone's television set, no matter how much work's been done to it? And if anyone here so much as mentions moving in a mysterious way, I shall get cranky. Quite seriously and violently cranky."

"If there were such communications, on a regular basis, we would know about it," Dagon said firmly. "It's our job to provide mysteries and wonder, not grubby little facts."

"But what if it is true," Stack! said wistfully. "Was this interception of the broadcast a mistake, or deliberate? Are we supposed to know, at last? And who or what is behind it; and what could they hope to gain?"

"Money, probably," said the Elegant Profundity, and everyone nodded solemnly.

"Maybe we should all do our own DVDs," Stack! said.

"Can't risk falling behind . . . Let's face it, you can't have too much publicity."

"Sure," said the Elegant Profundity. "I've been releasing CDs on a regular basis ever since I got here. Rock and Roll Heaven won't build itself, you know."

"Yes, yes!" said Bettie Divine. "The *Unnatural Inquirer* could give away a new DVD every week, with the Sunday edition! Build your own collection!"

"We don't want the faithful sitting at home in front of their televisions," Dagon said firmly. "We want them here, in our Churches."

"We already sell religious statues, and reliquaries, and blessed artifacts," Stack! said reasonably. "DVDs are the future. For now. Does anyone here know about this Extra Definition thing?"

"New formats are the invention of the Devil," said the Elegant Profundity. "He's always been big on temptation. But people would pay through the nose for teachings direct from their God! And even second-hand faith is better than none."

"Royalty cheques outweigh collection plates any day," Stack! said. "I want you all to concentrate on one word: *franchise* . . ."

"Oh, come on!" said Dagon. "Where's that going to lead, the McChurch? You'll be talking about bringing in image consultants and focus groups next."

"Why not?" Stack! replied. "We have to move with the times. Faith is fine, but wealth lasts longer."

"Heretic!" said Dagon, and punched Stack! out with a very unpriestly left hook.

I took Bettie firmly by the arm, and we hurried away. Believers were coming running from all directions, eager to join the fray, and you really don't want to get caught in the middle of a religious war on the Street of the Gods. Especially not when the smiting starts. Someone always ends up throwing lightning bolts, and then it's bound to escalate. We headed back to the Underground station, discussing what we knew about previous attempts to communicate with the Other Side, so we wouldn't have to listen to the rising sounds of conflict and unpleasantness behind us.

It was already raining frogs.

"Surprisingly, Marconi is supposed to be the first man to use technology to try and make contact with the Hereafter," I said. "Some sources claim he only invented radio because he was trying to find a way to talk to his dead brother. There are even those who say he succeeded; though reports of what he heard are . . . disturbing."

"Then there are people who approach dying people in hospitals," said Bettie. "And persuade them to memorise messages from a bereaved family, to pass on to people already dead. There's usually money involved—to pay hospital bills or look after the dying person's family. The *Unnatural Inquirer* paid good money for a dozen messages to Elvis, but we never got a reply. What *was that*?"

"Don't look back," I said. "Then there are the Death-walkers. A disturbing bunch of action philosophers with a very hands-on approach to the Near Death Experience. They kill themselves, a necromancer holds them on the very brink for a while, and then he brings them back to life. The briefly departed are then questioned on what they saw, and who they spoke to, while they were dead. I've read some of the transcripts."

"And?"

"Either the dead lie a lot, or they have a really nasty sense of humour."

"I once did a piece on people who hear messages on radios trained to dead stations, or tape recorders left running in empty rooms," said Bettie. "I listened to a whole bunch of recordings, but I can't say I was convinced. It's all hiss and static, and something that might be voices, if you wanted it badly enough. It's like Rorschach ink-blots, where people see shapes that aren't really there. You hear what you want to hear. Was that a Church blowing up?"

"It's the pillars of salt that worry me," I said. "Just keep walking and talking."

"Then there's psychic imprinting," said Bettie, staring determinedly straight ahead. "You know, when a person stares at a blank piece of film and makes images appear. I did this marvellous piece on a man who could make naughty pictures appear on bathroom tiles, from two rooms away! The paper did a full colour supplement on most of them. You could only get the full set by mail order, under plain cover."

"Psychic imprinting is more common than most people like to think," I said. "That's where most ghost images come from. And genius loci, where bad things happening poisons the surroundings, to produce Bad Places. Like Fun Faire."

"Wait just a minute, darling," said Bettie. "I heard about what just happened there! Was that you?"

I simply smiled.

"Oh, poo! You're no fun at all sometimes."

"That augmented television set bothers me," I said. "Could Pen Donavon have accidentally invented something that allowed him to Listen In, however briefly, on something Humanity was never supposed to know about? Stranger things have happened, and most of them right here in the Nightside. This place has always attracted rogue scientists and very free thinkers, come here in pursuit of the kinds of knowledge and practices that are banned everywhere else, and quite properly, too. Walker has a whole group of his people dedicated to tracking these idiots, then shutting them down, with extreme prejudice if necessary. Unless what they're doing looks to be unusually interesting, or profitable, in which case their work gets confiscated for the greater good. Which means the scientists get to work exclusively for the Authorities, somewhere very secure, for the rest of their lives."

"Except there aren't any Authorities, any more," said Bettie. "So who do these scientists work for now?"

"Good question," I said. "If you ever find out . . ."

"You'll read about it in the *Unnatural Inquirer*." Bettie smiled cheerfully. "I love the way you talk about these things so casually. I only get to hear about stuff like this at second or third remove, and there's rarely any proof. You're right there in the thick of things. Must be such fun . . ."

"Not always the word I'd use," I said. "And you are not to quote me. I don't care what you print, but Walker might. And he'd be more likely to come after you than me."

"Let him," Bettie said airily. "The *Unnatural Inquirer* looks after its own. John, you're frowning. Why are you frowning? Should we start running?"

"If Pen Donavon had found a way to Listen In and got noticed," I said slowly, "he might have attracted the attention of Heaven or Hell. Which is rarely a good thing. They might send agents to silence him, and destroy the Recording."

"Oh, dear," said Bettie. "Are we talking angels? The Nightside's still putting itself back together after the last angel war."

"I wish people would stop looking at me like the angel war was all my fault," I said.

"Well, it was; wasn't it?"

"Not as such, no!"

"You can be such a disappointment, sometimes," said Bettie Divine.

FOUR

# WHEN
# COLLECTORS
# GO BAD

Back in the Nightside proper, I headed for Uptown, that
relatively refined area where the better class of establishments and members-only clubs gather together and circle
the wagons, to keep out the riff-raff. People like me, and
anyone I might know. I had a particular destination in
mind, but I didn't tell Bettie. Some subjects need to be
sneaked up on, approached slowly and cautiously, so as
not to freak out the easily upset. Bettie clearly thought
she'd been around and seen it all, but there are some people and places that would make a snot demon puke, on
general principles.

"Where exactly are we going?" said Bettie, looking eagerly about her.

"Well," I said, "when you're on the trail of something rare and unique, the place to start is with the Collector. He's spent the best part of his life in pursuit of the extraordinary and the uncommon, often by disreputable, underhanded, and downright dishonest means. He's a thief and a grave-robber, a despoiler of archaeological sites, and no museum or private cabinet of curiosities is safe from him. He's even got his own collection of weird time machines, so he can loot and ransack the Past of all its choicest items. If there's a gap in history where something important ought to be, you can bet the Collector's been there. He's bound to have heard about the Afterlife Recording by now, and, faced with the prospect of such a singular and significant item, you can bet he won't rest till he's tracked it down."

Bettie looked actually awe-struck. "The Collector . . . Oh, wow. The paper's been trying to get an interview with him for years. Mind you, half the people you talk to swear he's nothing more than an urban myth, something historians use to frighten their children. But you know him personally! That is so cool! Has he really got the Holy Grail? The Spear of Destiny? The Maltese Falcon?"

"Given the sheer size of his collection, anything's possible," I said. "Except maybe that last one."

"There are those who say the two of you have a history," Bettie said guilelessly.

"If you're fishing in your pocket for your mini tape recorder, forget it," I said pleasantly. "I lifted it off you before we even left the *Unnatural Inquirer* offices. I don't do *on the record*."

"Oh, poo," said Bettie. And then she smiled dazzlingly. "Doesn't matter. I have a quite remarkable memory. And what I can't remember, I'll make up. So, tell me all about the Collector. How did you meet?"

"He was an old friend of my father's," I said.

Bettie frowned. "But . . . some of the stories say he's your mortal enemy?"

"That, too," I said. "That's the Nightside for you."

"Where's he based these days?" Bettie said casually.

I grinned. "That really would be a scoop for you, wouldn't it? Unfortunately, I have no idea, at present. He used to store his collection in a secret base up on the Moon, sunk deep under the Sea of Tranquility, but he moved it after I . . . dropped in, for a little visit."

"Couldn't you have used your gift to find it again?"

"The Collector is seriously protected. By Forces and Powers even I would think twice about messing with."

"Still . . . you've actually seen his collection! How cool is that? What did you see? What has he got? *Did you take any photos?*"

I smiled. "I never betray a confidence."

"But he's your mortal enemy!"

"Not always," I said. "It's . . . complicated."

Bettie shrugged easily and slipped her arm through mine. My first impulse was to pull away, but I didn't. Her arm felt good where it was. I looked at her thoughtfully, but she'd given up on grilling me for the moment and was looking interestedly about her.

"I don't think I've ever been this deep into Uptown. You don't come here unless you are almost obscenely wealthy. I'll bet there are shops here where a pair of shoes would cost more than my annual salary. Remind me to steal a pair before we leave. Where are we going, exactly?"

"I need to talk to Walker," I said.

Bettie slammed to a halt, stopping me with her. "The head man himself? Darling, you don't mess around, do you?"

"If anyone knows where the Collector hangs his hat these days, it'll be Walker," I said. "Can we start moving again?"

She nodded stiffly, and we set off at a somewhat slower pace than before.

"But, gosh, I mean . . . *Walker*," said Bettie, giving me her wide-eyed look again. "Our very own polite and civilised and extremely dangerous lord and master? The man who can make people disappear if he doesn't like the look of them? That Walker? There is a definite limit as to how far I'm prepared to go for this story, and annoying Walker is right there at the top of my list of Things Not To Do."

"You'll be fine, as long as you're with me." I tried hard to sound calm and confident. "He'll talk to me. Partly because Walker is another old friend of my father's. Partly because he's an old friend of the Collector. But mostly because I shall dazzle him with my charming personality."

"Maybe I'll stay outside while you talk to him," said Bettie.

I grinned at her and noticed abruptly that she wasn't wearing her polka-dot dress any more. She was now wearing a creamy off-the-shoulder number, very chic, and a pink pill-box hat with a veil. The horns on her forehead peeked demurely out from under the brim of the hat, lifting the veil just a little. I decided not to say anything.

"Is this really such a good idea, sweetie?" Bettie said finally. "I mean, *Walker* . . . That man is seriously scary. He's disappeared at least nine of the *Unnatural Inquirer*'s reporters because they were getting too close to something he didn't want known. Or at least discussed. We know it was him, because he sent us personally signed *In Deep Condolence* cards."

"Yeah," I said. "That sounds like Walker."

"I don't want to be disappeared, John! It would be very bad for my career. Promise me you'll protect me. I am too young, too talented, and too utterly gorgeous in a fashionably understated way to be disappeared! It would be a crime against journalism."

"Relax," I said. "You'll be fine. I can handle Walker."

I don't like to lie to people, unless I have to, but sometimes you have to say what people want to hear to get them to do what you want them to do. And I had to talk to Walker. He was the only one who might know where the Collector was hiding out these days, who might be willing to tell me. It was always a calculated risk, talking to Walker. In the end, when we finally run out of excuses, one of us is going to kill the other. I've always known that. And so has he.

We like each other. We've saved each other's lives. It's complicated. It's the Nightside.

"Do you need your gift to find Walker?" Bettie asked, staring distractedly about her as though half-expecting him to suddenly appear out of some door or side alley, just from the mention of his name.

"No," I said. "I know where he'll be. Where he always is at this time. Taking tea at his Gentleman's Club."

"Walker belongs to a club?" said Bettie. "Result, darling! A definite exclusive! Which club?"

"There is only one club for those of Walker's exalted position," I said. "The oldest and most exclusive club in the Nightside. The Londinium Club."

Bettie looked sharply at me. "But . . . that was destroyed. During the Lilith War. We published photos. That was where the Authorities were killed. And eaten."

"Quite right," I said. "But it's back. Word is, the Club rebuilt itself. Any building that's survived everything the Nightside can throw at it for over two thousand years isn't going to let a little thing like being destroyed in a war slow it down."

"Oh," said Bettie. "Do you mind that I'm holding your arm?"

"No," I said. "I don't mind."

• • •

The last time I'd seen the Londinium Club, during the height of the Lilith War, it had been one hell of a mess. The magnificent Roman façade had been cracked and holed, smoke-blackened and fire-damaged. The great marble steps leading up to the single massive door had been fouled with blood and shit. And the Club's legendary Doorman, who had kept out the uninvited and unwelcome for centuries beyond counting, had been torn apart, his severed head impaled on the railings. Inside, it had been even worse.

But now everything seemed back to normal, right down to the fully restored Roman façade. Which I'd always found rather crude, to be honest. There was a new Doorman, however. It seemed the Club could only restore itself, and not those who'd died defending it. Just as well, really. A lot of the Club's members were no loss to anyone, for all their wealth and power. Anyone rich and powerful enough to belong to the Londinium Club had almost certainly done appalling and unspeakable things to get there. And that very definitely included Walker.

The new Doorman was a tall and elegantly slender fellow dressed in the full finery of Regency fashion. Right down to the heart-shaped beauty mark on his cheek, the poser. He moved deliberately forward to block my way as I started up the steps towards the door. I stopped right in front of him and eased my arm out of Bettie's so I could give the Doorman my full attention. He looked down his nose at me, and there was a lot of it to look down. His eyes were cold and distant, and his thin smile was carefully calculated to be polite without containing the slightest trace of warmth or welcome. I was sure Bettie was giving him her brightest smile, but the Doorman and I only had eyes for each other.

"I have the name and face of every current Member of the Londinium Club committed to memory, sir," said the Doorman. He made the *sir* sound like an insult. "And I believe I am correct in saying that you, sir, and this . . . person, are not Members in good standing. Therefore, you have no business being here."

"Wrong," I said. "I'm here to see Walker."

"He does not wish to be seen, sir. And particularly not by the likes of you. You may leave now."

"I don't think so," I said. "Being faced down by a little snot like you would be bad for my reputation. One last chance—go and tell Walker I'm here."

"Leave," said the Doorman. "You are not welcome here. You will never be welcome here."

"Just once, I'd love to do this the easy way," I said wistfully. "Now step aside, fart face, or I'll do something amusing to you."

The Doorman sniffed disdainfully, gestured languidly with one hand, and a shimmering wall of force sprang up between us. I fell back a step, sensing the terrible power running through the field. This was new. The old Doorman had relied on sheer obnoxious personality, of which he had a lot, to keep the riff-raff out. That, and a punch that could concuss a cow. Presumably the Club had decided it needed a more sturdy defence these days. The new Doorman wasn't actually sneering at me, he wouldn't lower himself that much; but it felt like he was. And I couldn't have that.

I stepped forward again, so close to the field I could feel it prickling on my skin, and looked the Doorman right in the eye. He met my gaze coldly, with a supercilious stare. I kept looking at him, and he began to shake, as he realised he couldn't look away. Beads of sweat popped out all over his face as I held his gaze with mine, and he started to make low, whimpering sounds.

"Drop the screen," I said. "We're coming in."

The screen snapped off. I looked away, and the Doorman collapsed, sitting down suddenly on the steps as though all the strength had gone out of his legs. He actually flinched back as I led Bettie up the steps past him. She looked at me, frowning, as we approached the massive front door of the Londinium Club.

"What the hell did you do to him?"

"I stared him down," I said.

"That really wasn't a very nice thing to do, sweetie. He was only doing his job. I'm not sure I want you holding my arm any more."

"Suit yourself," I said. "I don't always have time for nice. Or the inclination."

"You're full of surprises, aren't you?"

"You have no idea," I said.

The huge door swung open before us. Just as well; I'd had something particularly unpleasant and destructive in mind in case it hadn't. Inside, the main foyer was exactly as I remembered it, intimidatingly large, unbearably stuffy, and smotheringly luxurious. Mosaics and paintings and marble pillars, and a general air of smug exclusivity. The last time I'd been here there'd been blood and bodies everywhere, but you'd never know it now. Wars came and apocalypses went, but the Londinium Club goes on forever.

Some say there are terrible caverns deep beneath the Club, where the oldest Members still gather to worship something ancient and awful. Baphomet, some say, or the King in Yellow, or the Serpent in the Sun. But there are always rumours like that in the Nightside.

A few people passed us, looking very prosperous and important. They studiously ignored me, and Bettie. I caught the eye of a liveried footman, and he came reluctantly over to see what I wanted.

"You've been here before," said Bettie, her voice hushed for once by the sheer presence of the place.

"I've been everywhere before," I said. "Mind you, I've also been thrown out of practically everywhere, at one time or another."

"I've never seen anything like this . . ."

"Don't let it get to you. For all the Club's opulence, you couldn't spit in the dining-room without being sure of hitting at least one complete scumbag."

She giggled suddenly and put one hand to her mouth. The footman came to a halt before me and bowed politely. Since I was in the Club, I obviously belonged there. His was not to question why, no matter how much he might want to. He'd bowed to worse, in his time. He managed to imply all this without actually saying a word. It was a remarkable performance. I felt like applauding.

"Walker," I said.

"In the main dining-room, sir. Dining, with guests. Should I announce you, sir?"

"And spoil the surprise?" I said. "Heaven forfend. You run along. We can look after ourselves."

The footman backed away at speed, not even waiting for a tip. Which was just as well, really. I headed casually for the main dining area, with Bettie tagging along at my side like an over-excited puppy. No-one challenged us. It's all about attitude. You can get away with murder if you look like you belong.

I pushed open the dining-room door, stepped inside, then stopped right there, pushing Bettie slightly to one side so that we were concealed from the crowded room by a fortuitously placed potted aspidistra. I hushed her before she could say anything and peered between the leaves. All the tables were full, mostly occupied by large sturdy types in formal suits, eating basic stodgy food because it reminded them of the good old days of school dinners. None of them looked at each other. They were there for peace and quiet, not to socialise.

Walker had to be the exception, of course. He was currently holding court with some of the more august personages jockeying for position to take the place of the recently deceased Authorities. They sat stiffly in stiff-backed chairs, nursing expensive liqueurs and oversized cigars and talking loudly to show they didn't give a damn who overheard them. They smiled and nodded and were polite enough, and you'd never know they were deadly rivals who'd happily slaughter each other at the first sign of weakness. This was politics, after all, and there were rules of etiquette to follow. Yesterday's enemy might be tomorrow's friend, or at least ally.

"Hush," I said quietly to Bettie. "Watch and listen. You might learn something interesting. You know who those people are, with Walker?"

"Of course," she said, putting her mouth so close to my ear I could feel her breath on the side of my face. "Walker's the smart city gent. The older gentleman to his left in the military uniform is General Condor. The revolting specimen to Walker's right is Uptown Taffy Lewis. And the woman sitting opposite Walker is Queen Helena, ex-Monarch of the Ice Kingdoms."

"Very good," I said. "Now let's see if you read anything more than the gossip columns. What can you tell me about Walker's guests?"

Bettie smiled, glad of a chance to show off her reporter's expertise. "General Condor comes from a future time-line. Arrived here through a Timeslip and got stranded in the Nightside when it closed. Word is he used to be in charge of some kind of Space Fleet, star-ships and the like, keeping the peace in some future Empire or Federation. He was leading the troops into battle against some kind of Rebellion, when his flagship came under fire and was blown apart. He only escaped at the last moment in a life-boat." She laughed briefly. "He doesn't approve of us. A very upright and moral man, is our General. Since he arrived here he'd made it his business to first support, and then lead, all the right causes. He wants to reform us and save our souls, the poor fool. The *Unnatural Inquirer*'s been trying to dig up some dirt on him for ages, but unfortunately it seems he really is as worthy and boring as he claims."

I nodded, looking the General over. Condor was a tall, straight-backed military type, in a surprisingly old-fashioned bottle-green uniform, complete with peaked cap. Even sitting down, he looked like he was still at attention. His face was deeply lined, scarred here and there, but his blue eyes were cold and piercing under bushy white eyebrows. He had to be in late middle age, but there didn't look to be an ounce of give in him.

I'd run into him a few times, here and there. He didn't approve of me, or people like me, but then it would be hard to find anyone or anything he did approve of in the Nightside. Our free trade in vice and depravity and damnation appalled him. A good man, perhaps, and no doubt brave enough standing on the poop-deck of his star-ship, facing terrible odds; but his stark black-and-white philosophy had no place in the Nightside. On the one hand, he was desperate to return to his own time and his own people, and take up the battle again, but on the other he was realistic enough to know he might never get back. And so he had decided to take on the Nightside, as a challenge. As an evil to be overcome. He now led, or at least represented, all those various interests inside the Nightside who wanted to clean the place up, for their own philosophical, financial, or political reasons.

General Condor liked to talk about redemption, and potential, and all the things we might achieve, if only we could control our darker urges and learn to work together. He couldn't seem to understand that people only came here to indulge their darker urges. He was a good man, in the wrong place. And the Nightside does so love to break a hero.

"How about the slug in the ill-fitting dress jacket?" I said.

"Easy. Everyone knows Uptown Taffy Lewis," said Bettie. She made brief retching noises. "He owns most of the prime real estate in the Nightside, now the Griffin is finally dead and gone. He has enormous economic leverage and isn't shy about using it to get his own way. Word is he can't get any richer, so now he wants power. He maintains his own private army of bully-boys, enforcers, and leg-breakers, and anyone who speaks out against Taffy tends to find out why terribly quickly. He wants to be the new Griffin, the new king of the castle, and have us all bow down to him. He has pretensions to style and elegance and gentility, but wouldn't recognise them if he fell over them in the gutter. The man was born a cheap thug, and he'll never change. The *Inquirer*'s run any number of exposés on him and said all kinds of nasty things, but he's rich enough that he doesn't care. Hateful man. They say he ate his brother."

"Completely accurate," I said.

Uptown Taffy Lewis was a large man, in all the wrong ways. The expertly cut suit couldn't conceal his many rolls of fat, any more than his current polite expression could hide his cold piggy eyes or cruel mouth. Taffy didn't just want to be big man at the trough, he wanted to keep everyone else out, simply because he could. Own it all, control it all, and have the power to destroy it all. And then use that power to make everyone else beg for the scraps from his table. Probably had a really small penis. Uptown Taffy Lewis wanted the Nightside because it was there.

He'd tried to have me killed on several occasions. I didn't take it personally. For Taffy, it was always just business.

"And ex-Queen Helena?" I said to Bettie.

"Nasty piece of work, by all accounts." Bettie curled her perfect upper lip. "Powerful, talented, and dangerous in all sorts of unpleasant ways, though it's hard to say whether her power derives from science or sorcery. She can kill with a look or a touch, and they say she can enslave a man by whispering his name. The official word is that she arrived here via a Timeslip from some far future time-line, where the sun is going out and the ice covers everything. A cold woman from a cold world. But you can take that with as many grains of salt as you like; people who turn up through Timeslips tell all sorts of tales, and there's rarely any way of checking. She claims to have been the Queen of the whole world, and she has the way of royalty about her, but . . . Odd that a Queen should be travelling alone, don't you think? Anyway, she's certainly single-minded enough about becoming royalty again, either back in her own time or right here in the Nightside. She has a lot of followers here; people who like to think they know a real monarch when they see one. She's been selling titles to anyone who can raise the money."

I nodded. I knew the type. (Ex-)Queen Helena was a disturbing sight. Tall, regal, haughty, and more impressive than God, she sat on her chair as though it was a throne fashioned from the bones of her enemies. She wore thick white furs, a diamond tiara, and her long flat hair was so blonde as to be practically colourless. Her deathly pale skin was tinged with blue, and her face and bare arms were covered with intricate patterns of painted-on circuitry. There were subtle bulges here and there under her skin, suggesting concealed high-tech implants. They raised and lowered themselves, apparently according to her moods.

"Well done, Bettie," I said. "Very accurate descriptions, nicely succinct and more than usually informed. There are investigative journalists on the *Night Times* who wouldn't have been able to tell me that much. You're not just a pretty face, are you?"

She smiled easily. "I was wondering how long the wide-eyed act would fool you. You don't get to be one of the *Unnatural Inquirer*'s top reporters by batting your eyes and simpering at people. Though you'd be surprised how far that can get you, even with important people. Men are such simple, basic creatures, bless them. For the others, it's amazing how many weak spots and vulnerabilities good research can turn up. I smile, I watch, I listen, I draw conclusions, and I write it all up afterwards. You weren't fooled by the act for one minute, were you?"

"It's a good act," I said, generously. "Now hush and observe Walker at work. See how he influences and manipulates people, without them even realising."

"Things have got to change," General Condor was saying heavily. He leaned forward across the table to glare at Walker, who seemed entirely unperturbed. The General's voice was slow and deliberate, used to giving orders and having them obeyed. He had the air of a man people would follow: bluff, experienced, sure, and certain. A man who knew what he was doing. He jabbed a heavy finger in Walker's face. "The Nightside can't continue as it has—a haven for all human depravity and weakness. It'll tear itself apart with the Griffin and the Authorities gone. The signs are clear for everyone to see, first the angel war, and then the Lilith War . . . Left to its own devices, the Nightside will inevitably tear itself apart."

"There have always been wars, and destruction, and changes at the top," Walker said calmly. "But the Nightside goes on. It has survived for thousands of years, and I see no reason why it shouldn't continue as it is for thousands more. The world has always had a taste for freak shows."

General Condor scowled. "That might have been true while the Authorities were running things and supporting the Nightside in the same way a farmer looks after the goose that lays golden eggs; but they're gone now. Along with their blinkered preoccupation with trade and profit. It's time for someone to take the longer view and make the Nightside into something better."

"Nothing wrong with making money," Uptown Taffy Lewis said immediately. His voice was soft and breathy, his great chest and belly rising and falling as though every breath cost him something. "The Nightside exists to provide people with the pleasures and pursuits they can't get anywhere else. The things civilised people aren't supposed to want, but do anyway. And they'll pay through the nose for it, every time. Keep your rigid morality to yourself, General. We don't need simple-minded do-gooders coming in from outside and meddling with a system that's worked fine for thousands of years."

"The man has a point, General," said Walker. "It's hard to argue with success."

"All the things I've seen here," said the General, "the marvels and wonders, the amazing achievements, the incredible possibilities . . . If you would only work together instead of cutting each other's throats over a penny's profits, the things you could do . . . The Nightside could become the pinnacle of human civilisation! Instead of the moral cesspit it is now. You could all be gods if you'd only throw off the chains that hold you back!"

"Not everyone wants to be a god," said Walker. "In fact, I'd say we already have far too many. I've been thinking about ordering a cull . . . Too many Chiefs only confuse the Indians. Wouldn't you agree, Helena?"

"You may address me as Queen Helena, or Your Majesty," she said immediately, her voice suitably chilly. The other two looked at her sharply. You didn't talk that way to Walker if you liked breathing, and having your bones stay where they were. But he nodded thoughtfully to Queen Helena, and she continued.

"People must know their place. For many, it is their nature to be ruled. To have someone ready to make the important decisions for them. I am not a lone voice in this. I speak for others such as I in the Nightside."

"The Exiles," said Walker. "All the other kings and queens and emperors who wound up here, via Timeslips or other unfortunate accidents. So many that there seems to be something of a glut of rulers on the market, at the moment."

"People of power and prestige," Queen Helena said firmly. "People who do not care for the way things are. The Nightside needs to be taken in hand and ruled by people suited to the task."

"Would you agree with that, Taffy?" said Walker.

"No-one tells me what to do," said Uptown Taffy Lewis. He almost sounded amused. "No-one rules the Nightside. Never has, never will. We make our own way. This is the last truly free place left on Earth, where everything and anything is possible. Even the Authorities knew enough to keep their distance. Right, Walker? I represent people, too. I speak for the businesspeople of the

Nightside, and we will not stand by and see our rights trampled on." He glared at Helena, and then at General Condor. "You don't belong here, either of you. We like the Nightside just the way it is; and neither of you have the support or the power to change anything that matters. I own most of the land the Nightside stands on; my associates own most of the rest. We can bankrupt anyone who doesn't back us up. And we can raise armies, if necessary, to defend what is ours."

"I have led armies," said General Condor. "There's more to it than giving orders."

"I have led armies, too," said Queen Helena. Something in her voice made the others look at her. She smiled coldly. "I did not come here by accident. No arbitrary Timeslip brought me here; I can go home anytime I want. To the ancient and melancholy Ice Kingdoms, where my armies wait for me. It has been a long time since the Armies of the Evening have had a cause worth fighting for. Because we killed everyone else who stood against us, in the long twilight of Earth. I have no wish to be Queen of an empty world. Not when I can bring my armies here and make the Nightside my own."

General Condor and Uptown Taffy Lewis looked at her, then at each other, and finally at Walker, who smiled easily.

"Why risk your armies, and your life, to secure a city, when you already have a world of your own?"

Queen Helena smiled back at him coldly, her blue-tinged lips drawing back to reveal perfect sharp teeth. "I like it here. It's warm."

"Ice melts when the going gets hot," said Taffy.

"You dare?" Queen Helena stood up, glaring down at them all. Strange metallic shapes surfaced in the blue-white flesh of her arms. Silver-grey barrels targeted Taffy and the General.

*"That's enough!"* Walker didn't stand up. He didn't need to. He was using the Voice. *"Put your weapons away, Helena."*

The Queen of the Evening shook and shuddered, her lips drawing back in a frustrated grimace, as she fought the Voice and failed. The implanted technology sank back into her arms, bluish skin closing seamlessly over it. She snarled furiously at Walker, a fierce, animal sound, then she turned abruptly and stalked away. Servants hurried to get out of her way. General Condor and Uptown Taffy Lewis rose to their feet, bowed stiffly to Walker, and then they left, too, careful to maintain a respectful distance between them. Perhaps they were worried Walker would use the Voice on them. He watched them go thoughtfully, and then turned unhurriedly in his chair and looked right at me.

"I'll see you now, Taylor."

I nodded and smiled, and moved unhurriedly forward to join him at his table. Bettie stuck close to my side.

"How did he know we were there?" she whispered.

"He's Walker," I said.

Bettie and I sat down in the newly vacated seats, facing

Walker. He looked perfectly calm and at ease in his elegant city suit, his public school tie neatly tied in a Windsor knot. He didn't seem particularly pleased to see me, but then he rarely did.

"Nicely played," I said. "You set them at each other's throats without once having to make clear your own position. It's always good to see a real professional at work."

Walker smiled briefly and turned his attention to Bettie. "I see we have a representative of the Press with us. And a more charming example than most. I feel I should warn you that recording devices won't function inside the Club. And I am very definitely not available for an interview. I've read some of your work, Miss Divine. You show promise. I'm sure you'll make a name for yourself once you get a job at a real newspaper."

Bettie smiled widely, almost overwhelmed that Walker had heard of her and was familiar with her work. I could have told her; Walker knows everyone.

"Looks like the vultures are gathering over the Nightside," I said. "Would I be right in thinking that people are being encouraged to choose sides? Whether they want to or not?"

"Which side would you be on, Taylor, if push came to shove?" said Walker.

"My side," I said.

Walker nodded slightly. And perhaps it was only my imagination that he looked a little disappointed in me.

"You've heard about the Afterlife Recording?" I said.

"Of course you have. It's gone missing, and I've been hired to find it."

"Then find it quickly," said Walker. "Before forces from Above or Below decide to get involved. The last time that happened was a disaster for all of us."

"I wish everyone would stop looking at me like the angel war was all my fault!"

"It was," said Walker.

"Can I quote you?" said Bettie.

"No," said Walker. "What do you want from me, Taylor?"

"I want to know where the Collector is hiding out these days," I said. "If anyone knows anything about the Afterlife Recording, it will be him. That's if he hasn't already got his fat sweaty hands on it, of course."

"Of course," said Walker. "Mark never could resist the challenge of the chase . . . Very well. The Collector is currently hiding his collection inside another collection. To be exact, inside the Museum of Unnatural History."

"An exclusive!" said Bettie, beaming happily.

"Not for long," said Walker. "He'll move again once he's been found. Poor Mark."

"You know the Collector personally?" said Bettie. "Is that how you know where he's been hiding?"

"I know where everyone is," said Walker. "That's my job."

"Do you know where the offices of the *Unnatural Inquirer* are located?"

"Yes."

"Ah," said Bettie Divine. "Then I'd better contact the Sub-Editor and tell him to tone down tomorrow's editorial."

"I would," said Walker. He looked back at me. "I can't speak for what kind of reception you can expect from Mark. The three of us might have worked together to end the Lilith War, but you can't rely on that to mean anything. His collection is all that really matters to him these days. He's come a long way from the man I and your father once knew. Don't turn your back on him."

I considered the point. "Can I say you sent me?"

Walker shrugged. "If you think it'll do any good. Find the Recording, John. And then, if you've got any sense, destroy it."

"The *Unnatural Inquirer* owns exclusive rights to the Afterlife Recording!" Bettie said immediately.

"There is that," said Walker. "Certainly I couldn't think of a better way to discredit it."

Bettie started to say something else, but I took her firmly by the elbow, levered her up out of her chair, nodded quickly to Walker and moved her off towards the door. She made a show of fighting me, but I could tell she was glad of a way to leave Walker without losing face.

"The way you and he talked," she said, as we walked across the lobby. "You two are close, aren't you? I never knew that. I don't think anyone does . . . There's a lot going on there that you're not telling me."

"Of course," I said. "I'm protecting you."

"From what?"

"From never being able to sleep again."

• • •

We left the Londinium Club, and strolled unhurriedly through the sleazy streets of the Nightside. Amber light from the street-lamps was easily shouldered aside by the fierce electric colours of the flashing neon signs, and the grubby pavements were crowded with preoccupied, anxious figures, all intent on their own private dreams and damnations. Sweet sounds and madder music blasted out of the open doors of clubs where the fun never stopped, and you could dance till you dropped. Brazen windows showed off all the latest temptations, barkers boasted of the attractions to be found inside for the discerning patron, and sin went walking openly down the street in the very latest fuck-me shoes.

The traffic roared past, never slowing, never stopping, because it wasn't there for us.

Visiting the Londinium Club's dining-room had made me peckish, so I stopped at a concession stand and treated Bettie and me to something wriggling on a stick. The meat was sharp and spicy, and just a bit crunchy.

"Would I regret it if I was to ask exactly what this is that I'm eating?" said Bettie, as we continued down the street.

"Almost certainly," I said cheerfully.

"Then I won't ask. Am I supposed to eat the head, too?"

"If you want."

"But it's looking at me!"

"Then eat it from the other end."

"You really know how to show a girl a good time, Taylor."

We walked a while in silence, chewing thoughtfully.

"I've never been to the Museum of Unnatural History," Bettie said finally. "I always meant to go and take a look at what they've got there. I understand they have some really interesting exhibits. But it's not really me. I don't do the educational thing."

"They've got a *Tyrannosaurus rex*," I said.

Bettie threw away her stick and looked at me. "What, the complete skeleton?"

"No, in a cage."

Her eyes widened. "Wow; a real *T. rex*! I wonder what they feed it . . ."

"People who litter, probably."

The Museum of Unnatural History is very modern-looking. The French may have a glass pyramid outside the Louvre, but we have a glass tesseract. An expanded cube that exists in four spatial dimensions. A bit hard on the eyes, but a small price to pay for style. The tesseract isn't merely the entrance to the Museum, it contains the whole thing inside its own very private and secure pocket dimension. The Museum needs a whole dimension to itself, to contain all the wonders and marvels it has accumulated down the years; from the Past, the Present, and any number of Future time-lines.

I walked steadily forward into the glass tesseract,

Bettie clinging firmly to my arm again, and almost immediately we were standing in the Museum's entrance
lobby. I say almost immediately; there was a brief sensation of falling, of alien voices howling all around, and a
huge eye turning slowly to look in our direction . . . but
you tend to take things like that in your stride in the
Nightside. The lobby itself was quaintly and pleasantly
old-fashioned. All polished oak and brass and Victorian
fittings, marble floors with built-in mosaics, and any
number of wire stands packed with books and pamphlets
and learned volumes on sale, inspired by the many famous
(or currently fashionable) exhibits. Once again the ticket
barrier opened itself for me, and Bettie looked at me, impressed.

"This is even better than having an expense account.
Did you do something important for the Museum, too?"

"No," I said. "I think they're just scared of me."

The uniformed staff were all Neanderthals—big and
muscular, with hairy hands, low brows, and chinless jaws
filled with large blocky teeth. The deep-set eyes were
kind, but distant. Neanderthals performed all the menial
work in the Museum, in return for not being exhibits.
They were also in charge of basic security, and rumour had
it they were allowed to eat anyone they caught. I asked
one to take us to the Director of the Museum, and he
hooted softly before beckoning us to follow him. He had
a piercing in one ear, and a badge on his lapel saying
UNIONISE NOW!

He led us deep into the Museum, and Bettie's head

swung back and forth, trying to take in everything at once. I was almost as bad. The Museum really does have something for everyone. A miniature blue whale, presented in a match-box, to give it some scale. I wondered vaguely how it would taste on toast. More disturbingly, half of one wall was taken up with a Victorian display of stuffed and mounted wee winged fairies, pinned through the abdomen. Only a few inches tall, the fairies were perfectly formed, their stretched-out wings glued in place and showing off all the delicate colours of a soap bubble. They had many-faceted insect eyes, and vicious barbed stingers hung down between their toothpick legs. In the next room there were tall glass jars containing fire-flies and iceflies, mermaids with monkey faces, and a display of alien genitalia through the ages. Bettie got the giggles.

On a somewhat larger scale, one whole room was taken up with a single great diorama featuring the fabled last battle between Man and Elf. The dozens of full-sized figures were very impressive. The Men, in their spiked and greaved armour, looked brave and heroic, while the Fae looked twisted and evil. Which was pretty much the way it was, by all accounts. There was a lot of blood and gore and severed limbs, but I suppose you need that these days to bring in the tourists. Another huge diorama showed a pack of werewolves on the prowl, under a full moon. Each figure showed a different stage of the transformation, from man to wolf. They all looked unnervingly real; but up close there was a definite smell of sawdust and preservatives.

Another group of figures showed a pack of ghouls, teaching a human changeling child how to feed as they did. The Museum of Unnatural History presented such things without comment. History is what it is and not what we would have it be.

There were a fair number of people around, but the place wasn't what you'd call crowded, despite all the wonders and treasures on display. People don't tend to come to the Nightside for such intellectual pleasures. And tourism's been right down since the recent wars. The Museum is said to be heavily subsidised, but I couldn't tell you who by. Most of the exhibits are donated; the Museum certainly didn't have the budget to buy them.

The uniformed Neanderthal finally brought us to the Museum's current pride and joy, the *Tyrannosaurus rex*. The cage they'd made to hold it was huge, a good three hundred feet in diameter and a hundred feet high. The bars were reinforced steel, but the cage's interior had been made over into a reconstruction of the *T. rex*'s time, to make it feel at home. The cage contained a primordial jungle, with vast trees and luxurious vegetation, under a blazing sun. The illusion was perfect. The terrible heat didn't pass beyond the bars, but a gusting breeze carried out the thick and heavy scents of crushed vegetation, rotting carrion, and even the damp smells of a nearby salt flat. I could even hear the buzzing of oversized flies and other insects. The trees were tall and dark, with drooping serrated leaves, and what ground I could see was mostly mud, stamped flat.

But it was all dominated by the tyrant king himself, *Tyrannosaurus rex*. It towered above us, almost as tall as the trees, much bigger than I'd expected. It stood very still, half-hidden amongst the shadows of rotting vegetation, watching us through the bars. There was a definite sense of weight and impact about it, as though the ground itself would shake and shudder when it moved. Its scales were a dull grey-green, splashed here and there with the dried blood of recent kills. It panted loudly through its open mouth, revealing jagged teeth like a shark's. The small gripping arms high up on the chest didn't seem ridiculous at all, when seen full size. I had no doubt they could tear me apart in a moment. But it was the eyes that troubled me the most; set far back in the ugly wedge-shaped head, they were sharp and knowing . . . and they hated. They looked right at me, and they knew me. This was no mere animal, no simple savage beast. It knew it was a prisoner, and it knew who was responsible; and it lived for the moment when it would inevitably break free and take a terrible revenge.

"How the hell did they get hold of a *T. rex*?" said Bettie, her voice unconsciously hushed.

"You should read your own paper more often," I said. "There was a sudden invasion of dinosaurs through a Timeslip, earlier this year. Some fifty assorted beasts got through, before Walker sent in an emergency squad to shut down the Timeslip. Most of the creatures were killed pretty quickly; the members of the Nightside Gun Club couldn't believe their luck. They came running with every kind of gun you can think of, and the dinosaurs never stood a chance, poor bastards. The only reason the *T. rex* survived was because the big-game hunters spent too long squabbling over who had the right to go first. Walker claimed it for the Museum before they started a shooting war over it."

"How did they get it here?" said Bettie, standing very close to me. "I mean, look at it; that is big. Seriously big. There can't be that many tranquilliser darts in the world."

"Walker had one of his pet sorcerers put the thing in stasis while the Museum got its accommodations ready. Then the sorcerer transported it right into its cage. The Japanese have been pouring in to have their photographs taken with it ever since."

While we were watching the *T. rex*, and it was watching us, the uniformed Neanderthal had gone off and found the Museum's Director. He turned out to be one Percival Smythe-Herriot, a tall spindly figure in a shiny suit, with some of his breakfast still staining his waistcoat. He stamped to a halt before me and gave both Bettie and me a brief, professional, and utterly meaningless smile. He didn't offer to shake hands. He had a lean and hungry look, as though he was always ready to add a new exhibit to his beloved Museum and was already wondering how I would look stuffed, mounted, and put on display.

"John Taylor," he said, in a voice like someone trying to decide whether snail or octopus would make the least distressing starter. "Oh, yes; I know you. Or of you.

Trouble-maker. Or at the very least, someone trouble follows around like a devoted pet. Tell me what it is you want here, so I can help you find it, then escort you quickly to the nearest exit. Before something goes horribly and destructively wrong in my nice and carefully laid-out Museum."

"Are you going to let him talk to you like that?" said Bettie.

"Yes," I said. "I find his honesty and grasp of reality quite refreshing." I gave Percival my own professional smile and was quietly pleased to see him wince a little. "Walker sent me. I need to talk to the Collector."

"Oh, *him*. Yes . . . I'd never have let him in here, but Walker insisted. Part of the price tag for his help in acquiring the *T. rex*. Beware civil servants bearing gifts . . . I mean, giving the Collector free access to a museum is like letting a fox with a chain-saw into a hen-house. Thief! Grave-robber! *Amateur!* All the great historical treasures he's supposed to have, kept locked away so he can gloat over them in private, when by rights they should be on open display in my Museum! It doesn't bear thinking about. My doctor told me not to think about it; he said it was bad for my blood pressure. I have to take these little pink pills, and I'm always running out. I'd have the Collector thrown out . . . if I didn't think he'd kill me and all my staff and burn down the Museum as he left . . . So go ahead, talk to him. See if I care. I'm just the Director of this Museum. I can feel one of my heads coming on . . ."

"Where is the Collector?" I said patiently.

For the first time, Percival gave me a real smile. It wasn't at all a nice smile, but I had no doubt he meant it.

"Through there," he said, pointing at the *T. rex*'s cage. "There's a door, right in the middle of our artificial jungle. You'll find the Collector in his lair, on the other side of the door."

"Oh, joy," I said.

"Deep joy," said Bettie, staring in horrified fascination at the jungle in the cage. "The Collector really doesn't want visitors, does he? Why couldn't he have settled for a BEWARE OF THE DOG sign like anyone else?"

I looked at Percival. "I don't suppose . . ."

"My position is purely administrative," he said, still smiling his nasty smile. "You're on your own, Mr. Taylor."

He turned his back on us and strode away, snapping his fingers for the Neanderthal to follow him. I gave the cage my full attention. I wasn't sure if I really needed to see the Collector that badly. I moved slowly forward, going right up to the bars of the cage for a better look. Bettie stuck really close beside me. With my face next to the bars, I could feel the savage heat of the jungle. My bare skin smarted just from the feel of it.

The *T. rex* surged forward, exploding out of its cover, throwing broken vegetation in all directions. It crossed the intervening space in a few seconds, driven forward by its massive legs, and its slavering mouth slammed against the other side of the bars while I was still reacting to its first movement. The bars held, and the *T. rex* smashed its great head against them again and again, determined to reach me. I stumbled back, Bettie clinging desperately to my arm. The *T. rex* howled, a deafening roar of hate and frustration. The smell of rotting meat from its mouth was almost overpowering. I backed away some more, and Bettie turned and buried her face in my chest. I put my arms around her and held her. Both of us were shaking.

The *T. rex* snorted once, threateningly, and then turned its great bulk around and stalked back into the jungle. The ground really did tremble when it moved.

I was still holding Bettie. We were both breathing hard. I could feel her heart beating fast, close to mine. She raised her face to look at me. Her eyes were very big. I could feel her breath on my face. Her scent filled my head. Our faces were very close. It had been a long time since I'd held a woman this close to me.

It felt good.

I pushed her away gently, and immediately we were both two professional people again. I looked at the jungle. I thought I could make out the silhouette of the *T. rex*, lurking silently, concealed amongst the tall trees.

"Big, isn't it?" I said. "Fast, too."

"It smells of meat and murder," said Bettie. "It smells of death."

"It's a killer," I said.

"How the hell are we going to get past it?"

I looked at her. "You sure you want to try?"

"Hell yes! No oversized iguana is going to intimidate

me! Besides, never let anything distract you from following the story. First thing they teach you at the *Unnatural Inquirer*. Right after how to fill out an expenses claim and next-of-kin forms." She looked at me consideringly. "You couldn't just kill it, could you?"

"I think an awful lot of very well-connected people would be exceedingly upset."

"That's never stopped you before."

"True. But a *T. rex* is too damned special to kill unless I absolutely have to."

"So what do we do? Call in some of your more dangerous friends and allies for backup? Shotgun Suzie? Razor Eddie? The Grey Eidolon?"

"No," I said. "I solve my own problems."

I studied the artificial jungle, hot and sweaty and stinking under its artificial sun. Flies buzzed hungrily, along with foot-long dragonflies and other less familiar insects. The jungle on its own would be hard enough to take, even without the *T. rex*. I could see it more clearly now, shifting its weight slowly from one great leg to the other, its long tail twitching restlessly. It stood there, huge and menacing, waiting for me to try something. Waiting for its chance. There was no sign of the Collector's door; but it couldn't be far. The cage wasn't that big . . . I smiled slowly. The *T. rex* would know where the door was. It would know it was important. So it would put itself between me and the door. Which meant . . . My smile widened as I looked at the *T. rex*'s massive legs, and then at the space between them.

"That is a really unpleasant smile," said Bettie. "Whatever you're thinking, please stop it."

"I have a plan," I said.

"I'm really not going to like it, am I?"

"How fast can you run?" I said.

"Oh, no," she said. "You're not suggesting . . ."

"Oh, yes I am," I said.

I marched back to the cage bars, Bettie moving unhappily along with me. The *T. rex* stepped out into the open, grinning at me with its terrible jaws. The feeding arms high up on the barrel chest clutched spasmodically at the air. I reached into my coat-pocket and took out a flashbang. I gestured for Bettie to cover her eyes and ears, then tossed the flashbang into the cage. The *T. rex* started forward. I closed my eyes, covered my ears, and turned my head away, and the flashbang exploded, filling the world with a fierce incandescent glare. I could still see it through my clenched-shut eyes. The *T. rex* screamed like a steam whistle. I turned back, grabbed Bettie's hand, and we squeezed quickly between the steel bars. Designed to keep the *T. rex* in, not people out. The *T. rex* stamped its great feet up and down, swinging its wedge-shaped head back and forth, trying to shake off the pain in its dazzled eyes. And I ran straight at the creature, with Bettie pounding gamely along at my side.

The heat hit me like a blast furnace, and the stench was almost unbearable. The *T. rex* knew we were coming, but it was too confused to place us. It snapped at the empty air, the heavy jaws slamming together like a man-trap. I headed for the gap between its legs. I think it sensed how close we were, because the great head came sweeping down. Bettie and I ran straight between its wide-set legs and out the other side, hardly having to duck at all. The *T. rex*'s head smashed into the ground as it missed us.

By the time the *T. rex* had shaken off its daze and its new headache, and got itself turned around, I'd already found the Collector's door and got it open. It wasn't even locked, the smug bastard. I pushed Bettie through and followed her in. I turned to shut the door, and there was the *T. rex*, shrieking with rage as it lurched towards the door. I blew a raspberry at it, and shut the door in its face.


Inside the Collector's lair, it was blessedly cool. I took a moment to get my breath back. I wasn't worried about the door. Any door the Collector trusted to guard his treasures could take care of itself. I looked around, while Bettie got her breathing back under control and cursed me with a whole series of baby swear-words. The Collector's new domain looked a lot like his old one. It stretched away in all directions, for as far as the eye could follow, and most of it was pretty damned hard on the eye. Walls, floor, and ceiling were all painted in bright primary Technicolor, with gaudy hanging silks to separate one area from another. The Collector's tastes had been formed in the psychedelic sixties, and he never really got over it.

But whereas his old collection up on the Moon had all

been stored away in rows and rows of wooden crates, here they were all set out in the open, presented carefully on rows and rows of glass shelving. Jewels and weapons, books and documents, machines and artifacts from all of recorded history. I recognised a few of the bigger items, like the wooden horse of Troy, and a half-burned giant Wicker Man with a dead policeman inside it, under carefully arranged spotlights; but I didn't have to know what the rest were to know they were important. They all but radiated glamour.

I looked round sharply as the Collector's security staff arrived, pattering across the bright blue floor towards us. Gleaming humanoid robots from some future Chinese civilisation, graceful and deadly with steel-clawed hands, and stylised cat faces complete with jutting metal whiskers. Their slit-pupilled eyes glowed green. A dozen of the robots moved swiftly to surround us, and I gestured quickly for Bettie to stand still. The robots hadn't been sent to kill us, or I'd never have heard them coming. Bettie stood firm, glaring about her.

"Call them off, Collector," I said, in a loud and carrying voice. "Or I'll turn them into scrap metal."

"You never did have any respect for other people's property, Taylor."

The cat robots fell back silently, to allow the Collector to approach. A pudgy, middle-aged man with a flushed face and beady little eyes, wearing a wraparound Roman toga, white with purple trimmings. There were knife holes and old blood stains on the toga's front. Lots of them.

"Do you like it?" he said, stopping a respectful distance away. "A new acquisition. The robe the Emperor Caligula was wearing when he was assassinated by his own security people. Partly because he was a monster, but mostly because he embarrassed the hell out of them." He looked at me, then at Bettie, who I now noticed was wearing a deep burgundy evening gown, with her long dark hair tumbling in ringlets to her shoulders. Her curved horns gleamed dully under the bright lights. The Collector smiled suddenly. "They've been feeding that *T. rex* too much; he's getting slow and sloppy. I shall have to have words with that little snot Percival. What do you want here, Taylor?"

I looked around, evading the subject for the moment. Some things you need to sneak up on, and ease into. Especially when you've known the Collector as long as I have.

"I like what you've done with the place," I said. "Up on the Moon, you had everything packed away in boxes. You thinking of opening up to the public?"

"They wish," said the Collector. "What's mine is mine, and not for other eyes. But I had something of an epiphany during the Lilith War; it reminded me of how short life can be, and the necessity for enjoying things while you still can. It's not enough just to own things, any more; I need to be able to walk amongst them, enjoy them, savour them. And I do. What do you want, Taylor?"

"I need a favour," I said. "And you do owe me, Mark."

He looked at me for a long moment, but in the end he looked away first. He seemed suddenly older, and tired.

"How much am I expected to pay for my sins against you?"

I could sense Bettie's ears pricking up, as she realised we were talking about secret, important things, but I didn't feel like enlightening her.

"Only you can answer that," I said. "Just tell me what I need to know, and I'll leave."

"I should kill you," he said, almost casually.

"You could try," I said, easily.

"This is about the Afterlife Recording, isn't it? I haven't got it. Heard about it, of course. The whole damned Nightside is buzzing with news of it, mostly inaccurate, and all the little collectors and speculators are driving themselves crazy running in circles, chasing down every rumour . . ."

"But not you?" I said.

"I want it. And when I'm good and ready, I'll go and get it. But right now I'm busy with something . . . something important. I have yet to be convinced that the Recording is the genuine article. But whether it's the real deal or not, I will have it, because it's a unique item, and it belongs here with me, as someone who will appreciate it . . . What is that woman doing?"

I looked around. Bettie had a small camera in her hands. I reached out and took it away from her.

"Give that back!" she said hotly. "It belongs to the paper! I had to sign for it!"

"Restrain yourself," I said. "We're guests here."

"Oh, but look at all the lovely things he's got," said Bettie, pouting in a very winning way. "The world deserves to know what's here!"

"No they don't," said the Collector. He gave me a thoughtful look. "Is she your latest?"

"No," I said. "I'm still with Suzie."

"Oh. Nice horns." He gave me a hard look. "You always were more trouble than you were worth, Taylor. You know how long it took me to regrow my leg after those insects gnawed it off? All because of you? Give me one good reason why I shouldn't have my lovely cat robots kill you, stuff you, and put you on display?"

"Because I'm my father's son."

"You always did fight dirty, John." He smiled briefly. "The sins of the father . . ."

"And the mother," I said. "And the man who put them together."

"Walker had sons," said the Collector. "Charles had you. And I . . . have my collection. Funny how things turn out. Get out of here, Taylor. I don't have the Afterlife Recording, and I don't know who has. Leave. And don't come looking for me again. I won't be here."

He turned and walked away, followed by his cat robots. Bettie looked at me.

"What was that all about?"

"The past," I said. "And how it always ends up haunting the present. Let's go."

"You're sure he doesn't have it, hidden away somewhere?"

"He wouldn't lie to me," I said.

We headed back to the door. Bettie was still frowning thoughtfully.

"Once we're back in the artificial jungle, we've still got to face one very pissed-off *Tyrannosaurus rex*. How are we going to get past it this time?"

"Don't worry," I said. "I'll think of something."

And I did.

# FIVE

# The Devil's in
# the Details

Back out on the Nightside streets again, we still carried the smell of the jungle with us. A harsh and murky mixture of sweat, rotting vegetation, and *T. rex* musk. It could have been my imagination, but people on the street seemed to be giving me even more room than usual. I felt like buying half a dozen air fresheners and hanging them round my neck. I did my best to rise above the situation, while debating what to do next with the delightful Bettie Divine.

"I still don't get it," she said, a bit pettishly. She was holding my arm again. "Why isn't the Collector out chasing round the Nightside, trying to grab the Afterlife Recording for himself? He said he wanted it."

"He also said he was busy with something," I said. "Odd, that; he didn't say what with. He's never been bashful with me before; usually can't wait to boast about what he's up to . . . Still, he's the Collector. Which means he's always busy with something."

"Unless . . . he's scared of someone else who's after the Recording," said Bettie. "You, perhaps?"

"I'd like to think so, but no. It would have to be someone really bad, and really powerful. The Collector is a Major Player in his own right, and he doesn't scare easily."

"Walker?"

"You have a point there," I admitted. I was getting used to walking arm in arm with Bettie. It felt good, natural. "Could Walker have been lying to us, to hide the fact he already had the DVD? No, I don't think so. He would have told me if he'd had it, if only to put me in my place. And his reasons for wanting me to find it before anyone else sounded pretty good to me."

"You mean the angels?" said Bettie.

"Please," I said. "Let us not use the a-word in public."

"All right, if it isn't Walker, then who? Razor Eddie?"

I shook my head. "He might be the Punk God of the Straight Razor, but Eddie's never been very interested in religion. In fact, he's pretty much the only god all the other Beings on the Street of the Gods are afraid of."

"How about the Lord of Thorns, then?"

"You have been doing your homework, haven't you? No, he's still recovering from the Lilith War and the trauma of finding out he's not who he thought he was."

"You know everyone, don't you?" Bettie said admiringly. "Who did he think he was?"

"Overseer of the Nightside."

Bettie thought about that. "If the Lord of Thorns isn't watching over us, who is?"

"Good question," I said. "Lot of people are still arguing about that."

She gave me a sly, sideways look. "Lot of people say you could have been King of the Nightside, if you'd wanted."

I smiled. "You shouldn't listen to gossip."

"Don't be silly, darling! That's my job!"

"Damn," I said, as a thought occurred to me.

"You're frowning, John, and I do wish you wouldn't. It usually means you've suddenly thought of something unpleasant, spooky, and probably downright dangerous."

"Right on all three counts," I said. "There is one man the Collector is afraid of, and quite rightly, too. Anyone with any sense is afraid of the Removal Man."

Bettie pulled her arm out of mine and stopped dead in the street. I stopped with her. She gave me a hard look.

"Hold everything, reverse gear, go previous. Are you having fun with me, John? Thinking I'll believe anything simply because it's you saying it? The Removal Man is just an urban legend. Isn't he?"

"Unfortunately, no," I said.

"But . . . I don't know anyone who's seen him, or even claimed to have seen him! The *Unnatural Inquirer*'s been offering really quite serious money for a *photo* . . . No-one's ever come forward."

"Because they're too scared," I said. "You don't mess with the Removal Man; not if you like existing."

"Have you ever met him?" said Bettie, her voice carefully casual.

"No," I said. "And I was hoping to keep it that way. I don't think he approves of me. And people and things the Removal Man disapproves of have this unfortunate tendency to disappear without a trace. The Removal Man has made it his personal crusade to wander the Nightside anonymously, removing all the things and people that offend him. Removing, as in making them vanish so completely that even really Major Players have been unable to confirm exactly what it is he's done with them."

"He removes people from reality because they offend him?" said Bettie.

"Pretty much." I started off down the street again, and Bettie came along with me. Not holding my arm. "Basically, the Removal Man drops the hammer on people if he considers them to be a threat to the Nightside, or the world in general . . . or because who or what they are offends his particular moral beliefs. Judge, jury, and executioner, though no-one's ever seen him do it."

"Like . . . Jessica Sorrow?" said Bettie, frowning.

"No . . . Jessica made bits of the world disappear because she didn't believe in them, and her disbelief was stronger than their reality. Very scary lady. Luckily she sleeps a lot of the time. No, the Removal Man chooses what he wants to disappear. No-one's ever been able to bring any of his victims back; and a whole lot of pretty powerful people have tried . . . I've never heard a single guess at his name, or who he used to be before he came here and took on his role. And this in a place that runs on rumours. He's a mystery, and all the signs are he likes it that way."

"You are seriously spooking me out, sweetie," said Bettie. "Are you sure he's involved with this?"

"No; but it sounds right. The Afterlife Recording is exactly the sort of thing that would attract the Removal Man's attention. Rumour has it he only ever reveals his identity to those he's about to remove, and not always then. There's some evidence he can work close up, or from a distance. Certainly he doesn't give a damn about celebrity, or notoriety, or even reward. He works for his own satisfaction. It's hard to be a shadowy urban legend in a place full of marvels and nightmares, but he's managed it. I'm almost jealous."

"I did hear one rumour," Bettie said carefully. "That he once tried to remove Walker . . . but it didn't take."

I shrugged. "If it did happen, Walker's never mentioned it. I suppose it's possible that Walker secretly approves of the Removal Man. In fact, it wouldn't surprise me if the Removal Man did the occasional job for him, on the quiet, disappearing people that Walker considered a threat to the status quo . . . No . . . No, that can't be right."

"Why not?"

"Because Walker would have sent the Removal Man after me long ago."

Bettie laughed and took my arm again. "You don't half fancy yourself, John Taylor. Any idea where the Removal Man might have gained his power?"

"The same way everybody else does," I said. "He made a deal with Someone or Something. Makes you wonder what he might have paid in exchange . . . I suppose it could be the Removal Man, or his patron, who's been interfering with my gift. I really do hope it isn't the Devil again."

"I could ask Mummy for you," said Bettie. "She still has contacts with the Old Firm."

"Think I'll pass," I said.

Bettie shrugged easily. "Suit yourself. You know, if we don't get to Pen Donavon before the Removal Man does, we could lose both him and his DVD. And my paper has paid a lot of money for that DVD."

"It might not be the Removal Man," I said. "I was thinking aloud. Speculating. I could be wrong. I have been before. In fact, this is one time I'd really like to be wrong."

"He worries you, doesn't he?"

"Damn right he does."

"Tell you what," said Bettie, snuggling up against me and squeezing my arm companionably against her breast. "When you want the very latest gossip on anything, ask a reporter. Or better yet, a whole bunch of reporters! Come with me, sweetie; I'm taking you to the Printer's Devil."

• • •

Luckily, the Printer's Devil turned out to be a bar where reporters congregated when they were off work; *printer's devil* being old-time slang for a typesetter. The bar catered almost exclusively to journalists, a private place where they could let their hair down amongst their own kind and share the kinds of stories that would never see print. Situated half-way down a gloomy side street, the Printer's Devil was an old place, and almost defiantly old-fashioned. It had a black-and-white timbered Tudor front, complete with jutting gables and a hanging sign showing a medieval Devil, complete with scarlet skin, goatee beard, and a pair of horns on his forehead that reminded my very much of Bettie's, operating a simple printing press. Reporters can be very literal, when they're off duty.

Bettie breezed through the door like a visiting princess, and I wandered in after her. The interior turned out to be equally old-fashioned, with sawdust on the floor, horse brasses over the bar, and a low ceiling with exposed beams. A dozen different beers on tap, with distressingly twee olde-worlde names, like *Langford's Exceedingly Old Speckled Hen. Taste that albumen!* A chalked sign offered traditional pub grub—chips with everything. And not a modern appliance anywhere in sight, including, thankfully, a juke-box. There was a deafening roar of chatter from the mob of shabby and shifty characters crowded round the tables and filling the booths, and the atmosphere was hot, sweaty, and smoky. There was so much nicotine in the air you could practically chew it. A great clamour of greeting went up as Bettie was recognised, only to die quickly away to a strained silence as they recognised me. Bettie smiled sweetly around her.

"It's all right," she said. "He's with me."

The reporters immediately turned their backs on us and resumed their conversations as though nothing had happened. One of their own had vouched for me, and that was all it took. Bettie headed for the crowded bar, and I moved quickly after her. She smiled and waved and shouted the odd cheery greeting at those around her, and everyone smiled and waved and shouted back. Clearly, Bettie was a very popular girl. At the bar, I asked her what she was drinking, and she batted her heavy eyelashes and asked for a Horny Red Devil. Which turned out to be gin, vodka, and Worcester sauce, with a wormwood-and-brimstone chaser. To each their own. At least it didn't come with a little umbrella in it. I ordered a Coke. A real Coke, and none of that diet nonsense. Bettie looked at me.

"Never when I'm working," I said solemnly.

"Really? It's the other way round with me, darling. I couldn't face this job sober." She smiled happily. "I notice the bartender didn't ask you to pay for these drinks. Don't you ever pay for anything?"

"I pay my way at Strangefellows," I said. "The owner is a friend."

"Ooh, Strangefellows, sweetie! Yes, I've heard about that place! There are all kinds of stories about what goes on in Strangefellows!"

"And most of them are true. It is the oldest pub in the world, after all."

"Will you take me there after we've finished with this assignment? I'd love to go dancing at Strangefellows. We could relax and get squiffy together. I might even show you my tail."

"We'll probably end up there, at some point," I said. "Most of my cases take me there, eventually."

The bartender slammed our drinks down on the highly polished wooden bar top, then backed away quickly. I didn't care for the man, and I think he could tell. He was one of those stout jolly types, with a red face and a ready smile, always there to make cheerful conversation when all you want is to drink in peace. Probably referred to himself as Mine Host. I gave him a meaningful look, and he retreated to the other end of the bar to polish some glasses that didn't need polishing.

"Can't take you anywhere," said Bettie.

Behind the bar hung a giveaway calendar supplied by the *Unnatural Inquirer*, with a large photo featuring the charms of a very well-developed young lady whose clothes had apparently fallen off. At the bottom of the page was the paper's current slogan: ARE YOU GETTING IT REGU-LARLY? Some rather shrunken-looking meat pies were on display in a glass case, but one look was all it took to convince me I would rather tear my tongue out. A stuffed-and-mounted fox head winked at me, and I snarled back. Animals should know their place. Not a lot further down the bar, an old-fashioned manual typewriter was being operated by the invisible hands of a real ghost writer. I'd met it once before, at the *Night Times* offices, and was tempted to make a remark about spirits not being served here, but rose above it. I leaned over towards the type-writer, and the clacking keys paused.

"Any recent news on the whereabouts of the Afterlife Recording?"

Words quickly formed on the page, reading *Future's cloudy. Ask again later.*

I persuaded Bettie to hurry her drink, politely evaded her attempts to chat, bond, or get personal, and finally we moved away from the bar to mingle with the assembled reporters. With Bettie as my native guide, we passed eas-ily from group to group, with me doing my best to be courteous and charming. I needn't have bothered. The re-porters only had eyes for Bettie, who was in full flirt mode—all squeaky voice, fluttering lashes, and a bit of laying on of hands where necessary. Bettie was currently wearing a smart white blouse with half the buttons un-done, over a simple black skirt, fish-net stockings, and high heels. Her horns showed clearly on her forehead, per-haps because she felt safe and at home here.

All the journalists seemed quite willing to talk about the Afterlife Recording; they'd all heard something, or swore they had. No-one wanted to appear out of the loop or left behind in company like this. Unfortunately, most of what they had to tell us turned out to be vague, mis-leading, or contradictory. Pen Donavon had been seen here, there, and everywhere, and already all sorts of people were offering copies of the DVD for sale. Only to be expected in the Nightside, where people have been known to rip off a new idea while it was still forming in the originator's mind. Rumours were already circulating that some people had managed to view what was on the DVD and had immediately Raptured right out of their clothes. Though whether Up or Down remained unconfirmed.

Bettie stopped at a table, and greeted one particular reporter with particular cold venom, along with a stare that would have poisoned a rattlesnake at forty paces. He seemed bright and cheerful enough, in an irredeemably seedy sort of way. He wore a good suit badly, and had a diamond tie-pin big enough to be classed as an offensive weapon.

"Aren't you going to introduce us?" I said innocently to Bettie.

She sniffed loudly. "John, darling, this particular gusset stain is Rick Aday, reporter for the *Night Times*."

"Investigative reporter," he corrected her easily, flashing perfect but somewhat yellow teeth in a big smile. He put out a hand for me to shake. I looked at it, and he took it back again. "You must have seen my by-line, Mr. Taylor, I've written lots of stories about you: *Rick Aday; Trouble Is My Middle Name*."

"No it isn't," Bettie said briskly. "It's Cedric."

Aday shot her a venomous glare. "Better than yours, *Delilah*."

"Lick my scabs!"

"They used to date," another of the reporters confided quietly to me. I nodded. I'd already guessed that.

"I've been hot on the trail of the Afterlife Recording for some time now," Aday said loftily. "Pursuing several quite credible leads, actually. Just waiting for a phone call from one of my extremely clued-in informants, then I'll be off to make Mr. Donavon a generous offer for his DVD."

"You can't!" Bettie snapped immediately. "My paper has a legitimate contract with Pen Donavon, granting us exclusive rights to his material!"

Aday just grinned at her. "Finders keepers, losers read about it in the *Night Times*."

"I suppose all's fair in love and publishing," I said, and Bettie actually hissed at me.

I moved away, to allow Bettie and her old flame to exchange harsh words in private. I'd noticed that the nearby wall boasted a whole series of framed cartoons and caricatures of noted Nightside personalities. Good likenesses, if often harsh, exaggerated, and downright cruel. They were all signed with a name I recognised. Bozie's work was well-known in the Nightside, appearing in all the best papers and magazines. He excelled at bringing out a subject's worst attributes and qualities, making them seem monstrous and laughable at the same time. Those depicted usually gritted their teeth and smiled as best they could, because you weren't anybody in the Nightside unless you'd been caricatured by Bozie.

There were rumours that Bozie had been known to accept quite large sums of money to kill a particular creation of his before the public got to see it. No-one mentioned blackmail, of course. Thus are reputations made in the Nightside.

I've never approved of needless cruelty. You should save it for when it's really necessary.

I moved slowly along the wall, checking out the various pen-and-ink creations in their softwood frames. All the usual suspects were there. Walker, of course, looking very sinister with more than a hint of in-breeding. Julien Advent, impossibly noble, complete with halo and stigmata. The Sonic Assassin, in his sixties greatcoat, gnawing on a human thigh-bone while making a rude gesture at the viewer. And . . . Shotgun Suzie. My Suzie. I stopped before the caricature and studied it impassively. Bozie had made her look like a monster. All fetishy black leathers and unfeasibly big breasts, with a face like an axe murderer. He'd exaggerated every detail of her looks to make her seem ugly and crazy. This wasn't just a caricature; it was an assault on her character. It was an insult.

"Like it?" said a lazy voice at my side. I looked round, and there was the artist himself—the famous or more properly infamous Bozie. A tall, gangling sort, in scruffy blue jeans and a T-shirt bearing an idealised image of his own face. He had long, floppy hair, dark, intense eyes, and an openly mocking smile. He gestured languidly at Suzie's caricature. "It is for sale, you know. If you want it?"

I had a feeling I knew how this was going to play out,

but I went along with it. "All right," I said. "How much?"

"Oh, for you . . . Let's say a round hundred thousand pounds." He giggled suddenly. "A bargain at the price. Or you can leave it here, for all the world to see. Who knows how many papers and magazines might want to run it?"

"I've got a better idea," I said.

"Oh, do tell."

I hit the glass covering the caricature with my fist, and it shattered immediately, jagged pieces falling out of the frame. Bozie stepped quickly backwards, his hands held protectively out before him. I tore the caricature out of the frame, and ripped it up, letting the pieces fall to the floor at my feet. Bozie goggled at me, torn between shock and outrage.

"You . . . You can't do that!" he managed finally.

"I just did."

"I'll sue!"

I smiled. "Good luck with that."

"I can always draw another one," Bozie said spitefully. "An even better one!"

"If you do," I said, "I will find you."

Bozie couldn't meet my gaze. He looked around him, hoping for help or support, but no-one wanted to know. He sat down at his table again, still not looking at me, and sulked. I went back to Bettie's table, and sat beside her. She patted me on the arm.

"That was very sweet, dear. Though a bit harsh on poor Bozie."

"Hell," I said. "I saved his life. Suzie would have shot him on sight. She doesn't have my innate courtesy and restraint."

There was a certain amount of coughing around the table, and then everyone went back to their discussion on what the Afterlife Recording might actually contain. The suggestions were many and varied, but eventually boiled down to the following:

1. There was a new rebel angel in Heaven, rebelling against the long silence of millennia to finally broadcast the truth about Humanity. Why we were created, what our true purpose is, and why we are born to suffer.

2. It was a transmission from Hell, saying that God is dead and they can prove it. Satan runs our world, tormenting us for his pleasure. Which would explain a lot.

3. An exact date for the final war between Heaven and Hell. Broadcast now because . . . it's all about to kick off.

4. There is a Heaven, but it's only for the innocent animals. People just die.

5. There is a Heaven, but no Hell.

6. There is a Hell, but no Heaven.

7. It's all bullshit.

There was a lot of nodding and raising of glasses at that last one. Once the subject of the DVD's contents had been thoroughly exhausted, I took it upon myself to raise the possibility of the Removal Man's involvement. Everyone perked up immediately and tumbled over each other to provide anecdotes and stories they'd come across but had been unable to get printed. Because no-one could prove anything.

"Remember Jonnie Reggae?" said Rick Aday. "Used to headline at the old Shell Beach Club? Rumour has it he vanished right in the middle of his set because the Removal Man was in the audience and decided his material was offensive. Management was livid. They'd booked Jonnie for the whole season."

"He's supposed to have made a house disappear, on Blaiston Street," said Lovett, from the *Nightside Observer*.

"Actually, no," I said. "That was me."

There was some more awkward coughing before Bettie determinedly got the conversation back on course.

"Remember Bully Boy Bates?" she said brightly. "Used to run a protection racket in the sweat-shop districts? Julien Advent was just getting ready to run an exposé on him in the *Times*, then suddenly didn't need to because Bates and all his cronies had gone missing. Or how about that alien predator, that disguised itself as an ambulance so it could eat the people put into it? That was the Removal Man. Supposedly. He has done some good."

"Yes," said Aday, drawing the word out till it sounded more like no, "but on the other hand, look what he did to the first incarnation of the Caligula Club. You know, that place that caters to all the more extreme forms of sexuality. Lots of people having a good time, according to their lights, all of it adult and consensual . . . but too much for the Removal Man's puritan tastes. He made the whole Club disappear, along with everyone in it. Just like that! Which is why the current version of the Club has such heavy-duty protections, and it's so hard to get in. Or so they tell me . . ."

And then the whole place fell suddenly silent as the door crashed open and General Condor entered, along with a dozen heavily armed and armoured body-guards. They made sure the place was secure and only then put their guns away. The General strode forward and looked the place over. He didn't appear especially impressed—by the bar or its customers. He was still wearing his Space Fleet uniform, complete with golden bars on his shoulders and rows of medal ribbons on his chest. He had the look of the old soldier, the calm steady look that said he'd seen a lot of men die, and your death wouldn't bother him in the least.

"John Taylor," he said, his heavy deliberate voice crashing into the hush. "I want him."

I stood up. "Get in line," I said. "I'm busy."

He looked me over, then surprised me by smiling

briefly. If anything, it made him look even more dangerous. "I need to talk to you, Taylor. And you need to listen."

I looked at him, then at the body-guards, and then at
the reporters, all staring at us with wide eyes, impressed
out of their minds. That settled it. I couldn't let them
down. I nodded to the General, who gestured stiffly at a
corner booth. The young man and woman sitting in it
got the message, and vacated immediately, leaving their
drinks behind. The General sat down stiffly in the booth,
and I went over to join him. Bettie wanted to come with
me, but I was firm. She pouted and stamped her little
foot, but she did stay put. I sat down facing the General,
and his body-guards moved quickly to form a defensive
barrier between the booth and the rest of the bar, their
hands resting on the butts of their guns. The reporters
turned up their noses at them and ostentatiously went
back to their own conversations.

I looked thoughtfully at the General. "I'm not sure I
want to hear anything you have to say, General. I'm not
the military type, I have problems with authority figures,
and I don't play well with others."

"A lot of people don't want to hear what's good for
them. The order of things in the Nightside is changing.
The Authorities are gone, and someone has to replace
them before this whole place tears itself apart fighting
over the spoils. I can put the Nightside on the right
course, John. Make it a place to be proud of. I have support from many fine and influential people, but I could
use you on my side."

"Why me?" I said, genuinely curious.

"Don't be disingenuous." General Condor sighed tiredly and leaned forward across the table. "You've been a force for good in the Nightside. You help people. You've even been known to dispense your own kind of justice when necessary. Help me to save the Nightside from its own excesses."

"You can't force change in the Nightside," I said. Something in me warmed to the General's blunt honesty, if not his cause, so I gave him the truth, and not what he wanted to hear. "The Nightside is what it wants to be. It's fought wars with Heaven and Hell for the right to go its own way. The best you can do, the best any of us can do, is encourage change for the better, one small step at a time."

"The Nightside has had thousands of years to grow up," said the General. "If it was capable of saving itself, it would have done so by now. It needs a firm hand on the tiller, it needs control and discipline imposed from above, like any military unit that's gone bad. Walker tried, but he was only ever the Authorities' puppy. He can't run things on his own. He must be replaced."

"Good luck with that," I said.

He smiled again. "If I thought it would be easy, I wouldn't be here talking to you."

"He has the Voice," I said.

"It doesn't work on you," said the General.

I raised an eyebrow. "You want me to kiss him on the cheek while I'm there?"

"I want you to do what's right. What's best for everyone."

"Even I don't know what that is," I said. "And I've been looking for it a lot longer than you have."

"If you're not with me, you're against me," General Condor said flatly. "And if you don't choose a side soon, one may be chosen for you."

I smiled. "Good luck with that, too."

He laughed briefly, quietly. "I could have used a man like you on my flagship, John. You won't bend or yield for anyone, will you?"

"Why is this so important to you?" I said, seriously. "You haven't been here long. Why this need to save the Nightside from itself?"

"I have to do something," said the General. "I couldn't save my Fleet. I couldn't save my men. I have to do *something* . . ."

He got up from the table, and I stood up with him. He offered me his hand, and I shook it. The General left the Printer's Devil with his body-guards, and I went back to join Bettie Divine.

"Well?" she said, almost bouncing up and down in her seat. "What was that all about?"

"Just politics," I said. "Nightside style. Anything new or useful come up, while I was gone?"

"But John . . . !"

"Move along," I said.

"You need to talk to the Collector," said Rick Aday.

"Been there, done that," said Bettie.

"Oh." Aday looked crest-fallen for a moment, and then brightened again. "All right, how about the Cardinal? You know, used to run the Vatican's Extremely Forbidden Library. Until they discovered he was sneaking things out for his own private collection. Had to go on the run and ended up here, where he's supposed to have built up a really impressive hoard of religious artifacts. He's your man. If anyone's got close to the Afterlife Recording, it'll be the Cardinal."

"Good call," I said. "Bettie, I think we need to pay the Cardinal a visit. It's been a while since I scared the shit out of him, for the good of his soul."

"Ah," said Aday, smiling craftily. "Word is, he's moved, and taken his collection with him. Hardly anyone knows where he is now."

"But you know," said Bettie.

"Of course."

"Oh, please, please, Ricky sweetie, tell us where he is," said Bettie, giving him the full fluttering eye-lashes treatment. "I'll be ever so grateful, I promise."

Aday smirked triumphantly. "And what makes you think I'll just give up a valuable piece of information like that?"

"Because she asked you nicely," I said. "I won't."

Aday gave us the Cardinal's new address, and directions on how to find it. Bettie and I left the Printer's Devil. She waved good-bye and blew kisses in all directions. I didn't. I had my dignity to consider.

SIX

# Heated Emotions from Unexpected Directions

It's hard to maintain a reputation for being grim and mysterious when you're accompanied by a brightly clad young thing, skipping merrily along at your side, holding your hand, and smiling sweetly on one and all. Still, it felt good to have Bettie with me. Her constant enthusiasm and optimism helped relieve a weight and burden I hadn't even realised I was carrying. She made me feel . . . alive again.

Following Rick Aday's directions, we were heading into one of the more seedy areas of the Nightside, where the narrow streets are lined with scruffy little shops and emporiums, where half the street-lights never work, and most of the neon signs have letters missing. The kind of shop where there's a sale on all the year round, where they specialise in only fairly convincing knock-offs of whatever brand-names are currently fashionable or in demand, where the buyer had better not only beware, but carry a large stick and count his fingers on the way out. Shops that sell tarnished dreams and tacky nightmares, misleading miracles and wondrous devices, most of whose batteries have run down. Bottom feeders, in other words; tourist traps, and home to every cheap and nasty con you can think of. The crowds were just as heavy here, jostling each other off the pavement and shouldering each other out of the way. Everyone loves a bargain.

And then, suddenly, everyone was yelling and running. I stopped and looked quickly around me. I hadn't done anything. The crowds scattered quickly, to reveal Queen Helena striding down the street, staring grimly at me, at the head of her own small army of sycophants, followers, and armed men. I stood my ground, doing my best to appear casual and unconcerned. Bettie stuck close to me, quivering with excitement. Queen Helena finally crashed to a halt right in front of me, fixing me with her cold faraway eyes. She was wrapped from head to toe in thick white furs, parting now as she struck a regal pose, to reveal glimpses of blue-white skin. She looked like someone who had died and then been buried in the permafrost. There was no warmth anywhere in her harsh, regal features, but her eyes blazed with arrogant superiority. She looked at me expectantly, waiting for me to kneel or bow or offer to kiss her hand. So I ignored her completely, con-

426

centrating on the colourful figures who'd moved forward out of her army to back her up.

"Take a good look," I said cheerfully to Bettie. "It's not every day you see so many prominent members of the Exiles Club out in public. Mostly, these aristocratic nobodies prefer to skulk inside their very own members-only club, addressing each other by their old titles because they're the only ones that will. They trade grievances about lost lands and abandoned kingdoms, how nobody recognises true quality in this dreadful place, and how you just can't get good servants any more.

"The bald, stooped, and vulturelike figure to Queen Helena's left is Zog, King of the Pixies. Word has it he's been wearing those scabby feathered robes ever since he turned up here thirty years ago, and he hasn't washed them once. Try to avoid standing downwind. Queen Mab herself kicked him out of the Fae Court, for using glamour spells to lie with human women. He always killed them after he'd had his way with them, but Mab didn't care about that. Sex outside their race is one of the Fae's greatest taboos. So here he is now, stripped of his glamour, just another rapist and murderer with a title that means nothing at all.

"Next to him we have His Altitude Tobermoret, monarch of all he surveyed in Far Afrique. A dark and distinguished gentleman indeed, in his zebra-hide suit and his lion-claw necklace. Tobermoret used to be War Chief of an entire continent, until his people realised he was starting wars and rebellions just for the fun of it. He did so love sending young men out to die while he sat at his ease in a tent overlooking the battle-field, enjoying the show. I did hear tell his people castrated him before they shoved him through the Timeslip, which is why he's always in such a bad temper.

"On Queen Helena's other side is Prince Xerxes the Murder Monarch. And yes, those really are preserved human eyes and organs and other bits and pieces hanging from all those chains he's got wrapped around him. Though given how much he's gone to seed since he got here, one can't help wishing he'd wear something else apart from just the chains. He practises necromancy, the magic of murder. Partly because it's traditional where he comes from, but mostly because he gets off on it. Though he's learned to leave the tourists alone ever since Walker had a quiet word with him.

"And finally, next to Xerxes we have King Artur, of Sinister Albion. For every glorious dream, there's a nightmare equivalent, somewhere in the time-streams. For every helping hand, a kick in the face. In Sinister Albion, Merlin Satanspawn decided to embrace his father's qualities instead of rejecting them, and brought up young Artur in his own awful image. Under their direction, Camelot became a place of blood and horror, where knights in terrible armour feasted on the hearts of good men, and Albion blazed from end to end with burning Wicker Men. The only reason I haven't killed Artur on general principles, is because I've been too busy with other things."

I smiled at Queen Helena. "I think that's it. Have I missed anything important?"

"You do so love the sound of your own voice, Taylor," said Queen Helena. "And you will address me as Your Majesty."

"That'll be the day," I said cheerfully. "What do you want with me, Helena? Or are you just taking the Exiles out for a walk?"

It took her a moment to work out how to answer me. She wasn't used to open defiance, let alone ridicule. "You were seen," she said finally, "talking with the General Condor. You will tell me what you talked about. What you decided. What plans were made. Tell me everything, and I shall make a place for you in my army. Power and riches shall be yours. I could use a man like you, Taylor."

"Ah, what it is to be popular and desired," I said. "The leadership of the Nightside is up for grabs, and suddenly everyone wants me on their side. Flattering, but . . . annoying. I'm busy right now, Helena. And I have to say, even if I wasn't . . . there isn't enough gold in the Nightside to persuade me to work for you, let alone this bunch of titled scumbags."

"Why do you say these things to me?" said Queen Helena. "When you know I will kill you for it?"

I shrugged. "I think you bring out the worst in me. There's some shit I simply will not put up with."

Her arms came out from under her robes, bulging tech implants already thrusting up through the blue-white skin. Dull grey gun muzzles orientated on me. Zog raised a withered arm to show off a beaten-copper glove with sharpened claws, buzzing with arcane energies. Tobermoret slammed the end of his long wooden staff on the pavement, and all the runes and sigils carved deep into the wood began to glow with a disquieting light. Xerxes produced a pair of long, curved daggers with serrated edges that looked more like butcher's tools. He grinned at me, showing off dull brown teeth filed to points. And Artur's bleak and brutal battle armour slowly came to life, its metal parts creeping and crawling over him, muttering to themselves in hissing otherworldly voices. Behind his blank steel helmet, his eyes glowed like corpsefires.

And behind Queen Helena and her Exiles, armed and armoured men hefted their various weapons, impatient for the order to attack.

Bettie Divine made quiet whimpering noises and looked like she'd rather be anywhere else than here, but still she held her ground at my side.

I took a sudden deliberate step forward, so I could look Queen Helena right in the eye. "I could have been King of the Nightside if I'd wanted. I didn't. Did you really think I'd bend the knee and bow my head to such as you?"

"I have powerful allies!" said Queen Helena. "I have an army in waiting! I have potent weapons!"

I laughed in her face. "You really think that's going to make a difference? *I'm John Taylor.*"

Queen Helena held my gaze longer than I'd thought she would, but in the end she looked away and stepped back a pace, her tech implants ducking back under her skin. I looked unhurriedly about me, and the Exiles fell back, too, powering down their weapons. Their followers stirred uneasily, looking at each other. Some of them were muttering my name.

Because I was John Taylor; and there was no telling what I might do. It was all I could do to keep from smiling.

And then, just when it was all going so well, Uptown Taffy Lewis came storming up the street from the other direction, at the head of his own small army of bully-boys, body-guards, and enforcers. All of them heavily armed. I turned my back on Queen Helena to face him. Bettie made a sound deep in her throat and stuck so close to me she was practically hiding inside my coat-pocket. Taffy stamped up to me, planted his expensively tailored bulk in front of me, paused a moment to get his breath back after his exertions, and then ignored me to scowl at Queen Helena and the Exiles.

"Why are you talking with these has-beens?" he growled to me. "You know where the real power is in the Nightside. Why didn't you come and talk to me?"

"I don't really want to talk to anyone," I said wistfully. "I keep telling everyone I'm busy right now, but . . ."

"Whatever they've offered you, I'll double it," said Taffy. "And unlike them, you can be sure I'll deliver. I want you on my side, Taylor, and I always get what I want."

"I suggest you take this up with Helena," I said. "She seems to believe she has exclusive rights to me. And you wouldn't believe some of the nasty things she's been saying about you."

And then all I had to do was step quickly to one side, as Uptown Taffy Lewis lurched forward to confront Queen Helena, screaming insults into her cold and unyielding face. She hissed insults right back at him, then the Exiles got involved with Taffy's lieutenants, and suddenly both armies were going for each other's throats. I had already retreated to a safe distance, hauling Bettie along with me, and we watched fascinated as open warfare broke out right in front of us. The tourists loved it, watching it all from a safe distance, and even recording it so they could enjoy it again later.

Queen Helena had her implants, the Exiles, and her followers, but Taffy had the numbers. They swarmed all over Queen Helena and her people, dragging them down despite their elite weapons. I saw Zog thrown to the ground and trampled underfoot, and Tobermoret beaten down with his own staff till it broke. Xerxes was cut open with his own daggers. Helena and Artur stood back to back, killing everyone who came within reach until finally the odds were too great; and then the pair of them disappeared in a sudden blaze of light, leaving the two armies to fight it out in the street. The bodies piled up, and blood flowed thickly in the gutters.

Politics is never dull in the Nightside.

I started off down a side street, leaving the violence behind. Bettie trotted along beside me, still staring back over her shoulder.

"Is that it?" she said. "Aren't you going to do any-thing?"

"Haven't I done enough?" I said. "By the time they're finished with each other, the two most dangerous armed forces in the Nightside will have wiped each other out. What more do you want?"

"Well, I thought . . . I expected . . ."

"What?"

"I don't know! Something more . . . dramatic! You're the great John Taylor! I thought I was going to see you in action, at last."

"Action is overrated," I said. "Winning is all that mat-ters. Aren't you getting enough good material for your story?"

"Well, yes, but . . . it's not quite what I expected. You're not what I expected." She looked at me thought-fully. "You faced down Queen Helena and the Exiles, and their army. Told them to go to Hell and damned them to do their worst. And they all backed down. Were you bluffing?"

I grinned. "I'll never tell."

Bettie laughed out loud. "This story is going to make my name! My day on the streets with John Taylor!"

She grabbed me by the shoulders, turned me round, and kissed me hard on the lips. It was an impulse mo-ment. A happy thing. Could have meant anything, or nothing. We stood together a moment, and then she pulled back a little and looked at me with wide, ques-tioning eyes. I could have pushed her away. Could have defused the moment, with a smile or a joke. But I didn't. I pulled her to me and kissed her. Because I wanted to. She filled my arms. We kissed the breath out of each other, while our hands moved up and down each other's bodies. Finally, we broke off, and looked at each other again. Her face was very close, her hurried breath beating against my face. Her face was flushed, her eyes very bright. My head was full of her perfume, and of her. I could feel her heart racing, so close to mine. I could feel the whole length of her body, pressing insistently against mine.

"Well," she said. "I didn't expect that. Has it really been such a long time since you kissed anyone? Since you . . . ?"

I pushed her gently away, and she let me. But her eyes still held mine.

"I can't do this," I said. My voice didn't sound like mine. Didn't sound like someone in control of himself.

"It's true what they say about Suzie, then," said Bettie. She sounded kind, not judgemental. "She can't . . . The poor dear. And poor you, John. That's no way to live. You can't have a real relationship with someone if you can't ever touch her."

"I love her," I said. "She loves me."

"That's not love," said Bettie. "That's one damaged soul clinging to another, for comfort. I could love you, John."

"Of course you could," I said. "You're the daughter of a succubus. Love comes easy to you."

"No," she said. "Just the opposite. I laugh and smile

and flutter my eye-lashes because that's what's expected of me. And because it does help, with the job. But that's not me. Or at least, not all of me. I only show that to people I care about. I like you, John. Admire you. I could learn to love you. Could you . . . ?"

"I can't talk about this now," I said.

"You'll have to talk about it sometime. And some-times . . . you can say things to a stranger that you couldn't say to anyone else."

"You're not a stranger," I said.

"Why thank you, John. That's the nicest thing you've said to me so far."

She moved forward and leaned her head on my shoulder. We held each other gently. No passion, no pressure, only a man and a woman together, and it felt good, so good. It had been a long time since I'd held anyone. Since anyone had held me. It was like . . . part of me had been asleep. Finally, I pushed her away.

"We have to go see the Cardinal," I said firmly. "Pen Donavon and his damned Recording are still out there, somewhere, and that means people like Taffy and Helena will be looking for it, hoping it will turn out to be something they can use to further their ambitions. I really don't like the way they were willing to flaunt their armies openly in public."

"Walker will do something," said Bettie.

"That's what I'm afraid of," I said.

·  ·  ·

Rick Aday's directions finally brought us to a pokey little shop called The Pink Cockatoo, a single-windowed front, in the middle of a long terrace of shops, set between a Used Grimoires book-shop, and a Long Pig franchise. The window before us was full of fashionable fetish clothing that seemed to consist mostly of plastic and leather straps. A few corsets and basques, and some high-heeled boots that would have been too big even for me. Incense candles, fluffy handcuffs, and something with spikes that I preferred not to look at too closely. I tried the door, but it was locked. There was a rusty steel intercom set into the wooden frame. I hit the button with my fist and leaned in close.

"This is John Taylor, to see the Cardinal. Open up, or I'll huff and I'll puff and I'll blow your door right off its hinges."

"This establishment is protected," said a calm, cultured voice. "Even from people like the infamous John Taylor. Now go away, or I'll set the hell-hounds on you."

"We need to talk, Cardinal."

"Convince me."

"I've just been with the Collector," I said. "Discussing the missing Afterlife Recording. He didn't have it. Now either you agree to talk to me, or I'll tell him you've got it and exactly where to find you. And you know how much he's always wanted to make your collection part of his own."

"Bully," the voice said dispassionately. "All right; I

suppose you'd better come in. Bring the demon floozy with you."

There was the sound of several locks and bolts disengaging, and then the door slowly swung open before us. I marched straight in, followed by Bettie. There might have been booby-traps, trap-doors, or all kinds of unpleasantness ahead, but in the Nightside you can't ever afford to look weak. Confidence is everything. The door shut and locked itself behind us. Not entirely to my surprise, the interior of the shop wasn't at all what its exterior had suggested. For one thing, the interior was a hell of a lot bigger. It's a common enough spell in the Nightside, sticking a large space inside a small one, given that living and business space are both in such short supply. The problem lies with the spell, often laid down in a hurry by dodgy backstreet sorcerers, the kind who deal strictly in cash. All it takes is one mistake in the set-up, one mispronunciation of a vital word; and then the whole spell can collapse at any time without any warning. The interior expands suddenly to its full size, shouldering everything else out of the way . . . and they'll be pulling body parts out of the rubble that used to be a street for days on end.

The shop's interior stretched away before me, warmly lit and widely spacious, with gleaming wood-panelled walls, and a spotless floor. The huge barnlike structure was filled with miles and miles of open glass shelving and stands, showing off hundreds of weird and wonderful treasures. Bettie made excited *Ooh!* and *Aah!* noises, and I had to physically prevent her from picking things up to examine them. The Cardinal had said his place was protected, and I believed him. Because if it wasn't seriously protected, the Collector would have cleaned him out by now.

The Cardinal came strolling down the brightly lit central aisle to greet us. A tall and well-proportioned man in his late forties, with a high-boned face, an easy smile, and a hint of mascara round the eyes. He was wearing skin-tight white slacks, a red shirt open to the navel to show off his shaven chest, and a patterned silk scarf gathered loosely round his neck. He carried a martini in one hand and didn't offer the other to be shaken.

"Wow," I said. "When the Church defrocked you, they went all the way, didn't they?"

The Cardinal smiled easily. "The Church has never approved of those of my . . . inclination. Even though we are responsible for most of the glorious works of art adorning their greatest churches and cathedrals. They only put up with me for so long because I was useful, and a respected academic, and . . . discreet. None of which did me any good when I was found out, and accused . . . It's not as if I took anything important, or significant. I simply wanted a few pretty things for my own. Ah, well; at least I don't have to wear those awful robes any more. So drab, and so very draughty round the nether regions."

"Excuse me," said Bettie, "But why is your shop called The Pink Cockatoo? What has that got to do with . . . well, anything?"

The Cardinal's smile widened. "My little joke. It's called that because I've had a cockatoo in my time."

Bettie got the giggles. I gave the Cardinal my best *Let's try and stick to the subject* look.

"Come to take a look at my collection, have you?" he said, apparently unmoved by the look. He sipped delicately at his martini, one finger elegantly extended. "By all means. Knock yourself out."

I wandered down the shelves, just to be polite. And because I was a bit curious. I kept Bettie close beside me and made sure she maintained a respectful distance from the exhibits at all times. I was sure that the Cardinal believed in *You broke it, you paid for it*. He wandered along behind us, being obviously patient. I recognised some of the things on the shelves, by reputation if not always by sight. The Cardinal had helpfully labelled them in neat copperplate handwriting. There was a copy of the Gospel According to Mary Magdalene. (With illustrations. And I was pretty sure which kind, too.) Pope Joan's robes of office. The rope Judas Iscariot used to hang himself. Half a dozen large canvasses by acknowledged Masters, all unknown to modern art history, depicting frankly pornographic scenes from some of the seamier tales in the Old Testament. Probably private commissions, from aristocratic patrons of the time. A Satanic Bible, bound in black goat's skin, with an inverted crucifix stamped in bas-relief on the front cover.

"Now that's a very limited edition," said the Cardinal, leaning in close to peer over my shoulder. "Belonged to

Giles de Rais, the old monster himself, before he met the Maid of Orleans. There are only seventeen copies of that particular edition, in the goat's skin."

"Why seventeen?" said Bettie. "Bit of an arbitrary number, isn't it?"

"I said that," said the Cardinal. "When I inquired further, I was told that seventeen is the most you can get out of one goat's skin. Makes you wonder whether the last copy had a big floppy ear hanging off the back cover . . . And I hate to think what they used for the spine. Ah, Mr. Taylor, I see you've discovered my dice. I'm rather proud of those. The very dice the Roman soldiers used as they gambled for the Christ's clothes, while he was still on the cross."

"Do they have any . . . special properties?" I said, moving in close for a better look. They seemed very ordinary, two small wooden cubes, with any colour and all the dots worn away long ago.

"No," said the Cardinal. "They're just dice. Their value, which is incredible, lies in their history."

"And what's *this*?" said Bettie, wrinkling her nose as she studied a single, small, very old and apparently very ordinary fish, enclosed in a clear Lucite block.

"Ah, that," said the Cardinal. "The only surviving example of the fish used to feed the five thousand . . . You wouldn't believe how much money, political positions, and even sexual favours I've been offered, by certain extreme epicures, just for a taste . . . The philistines."

"What brought you here, to the Nightside, Cardinal?"

said Bettie, doing her best to sound pleasant and casual and not at all like a reporter. The Cardinal wasn't fooled, but he smiled indulgently, and she hurried on. "And why collect only Christian artifacts? Are you still a believer, even after everything the Church has done to you?"

"Of course," said the Cardinal. "The Catholic Church is not unlike the Mafia, in some ways—once in, never out. And as for the Nightside—why this is Hell, nor am I out of it. Ah, the old jokes are still the best. I damned myself to this appalling haven for the morally intransigent through the sin of greed, of acquisition. I was tempted, and I fell. Sometimes it feels like I'm still falling . . . but I have my collection to comfort me." He drained the last of his martini, smacked his lips, put the glass down carefully next to a miniature golden calf, and looked at me steadily. "Why are you here, Mr. Taylor? What do you want with me? You must know I can't trust you. Not after you worked for the Vatican, finding the Unholy Grail for them."

"I worked for a particular individual," I said carefully. "Not the Vatican, as such."

"You really did find it, didn't you?" said the Cardinal, looking at me almost wistfully. I could all but sense his collector's fingers twitching. "The Sombre Cup . . . What was it like?"

"There aren't the words," I said. "But don't bother trying to track it down. It's been . . . defused. It's only a cup now."

"It's still history," said the Cardinal.

Bettie stooped suddenly, to pick up an open paperback from a chair. "*The Da Vinci Code*? Are you actually reading this, Cardinal?"

"Oh, yes . . . I love a good laugh."

"Put it down, Bettie," I said. "It'll probably turn out to be some exotic misprinting, and he'll charge us for getting fingerprints all over it. Cardinal, we're here about the Afterlife Recording. I take it you have heard of Pen Donavon's DVD?"

"Of course. But . . . I have decided I'm not interested in pursuing it. I don't want it. Because I know myself. I know it wouldn't be enough for me simply to possess the DVD. I'd have to watch it . . . And I don't think I'm ready to see what's on it."

"You think it might test your faith?" I said.

"Perhaps . . ."

"Aren't you curious?" said Bettie.

"Of course . . . But it's one thing to believe, another to know. I do try to hope for the best, but when the Holy Father himself has told you to your face that you're damned for all time, just for being what God made you . . . Hope is all I have left. It's not much of a substitute for faith, but even cold comfort is better than none."

"I believe God has more mercy than that," I said. "I don't think God sweats the small stuff."

"Yes, well," said the Cardinal dryly, "you'd have to believe that, wouldn't you?"

"If you learn anything, let me know," I said. "As long as the Afterlife Recording is out there, loose in the wind, more people will be trying to get their hands on it, for all the wrong reasons. There's even a chance the Removal Man is interested in it."

All the colour dropped out of the Cardinal's face, his brittle amiability replaced by stark terror. "He can't come here! He can't! Have you seen him? You could have led him here! To me! No, no, no . . . You have to leave. Right now. I can't take the risk!"

And he pushed both Bettie and me towards the door. He wasn't big enough to budge either of us if we didn't want to be budged, but I didn't see any point in making a scene. He didn't know anything useful. So I let him shove and propel us back to the door and push us through it. Once we were back on the street, the door slammed shut behind us, and a whole series of locks and bolts snapped into place. It seemed the Cardinal believed in traditional ways of protecting himself, too. I adjusted my trench coat. It had been a long time since I'd been given the bum's rush. And then from behind the door came a scream, loud and piercing, a harsh shrill sound full of abject terror. I beat on the door, and yelled into the intercom, but the scream went on and on and on, long after human lungs should have been unable to sustain it. The pain and horror in the sound was almost unbearable. And then it stopped, abruptly, and that was worse.

The locks and the bolts slowly opened, one at a time, and the door swung inwards. I made Bettie stand behind me and pushed the door all the way open. Beyond it, I could see the huge display room. No sign of anyone, anywhere. No sound at all. I moved slowly, and very cautiously forward, refusing to allow Bettie to hurry me. There was no sign of the Cardinal anywhere. And every single piece of his collection was gone, too. Nothing left but empty shelves, stretching away.

"The Removal Man," I said. My voice echoed on the quiet, saying the name over and over again.

"Did we lead him here, do you think?" said Bettie, her voice hushed. The echo turned her words into disturbing whispers.

"No," I said. "I'd have known if anyone was following us. I'm sure I'd have known."

"Even the Removal Man? Even him?"

"Especially him," I said.

# SEVEN

# THE GOOD, THE BAD AND THE UN-GODLY

"So," said Bettie Divine, sitting perched on one of the empty wooden shelves with her long legs dangling, "what do we do now? I mean, the Removal Man has just removed our last real lead. Though I have to say . . . I never thought I'd get this close to him. The Removal Man is a *real* urban legend. Even more than you, darling. We're talking about someone who actually does move in mysterious ways! Maybe I should forget this story and concentrate on him. If I could bring in an exclusive interview with the Removal Man . . ."

"You mean you're giving up on me?" I said, more amused than anything.

Bettie shrugged easily. She was now wearing a pale

blue cat-suit, with a long silver zip running from collar to crotch. Her hair was bobbed, and her horns peeped out from under a smart peaked cap. "Well, I am half demon, darling; you have to expect the odd moment of heartlessness."

"If you stick with me, at least there's a reasonable chance you'll survive to file your story," I said.

"Who'd want to hurt a poor sweet defenceless little girlie like me?" said Bettie, pouting provocatively. "And besides, we half demons are notoriously hard to kill. That's why the Editor paired me up with you for this story. Which, you have to admit, does seem to have petered out rather. I mean to say, if the Collector doesn't have the Afterlife Recording, and the Cardinal doesn't have it, who does that leave?"

"There are others," I said. "Strange Harald, the junkman. Flotsam Inc.; their motto: *We buy and sell anything that isn't actually nailed down and guarded by hellhounds.* And there's always Bishop Beastly . . . But admittedly they're all fairly minor players. Far too small to think they could handle a prize like the Afterlife Recording. They'd have sold it on immediately; and I would have heard. You know, it's always possible Pen Donavon could have realised how much trouble he'd let himself in for and destroyed the DVD."

"He'd better not have!" said Bettie, her eyes flashing dangerously. "The paper owns that DVD, no matter what's on it."

I looked at her thoughtfully. "If it is real . . . are you curious to see what's on it?"

"Of course," she said immediately. "I want to know. I always want to know."

"So you'll stick with me? Until we find it?"

"Of course, darling! Forget about the Removal Man. It was just an impulse. No; we're on the trail of something that could shake the whole Nightside if it is real. And you know what that means? I could end up covering a real story at last! Do you know how long I've dreamed about covering a real story, about something that actually matters? We can't let this end here! You're the private eye, you're the legendary John Taylor; do something!"

"I'm open to suggestions," I said.

My mobile phone rang. I answered and was immediately assaulted by the acerbic voice of Alex Morrisey, calling from Strangefellows. As always, Alex did not sound at all happy with the world, the universe, and everything.

"Taylor, get your arse over here at warp factor ten. A certain Pen Donavon has just turned up in my bar, looking like death warmed over and allowed to congeal. He's clutching a DVD case like it's his last life-line, hyperventilating, and crying his eyes out because he thinks the Removal Man is after him. He appears to be suffering from the sad delusion that you can protect him. He says you're the only person he can trust, which only goes to show he doesn't know you very well. So will you please come and get him because he is scaring off all my customers! Most of whom have understandably decided that they don't want to get caught in the inevitable cross-fire. Did I mention that I am not at all happy about this? You are costing me a whole night's profits!"

"Put it on my tab," I said. "I can cover it; I'm on expenses. Sit on Donavon till I get there. No-one talks to him but me."

I put the phone away and smiled at Bettie. "We're back in the game. Pen Donavon has turned up at Strangefellows."

Bettie clapped her hands together, kicked her heels, and jumped down from the wooden shelf. "I knew you'd find him, John! Never doubted you for a moment! And we're finally going to Strangefellows! Super cool!"

"You'll probably be disappointed," I said. "It's only a bar."

"The oldest bar in the world! Where all the customers are myths and legends, and the fate of the whole world gets decided on a regular basis!"

"Only sometimes," I said.

"Is it far from here?"

"Right on the other side of town. Fortunately, I know a short cut."

I took out my Strangefellows club membership card. Alex handed out a dozen or so, in a rare generous moment, and he's been trying to get them back ever since. Not that any of us are ever likely to give them up. They're far too useful. The card itself isn't much to look at. Just simple embossed pasteboard, with the name of the bar in dark Gothic script, and below that the words

*You Are Here*, in blood-red lettering. I pulled Bettie in close beside me, and she snuggled up companionably. I still wasn't used to that. It had been a long time since I'd let anybody get this close to me. This casual. I liked it. I pressed my thumb firmly against the crimson lettering on the card, and it activated at once, throbbing and pulsing with stored energy. It leapt out of my hand to hang on the air before me, turning end over end and crackling with arcane activity. Bright lights flared and sputtered all around it. Alex had paid for the full bells and whistles package. The card expanded suddenly to the size of a door, which opened before us. Together, Bettie and I stepped through into Strangefellows, and the door slammed shut behind us.

I put the card back in my coat-pocket and looked around. The place was unnaturally still and quiet, empty apart from a single drunk sleeping one off, slumped forward across his table. I knew him vaguely. Thallassa, a wizened old sorcerer who claimed to be responsible for the sinking of Atlantis. He said he drank to forget, but it was amazing how many stories he could remember, as long as you were dumb enough to keep buying him drinks. Everyone else had clearly decided that discretion was the better part of running for the hills, and that the combination of Pen Donavon, his DVD, and me in one place was just too dangerous to be around. Even the kind of people who habitually drink at a place like Strangefellows have their limit; and I'm often it.

Donavon was easy to spot. He was sitting slumped on a stool at the bar. No-one else could look that miserable, beaten down, and shit scared from the back. He peered round as Bettie and I approached, and almost collapsed off his stool before he recognised me. He was just a small, ordinary-looking man, no-one you'd look at twice in the street, clearly in way over his head and going down for the third time. Up close, he looked in pretty bad shape. He was shaking and shivering, his face drawn and ashen, with dark circles under his eyes as though he hadn't slept in days. Perhaps because he didn't dare. He couldn't have been half-way through his twenties, but now he looked twice that. Something had aged him and hadn't been kind about it. He clutched a long, shabby coat around him, as though to keep out a chill only he could feel.

He looked like a man who'd seen Hell. Or Heaven.

Alex Morrisey glared at me, and then went back to half-coaxing, half-bullying Donavon into putting aside his brandy glass and trying some freshly made hot soup. Donavon remained unconvinced. He watched, wide-eyed, until Bettie and I were right there with him. Then he sighed deeply, and some of the tension seemed to go out of him. He emptied his glass with a gulp and signalled for another. Alex put aside the soup bowl, sniffed loudly, and reluctantly opened a new bottle.

Alex owns and runs Strangefellows, and possibly as a result, has a mad on for the whole world. He loathes his customers, despises tourists, and never gives the right change on principle. He also had his thirtieth birthday just the other day, which hadn't helped. He always wore black, because, he said, he was in mourning for his sex life. (Gone, but not forgotten.) His permanent scowl had etched a deep notch between his eyebrows, right above the designer shades he always affected. He also wore a snazzy black beret, perched far back on his head to hide his spreading bald patch. I have known clinically depressed lepers with haemorrhoids who smiled more often than Alex Morrisey. Though at least he doesn't have to worry when he sneezes. I leaned against the bar and looked at him reproachfully.

"You never made me hot soup, Alex."

He sniffed loudly. "My home-made soup is full of things that are good for you, including a few that are downright healthful, all of which would be wasted on a body as ruined and ravaged as yours."

"Just because I don't like vegetables . . ."

"You're the only man I know who makes the sign of the cross when confronted with broccoli. And don't change the subject! Once again I am left clearing up the mess from one of your cases. Like I don't have enough troubles of my own. Bloody eels have got into the beer barrels again, the pixies have been at the bar snacks, which they will live to regret, the poor fools, and my pet vulture is pregnant! Someone's going to pay for this . . ."

He broke off as Pen Donavon suddenly reached out and grabbed my arm. There was so little strength left in him it felt like a ghost tugging at my sleeve. His mouth worked for a moment before easing into something like a smile, and there were real tears of gratitude in his eyes.

"Thank God you're here, Mr. Taylor. I've been so afraid . . . They're after me. Everyone's after me. You have to protect me!"

"Of course, of course I will," I said soothingly. "You're safe now. No-one's going to get to you here."

"Just keep them away," he said pathetically. "Keep them all away. I can't think . . . I've been running from everyone. Either they want to pressure me into selling the Recording, or they want to kill me and take it. I can't trust anyone any more. I thought I'd be safe, once I'd made my deal with the *Unnatural Inquirer*, but I was ambushed on my way there. I've been running and hiding ever since."

He let go of me and looked back at the full glass of brandy before him. He gulped half of it down in one go, and Alex winced visibly. Must have been the really good stuff, then. I looked at Bettie.

"Could someone in your offices have put the word out on Donavon coming in with the DVD?"

"For a percentage? Wouldn't surprise me. None of us are exactly overpaid at the *Inquirer*. And our Reception phones are always being tapped. We debug them at the start of every working day, but there's always someone listening in, hoping for an advantage. After all, we hear everything first. We're noted for it."

"I should never have recorded the broadcast," said

Donavon. He was sitting hunched over his brandy glass, as though afraid someone would snatch it away. "It was all a ghastly mistake. I was trying to contact the other side, yes, but I never thought . . . My life hasn't been my own since. And I'd certainly never have tried to sell the Recording if I'd known it would destroy my whole life."

"You saw the broadcast," said Bettie, leaning in close with her best engaging smile. "What did you see?"

Donavon started shaking again. He tried to speak, and couldn't. He squeezed his eyes shut, and tears ran down his trembling cheeks. Alex sighed heavily and topped up the brandy glass again. He smiled nastily at me.

"All these drinks are going on your tab, Taylor."

I smiled right back at him. "Do your worst. Expenses, remember?"

"Well," said Bettie. "You will get expenses if we deliver the DVD."

I looked at her. "What? What do you mean *if*? Nothing was ever said about my expenses being conditional!"

"This is the newspaper game, sweetie. Everything's conditional."

I scowled, and then had to stop because it was upsetting Donavon even more. I moved away down the bar and gestured for Alex to lean in close. "You can bet some of your recent customers will be out on the streets now, spilling the beans about who and what can be found in Strangefellows. Which means we can expect unfriendly visitors at any moment. Better lock the doors and slam down the shutters. Where are the Coltranes?"

"Out the back, doing exactly that," said Alex. "I can think for myself, thank you. My defences will keep out all but the most determined; but if anyone does get in, the resulting damage will also be going on your tab. I'd insure against you, but apparently you're classed along with Acts of Gods and other unavoidable nuisances."

"Call Suzie," I said. "I think we're going to need her help on this one."

"Damn," said Alex. "And I just had the place redecorated."

Bettie slipped her arm through mine and turned me round to face her. "I hate to sound disappointed," she said, "but I am, maybe a bit. I mean, darling, this isn't at all what I expected. It all looks so . . . ordinary. Well, ordinary for the Nightside. I was hoping for something more . . . extreme."

I refrained from pointing out the disembodied hand scuttling up and down the bar top. (Alex accepted it in payment for a bad debt.) The hand was busy polishing the bar top and refilling the snack bowls. Yet another good reason not to eat them, as far as I was concerned. Alex objected on principle to giving away anything, and it showed in his choice of snacks. Does anyone actually eat honeyed locusts any more? The vulture's perch was empty, of course, but there were other things to look at. Lightning, crackling inside a bottle. Bit hard on the ship, I thought. A small featureless furry thing, that sat on the bar top purring happily to itself, and occasionally farting. Until the hand grabbed it up and used it as a rag to polish the bar top. A small cuspidor of tanna leaves, with the brand-name *Mummy's favourite*. All nice homey touches.

"I want a drink," Bettie announced loudly. "I want one of those special drinkies you can only get here. Do you have a Maiden's Bloody Ruin? Dragons' Breath? Angel's Tears?"

"The first two aren't cocktails," I said. "And that last one is actually called Angel's Urine."

"Which was selling quite well," said Alex. "Until word got around it wasn't so much a trade name as an accurate description."

Bettie laughed and snuggled cosily up against me. "You choose, darling."

"Give the lady a wormwood brandy," I said.

Alex gave me a look, and then fished about under the bar for the really good stuff he keeps set aside for special customers.

"I do like this place, after all," Bettie decided. "It's cosy, and comfortable. It'd probably even have atmosphere if there was anybody else here but us. Ah, sweetie, you take me to the nicest places!"

She kissed me. As though it was the most natural thing in the world. Perhaps it was, for other people. I took her in my arms, and her whole body surged forward, pressing against me. When we broke apart, Alex was there, pushing a glass of wormwood brandy towards Bettie. She snatched it up with an excited squeak, sipped the brandy, and made appreciative noises. Alex looked at me. I looked at him. Neither of us mentioned Suzie, but we were both thinking about her.

And then we all looked round sharply at the sound of heavy footsteps in the entrance lobby upstairs. They were heading our way, and they didn't sound like customers. Alex cursed dispassionately.

"My defences are telling me that a bunch of combat sorcerers just walked right through them, without even hesitating. Really powerful combat sorcerers."

"How can you tell?" said Bettie

"Because only really powerful combat sorcerers could get through this bar's defences," I said.

Thirteen very dangerous men came clattering down the metal stairs into the bar proper, making a hell of a racket in the process. They moved smoothly, in close formation, and spread out at the bottom of the steps to cut us off from all the exits. They stood tall and proud, radiating professionalism and confidence. They were all dressed in black leather cowboy outfits, complete with Stetsons, chaps, boots, and silver spurs. Surprisingly, and a bit worryingly, they weren't wearing holsters. They all possessed various charms, amulets, fetishes, and grisgris, displayed openly around their necks or on their chests for all to see, and despair. These were major league power sources, for strength and speed, transformations and elemental commands. A bit generic but no less dangerous for that.

They all looked to be big men and in their prime. They all had that lazy arrogance that comes from having beaten down anyone and anything that ever dared to stand against them. You don't get to be a combat sorcerer without killing an awful lot of people in the process. There was an ideogram tattooed on all their foreheads, right over the third eye, showing their Clan affiliation. Combat sorcerers are too dangerous to be allowed to run around unsupervised. You either joined a Clan, or they joined together to wipe you out. This particular bunch belonged to Clan Buckaroo.

Their leader stepped forward to face me. He was a good head taller than me, broad in the shoulders and narrow in the waist. Probably ate his vegetables every day, and did a hundred and fifty sit-ups before breakfast. He had three different charms hanging from rolled silver chains around his neck and an amulet round his waist I didn't like to look at. This cowboy was packing some serious firepower. He fixed me with his cold blue eyes and started to say something that would only have been an insult or a demand, and I wasn't in the mood for either; so I got my retaliation in first.

"Those are seriously tacky outfits," I said. "What are you planning to do, line dance us to death?"

The leader hesitated. This wasn't going according to plan. He wasn't used to defiance, let alone open ridicule. He squared his shoulders and tried again.

"We are Clan Buckaroo. We work for Kid Cthulhu. And you've got something we want."

"Like what?" I asked. "Fashion sense?"

The leader's hand dropped to where his holster should

have been. The twelve other combat sorcerers all did the same. Some suddenly had guns of light in their hands, sparking and shimmering. Like the ghosts of guns steeped in slaughter. And a few, including the leader, just pointed their index fingers at me, like a child miming a gun. I looked at the leader and raised an eyebrow.

"Conceptual guns," he said. "Creations of the mind, powered by murder magic. They never miss, they never run out of ammunition, they can punch a hole through anything; and they kill whatever they hit. Allow me to demonstrate."

He pointed his finger at the bottles ranked behind the bar. I grabbed Bettie and Donavon and dragged them out of the way. One by one the bottles exploded, showering glass fragments and hissing liquids all over the bar. Alex stood his ground and didn't move an inch, even as liquors soaked his shirt, and flying glass cut his cheek. The leader raised his finger to his lips and blew away imaginary smoke. The disembodied hand flipped him the finger, and then disappeared under the bar. The watching cowboys were all grinning broadly. Alex glared right back at them.

"You needn't be so smug. You only got the stuff I keep for tourists. The good stuff can look after itself."

The leader looked at him for a moment. He'd used his favourite trick, and no-one was looking the least bit intimidated. He stuck out his chin and tried again.

"I've come for the Afterlife Recording."

"Don't worry, dear," said Bettie. "I'm sure you were just a bit over-excited."

I stepped forward, putting myself between her and the leader. I looked him square in the eye. "You don't want to be here," I said. "These aren't the people you're looking for."

I held his gaze with mine, and he stood very still. Behind him, the other combat sorcerers stirred restlessly. And then the leader smiled coldly right back at me.

"I've heard about your evil eye, Taylor. Won't work on any of us. We're protected."

He was right. I couldn't stare him down, couldn't even reach him. While I was still working out what to do next, Bettie stepped past me and put herself between me and the leader.

"Trevor!" she said. "I thought it was you, sweetie! Didn't recognise you at first, all tricked out in the Village People outfit. You never told me you were a combat sorcerer."

The other cowboys looked at their leader, and I could practically see them mouthing the word *Trevor?* at each other. The leader glared at Bettie.

"That is my old name," he said harshly. "I don't use it any more. My name is Ace now, Bettie, leader of Clan Buckaroo. I haven't gone by . . . that other name in ages."

"You were Trevor when I knew you," Bettie said briskly. "I did wonder why you insisted on wearing those black boots and spurs to bed, but I thought you were being kinky. Even though you went all bashful when I got out the fluffy handcuffs. What are you doing here, sweetie, dressed up as Black Bart and leading this bunch of overdressed thugs?"

"The money's good," said Ace.

"It would have to be," said Bettie.

"Don't get in the way," said Ace, giving her his best fierce glare. "We're here to do a job, and we're going to do it. I can't cut you any slack just because we used to be an item."

"You and he were an item?" I said to Bettie.

She shrugged. "He didn't last long."

There was some quiet sniggering from the other combat sorcerers that died quickly away as Ace glared around him.

"What exactly are you here for?" I said. "Maybe there's room for negotiation."

"We want Donavon, and we want the Afterlife Recording," said Ace, fixing me with his cold stare again. "No negotiations, no discussion. We work for Kid Cthulhu, and he wants sole ownership of the Recording."

"Now wait just a minute!" Bettie strode forward to glare right into Ace's face, and he was so startled he actually fell back a pace. "The *Unnatural Inquirer* has already purchased exclusive rights to all the material on that DVD! We have a binding contract! We own it!"

"Not any more you don't," said Ace. "Possession is everything, in the Nightside."

"Kid Cthulhu . . ." Alex said thoughtfully. "Thought I'd heard something about his having cash liquidity problems with his undersea-farming interests. And, of course, the bottom's dropped right out of the calamari market. He must be thinking he can make enough money out of the Afterlife Recording to bail him out. So to speak."

"You can't have the Afterlife Recording!" Bettie said firmly to Ace. "We got there first."

Ace looked at the cowboy next to him. "If she speaks again, kill her."

Bettie's mouth opened wide, outraged, and I clapped a hand across it and hauled her back. Ace didn't look like he was kidding to me. Thirteen combat sorcerers in one room can do pretty much whatever they feel like doing. But, on the other hand, I had a reputation to maintain . . . So I looked Alex in the eye and gave him my best disapproving stare.

"Now that was just plain rude," I said. "And if you threaten to kill me . . . I will smite the lot of you. Right here and now."

There was a pause, and the thirteen combat sorcerers looked at me uncertainly. With anyone else, they'd have dismissed it immediately as just talk. But I was John Taylor . . .

"Bettie Divine is under my protection," I said. "Along with everyone else in this bar. Very definitely including Pen Donavon. So you can all get your redneck wannabe big bad selves out of here, before I decide to do something quite appallingly nasty to you."

The combat sorcerers looked at each other, and then at their leader. Their magical guns or fingers were all pointing at the floor. And then Ace smiled at me and laughed softly, and just like that the mood was broken.

"Never make a threat you can't back up," he said.

Ace pointed his conceptual gun at the drunk sorcerer, still out cold despite all the drama going on around him. A tired old man, who might or might not have done a terrible thing in his younger days. Ace shot him three times, his pointed finger unwavering even as the invisible bullets punched large bloody holes in the sleeping man. Thallassa's body jumped and jerked under the impact of the bullets, but he never made a sound. He just lay where he was, slumped across his table, as the blood ran out of him. Murdered, for no reason he would ever know. Ace laughed briefly and turned back to me.

"Boys," he said, "kill everyone in this place except for Pen Donavon." He smiled at Bettie. "Sorry, sweetie. Just business. You know how it is."

"You little shit," Bettie said defiantly. "And I do mean *little*, Trevor. I've had more fun with a toothpick."

Women always fight dirty.

Ace pointed his finger at her. "Shut up and die, will you?"

"Not in my bar," said Alex. He produced a pump-action shotgun from under the bar, and when Ace turned to look, Alex shot him in the face. Ace was thrown backwards, blasted right off his feet, crashing into the cowboys behind him, who made shocked, startled noises. Alex worked the pump action, and all the combat sorcerers stood very still.

"Wow," I said. "Hard core, Alex."

He shrugged modestly. "Suzie left this behind, one night. Always thought it would come in handy one day. I loaded it with silver bullets, dipped in holy water, and blessed by a wandering god. I could shoot the head off a golem with this. And if golems had other things, I could shoot them off, too."

"You know," said Bettie, "I think I'd be rather more impressed if Trevor wasn't getting up again."

We looked round. Ace was already back on his feet, apparently entirely unaffected. Apart from the really pissed-off look on his face.

"Oh, shit," said Alex, putting down the shotgun. "Guys, you're on your own. If you want me, I'll be hiding behind the bar, whimpering and wetting myself."

"Really?" said Bettie, not bothering to hide her disappointment in him.

"Hell no," said Alex. "This is my bar! It's bad enough that the whole world conspires against me, messes with my beer and puts my vulture up the duff, without having a bunch of refugees from an S&M march walking in here like they own the place. And Thallassa hadn't even paid for his drinks yet, you bastards! You owe me money!" He vaulted over the bar, holding a glowing cricket bat. "Merlin made this for me, sometime back. For when you really, absolutely have to take out the trash."

"Alex," I said. "This isn't like you. It's an improvement, but it isn't like you."

"My new girl-friend's upstairs," said Alex. "Probably

watching on the monitors. You know how it is when you've got a new girl. You end up doing all kinds of stupid things."

"Yes," I said. "I know how it is."

"Is that it?" said Ace, smiling. "A glow-in-the-dark cricket bat?"

"No," said Alex. *"Oh, girls!"*

And Alex's two large, muscular, body-building bouncers, Betty and Lucy Coltrane, came charging in from the back of the bar and threw themselves at the startled combat sorcerers. They ploughed right into the group before the cowboys even had time to react, knocking them arse over tit and kicking them while they were down, in the fine old tradition of bouncers everywhere. Alex hit the group a moment later, swinging his cricket bat with both hands as though it were a long sword. He smashed faces and broke bones, and the cowboys fell back, crying out in shock and distress. None of them had prepared for an irate bartender armed with a weapon enchanted by Merlin Satanspawn. The glowing cricket bat smashed through their magical defences like they weren't even there. Tougher magical shields flared up here and there, as some of the combat sorcerers got their act together enough to ward off the Coltranes, but the girls just dodged around the shields to get at those cowboys who weren't protected. Shrill cries of pain and anguish filled the air.

I said Ace's name, and when he turned to look at me I threw a handful of pepper into his face. An attack so basic and physical his magical shields couldn't do a thing to prevent it. He howled piteously, scrabbling at his tearing eyes with both hands. I kicked him in the nuts, and he folded up and fell to the floor. Top-rank combat sorcerer, my arse. Try having assassins at your throat and at your back ever since you were a small child and see what that does to your survival skills.

Some of the combat sorcerers got past their shock and surprise and charged up their amulets and charms. They fired spells in all directions, and everyone ducked for cover. I looked around for Pen Donavon, just in time to see him diving behind the bar. Best place for him. Then I had to throw myself to one side as an energy bolt seared through the air where I'd been a moment before. It hit the long wooden bar and cracked it from end to end. I winced. I knew I was going to end up paying for that. Betty and Lucy Coltrane were ducking and dodging, avoiding fireballs and transformation spells and conceptual bullets from all directions at once. They were fast on their feet for their size, but they couldn't protect themselves and press the fight at the same time.

Sparks flew from Alex's cricket bat as he clubbed his way through the cowboys before him. They blasted him with destructive spells at point-blank range, but the magic Merlin had built into the bat reflected the spells right back at their source. As a result, lightning bolts flashed back and forth across the bar, bouncing off magical shields and doing extensive damage to the bar's fixtures and fittings. Magical bullets ricocheted, punching holes in the walls and ceiling. And two rather surprised-looking toads blinked at each other from piles of cowboy clothes before reappearing as themselves again.

Meanwhile, I had my own problem. Ace was getting up again. I picked up a handy chair and hit him over the head with it. I'm a great one for tradition. But the chair didn't break, and Ace didn't go down. So much for Hollywood. I dropped the chair and looked around for something else to hit him with. Preferably something with big jaggedy edges. I saw one of the combat sorcerers grab Bettie by the arm and pull her to him. I think he intended to use her as a human shield, or as a way to get to me. He really should have known better. He pointed his shimmering gun at her, and she smiled dazzlingly at him. He hesitated, and was lost. He stood where he was, unmoving, fascinated. Bettie's mother was a lust demon, and had passed on some of her deadly glamour to her daughter. Bettie held the cowboy's eyes with hers, fished in her bag, brought out her Mace, and let him have it. He fell to the floor, writhing and howling, and clawing at his eyes with both hands.

And to think I'd been a bit worried that she might not fit in with my friends.

While I was distracted, Ace hit me with a transformation spell. I cried out in shock as the spell crawled all over me, cramping my muscles and coursing through my neural system. Pain bent me in two, and sweat dripped from my face. I could feel my skin stretching and distorting, trying to find a new shape. Discharging energies spat and crackled around me, but for all its power, the spell couldn't find a foothold in me. Slowly, I straightened up again, fighting back the effects of the spell, throwing it off through sheer force of will. I smiled slowly at Ace, a cold and nasty death's-head grin, and he fell back a pace as the last of his spell fell away from me, defeated.

"So," he said harshly. "It's true. You're not human. That spell would have worked on any man."

"A man might have shown you mercy," I said. "But we're beyond that now."

He thrust his conceptual gun in my face. I grabbed his pointing finger and broke it. And while he was distracted by the pain, I reached automatically for my gift, to find some weakness in his defences . . . and it was there, just waiting to be used. I didn't waste any time wondering why. I simply fired up my gift, reached out with my mind, and found the operating spells controlling the combat sorcerers' magical items. And then it was the easiest thing in the world to tear away all the items' controls and restraints and let the amulets and charms and fetishes release all their power at once.

I could have fixed it so they would discharge harmlessly, but I didn't feel like being merciful.

The magical items exploded like grenades, blowing their owners apart. Thirteen cowboys cried out in shock and pain and horror as their power sources punched holes through their chests, tore off their arms, or blew their heads apart. It was all over in a few moments, and then there were thirteen dead combat sorcerers lying on the bar-room floor, in slowly spreading pools of blood and gore. Alex lowered his glowing cricket bat, breathing hard. Betty and Lucy Coltrane looked around, kicked the bodies nearest them just in case, and then high-fived each other.

Bettie Divine looked at me, shock and horror in her face.

"John; what have you done?"

"He said *Kill them all.*"

"That doesn't mean you had to kill all of them!"

"Yes it did," I said. "I have a reputation to maintain."

"*What?*"

"They threatened me, and my friends, and they killed a poor drunk sorcerer. They broke my first rule. *Thou shalt not mess with me and mine.* I just sent a message to Kid Cthulhu and all his kind."

"You killed thirteen men to make a point?" Bettie was staring at me as though she'd never seen me before, and perhaps she hadn't. Not this me.

"They would have killed you," I said.

"Yes. They would have. But you're supposed to be better than that."

"I am," I said. "Sometimes."

She wasn't even looking at me any more. She knelt beside what was left of the man called Ace. He'd carried three magical charms, and they'd torn him apart as they detonated. The amulet had blown his hand right off his wrist. His head was still pretty much intact. He looked more surprised than anything. Bettie cupped his face with one hand.

"We were close, once. When we were both a lot younger. He wasn't always like this. We had dreams, of all the wonderful things we were going to do. And I became a reporter for a tabloid, and he ended up as a cowboy. He wasn't bad, not when I knew him. He liked silly comedies, and happy endings, and he held me on bad days and told me he believed in me. And yes, I know, he would have killed me if you hadn't stopped me. That doesn't change anything."

"Did you love him?" I said.

"Of course I loved him. The man he was then. But I don't think he'd been that man for some time." She stared down at the dead face, into his staring eyes. She tried to close the eyelids, but they wouldn't stay closed. Bettie made a sound, and sat back on her heels. "I thought I'd be stronger than this. Harder, more cynical. The things I've seen, and done . . . the death of someone who used to be a friend, long ago, shouldn't affect me like this. I didn't think I could still hurt like this."

"You get used to it," I said. And immediately knew it was the wrong thing to say. "Bettie, you've got nothing to feel bad about. This is all down to me."

"Yes," she said. "It is."

She got up, all calm and composed again, and walked straight past me to the bar. She picked up her drink and took a dainty sip. She didn't look at me once. And I knew she'd never look at me the same way again, after seeing what I could do, what I would do, when pushed to the wall.

I will always do whatever is necessary, to protect my friends, whether they approve or not.

Alex helped Betty and Lucy Coltrane loot the bodies of anything worth the having, and then directed them to haul the bodies out back and dump them in the alley outside. Where the Nightside's various scavengers would quickly dispose of them. There's not a lot of room for sentiment in the Nightside. I would have helped, but I was busy thinking. Why had control of my gift been returned to me, after being blocked twice already? Presumably, whoever had been interfering with my gift just didn't need to any more. Because they were watching over me and knew I'd located Pen Donavon.

Still musing, I wandered back to the bar. Alex had finally persuaded Donavon to come out from behind it, and he was emerging slowly, bit by bit, staring with horrified eyes at all the carnage and destruction.

"They'll always be coming after me, won't they?" he said sadly. "It's never going to be over. I'm never going to get my life back. It wasn't much, but it was mine, and it was safe."

"You'll be safe again once we get you and the Afterlife Recording back to the *Unnatural Inquirer*'s offices," Bettie said briskly. "You'll have the paper's full resources behind you. No-one will dare touch you."

"And once you've handed over the DVD, no-one will have any reason to go after you," I said.

"They might expect me to intercept another broadcast," said Donavon.

"We've seen your television," I said. "Smash it. End of problem."

"We'll never make it to the paper's offices," said Donavon. "They'll be lining up to get at me, all along the way."

"John will find a way," Alex said firmly. "It's what he does. When he isn't busy trashing my bar."

"He doesn't have his gift any more," said Bettie. "He's been neutered."

"Actually, no," I said. "I've got it back, now I've caught up with Donavon. Tell me, Pen, what made you think to come here, looking for me?"

"I got a phone call," said Donavon. "It said I'd be safe at Strangefellows. That John Taylor could protect me. I knew your name, of course. And the bar's reputation."

"Who called you?" I said.

"Don't know. Identity withheld. I didn't recognise the voice. But I was desperate, so . . ."

Alex looked at me. "Kid Cthulhu?"

"Maybe," I said. "Or maybe there's another player in this game. Someone powerful enough to shut down my gift until it didn't matter any more. And just maybe, someone who wanted me to find Donavon, eventually . . . The rules of this game seem to be changing. I wonder why."

"I'd better track down Suzie," said Alex.

"She might have her phone turned off if she's busy. You know Suzie's only really happy when she's working. If you can find her, tell her I need her the moment she's free. I've got a feeling this case is going to get seriously ugly."

"Got it," said Alex. He turned away to root through the mess at the back of the bar, searching through the debris for his phone.

Bettie was looking at me now, her expression hard to read. I looked patiently back, waiting for her to make the first move.

"Is that what you and Suzie have in common?" she said finally. "The thing that holds you together? That you're both killers?"

"It's not that simple," I said.

"I've never understood what you see in Shotgun Suzie. She's a monster. She lives to kill. How can you stay with someone like that?"

"No-one else has shared what we've shared," I said. "Seen the things we've seen, done the things we've had to do. There's no-one else we could talk to, no-one else who'd understand."

"I want to understand," said Bettie. She moved slowly forward, almost in spite of herself, then suddenly she was in my arms again, her face pressed against my shoulder. I held her lightly, not wanting to scare her off. She buried her face in my shoulder, so she wouldn't have to look me in the eye. "Oh, John . . . You killed to protect me. I know that. I know it was necessary. But . . . you don't have to be like this. So . . . cold. I could warm you." She finally looked up at me. Our eyes met, and she didn't flinch. She put her face up, and I kissed her. Because I wanted to. After a while, she stepped back, and I quickly let her go. She managed a small smile.

"Let me take you away from all this, John. Living in an insane world is bound to make you crazy. And living with a crazy woman . . ."

"She's not crazy," I said. "Just troubled."

"Of course, John."

"Suzie and I need each other."

"No you don't! Sweetie, you really don't. You need a normal, healthy relationship. I could make you happy, John, in all the ways that matter."

"How can I trust you?" I said. "You're a lust demon's daughter."

"Well," said Bettie, "no-one's perfect."

We both laughed. Sometimes . . . it's the little moments, the shared moments, that matter the most.

Alex came back, scowling as he looked from me to Bettie, and back again. "Suzie isn't answering her phone. But I've put the word out. Someone will bump into her. What do we do now?"

"I think it's way past time we sat down and watched this bloody DVD and see what's on it," I said. "You've got a player upstairs, haven't you, Alex?"

"Well, yes, but like I said I've got my new girl-friend up there . . ."

"If you think it's going to be too much for her, send her home," I said. "I'm not going one step further with this case without knowing exactly what it is I'm risking life and limb for."

"Do you really think we should?" said Bettie. " I mean, look what watching it did to poor Pen."

We all looked at Pen Donavon, back on his stool again, drinking brandy like mother's milk. He felt our gaze on him and looked round. He sighed and handed me an un-labelled DVD in a jewel case.

"Watch it, if you must," he said. "I think . . . it's supposed to be seen. But I couldn't bear to see it again."

"You don't have to," I said. "Stay here. The Coltranes will look after you."

But even as Alex and Bettie and I headed for the back stairs that led up to Alex's private apartment, I had to wonder what seeing the Afterlife Recording would do to us. And whether I really wanted to know the truth.

EIGHT

# ONE MAN'S HELL

Getting into Alex Morrisey's private apartment is never easy. He guards his privacy like a dragon with his hoard, and there are many pitfalls waiting for the unwary. I think a very specialised burglar got in once; and something ate him. First, you have to go up a set of back stairs that aren't even there unless Alex wants them to be. Then you have to pass through a series of major league protections and defences, not unlike air-locks; you can feel them opening ahead of you, then closing behind you. Any one of these traps-in-waiting would quite cheerfully kill you if given the chance, in swift, nasty, and often downright appalling ways, if Alex happened to change his mind about you at any point. I have known gang lords' crime dens that were easier to get into; and they often have their own pet demons under contract. I wouldn't even try getting into Alex's apartment without his permission unless I was armed with a tactical nuke wrapped in rabbit's feet.

But it wasn't until Alex let us into his apartment that I was really shocked. The living-room was so clean and tidy I barely recognised it. All his old junk was gone, including the charity shop furniture and his collection of frankly disturbing porcelain statuettes in pornographic poses. Replaced by comfortable furnishings and pleasant decorative touches. His books, CDs, and DVDs no longer lay scattered across all available surfaces or stacked in tottering piles against the walls; now they were all set out neatly on brand-new designer shelving. Probably in alphabetical order, too. It was actually possible now to walk across Alex's living-room without having to kick things out of the way, and his carpet didn't crunch when you trod on it.

In the end, it was the cushions on the sofa that gave it away. Men who live on their own don't have cushions. They just don't. It's a guy thing.

I looked accusingly at Alex. "You've let a woman move in with you, haven't you? Don't you ever learn?"

"I didn't say anything," Alex said haughtily, "because I knew you wouldn't approve. Besides, you're in no position to throw stones. You live with a psychopathic gun nut."

There was a noise from the next room. A small tic appeared briefly in Alex's face. I looked at him sternly. "What was that?"

"Just the vulture," Alex said quickly. "Morning sickness."

A sudden horrible thought struck me. "You haven't let your ex-wife move back in, have you?"

"I would rather projectile vomit my own intestines," said Alex, with great dignity.

"Sorry," I said.

"I should think so, too."

"Wait a minute. Downstairs in the bar, you said your new girl-friend was up here. So where is she? Why is she hiding from me? And why do I just know that I'm really not going to like the answers to any of these questions?"

"Oh, hell," said Alex. He looked back at the other room. "You'd better come in, Cathy."

And while I was standing there, struck dumb with shock, my teenage secretary, Cathy, came in from the next room. She smiled at me brightly, but I was still too stunned to respond. She was wearing a smart and sophisticated little outfit, and surprisingly understated make-up. I barely recognised her. Normally she favoured colours so fashionable they made your eye-balls bleed.

"*This* is your new girl-friend?" I said finally. "Cathy? My Cathy? My *teenage* secretary? She's almost half your age!"

"*I know!*" said Alex. "She took one look at my music collection and turned up her nose! Called it dad rock . . . But; she came into the bar one night with a message from you, and, well, we happened to get talking, and . . . we clicked. Next thing I know we're a couple, and she's moved in with me. Neither of us said anything to you because we knew you'd blow your stack."

"I am lost for words," I said.

"Bet that doesn't last," said Cathy.

I glared at her. "I did not rescue you from a house that tried to eat you, take you in, and make you my secretary, just so you could get involved with a disreputable character like Alex Morrisey!"

"I thought Alex was your friend?" said Bettie, who I felt was enjoying the situation entirely too much.

"He is. Mostly. It's because I know him so well that I'm worried! Alex has even worse luck with women than I do."

"I resent that!" said Alex.

"I notice you're not denying it," I said.

Cathy stood close beside Alex, holding his arm protectively. It reminded me of the way Bettie had been holding my arm recently. Cathy looked me square in the eye, her jaw set in a familiar and very determined manner.

"I am eighteen now, going on nineteen. I'm not the frightened little girl you rescued any more. Hell, I've been running your office for the last few years and kept all the paper-work in order, which is more than you ever did. I am old enough to run my own life and to be responsible for my own actions. Just like you always taught me. Go after what really matters to you, you said. And I did. Alex and I might not be the most . . . orthodox of couples; but then, neither are you and Suzie."

I smiled briefly. "Well. My little girl is all grown-up. All right, Cathy. You're clearly off your head and displaying quite appalling taste, but you have the right to make your own mistakes." I looked at Alex. "We will talk about this later."

"Oh, joy," said Alex.

"Quite," I said. "Now, show me how that fiendishly complicated-looking remote control works."

Alex picked up something big enough to land the space shuttle from a distance, turned on his television, dimmed the lights, and showed me how to work the DVD player.

"That button is for the surround sound, the toggle is for the volume. Don't touch that one; it turns on the sprinkler system. And stay away from that one because it operates the vibrating bed. Don't look at me like that."

"What's this big red button for?" said Bettie, sitting beside me on the sofa before the television.

"*Do not touch the big red button,*" said Alex. "That is only to be used in the event of alien invasion, or if someone not a million miles from here starts another bloody angel war."

"I did not . . ."

"Right," said Alex. "That's it. You two enjoy the show, Cathy and I will be down in the bar."

"Don't you want to see what's on the DVD?" said Bettie.

"I would rather stab myself in the eyes with knives," said Alex. "Come along, Cathy."

"But I want to watch it!" said Cathy.

"No, you don't," Alex said firmly. "Wait until John's test-driven it; then, if it's safe, we can have a peep at it."

"So I'm your guinea-pig now?" I said, amused despite myself.

"Hey," said Alex. "What are friends for?"

"If you do get Raptured," said Cathy, "can I have your trench coat?"

Alex hustled her out, leaving Bettie and me alone with the television and the Afterlife Recording. The disc looked quite remarkably ordinary, almost innocent, as I took it out of its case. I handled it gingerly, half-afraid the thing might try to bite me, or even burst into flames once exposed to the open air; but it was only a DVD. I slipped it into the machine, hit PLAY, and Bettie and I settled back to watch.

There was no menu, no introduction. It was a recording of an unexpected transmission, with the beginning missing. It just started, and the television screen showed a view into Hell. There were buildings, or more properly structures, great looming things, like impossibly huge cancers. The walls were scarlet meat traced with purple veins, sick and decaying. Suppurating holes that might have been windows showed people trapped inside, plugged into the breathing sweating architecture, sometimes sunk deep in cancerous flesh; and all of them were screaming in agony.

The structures were packed too close together, their malign presence like a concentration camp of the soul. Through the narrow streets ran an endless stream of naked sinners, burned and bleeding, sobbing and shrieking as horned demons drove them on. The sinners who fell or lagged behind were dragged down and torn apart by the demons. Only to rise again, made whole, so they could be driven on again, forever. Bodies hung from lamp-posts, still kicking and struggling, as demons tugged their intestines from great rips in their bellies.

The sky was on fire, spreading a blood-red light across the terrible scene. Huge bat-winged shapes circled overhead. And from far off in the distance, vast and terrible, came the laughter of the Devil, savouring the horrors of Hell.

I hit the PAUSE button, leaned back on the sofa, and looked at Bettie. "It's a fake. That's not Hell."

"Are you sure?" said Bettie. And then her eyes widened, and she actually leaned back a little from me. "Do you *know*? Are the stories true, that you've really been to Hell, and returned?"

"Of course not," I said. "Only one man ever returned from the Houses of Pain, and he was the Son of God. No; you can tell that isn't the real thing from looking at the sinners. They all have the same face, see? Pen Donavon's face."

Bettie leaned in close for a better look. "You're right!

All the faces are the same! Even the demons, just exaggerated versions of Pen's features. But what does this mean, John? If this isn't a recording of the Afterlife, what is it?"

I hit the STOP button and turned off the television. "It's psychic imprinting," I said. "We discussed this, remember? What we were looking at was one man's personal vision of Hell. All of Pen Donavon's fears and nightmares appeared on his television set, leaking out of his subconscious, and when he tried to record what he saw, he psychically imprinted his own vision onto the DVD. Poor bastard. He believes he belongs in Hell; though probably only he could tell us why."

"So there never was any transmission from Beyond?" said Bettie.

"No. All that junk Donavon bolted onto his television set was just junk, after all."

I removed the DVD from the player and slipped it back into its case. Such a small thing, to have caused so much trouble.

"It doesn't matter," Bettie said cheerfully. "It looks good enough to pass. Fake or no, the paper can still make decent money off it. Actually, it's even better that it's not the real thing; now we don't have to worry about upsetting anyone *Upstairs*. It looks impressive enough, and that's all the punters will care about. So what do we do now, John? Take the DVD back to the *Unnatural Inquirer* offices, along with poor Pen? We can keep him safe there, until the DVD's appeared, then we can leak the news that it's not the real thing after all, and everyone will leave him alone."

"It's not going to be that simple," I said reluctantly. "That might have worked, right up to the point where I killed all Kid Cthulhu's combat sorcerers over it. No-one will believe I'd go to so much trouble unless there was some truth to the story."

"Ah," said Bettie. "Then, what are we going to do?"

"Good question," I said. "I'm not entirely sure. We need to play this exactly right . . ."

I thought for a while, pacing up and down, rejecting one idea after another, while Bettie watched, fascinated. And finally, I got it. A very crafty and downright sneaky way out of this mess. I took out my mobile phone and called Kid Cthulhu, on his very private number.

"Hi, Kid," I said cheerfully. "This is John Taylor. How are the barnacles?"

"How did you get this number?" said Kid Cthulhu. As always, he sounded like someone drowning in his own vomit.

"I find things, remember? I know everyone's private number. Or at least, everyone who matters. You should be flattered you made the list. Now, I don't want a war with you. I've got the DVD of the Afterlife Recording right here in my hand, and I'm willing to sell it to you for a merely extortionate price."

"You killed all my combat sorcerers, didn't you?"

"Try not to dwell on the negative aspects, Kid; we can

still do business. How about I come over to your place, and we discuss it?"

"You're not coming anywhere near my place," said Kid Cthulhu. "I've just had it redecorated. How about The Witch's Tit? Down on Beltane Street? Lap dancers and the like. Very classy."

"Sounds it," I said. "Okay, meet you there in an hour."

"Why the rush?"

"Because the Removal Man is on my trail, and I want to be rid of the damned DVD before he catches up with me. You know he's already taken out the Cardinal over this? Once the DVD is yours, he'll be your problem."

"One hour," said Kid Cthulhu. "And don't bring Shotgun Suzie with you or the deal's off."

"Such a fuss, over one little tentacle," I said. "If she'd wanted you dead, you'd be dead."

"Have you seen what's on the DVD?" said Kid Cthulhu.

"Of course not," I said. "And yes; I guarantee there are no other copies. You're buying exclusive rights to the Afterlife Recording."

"One hour," said Kid Cthulhu.

The line went dead. I put the phone away, smiling. These gang bosses all think they're so smart.

"Right," I said to Bettie. "Let's go meet Captain Sushi."

"It's bound to be a trap," said Bettie. She'd had her head right next to mine, so she could listen in on the call.

"Of course it's a trap," I said. "Kid Cthulhu owns The

Witch's Tit. But since we know it's a trap going in, we can be ready to take advantage of it. What matters is setting things up so everyone will believe Kid Cthulhu has the Afterlife Recording."

"Wait a minute," said Bettie. "You can't just give it to him, John. My paper . . ."

"Relax," I said. "At exactly the right moment, you will distract him, and I will swap this DVD for one I will happen to have hidden about my person. Something from Alex's collection; he won't even know it's gone till it's too late. Kid Cthulhu will be bound to make a fuss about getting the DVD from me, and the news will be all over the Nightside by the time he actually works up the nerve to watch what he's bought. By which time we will have delivered the real thing to your paper's offices, where it will be safe. Until you give it away with this Sunday's edition. And Kid Cthulhu . . . will learn the cost of messing with me and mine."

"He'll kill you," said Bettie.

"He can join the queue."

I took an unlabelled disc from Alex's private collection of elf porn, slipped it into an inside pocket, and smiled again. The day I couldn't work a simple bait and switch like this, I'd retire.

There's a lot more to being a private eye than most people realise.

• • •

We went back down into the bar. I didn't need Alex's help to leave his apartment though I could still feel his defences, like so many spider's webs, trailing lightly against my face as I went down the stairs. Pen Donavon was still sitting slumped on his bar-stool, staring into his brandy glass. Alex was behind the bar, scowling at Donavon as he opened yet another bottle of the good brandy. For a tired, scared, and totally out-of-his-mind man on the run, Donavon could really put it away. I suppose when you believe you're going to Hell anyway, little things like hangovers and liver failure don't bother you any more.

Cathy was behind the bar with Alex, poking the meat pies with a stick to see if they needed replacing yet. Lucy and Betty Coltrane were still clearing up the general mess. Everyone turned to look as Bettie and I appeared from the back stairs.

"Well?" said Alex. "How was it? What was it? I've got a first-rate exorcist on speed dial, if you need him."

"Everyone relax," I said. "It's a fake."

Pen Donavon's head came up. "What?"

I started to explain, as kindly as I could, about psychic imprinting and guilt, but I could tell he wasn't listening. And I stopped as I realised the bar was getting darker. The light became suffused with red, as though stained with fresh blood, sinking into a deep crimson glow. Tables and chairs suddenly exploded into flames and burned fiercely, unconsumed. The Coltranes backed quickly away, and joined the rest of us at the bar. The walls slumped slowly inwards, swollen and inflamed, their fleshy texture studded with sweating tumours. A huge eye opened in the ceiling, staring down at us in cold judgement. The floor became soft and uncertain beneath my feet, heaving like the slow swell of the sea. Deep dark shadows were forming all around us, slowly closing in.

"It's him, isn't it?" said Bettie, gripping my arm with both hands. "It's Pen. He's imprinting his vision of Hell right here, with us."

"Looks like it," I said. "Only this doesn't look or feel like any illusion. I wouldn't go so far as to say it's real, as such, but it could be real enough to kill us."

"How is he doing this?" said Alex. "This bar has defences and protections laid down by Merlin himself!"

"Yes," I said. "Where is the power coming from to let him do something like this?"

I fired up my gift, and looked at Pen Donavon through my third eye, my private eye. And I found the hidden source of his unnatural power. I could See the thing, inside his body, tucked away under the sternum and over the heart. It must have come to his little shop as just another piece of interdimensional flotsam and jetsam; and he probably hadn't realised how powerful it was until he accidentally activated it. Probably hadn't even realised it was alive until it forced its way inside him. Now it was attached to him, a part of him, with long tendrils reaching into his heart and gut and brain. A mystical parasite, living off him while feeding him power in return.

I couldn't tear it out of him without killing him in the process. And I didn't want to kill Pen Donavon, even after all the trouble he'd caused. None of this was really his fault. I doubt he'd had a free and uninfluenced thought of his own since the parasite took up residence inside him.

Demons emerged from the shadows around us. Hunched and horned, with scarlet skin; medieval devils all with distorted versions of Donavon's face. They smiled to show their jagged teeth and flexed their clawed hands hungrily. Alex had his cricket bat out again. Cathy had the shotgun. Betty and Lucy Coltrane stood back-to-back, ready to take on all comers. Bettie looked at me. I looked at Pen Donavon.

"Why Hell?" I said bluntly. "Why are you so convinced of your own damnation? What could a small and insignificant little man like you have possibly done that could be so bad that all you ever think about is Hell?"

For a long moment I thought he wasn't going to answer me. The demons were getting very close. And then he sighed deeply, staring into his glass.

"I had a dog," he said. "Called him Prince. He was a good dog. Had him for years. Then I got married. She never took to Prince. Just wasn't a dog person. We all got along well enough . . . until the marriage hit problems. We started arguing over small things and worked our way up. She said she was going to leave me. I still loved her. Begged her to stay; said I'd do anything. She said I had to prove my love for her. Get rid of the dog. I loved my dog, but she was my wife. So I said I'd give Prince up. Find him a good home somewhere else. But no, that wasn't good enough. She said I had to prove she was more important to me than the dog, by killing him.

"Have Prince put down. Or she'd leave me. My choice, she said.

"I killed my dog. Took him to the vet's, said good-bye, held his paw while the vet gave him the injection. Took my dog home. Buried him.

"And she left me anyway. Prince was my dog. He was the best dog in the world. And I killed him." He looked slowly round the bar, at the Hell he'd made. Slow tears were running down his cheeks. "I deserve this. All of it."

The fires blazed up all around us. My bare skin smarted painfully from the heat. The air was thick with the stench of blood and brimstone. The demons were almost within reach. In his need to be punished, to make atonement for his sin, Pen Donavon had brought Hell to Earth; or something close enough to do the job. He could burn up the whole bar and everyone in it . . . but the parasite inside him would make sure he survived. To go on suffering. Suddenly I knew what the parasite fed on.

I got angry then. I could kill Donavon, rip the parasite right out of him. But he didn't deserve that. Not when there was a better way. I'm John Taylor, and I find things. Things, and people, and just sometimes, a way out of Hell for those who need it.

I raised my gift and forced my inner eye all the way open, making it look in a direction I normally had sense enough to avoid. I concentrated, drawing on every resource I had, and I Saw beyond this world and into the

Next. I found who I was looking for and called his name; and he came. A great door opened up in the middle of the bar, spilling a bright and brilliant light into the crimson glare, forcing it back. All the demons stopped and looked round, as a great mongrel dog with a shaggy head and drooping ears bounded out of the door and into the bar. He went straight for the demons nearest Donavon, and tore right through them, gripping them with his powerful jaws and shaking them back and forth like a terrier with a rat. The demons cried out miserably, and fell apart. Donavon looked at the dog, and his whole face lit up in amazed disbelief.

*"Prince?"*

"Typical," said the dog, spitting out a bit of demon, then trotting over to push his great shaggy head into Donavon's lap. "Can't turn my back on you for five minutes."

"I'm so sorry, Prince. I'm so sorry." Donavon could hardly get the words out. He bent over and hugged the dog round the neck.

"It's all right," said the dog. "Humans can't think for shit when they're in heat. It was her fault, not yours. You were just weak; she was the bad one."

"Do you forgive me, Prince?"

"Of course; that's what dogs do. Another good reason why all dogs go to Heaven. Now come along with me, Pen. It's time to go."

Donavon looked at the wonderful light falling out of

the door in the middle of the bar. "But . . . you're dead, Prince."

"Yes. And so are you. You've been dead ever since that parasite ate its way into you. Don't you remember? No; I suppose it won't let you. Either way, it's only the parasite's energies that have been keeping you going, so it could feed on your pain and fear." The dog paused. "You know, there's nothing like being dead for increasing your vocabulary. I've been so much more articulate since I crossed over. Anyone got a biscuit? No? Come with me, Pen. Heaven awaits."

"Will we be together, Prince?"

"Of course, Pen. Forever and ever and ever."

There was a bright flash of light, and when it faded the bar was back to normal again. The Hell that Pen Donavon had made was gone, and so was the door full of light. His dead body slumped slowly forward and fell off the stool, hitting the floor. It heaved suddenly, jerked this way and that by loud cracking and tearing sounds, and then the parasite appeared from under the body. It scuttled across the floor like a huge beetle, until I stepped forward and stamped down hard. It crunched satisfyingly under my boot, and was still.

Gone straight to Hell, where it belonged.

NINE

# Entrances and Exits

So, back to Uptown we went. It had been a long time since I'd been involved with a case that involved so much walking, and I was getting pretty damned tired of it. If I'd wanted to spend so much time tramping back and forth in the Nightside, wearing out good shoe leather and guaranteeing severe lower back pain for later, I'd have had my head examined. And to add insult to injury, a fog had come up, ghosting the Nightside in shades of pearl and grey. Fog is always a bad sign; it means the barriers between the worlds are wearing thin. You can never tell what might appear out of the mists or disappear into them.

The Witch's Tit aspired to dreams of class and opulence,

but it was really just another titty bar with a theme. A campy mixture of Goth come-ons and Halloween kitsch, where the girls danced naked, apart from tall witch's hats, and did obscene things with their broomsticks. The club was situated right on the very edge of Uptown, as though the other establishments were ashamed of it, and quite probably they were. The Witch's Tit was the only legitimate business Kid Cthulhu owned and certainly the only one he took a personal interest in.

Why? Well, here's a hint: word has it he's not a leg man.

The club itself looked cheap and tacky from the outside, all sleazy neon and seedy photos of girls who probably didn't even work there, but that wasn't what concerned me. There was no barker outside, singing the praises of the girls and cajoling passers-by to come on in and take a look. And when I cautiously pushed the door open and looked inside, there weren't any bouncers either, or any traces of security. Kid Cthulhu wasn't known for leaving his assets undefended, especially during an important meet like this. Had to be a trap of some kind. So I walked in, smiling cheerfully, with Bettie bouncing happily along at my side in a black leather outfit with chains and studs, and a perky little dog collar round her throat.

The club had been fitted out with all the usual Halloween motifs—black walls, witch's cauldrons, and grinning pumpkin-heads. The lighting was comfortably dim and inviting, save for half a dozen spotlights that stabbed down onto the raised stage at the back of the club, picking out the dancer's steel poles. But still; no girls, no customers, no bar staff. Kid Cthulhu had cleared the place out, just for me. The phrase *no witnesses* was whispering in the back of my head. I led Bettie through the empty tables and out into the open space before the stage, our footsteps loud and carrying in the quiet. Half a dozen human skeletons had been hung from stretchy elastic, bobbing gently at the edge of the open space, perhaps disturbed by our approach. At first I thought they were another example of the Halloween décor, but something made me stop and take a closer look. They were all real skeletons, the bones held together by copper wire. Some of the longer bones showed teeth-marks.

A new spotlight stabbed down from overhead, revealing Kid Cthulhu sitting on a huge reinforced chair, right in the centre of the open space. He looked like a man, but he wasn't. Not any more. You could tell. You could see it, feel it. There was a taint in the man, all the way through. He had been touched, and changed, by something from Outside. Kid Cthulhu was a large man, he had to be, to contain everything that was in him now. He was naked, his skin stretched taut and swollen, as though pushed out by pressures from within. He was supposed to be about my age, but his face was so puffed out no trace of human character remained in it. He sat slumped in his oversized chair, like King Glutton on his throne. His bare skin gleamed dully in the mercilessly revealing spotlight, colourless as a fish's belly, while his eyes were all black, like a shark's.

They say he broke men's bones with his bare hands. They say he ate the flesh of men, breaking open the bones to get at the marrow. They said there was something growing within him, or perhaps through him, from Outside. And right then, I believed every word they said.

"Hey, KC," I said cheerfully. "Where's the Sunshine Band?"

He studied me coldly with his flat black eyes. "John Taylor . . . Your name is bile and ashes in my mouth. Your presence here is an affront to me. Your continued existence an unbearable insult. You killed my combat sorcerers. My boys. My lovely boys."

"You have changed," I said. "You never should have gone on that deep-sea voyage. Or at the very least, you should have thrown back what you caught."

"You defy me," said Kid Cthulhu. "No-one does that any more. I shall enjoy killing you."

His voice was harsh and laboured, forced out word by word, with a distinct gurgle in it, as though he were speaking underwater. He sounding like a drowning man, venting his spite on the man who'd pushed him in.

"I thought we were here to do business," I said. "I have the Afterlife Recording right here with me."

"I don't care about that any more," said Kid Cthulhu. "Money doesn't matter to me. I have money. All that matters now is the satisfying of my various appetites and the destruction of my enemies. I will see you broken, suffering, and dead, John Taylor. And your pretty little companion. Perhaps I'll make you watch as I tear her guts out, and eat them as she dies, screaming."

"Oh, ick," said Bettie. "Nasty man . . ."

Kid Cthulhu rose suddenly up from his throne, a man twice the size a man should be, forcing his great bulk up onto its feet through sheer strength of will. His joints were buried deep under swollen flesh, and unnaturally distended genitals showed under the great swell of his belly.

"Double ick," said Bettie. "With a side order of not even for a million pounds."

Kid Cthulhu strode toward us, slowly and deliberately, each step shaking the floor, his deep-set eyes fixed on me. His purple pouting mouth parted to reveal jagged sharp teeth. His huge puffy hands opened to reveal claws. Someone that size shouldn't have been able to move unaided, let alone have such an air of strength and deadly purpose. I was still thinking what to do when Bettie stepped smartly forward, opened her purse, took out her Mace spray, and let Kid Cthulhu have it, right in the face.

"Nasty fat man," she said calmly. "And you smell."

Kid Cthulhu stopped before her, surprised, but showing no hurt at all from a faceful of Mace laced with holy water. His all-black eyes barely blinked as the Mace ran down his distended cheeks like so many viscous tears. He lashed out suddenly, one huge arm swinging round impossibly quickly, and the impact knocked Bettie off her feet and sent her flying. She crashed through a table, hit the floor hard, rolled over a few times, and lay still; and it was all over before I could even move a muscle. I called out to her, but she didn't answer. And then Kid Cthulhu turned his head and looked at me.

He was between me and Bettie, so I couldn't get to her. I backed away slowly, thinking fast. I hadn't planned for this. I'd heard he was going through changes, but I still thought of him as just another gang boss. Someone I could make a deal with. The Nightside runs on deals. But all this Kid Cthulhu wanted was me, preferably in large meaty chunks. I don't normally care to get involved with hand-to-hand combat, partly because it's coarse and vulgar and beneath my dignity, but mostly because I've never been that good at it. I've always preferred to talk or threaten or bluff my way out of trouble. But I didn't think that was going to work here.

I stopped, stood my ground, and stared him right in the eye. Sometimes the oldest tricks are the best. But for the second time that day, I found myself faced with someone I couldn't stare down. His flat black eyes stared right back at me, untouched and unmoved. I couldn't reach him. I wasn't even sure there was anything human left in him to reach. So I grabbed the nearest chair and threw it at him. It bounced off, without leaving a single mark on his veiny, distended skin.

Then he was coming right at me, a huge mass of colourless flesh like something you'd find at the bottom of the sea, driven on by some unnatural energy. I'd beaten so many threats in my time, faced down and defeated so many Major Players, gods, and monsters . . . It had never occurred to me that I might be killed by some oversized, implacable gang boss.

As he crashed forward, the floor shaking with every tread, I somehow found the time to notice that his flesh seemed to move more slowly than the rest of him, sliding across his deep-sunk bones like an afterthought, as though it wasn't properly connected any more. What little humanity he had left in him was sliding away. I glanced behind me. I could have run. I was pretty sure I could beat him to the exit. But that would have meant leaving Bettie behind, abandoned to Kid Cthulhu's inhuman appetites. He'd said he'd do terrible things to her, and I believed him. So I stepped forward, braced myself, and punched him right in his protruding belly. His impetus drove him forward onto my fist, and it sank deep into his gut. He didn't even make a sound. The cold, cold flesh closed around my hand, sucking it in. I had to use all my strength to pull it free again. Just the touch of his flesh was enough to set my teeth on edge.

A huge arm came swinging round out of nowhere and hit me like a club. I managed to get a shoulder round in time to take the worst of the impact, but the flesh seemed to just keep coming and slammed into the side of my face. The strength went out of my legs, and I hit the floor hard, driving the breath from my lungs. My left shoulder blazed with pain, and I could barely move my left arm. The whole left side of my face ached fiercely. There was blood in my mouth, and I spat it out. I sensed as much as saw Kid Cthulhu looming over me, and I rolled to one side as his great fist came slamming down like a pile-driver, cracking and splintering the floor where I'd been lying. I got my legs under me and forced myself back up onto my feet again. I didn't feel too steady, and I was breathing hard. Kid Cthulhu wasn't.

I backed away. My left eye was puffing shut, and it felt like my nose might be broken. I checked my teeth with my tongue. I didn't seem to have lost any, this time. I hate it when that happens. There was more blood in my mouth. Probably a cut on the inside of my cheek. I spat the blood in Kid Cthulhu's direction, but his flat dark eyes never wavered.

I couldn't fight a man like this. I had to be smarter than that.

I backed away some more, glancing round to make sure I was leading Kid Cthulhu away from Bettie, and then made myself concentrate past the pain. I called up my gift, and looked at Kid Cthulhu with my inner eye. If I couldn't fight the man, maybe I could fight what was inside him. I used my gift to find the taint, the inhuman corruption deep within his flesh, the thing from Outside that was slowly suffusing his human form. And having found it, it was the easiest thing in the world to rip the taint right out of him.

Kid Cthulhu screamed; and for the first time, he sounded human. He fell to his knees, no longer able to sustain his massive weight once the taint from Outside was gone. He fell forward onto his face, his flesh moving in great ripples of fat. And beside him stood the taint, a horrid twisting shape that made no sense at all in only three spatial dimensions. It howled its fury, in a voice I heard more with my mind than my ears. It didn't belong in this world, stripped of the host it had been transforming into something suitable to birth its new form. I wondered briefly what that might have been. Nothing like Kid Cthulhu, certainly. It hurt just to look at the taint. Like a colour too vile for our spectrum, a shape like a living Rorschach blot that suggested only nightmares. Its very presence in this world was like fingernails scraping down the blackboard of my soul.

It came after me, moving in ways unknown in my comfortable, three-dimensional world. I ran for the raised stage at the back of the club, and it followed. It moved more like energy than anything physical, and that gave me an idea. Up on the stage, I backed slowly away. A bolt of vivid energy snapped out, and I had to throw myself to one side to avoid it. The taint came after me, rising and falling in the air. My back slammed up against a steel dancer's pole. The taint fired another energy bolt. I ducked to one side, and the energy bolt hit the steel pole. The taint screamed as its energy grounded through the pole, discharging into the earth below, its howl rising and rising till it seemed to fill my head, and then the sound broke off as the taint disappeared, gone.

Now that I was out of danger, my arm and my shoulder and my face all hurt worse than ever, but I made myself get down from the stage and go over to where Bettie was still lying sprawled on the floor. As I approached, she raised her head a little, looked at me, then sat up easily.

"Is it over?" she said brightly. "I thought I'd better keep my head down, and not get in your way." And then she saw the state of my face and scrambled to her feet. "Oh, John, sweetie, you're hurt! What did he do to you?"

She produced a clean white handkerchief from somewhere, licked it briefly with a pointed tongue, and dabbed cautiously at my face, wiping the blood away. It hurt, but I let her do it. My left eye was puffed shut, but at least I'd stopped spitting blood.

"Looks worse than it is," I said, trying to convince myself as much as Bettie.

"Hush," she said. "Stand still. My hero."

When she'd finished, she looked at the bloody handkerchief, pulled a face, and tucked it up one black leather sleeve. I looked thoughtfully at Kid Cthulhu, still lying where he'd fallen like a beached whale. I walked slowly over to him, Bettie trotting at my side. She managed to make it clear she was there to be leaned on, if necessary, but was considerate enough not to say it out loud. I stood over Kid Cthulhu, and he rolled his flat black eyes up in his stretched face to look at me.

"Kill you, Taylor. Kill you for this. Kill you, and all your friends, and everyone you know. I have people. I'll send them after you, and I'll never stop, never. Never!"

"I believe you," I said. And I raised my foot and stamped down hard, right on the back of his fat neck. I felt as much as heard his neck break under my foot, and as easily as that the life went out of him. I stepped back. Bettie looked at me, horrified.

"You killed him. Just like that. How could you?"

"Because it was necessary," I said "You heard him."

"But . . . I never thought of you as a cold-blooded killer . . . You're supposed to be better than that!"

"Mostly I am," I said. "But no-one threatens me and mine."

"I don't know you at all, do I?" Bettie said slowly, looking at me steadily.

"I'm just . . . who I have to be," I said.

And then we both looked round sharply. Someone new was there in the club with us, though I hadn't heard him come in. He was standing on the raised stage, in a spotlight of his own, waiting patiently to be noticed. A tall and slender man with dark coffee-coloured skin, wearing a smartly cut pale grey suit, with an apricot cravat at his throat. He might have been any age, but there was an air of experience and quiet authority about him. As though he had so much power he didn't need to put on a show. His head was shaven, gleaming in the spotlight. His eyes were kind, his smile pleasant; and I didn't trust him an inch.

"You did well, in dealing with Kid Cthulhu," he said finally, in a rich, smooth and cultured voice. "A very unpleasant fellow, destined to become something even more unpleasant. I would have taken care of him myself, in time, but you did a good job, Mr. Taylor."

"And you are?" I said. "Though I have a horrible suspicion I already know."

"I am the Removal Man. An honourable calling, in a dishonourable world. And I am here for the Afterlife Recording."

"Of course you are," I said. "It's been that sort of a day. How did you know I was bringing it here?"

"Mr. Taylor," the Removal Man said reproachfully, "I know what I need to know. It's part of my function. Now be a good chap and hand over the DVD, and we can get through this without any . . . unpleasantness. It must be removed; it's far too great a temptation for all concerned."

"The *Unnatural Inquirer* owns exclusive rights to the Afterlife Recording," said Bettie automatically, though I could tell she was getting tired of having to tell people that.

"I do not recognise the Law, or its bindings," the Removal Man said easily. "I answer to a higher calling. Just hand over the DVD, Mr. Taylor, and I'll be on my way. This doesn't have to end badly. You must admit that the Nightside will be better off without the Recording. Look how much trouble it's already caused."

"You don't need to do anything," I said. I was trying very hard to sound casual and reasonable, like him. It's not easy talking to someone who can probably make you disappear off the face of the Earth just by thinking about it. I added the *probably* as a sop to my pride, but I really didn't want to get into a pissing contest with the Removal Man. I had the uneasy feeling that his legend might be a little bit more real than mine. "I've seen what's on the DVD, and it's nothing you need be concerned about. It's a fake, the psychic imprinting of a disturbed mind."

"You've seen it?" said the Removal Man, raising one elegant eyebrow. "Oh, dear. How very unfortunate. Now I have to take care of you as well."

"But . . . I've seen it, too!" said Bettie. "It's nothing! It's a fake!"

The Removal Man shook his shaven head sadly, still smiling his kind smile. "Yes, well, you would say that, wouldn't you?"

"You can't just make us disappear!" Bettie said defiantly. "I work for the *Unnatural Inquirer*! I have the full resources of the paper behind me. And this is John Taylor! You know who his friends are. You really want Razor Eddie or Dead Boy coming after you? And anyway, what makes you so sure you're always right? What makes you infallible? What gives you the right to judge the whole world and everyone in it?"

"Ah," he said, smugly. "The secret origin of the Removal Man; is that what you want, little miss demon girl reporter? Yes, I know who you are, Miss Divine. I know who everyone is. Very well, then; I sold my soul to God. In return for power over the Earth and everything in it. Not God himself, as such, one of his representatives. But the deal is just as real. I am here to pass judgement on the wicked; and I do. Because someone has to. I'm changing the Nightside for the better; one thing, one person, one soul at a time. You mustn't worry, Miss Divine. It won't hurt a bit. Though really, gentlemen should go first. Isn't that right, Mr. Taylor?"

Bettie moved immediately to put herself between me and the Removal Man. "You can't! I won't let you! He's a good man, in his way. And he's done more for the Nightside than you ever have!"

"Stand aside," said the Removal Man. "Mr. Taylor goes first, because he is the most dangerous. And please, no more protestations. I really have heard them all before."

Bettie was still searching for something to say, when I took her by the arm and moved her gently but firmly to one side. "I don't hide behind anyone," I said to the Removal Man. "I don't need to, you arrogant, self-righteous little prig."

"Mr. Taylor . . ."

"What did you have to kill the Cardinal for? I liked him. He was no threat to anyone."

"He betrayed his faith," said the Removal Man. "He was a thief. And an abomination."

"I've scraped more appealing things than you off the bottom of my shoe," I said.

I raised my gift again and Saw right through the Removal Man. It wasn't difficult to find out who he'd really made his deal with and show him the truth. Not God. Not God at all. I showed the Removal Man who'd really been pulling his strings all this time, and he screamed like a soul newly damned to Hell. He staggered back and forth on the raised stage, shaking his head in denial, even as he cried out in shock and loathing. Until finally, unable to face who and what he really was, he turned his power on himself and disappeared.

And that was the end of the Removal Man.

I hadn't wanted to destroy him. He really had done a lot of good in his time, along with the bad and the questionable. But no-one's more vulnerable than those who believe they're better than everyone else. His whole existence had been based on a lie. He'd been betrayed, and I knew who by. I'd Seen him. I looked into the shadows at the back of the raised stage.

"All right, you can come out now. Come on out, Mr. Gaylord du Rois, Editor of the one and only *Unnatural Inquirer*."

Bettie's gasp was so shocked it came out as little more than a muffled squeak as Gaylord du Rois stepped forward into the light to stare calmly down at both of us.

"Well done, Mr. Taylor. You really are almost as good as people say you are."

Du Rois was a tall, elderly gentleman, dressed in the very best Edwardian finery. His back was straight, his head held high, and there wasn't a trace of weakness or frailty in him, for all his obvious age. His face was a mass of wrinkles, and his bare head was undecorated save for liver spots and a few fly-away hairs. His deep-set cold grey eyes hardly blinked at all, and his mouth was a wet slash of colourless lips. His hands were withered claws, but they still looked like they could do a lot of damage. He burned with a harsh and unforgiving energy, determined and defiant, as though he could hold back death through sheer force of will. He nodded at the spot where the Removal Man had disappeared himself.

"Damned fool. Always was inflexible. He really did think he'd been given his power by God himself, to indulge his prejudices and paranoias. I suppose learning I was his puppet master, and had been all along, was just too much to bear. Such a come-down from God. It doesn't matter. I'd have had to replace him soon anyway. He was having delusions of independence. Still, I can always find another fool."

"I don't understand," said Bettie. "You're the Editor? You've always been the Editor? And . . . the Removal Man was your creature all along? Why?"

"Dear Bettie," du Rois said indulgently. "Always a reporter, always asking the right questions. Yes, my dear, I am your Editor and always have been. The *Inquirer* is mine, and mine alone, and has been for over a hundred years. And in that time I have created many Removal Men to serve my needs. They don't tend to last long. Such small, blinkered, black-and-white attitudes don't tend to survive long when faced with the ever-shifting greys of the Nightside. They burn out. But there's always someone who thinks they know better than everyone else, just itching for a chance to remake the world in their own limited image . . ."

"Why create them?" I said. "I don't see why the Editor of the *Unnatural Inquirer* should give much of a damn about the morality of the Nightside."

"Quite right, Mr. Taylor. I don't give a damn. Except for when it makes good copy. Reporting and condemning the sins and shames of the Nightside has filled the pages of my paper for generations. But one lifetime wasn't enough for me. I wanted more. There was still so much left to see, and know, and do. So I found a way. You can always find a way in the Nightside, even if some of them aren't very nice. When one of my Removal Men removes a thing, or a person, all their potential energy, from all the things they might have done, is left up for grabs; and it all comes to me. Those energies have kept me going long after I should have left this world, and made me very powerful indeed."

"You're the one who shut down my gift!" I said.

"Yes," du Rois said calmly. "It was necessary to neuter you, so you wouldn't find Pen Donavon too quickly. I needed time for rumours about the Afterlife Recording to spread, and grow, and fascinate the minds of my readers. Bringing you in guaranteed that people would pay attention. After all, if you were involved, it must be important. By the time my Sunday edition comes out, with my give-away DVD, people will be fighting for copies of my paper. And all because of you . . ."

"Sales?" I said. "This has all been about sales?"

"Of course. I don't think you appreciate exactly how much money I stand to make out of this, Mr. Taylor."

"Why are you here?" Bettie said suddenly. "Why reveal the truth about yourself now, to us?"

Du Rois smiled on her almost fondly. "Still asking the

right questions, Bettie, like the fine reporter you are. A pity you'll never get to write this story. Sorry, my dear, but I am here to protect my interests, and my paper's. And your story, of the truth behind the Afterlife Recording, can never be allowed to see print. I report the news; I have no wish to be part of it."

"You want the DVD?" I said. I took it out of my coat-pocket and threw it at him. "Have it. Damn thing's just a fake anyway."

He made no attempt to catch the disc, letting it fall to clatter on the stage before him. "Real or fake, it doesn't matter. I can still sell it, thanks to your involvement. You really have been very helpful to me, Mr. Taylor, spreading the story and stirring up interest, but that's all over now. I have my story. And since every story needs a good end-ing . . . what better way to convince everyone of the DVD's importance than that you should be killed, acquir-ing it for me? Nothing like a famous corpse to add spice to a story." He looked at Bettie. "I'm afraid you have to die, too, my dear. Can't have anyone hanging around to contradict the story I'm going to sell people."

"But . . . I'm one of your people!" said Bettie. "I work for the *Inquirer*!"

"I have lots of reporters. I can always get more. Now hush, dear. Your voice really is very wearing . . . Don't move, Mr. Taylor. I've already taken the precaution of shutting down your gift again, just in case you were thinking of using it on me. And you don't have anything else powerful enough to stop me."

"Want to bet?" I said. And I took out of my coat-pocket the Aquarius Key. I activated the small metal box, and it opened up, unfolding and blossoming like a steel flower. A great rip appeared in reality, right in front of Gaylord du Rois. He only had time to scream once before the void swallowed him, then he was gone. I hung on grimly to Bettie as the void pulled us forward, then I shut the Aquarius Key down again, and that was that.

It was suddenly very quiet in the empty club. Bettie looked at me with huge eyes.

"I really should have handed the Key over to Walker, after that nasty business at Fun Faire," I said. "But I had a feeling it might come in handy."

"You've had that all along?" said Bettie. "Why didn't you use it before?"

I shrugged. "I didn't need it before."

She hit me.

## EPILOGUE

I phoned Walker and arranged to meet him at the Londinium Club. Now that I'd used the Aquarius Key, Walker was bound to know I had it. And he'd want it. I could have hung on to the Key if I'd been ready to make a big thing out of it, but I wasn't. The Aquarius Key gave me the creeps. Some things you know are bad news for all concerned. They're just too . . . tempting. So back to the Londinium Club Bettie and I went. Plenty of time yet to take the damned DVD to the offices of the *Unnatural Inquirer*. Where Scoop Malloy would have to decide what to do with it, and the news that his paper no longer had an Editor.

"But how would Walker know you've got the Key?" said Bettie, skipping merrily along beside me. She was back in her polka-dot dress and big floppy hat look.

"Walker knows everything," I said. "Or at least, everything he needs to know."

"I still can't get over my Editor being the Bad Guy in all this. I wonder who'll replace him at the *Inquirer*?"

"Scoop Malloy?"

"Oh, please! I don't think so!" Bettie pulled a disparaging face that still somehow managed to look attractive on her. "Scoop's only Sub-Editor material, and he knows it. No; the new owner will have to bring in someone new, from outside. But you know what? I don't care! Because for the first time in my career I have a *real* story to write! The truth behind Gaylord du Rois, the Removal Men, and the Afterlife Recording. Real news . . . which means I'm a real reporter at last! Right?"

"I don't see why not," I said. "The *Inquirer* might make you the new Editor on the strength of it."

"Oh, poo! I'm not wasting a *real* story on the *Inquirer*!" Bettie said indignantly. "Far too good for them. No; I'm going to sell it to Julien Advent at the *Night Times*; in return for a job on his paper. A real reporter on a real newspaper! I'm going up in the world! Mummy will be so pleased . . ."

"What about your other story?" I said. "A day in the company of the infamous John Taylor?"

Bettie smiled and hooked her arm familiarly through mine. "Let someone else write it."

We came at last to the Londinium Club, and Bettie and I stopped at the foot of the steps to stare at the black iron railings surrounding the club. Impaled on the iron

SIMON R. GREEN

spikes were three recently severed heads. Queen Helena,
Uptown Taffy Lewis, and General Condor. Helena looked
as though she was still screaming. Taffy looked sullen.
And the General . . . had a look of sad resignation, as
though he'd known all along it would come to this. I'm
sure enough people warned him. The Nightside does so
love to break a hero.

"Admiring the display?" said Walker, unhurriedly de-
scending the steps to join us. "It makes a statement, I
think."

"Your work?" I asked.

"I ordered it done," said Walker. "They disturbed the
peace of the Nightside and threatened to plunge it into
civil war. So I did what I had to."

"And not at all because they challenged your authority," I said.

Walker just smiled.

"But . . . why kill the General?" said Bettie, staring
fascinated at the impaled heads. "I mean, he was one of
the good guys. Wasn't he?"

"There's no-one more dangerous to the status quo," I
said. "Right, Walker?"

He put out a hand to me. "You have something for me,
I believe?"

I handed over the Aquarius Key. Walker hefted it on the
palm of his hand. "You didn't really think you'd be allowed
to keep something as powerful as this, did you, John?"

I shrugged. "Be grateful. I could have given it to the
Collector."

He nodded to me, tipped his bowler hat to Bettie, and went back into his Club. Leaving his handiwork behind him, *pour décourager les autres*.

"You could have kept that Key," said Bettie. "He's not powerful enough to make you do anything you don't want to."

"Maybe," I said. "Maybe not. All depends on where he's getting his power from these days . . . But anyway, I'm not ready to go head to head with him, not just yet. Certainly not over a glorified magical waste disposal. We're still on the same side. I think."

"Even after this?" said Bettie, gesturing fiercely at the severed heads. "Look at them! Killed by one of his pet assassins, just because they threatened his position! You liked the General. I could tell."

"Walker's done worse, in his time," I said. "And so have I."

Bettie took both my hands in hers and made me face her, her eyes holding mine. "You're better than you think, John. Better than you allow yourself to believe. I know you've done . . . questionable things. I've seen some of them. But you're not the cold-blooded killer your legend makes you out to be."

"Bettie . . ."

"You're the way you are because of *her*! Because of Suzie Shooter, Shotgun Suzie! She wants you to be a killer, just like her. Because that's the only way you'll ever have something in common instead of what everyone else has.

You don't have to be like her, John. I can show you a better life."

"Bettie, don't . . ."

"Hush, John. Hush. Listen to me. I love you. I want to be with you, want you to be with me. You can't throw your life away on Suzie Shooter, simply because you feel sorry for her. She's cold, broken . . . she can never be a real woman to you. Not like I can. How can you have a real relationship with someone when you can't even touch her? I could make you so happy, John. We could have a home, a life, a sex life."

She moved in close, still holding on tight to my hands, her face so close to mine now I could feel the breath from her words on my mouth.

"I can be any kind of woman you want, John. Every dream you ever had. I'm exactly the right kind of woman for you, one foot in Heaven, one foot in Hell. Come with me, John. You know you want to."

"Yes," I said. "I want to. But that's not enough."

"What else is there? I can help you! You don't have to be a killer, don't have to be so cold . . . With my help you could be a better person, a real hero!"

"But that's not me," I said. "And never was. I am what I have to be, to get things done; and that includes the bad as well as the good. Suzie understands that. She's always understood me. She accepts me, all of me. I've never had to explain myself to her. She's my friend, my partner, my love. I love her, and she loves me as best she can. And she cares about the real me, not the legend you still insist on seeing when you look at me. I want you, Bettie. But I don't need you, not the way I need Suzie."

"But . . . *why?*"

"Perhaps because . . . monsters belong together," I said.

I looked at her until she let go of my hands. She was breathing hard.

"Hello, John," said a cold, steady voice above us. "Is that girl bothering you?"

"Not any more," I said. "Hello, Suzie."

She was standing at the top of the steps leading down from the Londinium Club, a tall blonde Valkyrie in black motorcycle leathers, one hand tucked into the bandoliers of bullets criss-crossing her chest. She came unhurriedly down to join us. Bettie looked at her, and then at me, and then tossed her head angrily.

"You deserve each other! I never want to see you again, John Taylor!"

She strode away, her high heels clacking loudly on the pavement, her head held high. She didn't look back once.

"Nice horns," said Suzie. "Did I miss something?"

"Not really," I said. "You finished work now?"

"Yes. Just picked up my payment from Walker. A little private work." Suzie looked at the three severed heads. "Didn't take me long."

I looked at her, and then at the heads. I could have said something, but I didn't.

"Come on, Suzie," I said. "Let's go home."

It's the Nightside.

# At Home with
# John and Suzie

Until Walker's people arrived, Suzie and I stuck around, talking to the newly awakened patients, and comforting them as best we could. Well, I did most of the talking and comforting. Suzie isn't really a people person. Mostly she stood at the door with her shotgun at the ready, to assure the patients that no-one was going to be allowed to mess with them any more. A lot of them were confused, and even more were in various states of shock. The physical injuries might have been reversed, but you can't undergo that kind of extended suffering without its leaving a mark on your soul.

Some of them knew each other, and sat together on the beds, holding each other and sobbing in quiet relief. Some were scared of everyone, including Suzie and me. Some . . . just didn't wake up.

Walker's people would know what to do. They had a lot of experience at picking up the pieces after someone's grand scheme has suddenly gone to hell in a hand-cart. They'd get the people help and see them safely back to their home dimension. Then they'd shut down the Timeslip, and slap a heavy fine on the Mammon Emporium for losing track of the damn thing in the first place. If people can't look after their Timeslips properly, they shouldn't be allowed to have them. Walker's people . . . would do all the things I couldn't do.

When Suzie and I finally left the Guaranteed New You Parlour, Percy D'Arcy was outside waiting for us. His fine clothes looked almost shabby, and his eyes were puffy from crying. He came at me as though he meant to attack me, and stopped only when Suzie drew her shotgun and trained it on him with one easy move. He glared at me piteously, wringing his hands together.

*"What have you done, Taylor? What have you done?"*

"I found out what was going on, and I put a stop to it," I said. "I saved a whole bunch of innocent people from . . ."

"I don't care about them! What do they matter? What have you done to my friends?" He couldn't speak for a moment, his eyes clenched shut to try to stop the tears streaming down his face. "I saw the most beautiful people of my generation reduced to hags and lepers! Saw their pretty faces fall and crack and split apart. Their hair fell out, and their backs bent, and they cried and shrieked and screamed, running mad in the night. I saw them break out in boils and pus and rot! *What did you do to them?*"

"I'm sorry," I said. "But they earned it."

"They were my friends," said Percy D'Arcy. "I've known them since I was so high. I never meant for this to happen."

"Percy . . ." I said.

"You can whistle for your fee!" said Percy, with almost hysterical dignity. And then he spun around and walked away, still crying.

I let him go. I saw his point, sort of. Some cases, no-one gets to feel good afterwards. So Suzie and I went home.

The Nightside doesn't have suburbs, as such. But a few areas are a little more safe and secure than anywhere else, where people can live quietly and not be bothered. Not gated communities, because gates wouldn't even slow down the kind of predators the Nightside attracts, but in-stead small communities protected by a few magical defences, a handful of force shields, and a really good mutual defence pact. Besides, if you can't look after yourself, you shouldn't be living in the Nightside anyway. Suzie and I lived together in a nice little detached house (three up, three down, two sideways) in one of the more peaceful and up-market areas. Just by living there, we were driving the house prices down, but we tried not to worry about that too much. Originally, there was a small garden out front, but since Suzie and I were in no way gardening people, the first thing we did was dig it up and put in a mine-field.

We're not big on visitors. Actually, Suzie did most of the work, while I added some man-traps and a few invisible floating curses, to show I was taking an interest.

Our immediate neighbours are a time-travelling adventurer called Garth the Eternal, a big Nordic type who lived in a scaled-down Norman castle, complete with its own gargoyles who kept us awake at night during the mating season, and a cold-faced, black-haired alien hunter from the future named Sarah Kingdom, who lived in a conglomeration of vaguely organic shapes that apparently also functioned as her star-ship, if she could only find the right parts to repair it.

We've never even discussed having a housing association.

Suzie and I live on separate floors. She has the ground floor, I have the top floor, and we share the amenities. All very civilised. We spend as much time in each other's company as we can. It's not easy being either of us. My floor is defiantly old-fashioned, even Victorian. They understood a lot about comfort and luxury. That particular night, I was lying flat on my back in the middle of my four-poster bed. The goose-feather mattress was deep enough to sink into, with a firm support underneath. Some mornings Suzie had to pry me out of bed with a crow-bar. Supposedly Queen Elizabeth I had slept in the four-poster once, on one of her grand tours. Considering what the thing cost me, she should have done cart-wheels in it.

A carefully constructed fire crackled quietly in the huge stone grate, supplying just enough warmth to ward off the cold winds that blew outside. The wood in the fire remained eternally unconsumed, thanks to a simple moebius spell, so the fire never went out. One wall of my bedroom is taken up with bookshelves, mostly Zane Grey and Louis L'Amour Westerns, and a whole bunch of old John Creasey thrillers, of which I am inordinately fond. Another wall is mostly hidden behind a great big fuck-off wide-screen plasma television, facing the bed. And the final wall holds my DVDs and CDs, all in strict alphabetical order, which Suzie never ceases to make remarks about.

I have gas lighting in my bedroom. It gives a friendlier light, I think.

A richly detailed Persian rug covers most of the floor. It's supposed to have been a flying carpet at some point, but no-one can remember the activating Words any more, so it's just a rug. Except I always have to be very careful about what I say out loud while I'm standing on it. Scattered about the room are various and assorted odds and ends I've collected and acquired down the years, often as part or even full payment for a case. A few purported Objects of Power, some antiques with interesting histories, and a whole bunch of things that might or might not turn out to be valuable or useful someday.

There's a musical box that plays top-twenty hits from thirty years in the future. Still mostly crap . . . Some *Tyrannosaurus rex* dung, in a sealed glass jar, labelled *For when any old shit just won't do.* A brass head that could supposedly predict the future, though I've never heard it utter a word. And a single bloodred rose in a long glass vase. It doesn't need watering, and it hisses angrily if anyone gets too close, so mostly I leave it alone. It's only there to add a spot of colour.

As I lay on top of the blankets on my huge bed, listening to the wind battering outside and feeling all warm and cosy, it occurred to me how far I'd come since I returned to the Nightside. Wasn't that long ago I'd been trying to live a normal life in normal London and being spectacularly bad at it. I'd been living in my one-room office, in a building that should have been condemned, sleeping on a cot pushed up against one wall. Eating take-away food and hiding under my desk when the creditors came calling . . . I'd left the Nightside to feel safe. And because I was afraid I was turning into a monster. But there are worse things than that. Failure tastes of cold pizza and over-used tea bags, and the knowledge that you're not really helping anyone, even yourself.

I'll never leave the Nightside again. For all its many sins, it's my home, and I belong there. Along with all the other monsters. And Suzie Shooter, of course. My Suzie.

I got up off the bed, with a certain amount of effort, and went downstairs to see what she was doing. We loved each other as best we could, but I was always the one who had to reach out. Suzie . . . couldn't. But then, I knew that going in. So down the stairs I went, and treading the patterned carpeting was like moving from one world to another. Suzie wasn't what you'd call house-proud.

Her floor looked a lot like her old place—a mess. Dirty and disgusting with overtones of appalling. It was somewhat more hygienic, because I insisted, but the smell always hit me first. Her floor smelled heavy, female, border-line feverish. I peered through the bedroom door in passing. It was empty apart from a pile of blankets in the middle of the floor, churned up like a nest. At least they were clean blankets. Since she wasn't there, I moved on to the living-room, careful to knock on the door first. Suzie didn't react well to surprises.

Suzie was crashed out on her only piece of furniture, a long couch upholstered in deep red leather. *So it won't show the blood,* Suzie had said when I asked, so I stopped asking. She ignored me as I entered the room, her attention fixed on the local news showing on her more modest television set. The room never ceased to depress me. It was bleak, and so empty. Bare wooden floor-boards, bare plaster walls, apart from a huge life-size poster of Diana Rigg as Mrs. Emma Peel in the old *Avengers* TV show. Suzie had scrawled *My Idol* across the bottom, in what looked suspiciously like dried blood.

Her DVDs were stacked in piles against one wall. Her Bruce Lee and Jackie Chan movies, her much-watched copies of *Easy Rider* and Marianne Faithful in *Girl on a Motorcycle.* She also had a fond spot for James Cameron's *Aliens* and his two *Terminator* movies. Plus a whole bunch of Roger Corman's Hells Angels movies, which Suzie always claimed were comedies.

She was wearing her favourite Cleopatra Jones T-shirt over battered blue jeans, and scratching idly at the bare belly between the two, while eating deep-fried calamari nuggets from a bucket. I sat down beside her, and we watched the local news together. The impossibly beautiful presenter was in the middle of a story about a proposed strike by the Nightside sewer workers, who were holding out for bigger flame-throwers and maybe even bazookas. Apparently the giant ants were getting to be a real problem.

Next, a new Timeslip had opened up in a previously un-affected area, and already members of the Really Dangerous Sports Club were racing to the location, so they could throw themselves in and be the first to find out where they'd end up. Nobody was trying to stop them. In the Nightside we're great believers in letting everyone go to Hell in their own way.

And finally, a fanatical Druid terrorist had turned up in the Nightside with his very own backpack nuke wrapped in mistletoe. Fortunately, he had a whole list of demands he wanted to read out first, and he hadn't got half-way through them before Walker turned up, used his commanding Voice on the Druid, and made him eat his bomb, bit by bit. People were already placing bets as to how far he'd get be-fore the plutonium gave him terminal indigestion.

Without looking away from the screen, Suzie reached out and placed her left hand lightly on my thigh. I sat very still, but she took the hand away again almost immedi-ately. She tries hard, but she can't bear to be touched, or to touch anyone else in a friendly way. She was abused as a child, by her own brother; and it left her psychologically scarred. I would have killed the brother, but Suzie beat me to it, years ago. We're working on the problem, taking our time. We're as close as we can be.

So I was surprised when she deliberately put down her calamari bucket, turned to me, and put both her hands on my shoulders. She moved her face in close to mine. I could feel her steady breath on my lips. Her cool, controlled expression didn't change at all, but I could feel the growing tension in her hands on my shoulders, the sheer effort she had to put into such a small gesture. She snatched her hands away and turned her back on me, shaking her head.

"It's all right," I said. Because you have to say something.

"It's not all right! It'll never be all right!" She still wouldn't look at me. "How can I love you when I can't touch you?"

I took her shoulders in my hands, as gently as I could, and turned her back to face me. She tensed under my touch, despite herself. She met my gaze unflinchingly for a moment, then lunged forward, pressing me back against the couch. She put both her hands on my chest and kissed me with painful fierceness. She kissed me for as long as she could stand it, then pushed herself away from me. She jumped up from the couch and moved away from me, hugging herself tightly as though afraid she'd fly apart. I didn't know what to say, or do.

So it was probably just as well that the doorbell rang. I went to answer it, and there at my front door was Walker himself. The man who ran the Nightside, inasmuch as anyone does, or can. A dapper middle-aged gentleman in a smart City suit, complete with old-school tie, bowler hat, and furled umbrella. Anyone else you might have mistaken for someone in the City, some nameless functionary who kept the wheels of business or government turning. But you only had to look into his calm, thoughtful eyes to know how dangerous he was, or could be. Walker had the power of life and death in the Nightside, and it showed. He smiled easily at me.

"Well," I said. "This is . . . unexpected. I didn't think you did house calls. I wasn't even sure you knew where we lived."

"I know where everyone is," said Walker. "All part of the job."

"As a matter of interest," I said, "how did you get past all the mines, man-traps, and shaped charges we put down to discourage the paparazzi?"

"I'm Walker."

"Of course you are. Well, you'd better come in."

"Yes," said Walker.

I took him into Suzie's living-room. He was clearly distressed by the state of the place, but was far too well brought up to say anything. So he smiled brightly, tipped his bowler hat to Suzie, and sat down on the couch without any discernable hesitation. I sat down beside him. Suzie leaned back against the nearest wall, arms tightly folded, glaring unwaveringly at Walker. If he was in any way disturbed, he did a good job of hiding it. Surprisingly, he didn't immediately launch into whatever business had brought him to my home for the very first time. Instead, he made small-talk, was polite and interested and even charming, until I felt like screaming. With Walker, you're always waiting for the other shoe to drop. Usually he speaks to me only when he absolutely has to—when he wants to hire me, or have me killed, or drop me right in it. This new friendly approach . . . just wasn't Walker. But I played along, nodding in all the right places, while Suzie scowled so fiercely it must have hurt her forehead.

Finally, Walker ran out of inconsequential things to say and looked at me thoughtfully. Something big was coming—I could feel it. So I did my best to avert it with other business, if only to assert my independence.

"So," I said. "Did you get all the Parlour's patients safely back to their home dimension?"

"I'm afraid not," said Walker. "Less than half, in the end. Many didn't survive being separated from their life-support technology. Many more died from the shock of what had been done to them. And quite a few were in no fit physical or mental state to be sent anywhere. They're being cared for, in the hope that their condition will improve, but the doctors . . . are not hopeful."

"Less than half?" I said. "I didn't go through all that just to save less than half!"

"You saved as many as you could," said Walker. "That's always been my job—to save as many people as possible."

"Even if you have to sacrifice some of your own people along the way?" I said.

"Exactly," said Walker.

"Why should you get to decide who lives and who dies?" said Suzie.

"I don't," said Walker. "That's up to the Authorities."

"But they're dead," I said. "We were both there when

they were killed and eaten by Lilith's monstrous children. So who . . . exactly . . . pulls your strings these days?"

"The new Authorities," said Walker, smiling pleasantly. "That's why I'm here. I need you to come with me and meet the new Authorities."

I considered him thoughtfully. "Now you know very well I've never got on with authority figures."

"These people . . . are different," said Walker.

"Why now?" I said.

"Because the Walking Man has finally come to the Nightside," said Walker.

I sat up straight, and Suzie pushed herself away from the wall. Walker's voice was as cool and collected as always, but some statements have a power all their own. I would have sworn the room was suddenly colder.

"How do you know it's really him and not just some wannabe?" said Suzie.

"Because it's my business to know things like that," said Walker. "The Walking Man, the wrath of God in the world of men, the most powerful and scariest agent of the Good, ever, has come at last to the Nightside to punish the guilty. And everyone here is either running for the horizon, barricading themselves in while arming themselves to the teeth, or hiding under their beds and wetting themselves. And every single one of them is looking to the new Authorities to do something."

Suzie paced up and down the room, scowling heavily, her thumbs tucked in the top of her jeans. She might have been worried, or she might have been relishing the challenge. She wasn't scared. Suzie didn't get scared or intimidated. Those were things that happened to other people, usually because of Suzie. She sat down abruptly on the edge of the couch, next to me. Close though she was, she still didn't quite touch me. I caught Walker noticing that, and he nodded slowly.

"So close," he said. "In every way but one."

I gave him my best hard look, but to his credit he didn't flinch. "Is there anything you don't know about?" I said.

He smiled briefly. "You'd be surprised."

"It's none of your business," said Suzie. "And if you say anything to anyone, I'll kill you."

"You'd be surprised how many people already know, or guess," said Walker. "It's hard to keep secrets in the Nightside. I am merely . . . concerned."

"Why?" I said bluntly. "What are we, to you? What have I ever been to you, except a threat to your precious status quo, or an expendable agent for some mission too dangerous or too dirty for your own people? And now, suddenly, you're *concerned* about me? Why, for God's sake?"

"Because you're my son," said Walker. "In every way that matters."

He couldn't have surprised me more if he'd taken out a gun and shot me. Suzie and I looked blankly at each other, then back at Walker, but he gave every indication of being perfectly serious. He smiled briefly, holding his dignity close about him.

"We've never really talked, have we?" he said. "Only shared a few threats and insults, in passing . . . or discussed the details of some case we had to work on together. All very brisk and businesslike. You can't afford to get too close to someone you know you may have to kill one day. But things are different now, in so many ways."

"I thought you had two sons?" I said. I didn't know what else to say.

"Oh yes," said Walker. "Good boys, both of them. We don't talk. What could we talk about? I've gone to great pains to ensure that neither they nor their mother has any idea what it is I do for a living. They know nothing about the Nightside, or the terrible things I have to do here, just to keep the peace. I couldn't bear it if they knew. They might look at me as though I were some kind of monster. I used to be so good at keeping my two lives separate. Two lives, two Walkers, doing my best to give equal time to both. But the Nightside is a jealous mistress . . . and what used to be my real life, my sane and rational life, got sacrificed to the greater good.

"My boys, my fine boys . . . are strangers to me now. You're all I've got, John. The only son of my oldest friend. I'd forgotten how much that time meant to me, until I met your father again during the Lilith War. Those happy days of our youth . . . We thought we were going to change the world; and unfortunately we did. Now your father is gone, again, and you're all I've got left, John. Perhaps the nearest thing to a real son I'll ever have. The only son who could ever hope to understand me."

"How many times have you tried to kill me?" I said. "Directly, or indirectly?"

"That's family for you," said Walker. "In the Night-side."

I looked at him for a long time.

"Don't listen to him," said Suzie. "You can't believe him. It's Walker."

"The words *manipulative* and *emotional blackmail* do spring to mind," I said. "This is all so sudden, Walker."

"I know," he said calmly. "I put it all down to midlife crisis myself."

"And where does all this leave us?" I said.

"Exactly where we were before," said Walker. "We'll still probably end up having to kill each other, someday. For what will no doubt seem like perfectly good reasons at the time. But it means . . . I'm allowed to be concerned. About you, and Suzie. And no, you don't get a say in the matter."

"We're doing fine," said Suzie. "We're making progress."

She let one arm rest casually across my shoulders. And I hope only I could tell what the effort cost her.

"Let us talk about the Walking Man," I said. Everything else could wait till later, after I'd had more time to think about it. "He's never come here before. So, why now?"

"In the past, the Nightside's unique nature kept out all direct agents of Heaven and Hell," said Walker. "But since Lilith was banished again, it appears a subtle change has come over the Nightside, and many things that were not possible before are cropping up now with regrettable reg-ularity."

"So all kinds of agents for the Good could be turning up here?" I said.

"Or agents of Evil," said Suzie.

"Well, quite," murmured Walker. "As if things weren't complicated enough . . ."

"Still," I said, "what's bringing the Walking Man here *now*?"

"It would appear he disapproves of the new Authorities," said Walker. "The group whose interests I now represent."

"That's why you're here!" I said. "Because if they're in danger, so are you!"

Walker smiled and said nothing.

"Who are they?" said Suzie. "These new Authorities? The old bunch were nothing more than faceless businessmen who ran things because they owned most of the Nightside. So, are we talking about their families? The next generation? Meet the new boss, same as the old boss, don't get screwed again?"

"The inheritors?" said Walker, with something very like a sniff. "They wish. We saw them off. One quick glimpse of what actually goes on here, and they couldn't sell their holdings fast enough. No . . . Certain personages in the Nightside have come together to represent the main interests in this place. Essentially, the Nightside is now determined to run itself."

"Who, exactly?" I said. "Who are these brand-new *self-appointed* Authorities? Do I know them?"

"Some of them, certainly," said Walker. "They all know you. That's why I'm here."

"How can you serve people from the Nightside?" I said, honestly curious. "You've never made any secret about your feelings for us. You always said the best thing to do would be to nuke the place and wipe out the whole damned freak show once and for all."

"I've mellowed," said Walker. "Just possibly, these new Authorities can bring about real change, from within. I would like to see that, before I die. Now, come with me and meet the new Authorities. Hear what they have to say; learn what they mean to do. Before the Walking Man tracks them down and kills them all."

"But what do they want with me and Suzie?" I said.

Walker raised an eyebrow. "I would have thought that was obvious. They want you to use your gift to find the Walking Man, then find a way to stop him. Shall we go?"

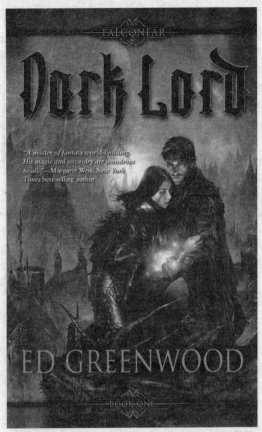

UK ISBN: 978 1 844166 17 6 • US ISBN: 978 1 844165 84 1 • £7.99/$7.99

*When he mysteriously finds himself drawn into a world of his own devising, bumbling writer Rod Everlar is confronted by a shocking truth - he has lost control of his creation to a brooding cabal of evil. In order to save his creation, he must seize control of Falconfar and halt the spread of corruption before it is too late.*

 **WWW.SOLARISBOOKS.COM**

*Follow us on Twitter! www.twitter.com/solarisbooks*

UK ISBN: 978 1 906735 63 0 • US ISBN: 978 1 844167 64 7 • £7.99/$7.99

Having been drawn into a fantasy world of his own creation, Rod Everlar continues his quest to defeat the corruption he has discovered within. With the ambitious Arlaghaun now dead, he sets off in pursuit of the dark wizard Malraun, only to find that he has raised an army of monsters and mercenaries in order to conquer the world...

 **WWW.SOLARISBOOKS.COM**

Follow us on Twitter! www.twitter.com/solarisbooks

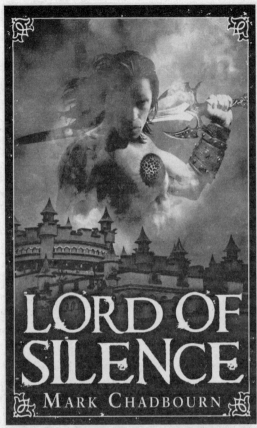

# LORD OF SILENCE

### MARK CHADBOURN

UK ISBN: 978 1 844167 52 4 • US ISBN: 978 1 844167 53 1 • £7.99/$7.99

When the great hero of Idriss is murdered, Vidar, the Lord of Silence, must take his place as chief defender against the terrors lurking in the forest beyond the walls. But Vidar is a man tormented — by his lost memories and by a life-draining jewel. With a killer loose within the city and a threat mounting without, he must solve an ancient mystery to unlock the secrets of his own past.

 **WWW.SOLARISBOOKS.COM**

*Follow us on Twitter! www.twitter.com/solarisbooks*

"Attractive characters and an imaginative setting combine
in an excellent, fast-moving quest novel."
— David Drake, author of the Lord of the Isles series

GAIL Z. MARTIN

# THE SUMMONER

Book One of the
CHRONICLES OF THE NECROMANCER

UK ISBN: 978 1 844164 68 4 • US ISBN: 978 1 844164 68 4 • £7.99/$7.99

*The world of Prince Martris Drayke is thrown into chaos when his brother murders their
father and seizes the throne. Forced to flee with only a handful of loyal followers, Martris
must seek retribution and restore his father's honour. If the living are arrayed against
him, Martris must call on a different set of allies: the living dead.*

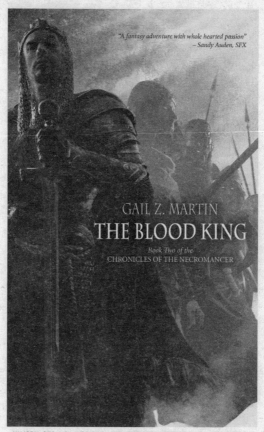

"A fantasy adventure with whole hearted passion"
– Sandy Auden, SFX

GAIL Z. MARTIN

# THE BLOOD KING

Book Two of the
CHRONICLES OF THE NECROMANCER

UK ISBN: 978 1 844165 31 5 • US ISBN: 978 1 844165 31 5 • £7.99/$7.99

Having escaped being murdered by his evil brother, Prince Martris Drayke must take control of his ability to summon the dead and gather an army big enough to claim back his dead father's throne. But it isn't merely Jared that Tris must combat. The dark mage, Foor Arontola, plans to cause an imbalance in the currents of magic and raise the Obsidian King...

 **WWW.SOLARISBOOKS.COM**

NATASHA RHODES

# CIRCUS OF SINS

*A KAYLA STEELE NOVEL*

UK ISBN: 978 1 906735 72 2 • US ISBN: 978 1 906735 73 9 • £7.99/$7.99

When young Hunter recruit Kayla Steele is bitten by a werewolf, she thinks it's the end
of her world; little does she know the real end of the world is not far off. Master vampire
Harlequin has made a deal with the Devil. He plans to commit the ultimate sin, killing an
angel, and trigger the Third War in Heaven, wiping out Mankind forever. Kayla must join
forces with her ultimate enemies - the werewolves - in order to stave off Armageddon and
save the man she loves from the clutches of Hell, or die trying.